THE WONDER THAT WAS OURS

A NOVEL

ALICE HATCHER

DZANC
BOOKS

DZANC BOOKS

5220 Dexter Ann Arbor Rd.
Ann Arbor, MI 48103
www.dzancbooks.org

Library of Congress Cataloging-in-Publication Data

Names: Hatcher, Alice, 1970- author.
Title: The wonder that was ours : a novel / Alice Hatcher.
Description: Ann Arbor, MI : Dzanc Books, 2018.
Identifiers: LCCN 2018005797 | ISBN 9781945814600
Subjects: LCSH: Taxicab drivers--Fiction. | Ex-convicts--Fiction. | Race
   relations--Fiction. | GSAFD: Suspense fiction
Classification: LCC PS3608.A86325 W66 2018 | DDC 813/.6--dc23
LC record available at https://lccn.loc.gov/2018005797

First US edition: September 2018

Printed in the United States of America

10   9   8   7   6   5   4   3   2   1

*To Lars, who set the stage,
and Melissa, who pushed me onto it.*

CHAPTER ONE

I NDIVIDUALS GOVERNED BY PREJUDICE will question our authority to recount the events of that week in November, when so much foul jetsam from the cruise ship *Celeste* washed up on St. Anne's shores and the heat inside Professor Cleave's cab, our classroom, nearly stifled our dreams—the week everything burned. They'll say we spent the week deep in sleep, addled by ingrained habits and sloth. What do they know? The subject of cockroaches' circadian rhythms is largely misrepresented in the scientific literature. Self-proclaimed experts on the affairs of insects will tell you we spend our days lazing beneath rocks and the floor mats of cars, napping in cupboards or slumbering in sewer pipes.

To quote J.B. Williams's *Entomological Atlas of the Americas*, "Pesky varieties of cockroaches generally lie dormant for all but four nocturnal hours in a twenty-four-hour cycle." In a typical oversight, Williams discounts the fact that, in cases of high population density ("infestation," he'd say!) and food scarcity, we extend our waking hours to forage. Though Williams and his ilk would never acknowledge it, crowding and scarcity have become the norm for cockroaches, and sleep deprivation endemic. Williams bases his spurious claims upon abstract conditions that hardly correspond to reality, unless one accounts for the practice of mass extermination. Williams concedes as much when he writes, "If cockroach populations are controlled, whether by standard commercial insecticides or boric acid applications, humans will rarely see them in daylight."

In pointing out the deficiencies in Williams's logic, our intent is not to quibble over an odd claim in a deeply flawed book, or to expose another apologist for the insecticide industry. We simply hope to defend our credibility. Sleep was a luxury that November. Thanks to a depletion of Freon and an ailing compressor, the air conditioning in Professor Cleave's cab was sporadic at best. We drifted in and out of feverish dreams, sleeping in short shifts that ended whenever Professor Cleave started to lecture us. Whatever dull-witted entomologists say, at least some of us were awake most of the time.

The day the *Celeste* docked at St. Anne's terminal, Professor Cleave had spent the entire afternoon scolding those of us sheltering in his cab, bartering our peace of mind for an occasional breath of air conditioning. He'd nearly outdone himself, calling us everything from "hopeless delinquents" to "irredeemable wastrels." To be fair, we'd been testing the limits of his patience, scurrying around the floor mats and darting through the vents. An "especially ill-mannered assembly" (his words) had spent hours idling at the base of the gearshift, making "lewd gestures" with our antennae. Each of Professor Cleave's reprimands only incited "further effronteries and grosser forms of misconduct." Some of us skittered around the radio with raised antennae, hoping to intercept DJ Xspec's *Heavy Vibes Hour* on Kingston's 103.5 Jams, which broadcast across most of the Caribbean on a clear day. Others scuttled across the windshield, hoping to preempt a lecture about the defection of common sense from St. Anne's electorate—a familiar topic in Professor Cleave's repertoire—or another recitation from *An Anthology of Classical Literature*, the most immediate (and obvious) source of our unrest.

Who could blame us? Professor Cleave had been parked on the curb before St. Anne's cruise ship terminal for almost an hour, drumming his fingers on the steering wheel and muttering about everything from the price of petrol to his latest bout of indigestion. When he wasn't staring at the policemen patrolling the streets around the duty-free mall, he read aloud from the anthology splayed across his lap. He trailed his fingertips over faded typeface, enunciating each syllable of Socratic dialogues to focus his flagging energy. Still, he felt distracted, and frustrated by our unwillingness—not our inability, he maintained—to quiet ourselves.

"You are not serious about anything of consequence, my six-legged students." He closed his book, and with a jaundiced eye regarded those of us near the radio. "You'll come to a very bad end with your lawless behavior. In mocking education and the rules that govern civil society, you have associated yourself with the growing criminal element on this island."

Mildly contrite, we let our antennae droop over the dashboard's edge, *as if* demoralized or dumbfounded by his allusions to etiquette and ethics. Members of a recidivist clique bristled around the gearshift.

Professor Cleave shook his head at these, his most recalcitrant students. "Many of you, I fear, have moved beyond the pale of reason and moral recall."

In the absence of our frenzied chatter, an unsettling silence and the full weight of the day's misery pressed upon him. He drew a fold of crumpled bills from the glove box and reviewed the morning's most unfortunate episode. At noon, three of us had emerged from the vents and brandished our antennae at two Canadians spraying some horrid substance (the latest toxin to be labeled "perfume") in the close confines of the cab. This, we admit, had been only one of our costly indiscretions.

"Through brazen acts, and in the most self-defeating manner, you have spurned the gratuities that sustain this cab, and, by extension, your sordid lifestyles." Professor Cleave slipped the bills into an envelope and peered at the overexposed world beyond his windshield.

Outside the terminal, a man in a straw fedora was trying to sell tourists photo opportunities with a diapered monkey. Americans and

Europeans wandered past battered card tables crowded with carved wooden pipes and shot glasses. Old women in headscarves shooed flies from piles of fruit. Men on rusted bicycles skirted potholes, spurred by the wailing horns of flatbed trucks.

Professor Cleave leaned forward to release the beads of perspiration pooling in the small of his back and looked into the rearview mirror, at the creases defining the dark planes of his face and the black and grey hairs competing for dominance at his temples. "I am tempted to get some traps. If my wife hears about your conduct, she will buy them herself. Cora can be quite severe, and this time I won't stop her."

He softened as he spoke, knowing (as did we) that he possessed neither the inclination nor the will to fumigate his cab. We'd long served as sounding boards for his lectures on international events, local politics, and St. Anne's General Transport Workers Union. If not model students, we possessed an ability rarely demonstrated by his family and friends to concentrate on his running—or, as some would say, droning—commentary. Who but the Earth's most down-trodden would suffer this sort of claptrap in exchange for a bit of air conditioning? In a more just society, we would have been listening to 103.5 Jams.

We did appreciate the times he read literary classics aloud, dramatizing dialogue and lingering over lyrical phrases to capture their cadence. Granted, we could be fickle. Only days earlier, we'd shown due deference to Dostoyevsky, lining up on the dashboard to the spellbinding sounds of *Crime and Punishment*. A week before that, in an admittedly unfortunate display, we'd hissed during *The Metamorphosis*, confirming Professor Cleave's troubling sense that there is no accounting for taste. Really, though, what did Franz Kafka know about cockroaches?

Whatever failings delusionals and cranks attribute to cockroaches, we're relatively ecumenical in our interests and generally subdued. During short recesses—for Professor Cleave always suspended his lectures when passengers entered his taxi—we withdrew behind the vents. We know how our bread is buttered—or in this case, from whence our air conditioning flows. In his excessive anxiety and frustration, Professor Cleave hardly differed from other humans. In other respects, he admirably distinguished himself. Over millions of years, our antennae have evolved into delicate receptors attuned to the most subtle gestures of those likely to harass us with aerosol cans and rolled-up newspapers. We know humans' very thoughts and feelings, for our survival depends on it (our collective mind reels, sometimes!). Professor Cleave, for all his faults, possessed a relatively peaceful disposition; he tyrannized us with philosophy and poetry rather than pesticides.

The day the *Celeste* docked, our "rude antics" had much to do with the weather. Like everyone else on St. Anne, we'd grown ill-tempered over three months of record-breaking heat and could think of little but our own misery. Unfortunately, our constant fussing had been a source of great annoyance, and worse, financial loss for Professor Cleave. We'd forced him to compensate for the day's losses by parking at the cruise ship terminal late in the afternoon. We warily observed his movements, our antennae twitching in currents of recycled air.

"If Cora knew what I was doing, she would insist upon your eradication. Let me tell you, her mood has been foul. She's been exceptionally parsimonious in her chocolate rations this week. I married a woman of minor vices made joyless by moral vanity."

Even the least observant among us noted the disjointed nature of his speech. He'd grown preoccupied, weighing his potential for profit against the complications often posed by difficult passengers—namely, those ejected from shuffleboard society and the food courts of floating shopping malls. What predictable specimens they were, these modern-day castaways.

Bellicose drunks forced to walk the proverbial plank usually kicked and screamed on their way out of the terminal, railing in defense of their democratic rights to drink. They filled the cab, our classroom, with their reeking tirades, registering their most bilious opinions on the floor mats. Ejected exhibitionists propounded libertarian theories about the nature of personal freedom in its most noble and epilated expressions. Indiscreet drug addicts excelled as backseat drivers, honing in on seedy establishments avoided by all but those drawn to nameless pushers and filthy bathroom stalls. Failed suicides, legal liabilities for frazzled captains, generally went one of two ways. Consigned to strange shores, some succumbed to despair, while others, graced with a sense of rebirth, countenanced life in a state of unparalleled bliss, equally enchanted by palm trees bending in the breeze and the duct tape peeling from the cab's cracked vinyl seats.

"They grow more dissolute each year." Professor Cleave scanned the sidewalk until he saw Portsmouth's harbormaster, Desmond James, at the terminal gate. "I'm sorry to do this, but your appearance disturbs Des, and we need information." He waved to Desmond and used his anthology to ferry us, in twos and threes, from the dashboard to a vent. "If you have any sense, you'll take this time to consider the monetary consequences of your latest outrages."

Need we elaborate on the indignity of being shuttled out of sight, even on the shoulders of master rhetoricians and philosophical giants? If only to atone for our misdeeds, we filed, chastened and infantilized, into the labyrinth beneath the hood. Professor Cleave closed the vent behind us, and we crowded against its loose slats to observe him.

Desmond slid into the cab and dragged a handkerchief across his brow. "This is a rotten game. You should go to the Ambassador. Behind the bar, you wouldn't be driven mad by the sun."

"I have time enough before my shift. What do you know?"

"Two are coming off the ship. Something to do with sex. It must be the kind of thing you read about in a blue magazine."

"Nothing less would do it."

"Often, much worse isn't enough. It was a bad lot coming through today. Duty-free was overrun with the worst sorts. Staggering about and fouling the pavement with whatever they feed them on that ship. I've had crews cleaning up all afternoon." Desmond glanced at Professor Cleave's anthology. "I doubt your Greeks would have much to say about carrying slop buckets."

"More than you would think. If you read any—"

"This heat will kill us. And here you have the air blocked." Desmond flipped open a vent and yanked his hand away from the dashboard, as if we had disturbed *his* niche. "You should exterminate these filthy things. There's not a driver who doesn't. You'll be an old man with nothing in your wallet if you let this go on."

"I have half that fixed up. I'm already an old man."

Desmond took this as an opportunity to offer unsolicited and insupportable advice about roach traps and insecticidal sprays.

"They're always creating situations when they're bored," Professor Cleave interrupted.

"They're rude things at any time." Desmond lit a cigarette. "Pestilence and nothing else."

"I'm talking about them." On the curb, policemen were using batons to disperse a group of homeless men. "They're a rougher bunch than when we were coming up." Professor Cleave picked at a callus on his thumb. "Now you wouldn't look at them sideways. Thugs to the last and crooked to the core. Paid to behave no better than criminals."

"Here you are again, like a fish circling its tiny glass bowl, surprised every time it sees the castle on the hill. Injustice. It will drive you mad."

"Did you know today is the anniversary? The day they took me from the courthouse in handcuffs. In front of my daughter."

"I didn't know." Desmond paused. "But I remember the day. Everyone talked of the trial and nothing else."

Professor Cleave rubbed a crease in his palm. "I can't stop thinking about it. Just when I think it's behind me, I feel the hatred coming back."

"No one would count that against you."

"But it's not just the police." Professor Cleave nodded at a group of young men sitting near the waterfront, staring at a line of rotted pilings. "Out of their heads. Selling drugs and scaring people off the streets at night. Not a thought to the future. Sometimes I think of them the same way I think of the police."

"Why wouldn't you? Those sorts landed you in prison. No different than that judge bought for the price of beer."

"But I can't let myself think of them as nothing but criminals. Most of them coming up now have nothing to call their own. No stake in things."

"You're arguing yourself in circles," Desmond said. "There wasn't much for us coming up either. But when we had opportunities, we took them."

"Not everyone can clean hotel rooms. Or leave." Professor Cleave watched a scrawny boy soliciting change in front of the terminal. "I wonder if anything has changed for the better."

"The bigger wonder is what's worse, but who's to say?"

We might have registered our opinion, had we not been suspended from class. Who better than cockroaches to speak of wonder, or of what's gotten worse? We've seen everything from the pyramids of Egypt to the sewers of Paris. Not that it matters. Education and experience count for so little in the minds of philistines.

"The anger feels like a sickness," Professor Cleave said. "I was hopeful, once."

"You've lost hope in an island that never had any. That's your problem."

"It's not just my problem. The ones getting paid the most are sweating the least. And those sweating the most are barely getting paid. Everyone takes it for granted."

"While you're reading your books, people are getting by. So what if a few are doing more than getting by?" Desmond leaned forward and blew smoke through a vent. "I'd smash them, but I'd hear one of your lectures. Something about the dignity everything deserves, as if these things had shoes on their feet and walked on two legs."

"You're stirring the pot, now."

Desmond settled back in his seat. "We should have gone to the States when we were young. How's your daughter? She was thinking about school."

"She's been thinking about a Jamaican." Professor Cleave looked down at his hands. "Not a thought to her mother. Or me."

"You should visit her. Spend some time. See something of the world before you leave it. Get away from these filthy things in your taxi."

Professor Cleave trailed his fingers along the edge of his anthology. "They have roaches in New York. Rats as big as dogs ride the trains."

"I'm hearing about the world from a man who's never been off this island."

"There's an argument for holding some ground. Working to find some common ground here."

"The only common ground you'll find is six feet under." Desmond held his hand out the window and tapped ash onto the curb. "There's no end to this heat. I should retire. Sit on the stoop and drink beer all day."

"I can tell you about a man who does that. It's the surest way to ruin."

"Your father's seen a few more days than most." The *Celeste*'s foghorn momentarily drowned out the shouts of young men hawking Bob Marley shirts. Desmond looked at his watch. "I should be off. Do something about these foul things."

We slipped through the vents after Desmond left the cab. Our relief at his departure was short-lived. As we assembled on the dashboard, Professor Cleave set aside his anthology and drew from beneath his seat one of the most boring books ever penned: *The Flora and Fauna of the Lesser Antilles*, the so-called magnum opus of early nineteenth-century British naturalist Geoffrey Morrow. We bristled.

We seethed. We fanned our wings and turned in circles. Professor Cleave had fallen into a mood, though. The gig, for us, was up.

An overbearing teacher on his best days, Professor Cleave had grown somewhat obsessed with certain passages in *The Flora and Fauna of the Lesser Antilles*. In these, he seemed to find comfort and even moral guidance when his feelings became too difficult to bear.

"Here you are, mired in hostility. Treading upon very dangerous ground. In this respect, you hardly differ from Desmond." He fingered the book's bent corners. "He says no one would hold my feelings against me. But even to speak the word *hatred* is to conjure something terrible, to give new life to an abomination by planting its seed in another's mind." He opened the book to a well-worn page. "I should not have said it."

He rubbed his fingertips together, and we quieted ourselves. All day, he'd been wracked by physical tics he'd developed in prison, and we were trying to be patient. He cleared his throat, and we drew our legs beneath our wings. He considered our drooping antennae and tapped a page to rouse us from a presumed stupor (not that he gave a bee's fuzzy ass about our opinions).

"'The splendorous Earth sustains infinite varieties of tree and flower and beast,'" he began. He'd quoted the same passage about tropical agriculture so many times before. "'Tend the ground beneath your feet as if there is no other, and with utmost vigilance, guard it against every noxious weed, contagion, and source of blight. By your example, others will do the same, and none shall want.'" Professor Cleave surveyed the dashboard. "From Morrow, we have much to learn. Hatred, in its spread, is a foul weed, the stem of violence."

Some of us edged toward the vents, and he lifted his finger.

"And violence must be refused without exception," he intoned. "It is a contagion. This, my students, is Morrow's lesson."

Where to begin? Morrow, like so many British naturalists of his era, held a fairly benign view of tilling the earth, little considering the disruptions modern agriculture has created in the lives of six-legged "beasts" who would happily live in the soil, unmolested, if not for humans' insatiable appetite for cereal. As for Professor Cleave, he'd taken considerable liberties with a simple text. Worse, he'd spoken of hatred without addressing the more compelling subject of love. In his omissions, we recognized the doubts of one treading upon uncertain ground. Professor Cleave was an awkward man, and he clearly wasn't getting enough at home. Love, we mean.

We almost felt relieved when the *Celeste*'s foghorn sounded. We rustled our wings and stretched our legs. Professor Cleave looked through his windshield at the people pressed against the *Celeste*'s deck railings, waving unsought farewells to sweaty rickshaw drivers.

"If the world could see what we have seen, would faith remain?" He slid *The Flora and Fauna of the Lesser Antilles* beneath his seat, turned back to his anthology, and lost himself in ancient dialogues between dead philosophers.

When he at last closed his book, he found us pacing beneath the windshield, shifting between sets of legs to escape the burn of magnified heat. A short distance away, Desmond was offering a cigarette to a man with a duffel bag slung over his shoulder. The man scratched the back of his neck, where blond hair brushed his collar. He exuded health, and with it, contentment verging on complacency.

"He knows I don't have much time, and there he is, smoking with strangers." Professor Cleave paused to listen to Desmond's conversation. We tuned our antennae to an American accent. The American cupped his hand around a match.

"No need," Desmond said. "There hasn't been a breath of wind in weeks."

"Habit. Been lighting them on deck for the past few months."

"You work on the ship, then."

"Until a few hours ago." The man lifted his face to the sky and exhaled. "My services are no longer required, as they say. Seeking my fortunes elsewhere now."

"Elsewhere is where you should go. You're in the wrong place to seek your fortunes."

The man rubbed his jaw. "If I was sticking around for a day or two, where'd I stay?"

"Most Americans stay at the Plantations. It has a golf course. A beach."

"Just need a few beers and a bed. Nothing special."

"Then you want the Ambassador Hotel. I'll get you a taxi."

The American glanced over his shoulder at a woman sitting on a suitcase, picking at the sleeves of her lime-green sweater and staring into the valley formed by her knees and the sagging fabric of a faded sundress. He tossed his cigarette to the ground and started toward her.

Professor Cleave rapped his knuckles on the dashboard and herded us toward a vent with his anthology. We scattered beyond Socrates's sweep and angled our antennae at a policeman.

"This book is not worse than a baton," Professor Cleave insisted. "Only intellectual invalids would make such a comparison."

We considered his prospective fares. The man was crouched beside the woman, pleading or quietly arguing. When he helped her to her feet, she wavered once, and he placed his hand on her back. They leaned into one another like exhausted lovers wilting in the heat and started toward the cab, joined at the hips in a drunken four-legged gait.

"Theirs is bound to be a questionable affair. One that can only end in tears." Professor Cleave watched Desmond wheel the woman's suitcase to the curb. "It's hardly his job to carry luggage. I'd help him, but I have all of you to contend with. Cora would not be pleased."

At the third mention of Cora Cleave, we surrendered the dashboard. There are times to take a stand, and there are times for quiet compromise behind the loose slats of air-conditioning vents. Professor Cleave stepped from the cab as the couple neared.

"I'm looking for a hotel with a bar," the man said. "More to the point, a hotel bar. Nothing special. Your friend said the Ambassador will do."

As his passengers lowered themselves into the backseat, Professor Cleave registered the man's blue eyes, as depthless as the cloudless sky, and the woman's anemic cast and stringy hair. Her ragged sweater, above all else, unsettled him. It was unseasonable, and, even by his standards, unfashionable. Its color suggested sickness, the wasting and weakness following an extended debauch, and its sleeves some wretched attempt at concealment. He saw a fresh bruise on the top of her hand and imagined needle marks along her arm. The pain of his anniversary had skewed his judgment; the medical disinfectants stinging our antennae spoke of suicide.

He stepped behind the taxi and watched Desmond lower a tiny suitcase with broken zippers into the trunk. "Never a good thing to say about this place. And you've riled them with your cigarettes."

"Get some traps." Desmond slammed the trunk. "So you can use proper air conditioning."

When Professor Cleave pulled from the curb, a few of us pushed our antennae through the vents to get some relief from the engine's heat.

"You have no civility or sense," he snapped.

He glanced into his mirror and muttered something about a flatbed truck without brake lights, though he had no need for caution. The man leaned into the window, lost in passing scenery. The woman skimmed the landscape with vacant eyes. Their intimacy was merely physical, Professor Cleave concluded, noting the woman's listless attitude. Professor Cleave would have been the last authority on the subject of carnal passion, but we stifled anything he might have construed as "rude commentary." We'd caused him enough grief already. We remained quiet until he parked in front of the Ambassador.

On the curb, the man considered the stunted palms beneath a portico. "Works for now."

The woman splayed her fingers across the cab's window for support. When she lowered her hand, its ghostly imprint remained on the glass. Professor Cleave glanced at the smudge and recoiled. To be fair, she bore an uncanny resemblance to the woman who had been seeding his mind with nightmares for years.

"The Ambassador is the oldest modern hotel on St. Anne. A historic landmark," he said, turning away from her.

The man nodded and pulled out his wallet. Some of us dropped from the cab's undercarriage and skittered across the sidewalk toward a crack in the Ambassador's wall. "Happy hour," to borrow an inapt phrase from the hotel's absentee managers, was about to commence in the lounge, and who, these days, is in a position to decline free snacks?

EDEN

IF WE EVER DISRUPTED Professor Cleave's lectures, it wasn't for the reasons he suspected: incomprehension or a sneering attitude toward education. Our threshold for irony simply fell short of what his lectures demanded, especially that week, when he fashioned strange gardening metaphors from *The Flora and Fauna of the Lesser Antilles*. As it was, nothing could have blossomed because of the withering heat and the poisons washing up on our shores. It's no wonder Professor Cleave missed the irony. He'd suffered misfortune, certainly, but he had never buried his fingers in soil or felt fungus on the undersides of rocks. He'd never dirtied his hands. Worse, he lectured us about tending some common ground, as if humans haven't driven us from almost every home we've known with toxic sprays (*Roach Out!* being the most wicked concoction in their arsenal).

We forgave him, though, and not only because we craved the air conditioning in his cab. He couldn't have foreseen the misfortune the *Celeste* would bring, but he sensed the earth giving way beneath him, the ground shifts of a world too quickly changing. He clung to his imaginary garden, his intellectual Eden, because he needed to believe in a common ground worth defending, in some unspoiled place still his to defend. If he patronized us, we empathized with him. Exile, after all, looms large in the collective memory of cockroaches.

We slept soundly in the New World until the Spaniards unleashed their pigs, scrofulous beasts that rooted us from our beds with ghastly yellow teeth and filthy snouts long after their owners moved on in search of gold. The English introduced their own disruptions and horrors, including bespectacled entomologists with wretched pins and matting boards. They destroyed our nests to build sugar mills and razed the earth for an open market, where they delivered slaves and indentured servants to unspeakable fates. They built a stone fort to protect their enterprise, a church to sanctify their unholy endeavors, and a governor's mansion to house corpulent men given to sloe gin and rapid dissipation. In time, they laid cobblestone streets, paved an airstrip, and dredged the harbor to ease the import of cars, crystal china, and claw-footed chairs—creature comforts from places some of them continued to call home.

The Ambassador Hotel was different than anything lodged in our memory of St. Anne. The American machines that attended its birth cast aside earth faster than some of us could run. One morning, we were slumbering beneath rocks and brush when a dreadful roar wrested us from dreams of compost and loam. We awoke to find the ground breaking apart and steel claws tearing at the earth around us. Many of us perished in the gaping hole that became the Ambassador's foundation. Rudely exposed, the rest of us scattered without sense or dignity and huddled among weeds that provided refuge in the absence of any other.

Hopefully without downplaying our grief, we can admit the awe we felt when the Ambassador first opened its doors. At eight stories, it was the first skyscraper on St. Anne, a towering monument to American ingenuity and ambition. Unapologetic in its proportions, it mocked gravity. Its pink walls glistened with excess. Beside each balcony, air conditioning units hummed incessantly, shedding heavy beads of condensation onto manicured lawns. It had an elevator. It was, far and away, the most luxurious hotel on the island, a cornucopia of delights equipped with all the modern conveniences.

Naturally, we established residence. We never questioned that the Ambassador Hotel belonged to us. It had been built on our homes, and, in some cases, on our backs. We claimed its air ducts and drainpipes and the space beneath its massive refrigerators. At night, we reveled in the kitchen trash, dining on spilled soda and potato chips—exotic fare, it seemed then—and the remains of prawn cocktails, iced melon, and meatballs. We enjoyed fare as exquisite as any (barring the puddings so adored by the British) found in the bins behind the Governor's Mansion. After dinner, we'd sit on the rooftop and remember the world when it was young, at times saddened and at others wondering what, if anything, we'd lost.

Few but Professor Cleave would deny that the Ambassador had become a somewhat déclassé establishment by the time the *Celeste* docked in St. Anne's harbor. Absentee owners had done little for its upkeep. Accretions of car exhaust and rainwater runoff from rusting balconies streaked its pink walls. Online reviewers described it as a second-rate hotel suitable for travelers willing to humor passé décor—mint-green tiles, splintered wicker tables, and faux bamboo headboards—time capsule oddities that added to the hotel's distinct personality, or as some wrote, its "decrepit character." They complained of missing light bulbs, shoddy service, and oddly, given the basis of their authority, the caliber of the clientele.

Few speak of the hotel now. Most have forgotten it, just as most have forgotten the days when it stood as a portent of prosperity and political change, when it was a source of wonder.

CHAPTER TWO

MONTHS BEFORE IT ROSE from a bluff overlooking Portsmouth Harbor, the Ambassador had already become the source of excited conversation and excessive drinking in Professor Cleave's village, Stokes Hill. The drinking started the evening Professor Cleave's father Topsy announced he'd just quit his job packing bananas on a moribund plantation. At the time, we were happily huddled behind a scrap bucket. Cora Cleave, with her folded newspapers and fastidious ways, had not yet sapped our precious joy; Professor Cleave's mother Rose, a woman of reason and restraint, still ruled the proverbial roost.

"I've been paid by the pound for the last time." Topsy tilted a half-empty bottle of rum in Rose's direction. "To hell with that knuckle-dragging boss and his crooked scales."

Rose crossed herself and lifted her eyes to the ceiling.

"Save your prayers for someone who needs them." Topsy threw his arms around Wynston, then still known by the name he'd been given at birth. Pressed against a taut paunch, Wynston listened to his father's drunken declaration of independence. "We don't need their jobs. The winds of change are blowing our way."

Rose lowered herself onto a rickety stool. "What did you do?"

"Today, we gave those red-assed monkeys the sack." Topsy released Wynston from his suffocating embrace. "All of us are going to work at the cement factory. My brother has it lined up. Everyone in Stokes Hill will be rich building hotels."

"Hotels?" Rose furrowed her brow. "There are no tourists here. This is not Jamaica."

Wynston studied his mother's face and drew his eyebrows together.

"Because we have no hotels. But the Americans are going to build one," Topsy said. "Eight stories and a pool. All cement."

"One hotel?" Rose said. "How long can this work last?"

"This is only the beginning." Topsy drew Rose from the stool and into his arms. "This, I can promise."

However tentatively, Rose soon embraced her husband's faith in St. Anne's future—a future that rudely presented itself in the middle of Sunday service in Stokes Hill's chapel. In a back pew, Wynston was sitting on his hands, shifting his weight to relieve the pressure on his bony haunches and daydreaming through the sermon of a preacher moved by the spirit as slowly as molasses. Beside him, Topsy was jotting cricket scores on a scrap of paper and making calculations related to a betting pool. In a small choir box, Rose violently fanned the air to distract herself from Topsy's gambling. We napped intermittently, alternately lulled by the opiate effects of the preacher's drone and stirred by creaking pews, until the distant shriek of an electric saw cut through the air. At that moment, hundreds of us were scrambling from the loosened earth around a tree's disturbed roots.

Topsy slapped Wynston's knee. "The Americans are starting."

Beneath Rose's mortified gaze, Topsy slid from the pew, dragging Wynston behind him. Outside, he lifted Wynston onto his shoulders and walked to the edge of a small cemetery.

"Look down near the water." He pointed toward the harbor. "See the treetops move. They're clearing ground for the hotel."

Wynston laced his fingers across his father's forehead and leaned forward. We perched atop crooked crosses and strained our antennae. In the distance, trees swayed in widening circles and toppled one by one. By the time the preacher surrendered to the screech of saws, twenty trees had fallen and a patch of cleared ground was visible from the hillside.

"They're cutting trees," Wynston shouted when Rose appeared. "Where the hotel will be."

"This noise. On Sunday. It's a disgrace." Rose pressed her Bible to her chest. "Nothing is sacred to these people. The Americans bow to nothing."

"Not even the English." Topsy gripped Wynston's ankle and lit a cigarette. "They'll change this place. Wynston will wear new shoes, and you'll have a new Sunday dress and hat."

Rose touched the brim of her straw hat. That morning she walked home with her Bible balanced precariously in the crook of her arm, indulging in fantasies of floral fabric and feather festoons— bold statements of faith better suited than straw to the celebration of God's infinite glory. Over the next few weeks, she accompanied Wynston to the schoolhouse at the top of Stokes Hill. She always stopped beside the chapel to view the clearing.

"Your father's a foolish man," she said at first. "We'll be in the workhouse."

As bulldozers displaced earth for a massive foundation and we grieved countless deaths, she celebrated the appearance of rumbling cement trucks. Who could blame her? She knew nothing of our suffering.

"Your father's a brilliant man," she said, squeezing Wynston's hand. "You will have a life we never dreamed of when we were your age."

Slowly but steadily, her worldly aspirations overturned scriptural revelations. Hats with satin sashes replaced sackcloth and ashes, and piety surrendered to a reverence for all wondrous things.

The wondrous things happening on St. Anne quickly became a source of occupational solidarity for those handed cement factory jobs on the greased palms of Wynston's uncle, John Cleave. Every night, seventeen dust-covered members of the United Gravel Grinders Union gathered around the Cleaves' front stoop to analyze cricket matches and deliver successive toasts to St. Anne's labor movement, however small, and the international brotherhood of workers, however dimly imagined. More often than not, Wynston fell asleep beneath his open bedroom window to the sound of UGG members complaining about cricket teams and drinking with Morris, a widower known for his unflagging generosity when it came to sharing a bottle.

Six weeks after the union's inaugural meeting, Rose complained. "Wynston will never sleep with this noise."

"This is grassroots organizing," Topsy said. "The labor movement depends on it."

"You know very well about grass roots, after spending so much time facedown in the dirt. There will be no union if you have no jobs," Rose insisted, bemoaning the price of hats in Portsmouth's tiny department store and the growth of Wynston's ungainly feet, now splitting the seams of his Sunday shoes.

One month later, when American investors cut a slender ribbon stretched across the Ambassador's glass doors, her fears faded. Her curiosity piqued by stories of guests signing checks with silver pens and firing champagne corks from their balconies, she suggested a trip to the hotel.

"Put on your best dress. We'll get something to drink." Topsy patted his wallet. "Ginger beer with ice cubes."

"In the canteen," Rose said, rubbing Wynston's back.

"The lounge," Topsy said.

By the time they stepped off the Portsmouth bus, the Cleaves were flecking sweat from their foreheads and nursing blistered feet. Wynston lifted his face and squinted at the Ambassador's bright pink walls. "It touches the sky."

The young Professor Cleave had echoed our very thoughts. By that time, we'd ridden in the Ambassador's brass elevators, sampled its unrivaled air conditioning, and gorged ourselves on scraps from overstocked buffets. A feast awaits at every turn for those with less refined palates, and we suffered a plague of riches.

So we understood Rose's fascination with bright green sod and her impulse to slip off her shoe and press her toes into soft grass. We understood her apprehension, too, when a valet standing beneath the portico narrowed his eyes. Suddenly conscious of the perspiration darkening her collar, she stepped back onto the sidewalk.

"Are we allowed here?" she whispered, forcing her foot back into her shoe.

Topsy glanced at the valet and gripped Wynston's hand. "Maybe we'll go inside another time. Let's look at the swimming pool."

At the edge of a patio enclosed by iron gates, Wynston observed Americans for the first time. He wedged his face between two bars, and with metal warming his cheeks, he grew transfixed by the lethargic occupants of two deck chairs.

"It's nine feet deep," Topsy said. "Do you know how deep that is?"

Wynston didn't answer. He was studying a woman wearing a bikini and oversized sunglasses. In her sunburn and lifeless black eyes, and in her red fingernails, fixed like pincers on an ice cube, he saw a lobster's features grafted onto a nearly naked woman and wailed. The woman's companion reached into a bowl of peanuts, struggled from his chair, and shuffled to the gate.

"Peanut, son?" He slipped his fingers between two bars. "Nothing a peanut can't cure."

Sniveling, Wynston accepted a peanut in his upturned palm.

"Say thank you for the peanut," Rose said, straightening her dress.

"Thank you for the peanut."

The man brushed a peanut husk from his chest hair, turned from Wynston, and flopped into the pool.

"Why don't they swim in the sea?" Wynston asked.

"They prefer bleached water," Rose said. "It keeps them white."

Topsy pinched Wynston's arm. "They're afraid the fish bite."

"Why did he talk that way?" Wynston asked.

"People sound different in the United States."

"He shouldn't have called our boy 'son,'" Rose said.

Sensing the edge in her voice, Wynston dug his thumbnail into the peanut's shell.

"Look at our little man," Topsy remarked. "So serious about pools and American talk."

❈

Wynston was right to be serious about pools and American patter. By then, the few British administrators on St. Anne were retreating further and further into exclusive clubs, where servants in white coats continued to serve tea and lemon tarts on eggshell saucers. In public, they maintained the stolid appearance of efficient bureaucrats. They defied the heat in linen suits and heavy nylons, and after sunset spent themselves in inconsequential bacchanals, swilling gin in elegant parlors and perspiring liquor and lime. They sensed what we knew, having witnessed the collapse of countless empires. Their sinecures had grown insecure. The era of endless puddings had come to an end.

Americans, when they arrived, easily distinguished themselves from the British. They were a bundle of contradictions. They spent hours in the sun "working" on tans and then drowned themselves in air conditioning. They spoke loudly and perplexed harried waiters by leaving loose change to complement their endless complaints. If their strange concepts of hygiene involved buckets of bleach and caustic detergents, they tossed half-eaten entrées into the trash, trailed crumbs everywhere, and left gobs of exhausted chewing gum in ashtrays. Outspending and talking over the British, they carried a promise of political change that, for some, mitigated their offenses.

"They'll drive the British back across the Atlantic," Topsy said to anyone who would listen. "We'll be raising our own flag soon enough."

In this, he exhibited an uncanny prescience. Within a year, Britain conferred self-government to St. Anne and designated a skeleton crew of administrators to manage the island's foreign affairs from the Governor's Mansion. In the weeks before the Assembly elections, dozens of political parties representing a bewildering array of occupational interests formed, including the Social Democratic Alliance—a cadre of taxi drivers bound by elaborate manifestos and a revolutionary aesthetic based on berets and, in the case of its male members, excessive facial hair—and the Progressive Workers Party, a cement mixers' association devoid of internal dissent due to its nightly affirmations of brotherhood.

Despite the insobriety of its disorganized members, the Progressive Workers Party won two of eleven seats in the new assembly. On Election Day, the Cleaves and their neighbors gathered in a wild celebration of modest victory. They guzzled rum and danced, kissed good friends and hugged old enemies, made regrettable declarations of love and shunned thoughts of impending hangovers. Topsy hung on his brother's shoulder, basking in the glow of victory and dispensing unsolicited advice.

"We wore the British down," he declared, talking around the soggy end of a cigarette.

"You're wearing yourself down. This has nothing to do with us." John took a bottle from Topsy's hand and raised it to his own lips.

"We're driving them out, straight into the sea. They see the tide turning."

"They're washing their hands."

Topsy reached for the bottle. "You're a gloomy bastard. At least those taxi-driving communists won't be driving us into the ground. Only one seat. They have their heads hanging low tonight. This is a day for celebration."

"Let me tell you, the real work is ahead," John said.

"But things are turning. You're a fool to go to New York now. If you had any sense, you'd tear up your ticket."

"The money's still in the States," John said, looking at a trampled ribbon on the ground.

Three weeks after taking a job in an aluminum mill in Newark, John started sending Topsy letters about acid baths, vats of molten metal, and voracious presses that consumed limbs and spit out sheets of shining foil. He wrote of squalid boarding houses, horizons obliterated by haze, and junkies lying in gutters. He wrote about rats as big as dogs and cockroaches as big as rats. He exaggerated only the size of the cockroaches.

Topsy spent hours digesting each of his brother's letters. After collecting his thoughts, he'd sit at the kitchen table and spin tales of sleek red convertibles and tinted glass towers for Rose and Wynston. Afterward, he'd hide the latest letter in a box beneath his bed and hope for his brother's return. When John finally returned to St. Anne, he stayed for only one month. He arrived in style, in a taxi loaded with three large suitcases.

"Look at your uncle," Rose murmured, staring at John's shimmering polyester shirt and the generous cut of his flared white pants. "They must wipe their asses with dollars."

Indirectly, John's visit resulted in the nickname Wynston would carry for the rest of his life, a name born of curiosity about his uncle's gifts—filtered cigarettes, bottles of cologne, and waxy chocolates filled with pale creams and translucent gels—and stories about floating suspension bridges and chicken fingers served in foam boxes.

"Do American chickens really have fingers?" Wynston asked, breathing through his mouth to avoid the smell of cologne drying on his mother's neck.

"They need to count their money," John said.

"Don't fill the boy with stories." Rose dipped her finger into the creamy cavity of a chocolate mint. "His mind wanders already."

If Wynston's mind was given to wandering, John's visit gave it direction. Every night, John, Topsy, and Morris gathered on the stoop to discuss the glories and perversities of American life while Wynston lay beneath his bedroom window, eavesdropping on the conversations of intoxicated adults. Stirred by the odd reference to our relations in Newark, we perched on the sill.

"You must think things have changed since you left." Morris coughed.

"It seems quiet. There's always noise in the States. Car horns. Gunshots. I don't stand near the window."

"American women must be nice," Topsy said, after a pause. "I suppose you've had a few."

"The ones who don't cost too much."

"A real romantic, buying them presents with your hard-earned money," Topsy mused.

"I give them my hard-earned money, fool. Too few women in the place I live."

"If the world was a fair place, you'd pay any woman double," Morris said.

"You wouldn't pay less than what they ask. End up like one man I saw, lying on the street, staring at the sky with his face skinned like a goat."

Wynston's scalp tingled, and for the rest of the night, and for many nights to come, he listened to conversations about gutted buildings, knife-wielding pimps, and scorched spoons, trying to reconcile his uncle's letters and stories and envisioning streets of gold covered in shredded skin. One week after his uncle returned to Newark, he issued a dinnertime proclamation.

"I'm never leaving St. Anne."

"Listen to him, so serious," Rose said. "After so much chocolate, you think he'd beg to live with his uncle."

Serious, he was. He soon began secreting letters, one at a time, from the box beneath Topsy's bed. With each letter, he grew more perplexed and more determined to answer questions about places he'd never seen. A broken-down bicycle enabled his self-education.

On Wynston's eleventh birthday, Morris conceded victory to emphysema and wheeled his twenty-year-old bicycle to the Cleaves' front stoop, where Wynston was digging in the dirt with his toes.

"No use to me," Morris said, tilting its misaligned handlebars toward Wynston.

A rusted one-speed contraption with bald tires, the bicycle carried Wynston, wobbling and elated, from Stokes Hill to Portsmouth's one-room library, and into adolescence and intellectual maturity. Wynston spent five years' worth of Saturdays poring through the abandoned books of British administrators and disintegrating Caribbean newspapers that, for years, we'd nibbled for want of less picked-over material on the library's termite-riddled shelves. He sought out news of the United States, absorbing stories about Black Panthers, campus protests, and political assassinations, and as years passed, a hotel called Watergate and Americans dangling from helicopters in Saigon. In the afternoon, he'd leave the library with bloodshot eyes and ride around the island, refining his thoughts and rehearsing ethical debates with imagined adversaries.

Hunched over books and crooked handlebars, he assumed the carriage of a brooding intellectual. Perpetually preoccupied, he ate sparingly. By the time he reached sixteen, his loose-fitting shirts hung awkwardly from his shoulders. He acquired a premature furrow between his eyebrows from squinting at faded newsprint.

"Look at him," Topsy said one afternoon, as Wynston coasted to a stop in front of his house. He was sunning himself in the company of Morris and the UGG's most dedicated drinkers. "The youngest member of this island's 'intellectual avant-garde.' That's the phrase he used the other day."

"The only member." Morris gathered a pinch of snuff between his stiff fingers. "You could learn something from him."

"He'll be at his pulpit soon enough, telling us what to do."

"My lectern," Wynston said, sealing his own fate.

"Listen to him. The Professor."

Bestowed in the presence of many, the title clung to its reluctant recipient. By the time Wynston took his first job, his friends and neighbors regularly addressed him as "Professor" with encouraging smiles or dismissive sneers, depending on their attitudes toward his erudition, or what some called his airs.

※

At the Ambassador, a starched bellboy uniform enabled Professor Cleave's entrée into a world of glowing televisions and glossy magazines that provided perspectives, however skewed, on places he'd known only through outdated books and crumbling newspapers. He worked overtime, using each paycheck to order academic monographs and literary classics from New York. Every day, he ascended the service stairwell to the Ambassador's roof and spent his breaks engrossed in words, oblivious to our presence.

He was, to us, a curiosity, an unassuming human with gangly limbs not entirely unlike our own. He seemed taken with the idea of flight, or so we incorrectly assumed from the amount of time he spent staring at clouds (probably to give his eyes a rest from the torturous sociological prose he so often read). Between paragraphs, he'd absentmindedly chew bits of fried plantain we hadn't ingested while he was absorbed in some social question. Who could blame us for taking a tiny share? To each according to his needs, as Karl Marx once muttered at us. Blame the great political economist for our sins! Remarkably, Professor Cleave was already reading Marx by then. He'd become consumed with questions of collective action and worker solidarity, though solitude seemed to suit him.

He socialized very little and might have continued in his lonely orbit, if not for a fortuitous encounter with an estranged cousin, James Brooks, the subject of endless editorializing among extended family members outraged by his unofficial marriage to a retired prostitute. One morning, while riding from the post office, he heard someone call his name and looked up to see a young man standing outside the taxi stand that doubled as the headquarters of the Social Democratic Alliance. He came to a halt and studied the dense beard covering the man's face.

"You blind? It's your cousin." James looked at the book resting in the basket beneath Wynston's handlebars. "*A Complete History of Empires through the Ages*. I hear you've become the little scholar."

Wynston picked at his disintegrating handlebar grips. "What are you doing now?"

"Organizing the movement. It's time for change, cousin. Come inside. I'll show you."

Speechless at the prospect of seeing the infamous communists of his father's harangues, Wynston propped his bike against a wall and gathered his book.

"Leave it." James nodded at the book cradled in Wynston's arms. "No one steals here. If they did, no one would steal that."

Wynston pressed the book to his chest and followed James past a warped screen door. Inside, dust motes drifted over card tables covered with old newspapers and coffee-stained pamphlets. Beneath a poster of Martin Luther King Jr., a bearded man wearing a black beret was speaking to a slender young man with flawless skin. Seeing James, he broke off his conversation and crossed the room.

"Brooks Brother," he said, pulling a thread from the split seam of James's sleeve.

"Cousin, this man you should know. Patrice Williams, President of the SDA."

"A cousin of James is welcome here," Patrice Williams said.

Fearing he might collapse from the dizzying effects of Patrice Williams's stare, Wynston looked at a newspaper lying on a table. "*The Guardian*," he mumbled, nodding at a grainy photograph of Welsh miners. "I read about that strike."

"You read British newspapers?"

"Guests at the Ambassador leave them sometimes. Usually, the *Miami Herald*."

"You're a cousin of our Brooks Brother how?"

"My ma is Rose Cleave, John's aunt."

"You're a Cleave?"

"My father is Topsy Cleave. A union man. UGG."

"He must have been pleased with the elections. 'Our future is America's.' Isn't that what the UGG says? Or is it 'America's future is ours'?"

"Not everyone agrees with him. With the UGG," Wynston stammered. "Some people think self-government is not the same as governing ourselves. That independence requires the end of economic dependence."

Patrice Williams stroked his goatee. "What are you reading?"

Wynston lowered the book from his chest, and Patrice Williams read its cover.

"He spends too much time with books, but he's all right," James said.

"Someone needs to read. Not everyone does." Patrice Williams glanced at the man with flawless skin and turned back to Wynston. "Come back another time and we'll talk about empires through the ages, including this age. James will give you a lift home."

Outside, James rolled Wynston's bicycle though a lot filled with rusting cars in various states of disrepair. "Patrice says the Americans are planting seeds of change, but their money isn't reaching our people. We give them tax breaks and then we pay for the roads and electric lines they use."

Wynston quietly absorbed his cousin's words.

"He was impressed with you," James continued. "I could see it."

Wynston followed James past stacks of bald tires to a 1972 Hillman Avenger with gleaming chrome fenders and polished windows. "What about my bike?"

"In the boot."

As Wynston lifted his bike from the ground, those of us dozing beneath a pile of scrap metal scrambled into the Avenger's undercarriage. A moment later, Wynston was sitting in the passenger seat, running his fingers over stitched leather. His breath caught as the engine roared to life.

"You've never been in a car before?"

"The bus to town. Not a car." Wynston tried to emulate his cousin's blasé demeanor. "Good for getting around, I suppose."

"You suppose? That library's done something to your head. You don't see the way the world's going. Taxis will be everywhere soon."

"I see the way things are going."

"Then you should get involved. Patrice is the only one talking about independence."

"Is he really a communist?"

"That's your father's talk."

"Who was the man with him?"

James tightened his grip on the steering wheel. "Lyndon Buttskell. Little Butts, we call him. He's a little ass."

"What does he do?"

"Every woman in town. He primps and preens. He's seventeen and I bet some of our mothers' friends have been with him. I don't think he sweats."

James turned on the radio, and the voice of Calypso Rose flooded the car. Beyond Portsmouth, he pressed the gas pedal to the floor. Wildflowers streaked past, the roadside fell away at the edges of steep cliffs, and those of us clinging to the car's fenders felt as though we had functional wings. For several delicious moments, Wynston dreamed of inclusion in a kinship based on considered convictions. He felt like Calypso Rose was singing directly to him, that he was more intelligent than strange, and that anyone with integrity could find a home.

When James pulled up to the gate, Topsy was sitting on the stoop with Morris. Rose had just come from the garden. At the sight of Wynston pulling his bike from a car, she dropped a basket of potatoes. We climbed atop piles of compost to watch James Brooks Brother execute a perfect three-point turn.

"What was that hairy thing doing driving?" Topsy asked as the Avenger disappeared. "And why are you keeping company with your foolish cousin?"

"He gave me a lift from town." Wynston leaned his bike against the house.

"He looks like Che Guevara. Like Castro himself."

Rose sucked air through her front teeth. "He should visit his ma."

"She wouldn't recognize him with that thing on his face," Topsy said.

"He's broken her heart with his doings and that low woman."

"It's that woman's parents that should be upset." Morris lit a cigarette.

"He did a fair job on the turn," conceded Topsy.

"He works at the taxi stand," Wynston said.

"Because he doesn't have a bit of sense. Patrice Williams wants everyone to live in shacks, but he wouldn't give up that car."

"They're communists," Rose said. "They don't believe in God."

"They don't know enough about communism to be communists," Morris said, wheezing.

"You don't need to know anything to be somebody," Topsy said. "What kind of car was that hairy boy driving?"

"A Hillman Avenger."

"You're coming up in a different world. I never dreamed of riding in a car at your age. I never talked about revolutions. I was too busy working. Pretty soon, you'll be lecturing everyone and offering lifts in a fancy car."

Topsy had stumbled upon two partial truths. Over the next few months, Wynston frequented the cabstand every afternoon and became acquainted with its hirsute denizens. There, he refined his ideas and authored numerous pamphlets, starting with *Whither St. Anne?: A Case for Self-Sufficiency* and *What Can Possibly Be Done?: Lenin's Philosophy and Taxis*. Through his erudition and impenetrable tracts, he assured his professorial status and secured his place in a society of taxi drivers. He started wearing a union pin, if not a beard or beret, on his seventeenth birthday.

"If you write about taxis, you should know what a gearshift is," James said.

An hour later, the newly appointed Professor Cleave was sitting in the driver's seat of a dusty car, lurching through the lot behind the taxi stand and suffering the attentions of Little Butts, leaning against a fence and sucking on a mint.

So, as Topsy had surmised, Wynston established himself as the Professor, if not a professor. He began driving a car, if not a fancy one. He divided his time between driving cabs, attending union meetings, delivering towels, and in time, mixing drinks at the Ambassador.

"Is socialism so bad, I wonder?" Rose said one evening, eyeing a stack of bills he'd placed on the table. "If God is merciful, better times on are on the way."

"If there's a god and he's merciful, you won't end up looking like that cousin of yours," Topsy said. "I can barely remember his face, and that can only be a good thing."

❈

The next year, Professor Cleave sprouted the sort of whiskers that might have made him a full-grown member of the Social Democratic Alliance. However, he studiously shaved every morning, not for reasons of ideological disaffection or the vanity that motivated Little Butts, but in opposition to prescribed political aesthetics. He contented himself to work on the fringes of the SDA, authoring pamphlets calling for St. Anne's independence. A six-week sanitation workers' strike in Britain provided the first real portent of political change.

"They don't have the money to pay for trash collection," Professor Cleave said, scanning a *Guardian* article about London streets congested with refuse and feasting rats. "Soon they won't have money to govern us."

We would have boarded the first plane for England but for the filth in the taxi stand and hopes of better days. Patrice Williams only encouraged our inertia with confident declarations.

"The winds of change are blowing," he said, tapping cigar ash into a foam cup. "If they carry the smell of garbage, so be it."

So, we lolled about in discarded food containers and contented ourselves to dream. History will be our judge, and that of our naiveté.

Within a year, a pale master of ceremonies lowered the Union Jack before the Governor's Mansion, and the SDA, the most prolific faction of St. Anne's nationalist movement, won a landslide victory in the first independent election. On election night, the UGG's dust-covered leaders gathered on the Cleaves' stoop to rue the decline of civilization.

"This place is overrun with communists," Topsy said.

"Social democracy isn't the same as communism," Professor Cleave insisted.

"The Americans will leave with their money. The whole thing reeks of communism."

Ultimately, distinctions between communism and socialism didn't matter as much as the place of Cuban cigars in the American imagination. Five months into his term as prime minister, Patrice Williams met with a U.S. attaché to discuss trade, and in a fateful moment offered his guest a Cohiba from the private reserves of Fidel Castro.

"Cuban," he said. "Only the best."

Three days later, the U.S. State Department issued a travel advisory for St. Anne. U.S. congressmen spoke of rotten banana republics and the creeping noon shadow of communism. American investors withdrew from St. Anne. Cement trucks disappeared from the roads. Hoarding and hard bargains became the norm. Desperate shopkeepers bartered batteries for eggs, toothpaste for chickens, and cigarettes for just about anything. We foraged amidst shrinking stores of rubbish in restaurant dumpsters. The UGG's members settled for the cheapest rum and cursed the island's communists.

"They say your man offered the American a cigar autographed by Castro," Topsy said. "What kind of monkey ass would offer an American that kind of thing?"

"The cigar wasn't autographed," Professor Cleave said. "The humidor had his stamp."

"What the hell is a humidor?"

"A box for cigars."

"Someone should put Castro in a box."

To evade his father's front-stoop gauntlet, Professor Cleave spent afternoons at the cabstand, enmeshed in discussions of the SDA's future. When Patrice Williams started packing his bags, Little Butts was the first to raise the white flag.

"We can expect a vote of no confidence. Patrice will step down and live with his sister in Liverpool." He picked a piece of lint from his shirt. "We'll face the United Independent Party in the general election."

Professor Cleave narrowed his eyes. "The United Independent Party didn't exist a month ago. It's an American creation."

Butts unwrapped a mint. "And when it falls, we'll be ready."

The afternoon Parliament ousted Patsy Williams, Professor Cleave approached his house in dread.

"Hard to have a workers' revolution with no one working," Topsy called, inaugurating months of smug commentary on the fall of St. Anne's communist regime.

Only "romance"—a singularly staid love affair with Cora Jones, a maid at the Ambassador—distracted Professor Cleave from his father's taunts. With religiously scrubbed skin and a smile as elusive as her sense of humor, Cora performed her tasks with joyless efficiency and murderous intent. She swept so thoroughly that hardly a crumb could be found. If she wasn't disrupting our naps by upending wastebaskets, she was spoiling our dinners with torrents of bleach. If idle distractions or illicit diversions ever tempted her, she resisted them with the forbearance of a willing martyr.

Schooled in everything but matters of the heart, Professor Cleave mistook her habitual industry for moral rigor and her seriousness for a studious bent. Smitten, he suffered the awkwardness of an isolated intellectual. He addressed Cora only to answer her pointed questions about towel inventories. Her brusque manners failed to quell his muddled passions. On short breaks, he'd sit in the staff lounge, alternately longing to see her face and dreading her appearance. He'd rehearse witticisms about the weather, and when he heard her footsteps, retreat helplessly behind a book.

He pined in silence for months. He'd almost forsaken hope when Cora chose to linger over a small cup of unsweetened tea, taking tiny sips and biding her time until Professor Cleave met her eyes.

"What is your name?"

"Professor."

"I am not interested in your nickname."

"Wynston," he said, his ears warming.

"My name is Cora."

"I'm sorry." He hadn't asked about her name because he'd already spelled it a thousand times in his mind, cherished its open syllables and languorous vowels.

"I am not sorry. I like my name."

Thus began a clipped exchange that, in fits and bursts, would fill a lifetime, or in this case, two lives spent in close proximity. Though her careful diction charmed him, Professor Cleave enjoyed only the most constrained conversations with Cora. She remained frugal in speech, even on the afternoons they strolled around the harbor.

"Do you ever think of leaving?" Professor Cleave gazed at the horizon. "For the States?"

"I don't think I'd care much for life over there."

"London?"

"I wouldn't like London. They say it rains every day."

"You think you'll stay here?"

"I think so."

"You wouldn't be leaving, then?"

"Are you asking?"

"I'm asking."

"Then I will stay."

This was as close as Professor Cleave ever came to proposing. He married Cora in Stokes Hill's chapel four weeks later, while Rose quietly wept at the loss of her son and Topsy nervously massaged a scrap of paper covered in cricket scores. Shortly after, Professor Cleave and Cora moved into a small house and settled into unbending routines and undemonstrative physical intimacies. The latter eventually produced a daughter, named Irma after the former head of Portsmouth's library. As Irma passed through childhood, she revealed a promising intellect, as well as a physical beauty that defied all genetic probabilities. She brought Professor Cleave a joy he fought to preserve in the face of emotional austerity at home and growing social disparity everywhere else.

With the United Independent Party in power, restored plantations welcomed wealthy patrons seeking the curative powers of mud baths and tropical breezes. Sprawling second homes appeared on St. Anne's southern peninsula. While water pipes and electric cables snaked into gated communities, small villages continued to rely on rooftop cisterns and temperamental generators. Portsmouth's shops sold cigars and gold jewelry to wintering Americans with well-worn credit cards, while St. Anne's schools and tiny hospital fell into disrepair, and then disgrace.

Anxious about his daughter's future, Professor Cleave spent every afternoon mixing drinks and every night ferrying drunks between parties. At midnight, he'd drive home and place his day's earnings in a biscuit tin. He'd wipe the oily prints of foreheads from his cab's windows and spray insecticide into its vents. It's hard to imagine how we managed in those years, dropping from gaskets like so many drunks, only to crawl back into the cab hours later to escape the sun. For our survival, we can thank the short half-life of the cheap pesticides Professor Cleave used and Professor Cleave's predictability, which enabled us to stay one step ahead of the stinging mist. What a dull existence he led! Still, he knew something of happiness for the first seventeen years of his daughter's life.

Change, when it arrived, came suddenly and with unprecedented cruelty. Within the span of four years, Professor Cleave helped his father bury his mother and Morris. He watched the SDA, under Little Butts, trade its values for vanities. He spent three years in prison and developed odd physical tics that, in anxious moments, overpowered his self-restraint. After his release, he drove his taxi only in the morning, in an attempt to avoid the company of nodding drug addicts and drunks. At night, he maintained a studied reserve behind the bar to distance himself from the slurred confessions of strangers. He sought refuge from painful memories in chimerical gardens and constructed intellectual bulwarks against tempestuous feelings. He talked to cockroaches.

We might have welcomed his social overtures more readily, had they not been so transparently inspired by loneliness. We have feelings, too, whatever rubbish Ivy League entomologists claim. Sometimes, though, it's easier to forgive than to fight. And if a sucker is born every minute, it stands to reason, statistically speaking, that some of them are cockroaches (chumps to the last, those of us who stayed in his cab!).

Hopefully, one can understand our low graduation rate from Professor Cleave's cab. As more and more Americans descended on St. Anne, maids and janitors and taxi drivers (excepting one) pursued their insecticidal regimens with ever-increasing ferocity and drove us from nearly every air-conditioned "public" space. It's hardly surprising, then, that we reached a strained accommodation with Professor Cleave.

The day the *Celeste* arrived, the sun was beating mercilessly. After the two Americans left his cab, Professor Cleave parked in the shade, thumbed the pages of his anthology, and tried to compose himself before the start of his shift at the Ambassador. Deflated, we listened to him dissect the appearance of his latest passengers—the man with depthless eyes and the woman with an unnerving pallor.

"She was all too familiar, my students. A hungry ghost desperate with need."

He scraped his thumb with his fingernail and examined a patch of inflamed skin. "We should have avoided her today, just as we should have avoided her sort back then, but these are lean days made leaner by your carrying on." He narrowed his eyes at those of us on the dashboard. "I see the affairs of others are of no concern to you, and that you are content to lapse into intellectual atrophy."

As it was, we'd begun to feel overwhelmed by strange emanations from the ship. He considered our limp antennae and splayed wings. "Here you are, lazing about, mired in willful ignorance."

He opened his book to a rabbit-eared page. He read aloud, at first, pausing once to pose a question about the motivations and morals of tragic figures. By then, we had withdrawn behind the vents. The most demoralized among us slipped into dreamless sleep beneath the hood. Professor Cleave tapped the dashboard, and when none of us reappeared, he read silently until the Ambassador's face grew ashen in the twilight.

EXILE

IXATED TO AN UNHEALTHY degree on our affinity for sewers, social commentators and petty moralists have long referred to us as the "Great Unwashed" and the "teeming masses." Even now, one will hardly see the words "cosmopolitan" or "sophisticated" attached to "roaches" in scientific journals, or in the sensationalist tracts written about us—publications designed to alarm more than edify. Despite the baseless aspersions cast by our human detractors, we're quite cosmopolitan. Ignorance is a luxury, as we discovered when Europeans destroyed our homes and exposed us to the merciless sun and untold misery.

Once the British began their abominable trade in sugar and slaves, we stowed away on ships bound for Liverpool and London, nestled among hogsheads and shuddered at the cursing of debauched captains and their scurvy-ridden crews. In England, we beheld poachers strung from gallows and clouds of poison massing above Blake's Dark Satanic Mills. We ate exquisitely aged cheese, mingled with pickpockets, and rode on the undersides of aristocrats' carriages. We lived in castles built for kings. We made our way around the world, drawn by tantalizing scents and distant horizons. We learned Swahili and Arabic, and in the packs of camel traders, crossed seas of rippled sand. We explored abandoned Mughal palaces and nearly lost ourselves in poppy fields. We ran amok in the Forbidden City, perched on golden pagodas and napped in jade vases. We heard Verdi performed in Vienna and sampled Lutefisk in the taverns of Oslo. We lived on the crumbs of croissants and literary conversation in Montparnasse. We dabbled in jazz with bedbugs and Beat poets in Greenwich Village and slept with hobos on trains rattling into Detroit and Chicago, mythical cities built upon mountains of coal.

Needless to say, we became intimately acquainted with human nature in its varied expressions, what some call "the ways of the world," and the outlandish behavior of humans blowing off steam in exotic locales. We clung to the prows of Venetian gondolas littered with beer cans and nearly suffocated in stretch limousines packed with stag parties trolling the streets of Manhattan (Jay Gatsby would have paled!). We disappeared in cocaine drifts in Ibizan dance clubs and got trampled in discos in Rio de Janeiro. We passed out in cheap hostels in Dublin and four-star hotels in Dubai. We found ourselves dumfounded by unspeakable doings in the back alleys of Bangkok.

Some of us returned to St. Anne as citizens of the world, bearing stories of wondrous things and the terrible weight of hard-earned wisdom. With little difficulty, we recognized the signs of moral depravity that marked the Ambassador's typical guests: discount travelers, individuals with undiscerning palates, and the unfortunates expelled from the drunk tanks and infirmaries of cruise ships. Any goodwill on the part of these anti-socialites rarely extended to our kind, so we studied them from a distance. We huddled in air ducts and observed their awkward movements, odd grooming habits and unsightly mating rituals. Once they departed, we'd sample the remnants of partially digested delicacies and the residue clinging to plastic cups ("What happens in St. Anne stays in St. Anne," guests used to say, and how true, for they always left their trash behind!). We lived off their garbage, and by their garbage, we knew them. We knew what they disregarded and most desperately treasured. We knew of their inexplicable anxieties and aversions. We often wondered whether the splendorous Earth described by Geoffrey Morrow could, in fact, sustain "infinite varieties of tree and flower and beast." Would Morrow, had he imagined the sorts expelled from the *Celeste*, have retained his precious faith?

CHAPTER THREE

THE TWO AMERICANS EXPELLED from the *Celeste* that November afternoon were more subdued than most. The man went to the Ambassador's lounge without bothering to book a room. With a cigarette burning between two fingers, he sat alone at the end of the bar, quietly contemplating the harbor through a glass door covered with dust and fingerprints. He ordered a beer and a rum chaser to mark the *Celeste*'s slow passage from the harbor, reveling in his release from its narrow service stairwells and the windowless rooms beneath its waterline. Who could blame him? The *Celeste* was a real shitshow for cockroaches, not to mention its crew members and more depressive passengers. Those of us who'd crawled off the ship earlier that day, sugar-addled and shattered, shared his relief.

He recalled his first moments on land and the sensation he'd experienced, struck by the vivid contrast between the sky's postcard blue and the patchwork of green and gold covering a rise of hills. He'd let his eyes wander down cobblestone streets and over the glistening skin of men loading crates onto flatbed trucks. He'd inhaled the scent of overripe bananas and exulted in his unexpected dismissal, an opportunity, he'd told himself, imagining unmeasured hours and unaccounted days unfolding before him. He'd turned to the *Celeste* and watched the last passengers board, delighted not to be among them.

Where the ship had been, gulls now skimmed the water. He considered wandering back into town to lose himself in dark clubs and light conversations with strangers. First, he decided, he'd have another drink.

He ordered a beer and a pack of Silk Cuts from the bartender, lit a cigarette and forgot about it, and then lit another before the first burned down in an ashtray. He swiveled unsteadily on his barstool and looked out at the patio, where two women sat at a tiki bar, sucking pink slush through straws and appraising a bellboy skimming debris from a pool with a shallow net. The steep arches of their penciled eyebrows reminded him of drag queens he'd known in Miami, and he smiled at the association until the phrase "pool boy" entered his mind. He turned from the patio and gripped the edge of the bar. When he looked outside again, the patio was empty. He met the blank gaze of a man dimly reflected upon smudged glass, spending his meager severance pay and drinking to forget.

"I've come to the wrong place to seek my fortune," he said.

He pulled an employee badge from his pocket. He studied the smooth face in a thumbnail photo and the barcode beside his name. Being fired was for the best, he thought. He'd spent too many years adrift at sea, delivering towels and mopping up spills and sleeping with strangers in expensive suites.

"A long fucking rut," he whispered.

He slumped against the bar and entertained disparate thoughts connected to the drawn-out day. He'd never been a victim, he assured himself. Even as a closet case growing up in a rustbelt Michigan town with four closed foundries, he'd never surrendered to circumstance. On streets lined with foreclosed houses, pawnshops, and bail bond offices, he'd been restless where others had been resigned. In high school, he scavenged from abandoned buildings, stripping copper pipes and light fixtures from the walls and carting abandoned furniture to consignment shops. He made his way by selling bits of the past in a place with no future. In his ability to find modest riches amidst rubbish, Dave Fowles was a man after our hearts.

Five months after he graduated from high school, he crawled into a house strewn with the mildewed blankets of departed squatters and discovered a porn magazine splayed open to a tribute to "The Boys of Miami Beach." He knelt down before a series of epilated men squeezing and swallowing each other, and fourteen seconds later, he shuddered and released a wordless prayer to the sound of hail beating against a cracked window. One year later, he boarded a Greyhound bus for Miami, carrying only a duffel bag, a fake driver's license, and directions to a cheap hostel. Again, who could blame him? He'd just spent twelve months making minimum wage in a subterranean garage, flushing out the oily intestines of rusted cars and dreaming of six-pack abdomens.

In the Ambassador's lounge, he recalled his first impressions of Miami as a place bathed in golden light. He recalled the astonishing array of foreign flags fluttering from convertibles' antennas, the Spanish names of tiny grocery stores, pastel Art Deco motels and rainbow decals on café windows. He recalled the bronzed skin of beautiful men. He recalled the absence of grey.

He'd spent his first few weeks in Miami cradling rum-filled coconut shells in beachfront bars, downing cocktails in dark clubs, blushing at the jokes of powdered queens, and throwing up in bathrooms bathed in black light, where we flourished in filthy stalls, our wings opalescent beneath glowing graffiti. He leased a room in a subdivided house (with a gorgeously begrimed communal kitchen), fed potato chips to seagulls perched on his windowsill, and learned fragments of French from a Haitian woman across the hall. He experimented with ecstasy and cocaine and eventually settled on rum and tequila. He browsed sex shops and local newspapers, learning equal amounts from each as he explored crowded streets filled with color and the promise of new life.

Just before his money ran out, he found his first in a long series of short-lived jobs, and with it, his first lover. At a club called Rough Riders—a place we rarely ventured unless tempted against our better judgment by the playlists on MasterMix Tuesdays—he loaded industrial dishwashers and picked up bartending tricks, along with an aspiring model from Belize. For months, Dave and Miguel spent every night together, each recounting stories of places exotic to the other. Dave spoke of county fairs and cinnamon-dusted elephant ears. Miguel described the emerald feathers of quetzal birds, sapphire lakes and volcanoes shrouded in mist, overgrown ruins carved with tributes to ancient kings, and a childhood spent chasing monkeys behind waterfalls. Dave never considered that Miguel's stories were soothing lullabies, fabrications as fantastic as any tale fashioned to draw children into pleasant dreams.

When Miguel decided to seek his fortunes in New York, he left Dave with visions of resplendent equatorial beauty and stirrings of restlessness. On the twelfth anniversary of his arrival in Miami, Dave applied for a job with Maiden Cruises, daydreaming of jungles teeming with monkeys as he checked boxes on a two-page aptitude test. He became a workout attendant aboard the *Celeste* one week later.

He never set foot in Belize. He beheld the country of his dreams as he viewed most Maiden Cruise destinations, through a fitness center's tinted windows or the plastic weave of a cyclone fence surrounding the staff sundeck. He spent his days sterilizing elliptical trainers and wiping sweat from the seats of sedentary bicycles. He spent his evenings in the windowless world below the waterline, a labyrinth of service stairwells and narrow corridors painted battleship grey, that is, until he began trespassing on the world of moonlit decks and swim-up bars to pursue illicit trysts with the besotted businessmen and college students he'd harnessed to the *Celeste*'s climbing wall. At least once a week, he strolled down a carpeted hallway with a fresh towel draped over his arm and a cabin number inked onto his palm. Had it been possible, we would have explained the risks of dalliance above the waterline, where maintenance crews employed the worst kinds of sprays, so that air seemed scarce and life uncertain. Once, his Latvian bunkmate tried to impart the hard-earned wisdom of exiles.

"Someday, you go too far," he said. "You know orientation? The only thing guest should remember is staff smile. There is not fraternizing. That word. In English is fucking, right?"

Perhaps only those who have been hunted to the ends of every five-star restaurant understand the importance of reading between the lines. Dave little understood euphemisms or the limits of fraternity. Six hours ago, he'd gone too far.

He considered a smudged number on his palm and remembered smooth hands on his hips and the world listing as everything grew warm and wet. He never heard the door or saw the mother until he felt the chill of saliva evaporating from his penis. He lifted his head from a pillow and yanked his pants over his dying erection, and two hours later, the cruise director gave him three hundred dollars in back pay and fired him for fraternizing with a seventeen-year-old who'd claimed to be in college.

He rubbed the smear of ink on his palm and looked across the harbor, at the outlines of shops and houses dissolving along the shore and the tiny crescent of yellow lights appearing in their place. He pushed aside an empty bottle. It was time to move on, he thought. He'd always extricated himself from moribund places and hopeless situations, even if he'd had to leave certain people behind, including the woman wearing a ragged sweater with misery ground into its threads.

When he first saw her, she'd just been escorted from the terminal and left on the curb by two security guards. She sat down on a suitcase and pulled her sweater over her narrow shoulders and, with a difficulty that sickened him, over the bandages covering her inner arms. She lifted her face once, beheld her surroundings with a stupefied gaze and turned in his direction. He'd grown agitated by a sense of uninvited responsibility, and against his better judgment he'd persuaded her to share a cab. She looked as insubstantial as the breeze, but as he led her toward the taxi, he'd felt the impossible pull of gravity, the weight of a broken albatross clinging to his neck.

When he flagged the bellboy and abandoned the woman in the lobby, he hadn't acted callously, he told himself, but in honest recognition of his own helplessness. Unsettled, still, he dedicated himself to spending his severance pay, flattening debased bills on the bar and dissolving lingering uncertainties in successive beers. When his fingertips went numb, he assured himself that everything had been for the best, and that his next beer would be his last before he wandered into town. At the end of the night, he'd sleep on a secluded beach, lulled by the sound of waves breaking beneath a pale moon.

Had it been possible, we might have told him how few can slumber on beaches without a care for incoming tides.

When Professor Cleave entered the lounge, he dragged his hand along his neck with a mild sense of displeasure, one he associated less with the chill of perspiration cooling too quickly than the sight of his last passenger slumped on a stool. Lost in his own reflection, the man evoked a perfect picture of intellectual dereliction. He had the pose of a man dissolving every thought flitting at the edge of a dulled conscience. Professor Cleave stepped behind the bar and began slicing limes into identical segments. The man had at least parted company with the woman, he thought, and then startled at the sound of his voice.

"I'll have another." Dave leaned across the bar. "Hey, I was in your cab."

Professor Cleave appraised Dave's lopsided smile and placed a bowl of peanuts on the bar.

"Ain't that the shit?" Dave lifted his badge and squinted at the image of his face until the card slipped from his fingers and fell to the floor. "My services are no longer required. Told the guy at the dock I'm seeking my fortunes here. Told me I came to the wrong place."

Professor Cleave set a bottle on the counter. "That would depend on what you want to do."

"Spent years mopping up sweat and helping people live out Everest fantasies on a climbing wall." Dave cracked open a peanut. "Time for a change is all I got to say."

"I suppose you know best." Professor Cleave looked at the rings of condensation beneath Dave's fingers. "It's no small thing to lose a job."

"I can pull a job on some other line." Dave shrugged. "Just glad to be off that ship. It was turning into a sick ward. Quarantine tape on doors. People mixing up plates at buffets. Kids shitting in pools. Too many fucking people in one place."

Dave was leaning forward, as if to speak in confidence, when two men in polo shirts stepped up to the bar.

"Two Cane Cutters," one said. He turned to his companion. "The national drink here. When in Rome, they say."

"Ain't exactly Rome." The second man tossed a credit card onto the bar. "I was pricing generators. Half are from Eastern Europe. The rest are from American companies that went belly up years ago."

"Soviet junk the Russians don't want and Midwestern scrap."

"Ted's pissed about the nickel-and-diming. He thinks St. Anne's an opportunity. There's still some beachfront real estate left."

Professor Cleave uncapped a bottle of rum and feigned concentration on the garnishes rimming two glasses.

"With workers from the DR, we'll stay under budget."

"Bring that up tomorrow at the Plantations. I'm shifting over first thing in the morning. Can't believe the secretary put me in the wrong hotel."

Dave listened quietly until the men collected their drinks and left for the patio. "Guys like that can really ruin a buzz," he said.

"Expense-account entrepreneurs." Professor Cleave trailed off.

"Midwestern scrap. What assholes." Dave picked at the label on his bottle. "So, Cane Cutters."

Professor Cleave turned a lime over in his hand. "They're popular with tourists. So they're the national drink."

"Watched you make them. Used to make a version when I was bartending in Miami. Rum. Red Bull. Chocolate liqueur. Called it a Bull Run."

"You left Miami to work on the ship?"

"Wanted to see the world. Ever been to Miami?"

"I've never left St. Anne. Years ago, my uncle lived in New York. Or Newark." Professor Cleave paused. "He always said I should join him, but there were too many things to do here."

"Good to know. I'm tempted to stick around."

"If it's paid work you want, you'll be a long time looking."

"That's what your friend at the dock said."

Professor Cleave swept a peanut husk from the bar. "Desmond is one to foul his own nest."

"A man after my own heart. Hiring cab drivers?"

"You'll need to join the union, and it helps to marry someone's sister or cousin."

Dave lit a cigarette. "Afraid that ain't in the cards, brother."

Professor Cleave turned to a mounted television and watched Lyndon Buttskell smile at a reporter. "There you go again, Little Butts."

"Who's that?"

"Our prime minister, Lyndon Buttskell."

"You just call him Little Butts?"

"That's what everybody calls him."

"Not liked much, I take it," Dave said.

"There's little of substance to like or dislike."

"Not a bad-looking guy."

"He's the best of a bad lot." Professor Cleave rubbed his fingertips together. "He belongs to the taxi drivers' union."

"He drives a cab?"

"He's never driven a car in his life. You don't get to be prime minister by driving a taxi."

"No shit." Dave took a drag off his cigarette. "Speaking of cabs, where do people go around here? Clubs, that kind of thing."

"You wouldn't go into Portsmouth at night. You'll find Americans at the Plantations. People on holiday from Minnesota, Michigan. The Midwest."

"You've heard of Michigan?"

"I read about it." Professor Cleave sliced a lime in half. "Henry Ford. General Motors."

"Riots. Recession. Grew up there and got the hell out. Didn't want to end up like my dad, drinking alone in windowless bars. Staggering home in the snow." Dave fingered the neck of his bottle. "Maybe I'll visit someday. Haven't been back. My dad's alone now."

Professor Cleave lost his grip on his knife, and when he looked down, blood was beading on the tip of his thumb. He pressed his thumb into a hand towel. "Where's the lady you were with?"

"She got a room. Probably just needed to pass out. Sure she's fine."

Professor Cleave watched Dave take a long swig of beer and wondered at the sordid nature of holiday trysts.

What did Professor Cleave know about sordid behavior? There was nothing sordid about Helen S. Mudge, except the damage she'd done to herself in such remarkably human fashion. She didn't move when we squeezed from behind the baseboards and examined the sweater she'd cast to the floor, alternately drawn and repulsed by the scents of sweat and disinfectants clinging to its threads, and encouraged by her obvious disinterest in doing violence to anyone but herself. She sat on the edge of a bed, rubbing Betadine stains from her palms, listening to the air conditioner's death rattle and observing our tentative movements with a meditative gaze. At sunset, she peeled off the gauze bandages taped to her arms, trailed her fingers along a line of sutures, and looked across the harbor at a thin red line rimming the horizon and the tiers of glowing windows giving shape to the *Celeste*'s receding form. Then, with a mystified expression, she considered her reflection in a smudged mirror. She was an anemically white wisp fading in the waning light.

If only the reasons for Helen Mudge's quiet accommodation with us had been less depressing. Only two days earlier, she'd become the ultimate paradox: a failed suicide. This, even more than the damage she'd done to herself, had left her utterly dumfounded. She was, after all, the daughter and granddaughter of two highly accomplished suicides.

She discovered this at the age of ten, at a family barbeque. While chasing toads in her backyard, she came upon a dead sparrow. A curious child, she lifted its broken wing with a stick and examined the maggots writhing in its chest cavity. Her father watched from the patio, stricken by the morbid curiosity of his only daughter.

"Don't ever play with dead things," he said, crossing the lawn to spread a fan of paper napkins over the bird. "You'll have nightmares."

An hour later, Helen sat alone in the backyard, just beyond the pale of glowing paper lanterns, eavesdropping on the conversations of intoxicated adults.

"Most girls would have run screaming," her father said. "But then, her mother always had that same morbid streak. I shouldn't have been surprised when she jumped from that roof." He took a long sip of gin. "I just didn't think she'd leave me with a newborn baby. A girl."

"Between that and her grandmother's arsenic cocktails, you have to wonder if suicide's hereditary," her aunt said. "You'd think it would be hard to pass along the genes, but I guess some people only get depressed after the kids show up."

After dinner, Helen sat down beside her father and listened to the crackle of mosquitoes electrifying themselves in a bug lamp. "I read mosquitoes only live for one day," she said hesitantly. "Do they fly into the bug zapper because they're sad?"

"It's in their nature." Her father gazed at a shriveled hot dog left on the grill. "It's inevitable."

That night, Helen spent hours staring at a Polaroid image of her mother, noting each similarity between her own features and those fading under a gloss finish, and anticipating the impulses that would bring about her own death.

"It's inevitable," she whispered over and over.

Conditioned by foregone conclusions, she lived her adult life by default. After graduating from law school, she accepted a job in the legal department of a Chicago gas company and adopted the life of an emotional ascetic. She shied away from close friendships and avoided long-term romantic entanglements, opting for casual encounters with incurably fatuous or terminally ill men. She renewed short-term leases on apartments furnished with items from down-scale chain stores—pressboard tables with peeling veneers, dressers with badly glued joints, and sagging plastic bins. She took her possessions' rapid depreciation for granted; she inhabited a world without a future, a world not worth saving. She ended up in St. Anne entirely by chance, after winning a voucher for a Caribbean cruise at a work party raffle. By the restricted terms of a special offer, she booked a Deluxe Interior Stateroom, a windowless cabin not far from the *Celeste's* massive engines. Death is inevitable, but the doomed need something to do in the meantime, after all.

On the *Celeste*, she passed joyless hours in the company of cheer-ful strangers. She exchanged pleasantries with Baptist missionaries in a cupcake-decorating class. She won eleven dollars from a slot machine and downed margaritas with a divorced dentist. She waltzed with a former U.S. ambassador and traded ping-pong tips with a defrocked priest. She watched diapered monkeys riding unicycles and chorus lines of sequined women dancing in feathered capes. With an arm-chair art critic from Montana, she wandered through carpeted gal-leries, appraising Picasso knock-offs and oil paintings of kittens. At a formal dinner, she drifted through conversation with a Texas ma-triarch hunched beneath the weight of gold chains. Later, in a quiet piano bar, she realized she couldn't remember the name of a single person she'd met on the ship, and that she hadn't tasted anything in days or enjoyed herself in decades.

"It's inevitable," she whispered.

She spent the following morning in her cabin, pacing before a painting of a sailboat foundering in the trough between bleeding watercolor waves. Each time a vibration moved through the floor, she shuddered at the sense of constant drift leading nowhere. In the afternoon, she wandered the decks alone, pausing in the shadows of lifeboats to contemplate cherry-red smokestacks and the black smoke trailing in their wake. She watched seagulls skim the ocean's surface for floating refuse, mesmerized by their graceful movements and the endless sky burial of trash. She imagined the end of ambivalence, the silence and peace after all struggle ceases.

When the *Celeste* docked in Barbados the following day, she remained on board, leaning against a deck railing. Beneath her, dead fish and foam containers floated on iridescent oil rainbows. Entranced by the water's metallic sheen, she drifted into decision. In a drugstore off the promenade deck, she bought a box of fat-free cookies, a bag of gumdrops, a pack of razor blades, a cheap magazine, and a bottle of aspirin. She threw everything but the aspirin and razor blades into a trash bin outside the store.

She expected a literary suicide, the weightlessness and release of Ophelia floating in warm water, the gentle ebb of life and the slow surrender of regret. The intensity of pain stunned her, and the rush of adrenaline filled her with panic. The edges of her vision blackened, and through a collapsing tunnel, she saw stark red fans unfolding across the water filling her bathroom sink. A chill seized her, the walls groaned, and she grasped the horror of solitary death in a windowless room. With her arms folded in a towel, she staggered from her cabin and into an elevator, down hallways and through a crowded restaurant, past melting ice sculptures of mermaids. Beyond a set of open French doors, she collapsed beside an empty deck chair. Silhouetted gulls circled in the afterglow of sunset and grew indistinct against the horizon. Regretting only their passing, she drifted in and out of consciousness, dimly aware of someone screaming and unmoored faces hovering above her.

From the Ambassador, she watched the *Celeste*'s lights fade and tried to recollect two days nearly effaced from her memory. That morning, she'd awoken to the stab of an intravenous needle sliding from beneath her skin. After receiving a vacuum-sealed pouch containing her dry-cleaned dress, she signed forms covered in fine print, naming herself as the sole party responsible for her injuries and waiving her rights to future claims. A security guard escorted her through a crowded infirmary, along monochromatic passages suffused with the smell of sickness, past dyspeptic crew members and small mounds of absorptive dust, and down a service gangplank. An American touched her shoulder and said something about the swiftness of Caribbean sunsets, and she'd followed him without question to a waiting cab. She'd let him carry her suitcase into the lobby and summon a bellboy.

For the first time, she imagined strangers going through her cabin and collecting her things, bleaching the sink and talking about the latest suicide, or worse, the weather. She broke into a sweat and slid from the bed to open her suitcase. She found her clothes, crumpled as she'd left them, and a pouch containing her toiletries, a bottle of aspirin, and a box of razor blades collected by an unsparingly efficient staff. She held the box in her hands, studied its torn cardboard edge, pressed her fingertip against an exposed blade and twitched.

She was staring at the blade when she heard knocking—muffled, it seemed, by the deepening gloom. She struggled to her feet and pressed her eye to a peephole. The bellboy was floating fish-eyed at the end of a tunnel. His knocking stopped and resumed, grew more insistent and intolerable as she forced her arms into her sweater. When her sutures caught in its sleeves, she cast the sweater aside and opened the door just enough to frame her face.

The bellboy held out her driver's license. "You left this at the front desk. They told me to bring it."

She slid two fingers past the door. He hesitated and then slipped her license between them.

"You carried my bag," she said. "I meant to give you something earlier. I wasn't feeling well."

She trailed off at the sight of his arms, covered in raised scars she hadn't noticed earlier, drew a sharp breath and pressed a hand to her lips.

"I won't bother you again," he began.

He stuttered, once, and shuddered. The muscles in his face rippled and his fingers curled into his palms. He pressed a loose fist against his temple, and she gripped the edge of the door. When his shaking subsided, she stepped back to open the door wide, but he'd already started down the corridor, trailing his fingers along the wall to steady himself.

Traces of his cologne and sweat, the presence of something pungent and cutting, lingered in the room. She listened to the erratic buzz of a fly skating around the sink and contemplated her own horror, no less cruel for being unintended. She stood shivering in the darkness and ruminating for nearly an hour. When she felt the first hunger pang in days, she placed the box of razor blades on the bathroom counter and glanced at a room service menu. Sick at the thought of the bellboy, she gathered her sweater from the floor.

She found Dave in the lounge, leaning over the bar and hanging (inexplicably, we thought) on every one of Professor Cleave's words.

"Whole crew's back together." Dave patted an empty stool. "Remember Wynston? His friends call him Professor."

Professor Cleave wiped his hands in a towel and considered her vacant expression. "You were in my cab."

"She could use a Cane Cutter," Dave said. "And I'll take another."

"What's a Cane Cutter?" Helen asked.

Professor Cleave reached for a bottle of rum. "A machete. For cutting cane."

"He'll give you a whole lecture. I should get a goddamn college degree for drinking here." Dave lit a cigarette and turned back to

Professor Cleave. "Anyway, these guys were fine getting arrested for stripping copper. Middle of winter. Happy to have three hots and a cot. Ended up being three hundred hots."

Professor Cleave pressed his thumb and finger together. From the edges of rubber floor mats, we ingested bits of rind and tried to quell the movements of our antennae. He was staunching a flood of memories, and we feared he'd be tempted to recite Geoffrey Morrow again on the way home. Helen sat quietly, grateful to be spared the demands of conversation by Dave's drunken monologue. She said nothing until Professor Cleave placed two drinks on the bar.

"Yours is different."

"Skipped the Coke," Dave said. "Skipped the ice, too, because of this drought he was telling me about. Extreme measures for extreme times."

"You mean double measures for difficult times," Professor Cleave said.

"Nothing difficult for me. I'm a free man now. It was a goddamn plague ship. Restaurants closing. Slipping on shit every time you walked down a hall."

"The infirmary was crowded." Helen looked down at her lap. "By the time I left."

"Hand-sanitizing stations everywhere. Hell, we got off just in time."

"You never mentioned what it was," Professor Cleave said.

"Some virus. Happens all the time. This one's just getting around faster than usual." Dave raised his glass. "Here's to freedom."

Helen tilted her head back and let her drink slide down her throat.

"Eat something before you go hard, sister." Dave slid a menu in her direction. "They got club sandwiches. Can probably get them anywhere in the world."

She nodded, and Professor Cleave wrote a note on a pink order slip. He considered her anemic cast and calmed himself with the fact that she'd ordered food.

"I'll have someone bring this order to the kitchen," he said, glancing at his watch and imagining the whereabouts of Tremor Prentice, the Ambassador's lone bellboy.

Happy Hour, for us, ended the moment Helen placed her order. The club sandwiches at the Ambassador were nearly indigestible, and given how long it took Tremor Prentice to deliver anything, the chances of the two Americans hailing a cab to Portsmouth before the night's end seemed slim indeed. Once again, we faced an evening of insurmountable boredom in the lounge. DJ Xspec's *Heavy Vibes Hour* was about the last thing we'd be likely to hear coming through the lounge's outdated sound system. However abysmal Portsmouth nightlife, the owner of Reef Wrecks at least had KRS-One and Fab 5 Freddy on vinyl. Despairing, we quietly seethed and slipped into the nearest air ducts in search of different company and tolerable snacks.

We might have expected too much in the way of easy entertainment. Still, we found ourselves incurably dissatisfied, bristling at loose comments about getting a "goddamn college degree" simply for drinking in the presence of Professor Cleave. How rudimentary Dave Fowles's education was, and how easily earned, relative to our own! Any cockroach subjected to Professor Cleave's endless lectures should have been given an honorary degree from Harvard and treated to a cruise on a garbage barge off the coast of New Jersey. What really frosted our collective ass, though, was our frustrated desire, our desperate need for decent music. This, Tremor Prentice, sitting high above on the Ambassador's roof, would have understood.

WONDER

THE VIEW FROM THE Ambassador's rooftop would hardly have merited comment by those who have watched, as we have, the sun set behind the Golden Gate Bridge from the Fairmont Hotel, or beheld the Nihonbashi River from the top of the Mandarin Oriental. Still, we often found ourselves drawn into the Ambassador's service stairwells and storm drains and onto the rooftop, which afforded views unrivaled, at least, on St. Anne.

After the British built an airstrip, we used to watch the occasional plane ascend over the mountains and disappear into clouds that seemed almost within reach. We'd marvel at their speed and wonder how we ever survived journeys in the cramped holds of sailing ships. On clear afternoons, we'd trail our antennae in the breeze and pick up radio transmissions from around the world. We'd spend hours listening to Calypso Rose, and as time passed, Miles Davis, the Ramones, and DJ Xspec's *Heavy Vibes Hour*. At night, we'd trace the shapes of constellations and wonder at the beauty of life so far above the ground. We'd forget that our wings were brittle and flight nearly impossible, and that gravity held sway over our affairs.

Trevor Prentice, or Tremor as he called himself, used to sit on the rooftop and smoke weed to escape the Ambassador's most boorish guests and Professor Cleave's constant harangues. He would have been surprised to learn that Professor Cleave, in his younger years, had spent quite a bit of time on the roof himself. Of course, Professor

Cleave went to the rooftop to read. On the rooftop, he first encountered the writings of Max Weber and James Baldwin and, much to our regret, Geoffrey Morrow. He'd survey the coastline and reflect upon historical contingencies and possible futures. He'd forget the watch on his wrist and the dirty towels lying beside the pool. He'd forget the sway of circumstance over lofty ambitions.

Both Professor Cleave and Tremor went to the rooftop to be alone, or so they thought. Little did Professor Cleave know that he was disturbing our quiet reveries each time he read aloud. Little did Tremor know that, whenever he lit a joint, we'd emerge from rooftop drains and enjoy, secondhand, God's greenest grass.

Without dwelling on specific ratios of THC, CBL, CBND, and CBT, we can say that Tremor grew tremendous weed, the sort best ingested in a relaxed frame of mind, in the company of compassionate sorts willing to overlook others' foibles and laugh at themselves. Simply, it was heavy shit with somewhat unpredictable effects. Tremor often menaced us with his lighter if we got too close, so we hid in the shadows when we partook, drawing thin trails of smoke from drifting clouds and tuning into radio stations around the world. For a succession of fleeting instants, we'd be as one, connected via tingling antennae to every cockroach on every rooftop on Earth, tripping through infinite space and meditating like six-legged bodhisattvas tasting something of Nirvana.

It's safe to say that Tremor Prentice lived in complete ignorance of Geoffrey Morrow. What's more, he would have scorned Morrow's purely academic interest in certain herb-bearing seeds. Yet Tremor was, far and away, one of the best gardeners on the island. He'd developed remarkable methods for conjuring and cross-fertilizing magical herbs in the ruts of abandoned cane fields. He possessed a subtle appreciation for the earth, a keen insight into its delicate yield and stubborn refusals. He knew how badly it had been poisoned. He'd been born, after all, amidst the pungent smell of tidal muck and grown up like a weed on St. Anne's most polluted ground.

CHAPTER FOUR

CHALK IT UP TO the Ambassador's miserable menu, but the night Helen and Dave arrived, quite a few of us were on the roof, engulfed in smoke and floating in streams of music only we could hear. But all happy hours come to an end, as did this one, thanks to an ill-timed order for a club sandwich. Just as we began to dissolve in waves of pale light reflected off distant planets, Professor Cleave's voice and a burst of static came through Tremor's radio. What a buzzkill. The proverbial snack bowl had run dry, we thought in our addled, metaphor-mixing state, and scattered into the shadows to escape Tremor's hostile vibes.

Tremor turned off the radio hanging from his belt and became a bellboy without a bell, a red-eyed renegade drawing from a joint in a futile attempt at forgetting. He tried to blot out the memory of Professor Cleave and the woman who had studied him from behind a nearly closed door, shunned physical contact, and stared at him as if willing his hands to shake. He entertained nebulous fantasies of revenge, momentarily exhilarated by the turmoil in his mind, and just as quickly succumbed to shame. Humiliation, while stoking his hatred, had marred its purity. He looked up at the attenuated arms of galaxies and the outlying stars pulsing beyond their reach and tried to quiet his mind, but the world was spinning too quickly, leaving white tracers across the sky. He gripped the polyester stretched across his knees and his eyes slipped out of focus. Slowly, he became aware of faint strains of music drifting across the harbor and stars assuming their places in familiar constellations. He uncurled his hands and massaged his thighs, struggled to his feet, and made his way across the roof on unsteady legs.

In the narrow enclosure of the Ambassador's service stairwell, he spat curse words and spiraled downward, past identical doors to identical floors. At the bottom of the stairs, he peered into the space between switchbacking flights and experienced a perverse sense of vertigo, a fear of falling upward. Stillborn laughter caught in his throat, and he pressed his hand against a wall to regain his balance. We should have fled his path, but between sleep deprivation and smoke, we felt cognitively clouded and emotionally stretched from our antennae to the tips of our tarsi. We were craving carbohydrates in the worst sort of way and hoping to discover some odd delicacy left in the staff lounge. Desperation knows no bounds.

The staff lounge had hardly changed in decades. White kitchen uniforms and smocks stained with dried sweat hung from exposed water pipes along the ceiling. They had the appearance, Tremor thought, of ghosts given form by bent wire hangers, limp specters of servitude resolved to haunt him. Unnerved, he rifled through the contents of dented lockers and then turned to a set of books stacked on a shelf. He considered their broken spines, selected a book at random, and collapsed on a couch with torn cushions. Hunched over a yellowed page, he ran his fingers over his scalp and traced the shape of his skull. He struggled through successive words, tripping over syllables and understanding little but hearing, still, echoes of Professor Cleave. Like drops of dirty water in his inner ear, they unbalanced him.

He scratched the side of his face and imagined Professor Cleave standing before him. "Shut your fucking mouth," he said.

Overcome by the static filling Tremor's mind, we crawled beneath the couch and lay down in dust. Our antennae had been strained to the point of exhaustion all day, and Tremor had become dangerously unpredictable. He clutched the book and closed his eyes, and his legs began to tingle. Again, Tremor had the tremors.

❧

Tremor hadn't always been called Tremor. He'd been given the name Trevor at birth, one week before the worst hurricane in St. Anne's history destroyed his home, a tiny fishing village nestled beneath a jagged outcropping of rock. Even before the storm, Rocky Point had been less a village than a line of shacks above a beach that seemed, at times, a receptacle for the world's refuse. Turning tides never reclaimed the bottles and bits of garbage that washed up or the innards of gutted fish left on the sand. Still, Rocky Point wasn't a stagnant backwater, as its smell might have suggested. (It was a tropical paradise offering every variety of edible trash for six-legged travelers.) Its human inhabitants enjoyed a livelihood that sustained them from year to year. Every morning, Rocky Point's men set out in tiny boats, and beneath the cliffs marking the edge of their world crossed themselves out of habit and cast their nets. No one went hungry. Destitution, unaddressed, would have been an embarrassment to all.

People even looked out for Mary Clay, or Crazy Mary, as everyone called her after her husband drowned. Overcome with grief and longing, she started leaving half-eaten pieces of fruit, offerings to unnamed gods, on her stoop to secure her husband's return. She erected crooked crosses of sticks and twine near her house, beside piles of stones and animal bones imbued with cryptic meanings. She drew abstruse signs in the air and held whispered conversations with the wind, and then with us. Over time, she began to feed us, placing scraps of food on her floor whenever she saw us. For that, and then for much nobler reasons, we fell madly in love with her.

Her house eventually slid into disrepair, but she spurned anyone who offered to buttress its sagging roof. Her husband, she insisted, would do this when he returned. If her neighbors avoided her, they engaged in thankless acts of charity, leaving squash and potatoes on her cinderblock stoop. Even after it became impossible to distinguish her ecstatic fits from her inebriated outbursts, some left bottles of cane liquor.

Except for Mary (and us), no one in Rocky Point anticipated the storm that would utterly transform their village. Three days before the storm, our antennae began to tingle. As if attuned to barometric imbalances, Mary buried her bone collections, pulled frayed ribbons from the trees around her house, and burned pages torn from her well-worn Bible. She started carrying her dead husband's compass, a rusting artifact of days filled with love. The day before the hurricane hit, she stood at the water's edge with outstretched arms to welcome her husband's return. For the first time, she shooed us away, and perhaps thinking we possessed functional wings, she urged us toward higher ground. Only at the last minute did she take shelter in the hills, sweeping us along in the folds of her skirt as rising swells brutalized the shoreline.

The hurricane left little on St. Anne untouched. It obliterated houses and swept away cars, carried the contents of storefronts out to sea and heaved silt onto streets. It saved its worst violence for Rocky Point. It left the beach strewn with shattered furniture, broken picture frames stripped of familiar faces, and boats half-buried in sand. It washed away Rocky Point's tiny cemetery and the abbreviated histories inscribed on wooden markers. It left shredded fishing nets dangling from uprooted trees and dead chickens and goats floating near shore. It left an embittered community of people who thereafter believed in God in the way of people who fear and hate him.

Within months of the storm, American developers descended upon St. Anne. They bought up devalued properties and dredged the harbor, constructed a cruise ship terminal, and converted derelict plantations into exclusive spas (creative destruction, indeed!). They imported Chinese shrimp, Australian lobster, and Pacific cod on massive cargo ships and laid a ring road for day-tripping tourists seeking panoramic views from brightly painted taxi vans. By design, the road curved inland at the island's northernmost point, away from the un-healed eyesore of Rocky Point. By the time Rocky Point's inhabitants salvaged their boats, the economies of scale had tipped against them. Despairing, they sold what they could in Portsmouth's open market and spent their afternoons drinking to forget while their malnour-ished children played amidst garbage and the scales of dead fish.

As years passed, Rocky Point's inhabitants embraced their isola-tion. They mistrusted outsiders and flaunted social conventions of every kind. They recycled scraps of fabric to fashion tattered trousers and formless dresses. They reviled books and newspapers and surren-dered the village school to the rule of spiders and mildew. They drank at unconventional hours, disregarding distinctions between morning and night. Lost in alcoholic reveries, they talked more often than not about the past, and their fading memories became both a refuge and a source of torment. As the generation raised in wreckage came of age, outsiders spoke of atavism in Rocky Point, basing their impres-sions on the scabby children who gathered in the weeds along the bypass to throw dirt clods at taxis and rental cars.

Trevor was one of these children, playing in the overgrowth cov-ering the concrete slabs of vanished houses and in waves laden with trash. One afternoon, he was standing to his waist in water when a riptide dragged him beneath the waves, over submerged engine parts and broken bottles and into darkness. When he regained conscious-ness, he was lying across his father's knees, coughing up the sea and convulsing. He lay wrapped in blankets for days, badly concussed and trembling. Even after his fever broke, he continued to suffer epi-sodic bouts of shaking induced by fear and, in time, rage. He never again ventured into the sea, though he often stood on the beach, staring at the waves with a haunted expression and remembering the rush of water that had blotted out the sun.

He was a curiosity at first, and then an object of ridicule. Other children followed him, shaking their hands, knocking their knees and mocking his dead mother for producing such an oddity. The only person they taunted more than Trevor was Mary. They followed her wherever she went, muttering and shuffling in grotesque exaggerations of her strange speech and limping gait. In the interest of self-preservation, Trevor joined their parades, sickened as much by self-betrayal as by his cruelty toward another, until the day he shook during a hazing of Mary. His hands trembled, his knees buckled, and he collapsed beside a rotting log to the calls of Crazy Mary, Crazy Trevor, and then Crazy Tremor. When he looked up, Mary was staring at him with unmistakable pity. He struggled to his feet, singled out the oldest of his persecutors, and bloodied the boy's face with his fists. When the boy's legs gave out, Tremor kicked him in the ribs. When he tired of kicking him, he beat the boy with a stick until the stick broke, and then he spat on his face. When he turned around, Mary was tracing signs in the air in a way that both disgusted and terrified him.

The beating established Tremor as a person to be feared and flattered. Seared by the memory of abuse, he shunned his peers and silently railed against Rocky Point. As an adolescent, he showed little interest in fishing and spurned the men who gathered on the crumbling pier to reminisce about days when the reefs teemed with fish, women were prettier, and young men had more courage. He renounced his father's stories as the alcoholic fantasies of a man so badly twisted by a hurricane that he could only look backward.

By the time he turned sixteen, his disgust had fermented into shapeless anxieties about the future. He spent hours walking along the ring road, breathing the exhaust of taxi vans and watching cloud shadows race across fields of feral cane. Returning to Rocky Point, he'd dread the sight of barefoot children covered in mosquito bites, women in patchwork dresses, and men with sunken eyes and sagging pants. Soon, he began stealing away to Portsmouth with change secreted from the jar beside his father's bed. He spent hours staring at window displays and willowy women sauntering down sidewalks in clinging dresses and bargain-bin jewelry. He envied young men standing on street corners, trading jokes and insults and ignoring the few tourists who ventured from the duty-free mall.

To gain admission to Portsmouth's street-corner society, he took a job as a bellboy at the Ambassador. He was less demoralized by the cost of bus rides from Rocky Point than bent on making the acquaintance of deliverymen and dishwashers familiar with Portsmouth's back streets. Within a year, he became a familiar if fringe member of a group dominated by EZ, a small-time smuggler who kept Trevor at bay because of his worn shoes and village ways.

Only a sudden seizure enabled Trevor's ascent through the ranks of EZ's friends. Squinting into the sun one day, he nearly walked into the path of a speeding car.

"I know that man," EZ said, watching the car round a corner. "We'll mess him bad."

Tremor's head bobbed and his fingers curled into trembling fists. When his shaking subsided, he braced himself for ridicule, but EZ slapped him on the back and laughed.

"You smoked some bad shit." EZ wiped away a tear. "Maybe I got some bad shit, too."

Looking into EZ's bloodshot eyes, Trevor grew lightheaded and incautious. "Get tremors sometimes. Used to be called that. Tremor."

"Trevor with the tremors," EZ said. "Tremor, our man."

From that point, Trevor carried the name Tremor. Rebranded, he bought new clothes, went to parties in apartments filled with smoke and old stereos, and drank liquor distilled in hillside villages. He formed friendships based on new phones and false stories about the origins of old scars. Most nights, he stayed in town, collapsing at dawn on a torn couch or dusty floor.

"You'll need another job to pay for those shoes on your feet," his father said one afternoon.

"The hotel gave me shoes with the uniform. Don't worry."

"You're the one who needs to worry. Looks like they paying you more than the prime minister."

"Working extra," Tremor said, trailing his fingers over the phone in his pocket.

On this rare occasion, Tremor was speaking the truth, thinking of the marijuana plants he'd cultivated in an abandoned cane field above Rocky Point, where he spent his nights away from Portsmouth admiring jagged leaves glittering with moonlit crystals. He showed his illegal tender more tenderness than he showed his many girlfriends, including the guileless maids who smoked his weed and slipped him keys to the Ambassador's empty rooms. With his most constant lover, a young mother with stretch marks across her breasts, he simply unzipped his pants and lay back on dirty sheets. He never met her eyes when she straddled his narrow hips or called out his name and collapsed. He never minded her callused hands or the smell of disinfectant clinging to her. That changed one afternoon, when she posed a question as cutting as her ragged nails.

"Why don't you shake when we lie together?" she asked. "It would be fun."

He thought to strike her, but she was already moving on top of him, so he closed his eyes and conjured an image from a magazine. A minute later, he slid from beneath her, buttoned his shirt, and slipped from a dirty room that seemed dirtier for her presence. On the rooftop, he lit a joint and looked down at the patio, where a white-haired American was waving a credit card to hold the unsteady attentions of a young woman. From that point, he hated those who took for granted all he desired, and in emulating those he hated, he came to loathe himself.

Not long after, he began stealing from guests' rooms, feigning interest in conversations with maids scrubbing toilets while he slipped jewelry and crumpled bills into his pockets. If his successive lovers were sacked for stealing, cheap seductions sustained his sloppy sex life. He curried favors by selling overpriced joints to gullible guests and distributing meaningless gifts to girlfriends. In this way, he only confirmed his worst suspicions of human nature. The only person Tremor despised more than his girlfriends and the Ambassador's guests, and even more than himself, was Professor Cleave, the straightest and most sexless man he knew.

To be fair, Professor Cleave was tightly wound on his best days. He would have blown the curve on the Friedman-Rosenman Test with his type A+ personality, and he was especially agitated when he wandered into the staff lounge in search of Tremor. His agitation and Tremor's hostility made us glad we don't have alphas fighting it out within our own ranks. Humans' massive heads, we've often thought, serve as little more than the seats of swelling egos, teacups for raging chemical storms. The irony, then, that Professor Cleave found Tremor on the couch, staring vacantly at a passage in *Select Essays from the Age of Reason*.

When we saw Professor Cleave, we nestled beneath gum wrappers and braced ourselves for a round of chest-beating and bipedal antics. It was Professor Cleave's most dreaded anniversary, and Tremor had the appearance of someone getting paid without breaking a sweat, between his new phone and smooth hands, and the glow of easy sex and smell of weed surrounding him.

"I've been looking all over," Professor Cleave said. "And here you are, smoking yourself into a stupid state."

Tremor tossed the book aside and looked down at his phone. "Makes no sense."

"You're thick in the head. You don't understand a thing because you don't put forth the effort." Professor Cleave snatched the book from the couch and placed it on the shelf. "And you've been going through things again."

Tremor slid his fingers across his phone's glowing screen. "Wasn't going to take it."

"You should know your lying and thieving have been noticed. When you steal, you lose something of yourself. You amputate part of your character. It's an abomination."

Tremor shook his head. "You make no sense to anyone."

"Shameful. A disgrace. That is the meaning of abomination."

"This place is an abomination. This hotel."

"That doesn't change what is right or wrong."

Tremor shrugged. "They say you ended up in jail for nothing. The laws are nothing. The police work for rich people. For white people. Didn't matter what you did."

A line of perspiration formed at Professor Cleave's hairline. "You can still control your thoughts and actions. You can keep your self-respect, even if you don't respect—"

"You think you control anything? They ask for peanuts, you give them peanuts. They ask for pineapple, you give them pineapple."

Professor Cleave slammed a locker door. "You have no direction. And no means of changing things, the way you're going."

"I am changing things." Tremor looked up from his phone. "One thing at a time."

"Let me tell you, the things you steal can never be yours. You carry them in secret. You can never be proud of them, because they belong to someone else. You elevate yourself through others' labor and none of your own. That is an abomination."

Tremor looked at the apron tied around Professor Cleave's waist. "The way you talk. Way you walk. Shoes splitting. Wallet falling apart. Don't know how you keep a wife."

"I see how you make yourself the big man in front of young girls." Professor Cleave gestured at Tremor's arms. "Lying about knife fights and filling your pockets when their backs are turned."

"I don't lie to them about—"

"You're lying now. What happens when everyone starts lying?"

Tremor leaned back and listened to the lurching hand of a broken clock. Professor Cleave dropped a pink slip onto the couch.

"Bring the sandwich to the lady at the bar. In the green cardigan."

Professor Cleave left the room, and we fumbled about beneath the couch for crumbs, our antennae twisted by strange transmissions moving across the harbor and the nature of the exchange we'd just witnessed. Some of us finally reconciled ourselves to the Ambassador's meager offerings, shook the dust from our wings, and adjourned to the lounge.

By then, Professor Cleave had calmed himself. When Tremor appeared, he gestured to Helen and walked to the end of the bar to retrieve the bottle of ketchup. Tremor's expression hardened as he set a plate on the counter.

While Helen struggled to pull a wallet from her sweater, Tremor looked down at the floor, at a badge bearing a corporate logo. On impulse, he swept it from the floor and into his pocket and pressed himself against the bar beside Dave.

"If you need something to relax on holiday, I can get it."

Dave turned on his stool and struggled to focus on Tremor. "How about some weed?"

Professor Cleave returned with a bottle of ketchup. "You need to collect the newspapers from the lobby. Some are three days old. Take them to the trash if you won't read them."

"Don't want to read them. Nothing for me in any of them," Tremor said, dragging his fingers along the bar on his way from the lounge.

"Pay him no heed," Professor Cleave said. "He's a foolish boy."

Dave tossed a matchbook on the bar. "Just young and stupid. We all were at one point."

Professor Cleave furrowed his brow and tried to remember such a point in his own life. Nothing came to his mind. Nothing came to ours either.

Helen picked at the flaccid lettuce edging her plate. We contented ourselves with dropped peanut shells. Last call came as a relief to us, and to Professor Cleave, too. He seemed grateful to avoid Tremor at the end of the night, when he carried a bag of trash to the dumpster behind the kitchen, keeping his face to the sky to escape the smell of decay. He even seemed grateful for our company when he climbed into the taxi.

"It was a long night. As long as the morning."

At the sound of his voice, we crawled from the vents and into the moonlight falling upon the dashboard. Professor Cleave fumbled with the radio dial, drifting over bits of static and opting, in the end, for silence.

"There is no accounting for taste, my students. Her sweater might have turned your antennae," he said, pulling from the curb. "Desmond always says you wouldn't ride a certain sort for practice, but then he can be crude."

We fluttered our wings, surprised by Professor Cleave's rare foray into gossip.

"He wasn't in much of a condition to choose. I wouldn't have thought either of them fit to walk. Hopefully he's not fit to do much else. She had the look of someone stumbling toward an open grave. Just like the other one, so many years ago."

He neared a group of men standing at the edge of an empty lot. One of the men stepped into the road, peered into the taxi, and then let Professor Cleave pass.

"Who knows how he'd act if I didn't know his father? These are strange times, with gunmen posing as politicians and a growing criminal element governing the streets." Our antennae quivered. "But you don't like to hear these things. You are content to squabble with one another and fiddle while Rome burns."

Beaten down by his deteriorating mood, we remained silent until we reached Stokes Hill.

As Professor Cleave pulled through his front gate, he looked at a light in the front window and took a deep breath. Naturally, we were thrilled to come home to Topsy, a man given to dispensing crumbs and compliments, except when it came to Little Butts and his well-scrubbed ilk, moralizing types, and those who chintzed on cigarettes or chocolate.

"I heard your man Butts on the news today, talking his usual garbage," Topsy said, rousing himself when Professor Cleave entered the house. He sat up in his chair and coughed. "I could smell his garbage coming right through the radio. Strange, because he's always drowning in some unfortunate woman's perfume."

"It's after midnight," Professor Cleave said, unbuttoning his shirt. "I suppose you didn't drink enough to sleep."

"You always have a word about everything. Everybody's doings." Topsy pulled a pack of cigarettes from his pocket. "I should never have mentioned that monkey's ass. Now I need to calm my nerves."

"It's any excuse with you—"

"Before you go to bed, remind me to tell you a story I got from Morris's daughter today. About the tailor who worked in the fabric shop years ago. The one who ran off with the rich English lady with big feet."

Professor Cleave pressed his fingers to his temples and stepped into the bathroom. Beneath a bare bulb, he peeled off his clothes, held his shirt to his nose and then hung it from a hook. To the sound of his father's voice coming from the front room, he considered a tangle of socks and underwear soaking in the sink, beneath a chalky film of disintegrated suds.

"He wouldn't give the first thought to anyone else."

He stepped into the concrete stall and dragged a cracked piece of soap across his arms, twisted his body beneath a miserly stream and watched water trickle down his chest and fall from the tip of his underappreciated penis in tiny beads.

We left him to his mutterings and wandered into the front room, safe in the knowledge that Cora Cleave had gone to bed. We, at least, wanted to hear the story about the rich English lady tripping on big feet into the proverbial sunset with a local shopkeeper of middling status. How improbable and fantastic their love must have been! The social censure their elopement must have inspired! We assembled beneath the buffet and listened, utterly rapt, savoring salacious details Professor Cleave would never have discussed. Love, in all its complexity and wonder, with all its concessions and compromises, often eluded Professor Cleave's full understanding, and so he generally avoided the subject. It was, far and away, our favorite subject.

That night, we dreamed about floppy feet kissed a thousand times and the joy inspired by a master tailor's skilled touch.

TEMPEST

Professor Cleave's father was a man given to telling dramatic stories, and for that reason often accused of embellishment by people lacking imagination. To be fair to some of his strained listeners, Topsy's presentation of certain events didn't always accord with narratives prevailing in sober circles. Still, we much preferred his stories to Professor Cleave's lectures. Our favorite story concerned the evening Topsy and his friends set fire to the Markeley house, the largest plantation manor on the island, back when Topsy was a young man and the British still "ruled the roost."

We remember the Markeley house well. Some of us settled there in 1758, only to find the Markeleys so miserly that their slaves were nearly starving. Miserliness, it turns out, trickles down. Nary a scrap could be found lying about after the Markeleys feasted like hogs. Naturally, we always welcomed the story of Topsy burning the house of "the most miserable rotters on St. Anne."

At the time of the events recounted, the Markeley place had been abandoned for twenty years. Ruined by the Great Depression, the Markeleys had quietly sold their land for "chicken squat" and abandoned the house, a manor too expensive for any local to buy. Too impoverished to transport their furniture and too proud to sell it, they simply announced plans to "summer in England," carted two dozen trunks to Portsmouth Harbor, and drove their Vauxhall convertible, "a fine automobile for foolish bastards," onto a waiting steamer, never to return.

The house stood empty for years. Unmolested, we feasted on stale crackers left in pantries, compost abandoned by goats set to permanent pasture, and crumbling paste on peeling wallpaper. In time, the house assumed an air of decrepitude that recalled the moral depravity of the Markeleys' slave-owning past, and rumors of troubled spirits haunting its hallways began to circulate. Superstition, more than any lock, kept most trespassers at bay.

Topsy declared the rumors "utter rubbish." One evening, after ten hours "packing bananas for a knuckle-dragging bastard," he and "a number of lads happened to wander past" the Markeley place and decided to "put foolish tales to rest." With three bottles of cane liquor and a crowbar, they worked up their courage and pried open a window. That evening, and for many to come, they lounged in dusty claw-footed chairs and toasted their own bravery. Without a music lesson between them, they played bawdy songs on a piano twenty years out of tune. They held boxing matches in the cobwebbed ballroom. At the time, certain elements on St. Anne had been taken with boxing fever on account of Floyd Patterson's knockout of Brian London, a "British bruiser with no business wearing gloves." For weeks following Patterson's victory, Topsy and his friends would wrap their hands in the Markeleys' moldering linen napkins and "have a go" at one another, rattling the crystal chandelier with each knockdown.

They generally kept us awake all evening, and we led a sleepless existence until Owen Jackson infamously muttered, "The British will never leave, and we'll be picking bloody bananas 'til the end of eternity." Incensed by Jackson's resignation, inspired by Patterson, and intoxicated by beer, Topsy challenged Jackson to "stand accountable for his nonsense." Without bothering to wrap his hands, he delivered a combination of jabs and hooks that had "his man against the ropes" (the piano) and stumbling into a lantern. Within seconds, the flame from the overturned lantern attached itself to a drape and smoke filled the room. With "fire at their heels and the law certain to follow," Topsy and his friends scrambled from the house and scattered in every direction. Topsy and Morris alone paused on a hilltop to watch smoke spiraling beneath black rain clouds, knowing they'd done something unpardonable, and in that way irrevocably bound themselves to one other.

If torrential rains extinguished the fire before it entirely destroyed the house, the night's events nevertheless "changed the course of St. Anne's history." In the week following the fire, the magistrate questioned every amateur boxer on the island. Not one divulged a single inciting circumstance. Their brush with the law and their "sworn silence to the last" confirmed a growing sense of solidarity among those who later formed the UGG. In that sense, the right hook that bloodied Jackson's nose represented a "decisive blow against the British ruling classes."

Although the magistrate did question Topsy and his friends, we could never confirm Topsy's version of events. We were in the pantry when the fire started, and by the time we scuttled from the house, Topsy had disappeared. When we returned the following morning to reclaim the cupboards, we found only two beer bottles lying on the ballroom floor.

None of that mattered, though, when Topsy told the story. We'd listen, rapt, as he described flames crawling up the side of the house and his sense, standing beside Morris, that he'd never felt more alive or possessed of such faith in the future, and that he'd just lived through a beautiful moment that would protect him forever against regret, whatever might happen on this earth or in the hereafter.

CHAPTER FIVE

How much our binges had changed since those hopeful bacchanals following the Markeleys' departure! On the night of Professor Cleave's anniversary, we indulged without joy in the remnants of club sandwiches and Cane Cutters to forget another day frittered away in dusty air ducts. We awoke the next morning feeling utterly wretched, with crumbs clinging to our carapaces and our antennae glued to the floor by pineapple juice residue. How desperately we wanted to fault others for our predicament, knowing we had only ourselves to blame. If the Americans had ordered round after round of Cane Cutters, we'd gone along, three sheets to the wind and without a single thought to the future.

The Americans were hardly in better shape. Dave lifted himself on an elbow and let his gaze wander from the cobweb filaments dangling from the ceiling to the harbor's glittering surface. He lowered his feet to the floor and studied the edge of a quivering puddle beneath the air conditioner, dizzied by the feeling of freedom after months of waking in a cramped cabin. He inhaled deeply and his erection stirred. We knew he was lingering in that wonderful moment when pleasant memories of recklessness still reign over incipient regrets and budding headaches. That moment was already fading.

He turned to Helen, curled into herself on the second bed. Her wrinkled sundress was clinging to her narrow frame and damp hair was plastered to the side of her face. She possessed the febrile appearance of someone lost in a labyrinth of nightmares. He massaged his forehead and struggled to remember something of their conversation. At the bar, he'd been relieved by the slow loosening of her speech and a burst of nervous laughter at some joke he'd made. Now, she seemed gripped by renewed misery. Anxious at the thought of her waking, he pulled a pair of shorts and a shirt from his duffel bag. We peeled our antennae from the tiles and sought the cover of dust ruffles and empty drawers.

In the bathroom, he splayed his hand across the wall to steady himself. His urine was streaming into the toilet when he noticed the box of razors and a square of stained gauze beside the sink. His hand grew numb, and when he looked down, his penis seemed disconnected from his body and the drops of urine on the toilet seat. He pressed his lips together to stanch a rising sickness and stepped in front of the mirror. His skin appeared ashen and fragile upon the glass. He was, he decided, more hungover than he'd first realized; she was a greater liability. He used a washcloth to sweep the box and gauze into a wastebasket, tossed the cloth on top of the blades, and scrubbed his fingers until they were raw. When he stepped from the bathroom, she was sitting up in bed, wrapped in her sheet, with her back against the headboard.

He wiped his mouth with the flat of his hand. "Hope you don't mind that I crashed here. Don't remember if we talked about it."

She folded him into a wide stare that encompassed her luggage, the sweater on the floor, and the smudged wall behind him, as if struggling to place him in her memories of the past twenty-four hours.

"I usually don't get hangovers," he continued, trying to stave off silence.

"I don't know what I'm going to do," she began.

Her voice cracked, and he imagined a deep fracture widening inside of her. He considered her drawn features and sensed the sorrow embedded in everything she'd touched—the cardboard box, the lifeless sweater, the damp sheet twisted by nightmares.

"Right now, I'm thinking about what I'm not doing. At work, I'd be delivering towels to trust-fund kids. Probably see what this place is like before I decide anything." He waited for her to speak and then walked to the air conditioner. "Want this thing on or off?"

"It doesn't matter," she said.

He turned off the air conditioner to silence its rattle, wishing she'd shown some preference or will of her own. He stepped onto the balcony and scanned the harbor, now a depthless metallic grey, and the narrow crescent of a town glutted with idling taxis and flatbed trucks. Beyond the terminal, streets lined with tiny shops trailed into a tinderbox slum. When he stepped back into the room, she hadn't moved.

"Not even ten, and it's brutal out there. Town's pretty small."

"They didn't tell me anything about this place. On the ship."

He nodded slowly. "I'll go downstairs to see what the front desk knows about flights." He searched her face for some response, and finding none, turned away.

When he left, she let the sheet slip from her shoulders and examined her arms with the bafflement of Lazarus waking to his botched resurrection. She rose from the bed, started pacing and then froze, recalling the blades she'd left on the counter, his stricken face when he emerged from the bathroom and the way he'd slumped against the balcony railing. Wishing he'd left before she woke and spared her the humiliation of facing him in daylight, she considered locking herself in the room, but he'd left his duffel bag beside his bed. And she was suddenly, and deeply, afraid of being alone. Averting her eyes from every mirror, she collected her sweater and left the room. She found him standing in front of the hotel, smoking.

"There's one flight a day to Miami. We just missed it." He surveyed the quiet street leading into Portsmouth. "Airport's probably an airstrip for puddle jumpers."

A trickle of perspiration slid down her arm. She tugged at her sleeves and the smell of spent adrenaline rose from her sweater.

"Are there flights to other places?"

"San Juan flight doesn't leave until this evening. We'd just be stuck there overnight. Probably better than here, but I'm too hungover to decide." He tossed his cigarette onto the sidewalk. "There's a tourist office at the terminal. We can book flights for tomorrow there."

"You can stay in my room tonight. To save money," she said quietly. "It doesn't matter to me."

Thinking only of his dwindling severance pay, he nodded.

They walked in silence with dust clinging to their feet, waving away flies drawn to the moisture in their eyes. At the harbor, they stood beside a retaining wall and watched eddies of brown foam turning along the shore.

"There's so much sea glass," she said. "And garbage."

"Ships dump shit in the ocean all the time. It's gotta wash up somewhere. Just like us."

She cradled her arms. He berated himself for upsetting her, and then blamed her for his worsening mood. To draw her attention from the beach, he nodded at a cruise ship approaching the harbor, trailing a cloud of black smoke.

"Surprised that one hasn't docked. We were always in port by ten."

She considered the ship with a bewildered expression, and he started down the road, feeling only mildly relieved when she backed away from the wall and followed him.

Near the terminal, men in sleeveless shirts pulled slabs of pork to the edges of oil drum grills to slow their cooking. Women hovered over tarps, arranging mangoes and bananas bruised from anxious handling. Rastafarians stood beside stacks of CDs, casting apprehensive looks at the ship's fading trail of exhaust, a solitary cloud in an otherwise barren sky.

"Wonder if it broke down," Dave said. "Somebody usually has to tow them."

"Like the one that floated off Mexico for days. The Coast Guard airlifted croissants."

"Almost looks like the *Celeste*. It's hard to tell. They all look alike."

She stared at the ship for a long moment. "Why did you get kicked off?" she asked.

"Sex with some seventeen-year-old from first class. His mom walked in." He shook his head. "Rich kid blowing the service. Supposed to go the other way."

"I was a liability. They didn't want to get sued if I tried again. They had me sign forms stating I'd violated my booking agreement by harming a passenger."

She trailed off at the approach of a man in a straw fedora. A diapered baby monkey perched on the man's shoulder trembled within a rope collar. "Photo with the monkey? Five dollars, American."

"Not interested," Dave said.

"He's well-behaved." The man rapped the monkey's head. "You see, he doesn't bite."

The monkey fanned its fingers over its face. Shaken, Helen turned away and started toward the terminal. Thinking only of his duffel bag, Dave followed her.

Inside the terminal, they walked along a shaded promenade, past window displays of cigarette cartons, coral necklaces, and plastic coconuts. They found the Tourist Office shuttered behind metal grating.

"We'll come back," Dave said. He glanced at Helen's sweater. "Later today."

For the next hour, they wandered along narrow streets, allowing stretches of shade to determine their direction. In a small park in the center of town, they sat on the rim of a dead fountain. A homeless man with yellow stubs for teeth wished them a good morning, as if it were. Some of us slipped between the loose tiles at the fountain's base and in short shifts dreamed of clear puddles and soft loam.

❈

It had not been a good morning for Professor Cleave. After an argument with his father about the distinction between class and class consciousness—one that abruptly ended when Topsy insisted that Professor Cleave, lacking the former, had no basis for judgment—he'd arrived at the terminal to find dozens of drivers standing on the curb, staring at the ship just beyond the mouth of the harbor. He parked behind a line of cabs and tapped the cover of Eric Williams's *Capitalism and Slavery*. Those of us dozing on the dashboard lifted our antennae.

"I count you among my honors students, though you enjoy only the most relative of distinctions, given the delinquency of your peers."

Our antennae stiffened, less in response to the qualified nature of Professor Cleave's praise than the appearance of Desmond, who leaned through the window and blew smoke in our direction.

"You shouldn't be paid to smoke as much as you do," Professor Cleave said.

"Rich talk for a taxi driver." Desmond tapped ash on the sidewalk. "There are times for breaks. I think your union has things to say about this. And your man Marx."

"Socialism has nothing to do with lazing—"

"This is no time for lectures. You'll be the first to know, and you didn't hear it from me. The ship that docked yesterday was turned back from St. Barts last night. Butts refused it here this morning and closed the port."

"It must be serious if Butts made a decision of any kind."

"I'd say he has his reasons, but he hasn't given a statement."

"He's never passed a chance to put his face on television."

"You're wasting your time here. Find what business you can elsewhere." Desmond nodded to a group of drivers milling on the sidewalk. "Soon, they'll give up, and you'll be competing for scraps. I'm carrying news I shouldn't, but there's no good seeing a friend suffer the heat."

"We scratch each other's backs."

"Because too many others would be happy to lash them." Desmond patted the cab's roof and started toward the terminal.

Professor Cleave snapped his fingers at those of us circling the radio. "This is not a holiday, and Desmond's words should not tempt you. I can hear members of your cohort making mischief behind the vents, and you'd have no business mixing it up with them."

As usual, he'd been too quick to judge. We had reasons for feeling agitated, and not all of them were related to our hangover. Those of us who'd jumped ship the day before had observed strange things aboard the *Celeste*—odd regurgitations and flecks of blood on crumpled tissues—and our antennae had been stinging all morning. But try to tell that to the judge! We crawled away from the radio, demoralized and dumbfounded, while Professor Cleave trolled cobblestone streets in the center of town. He pulled to the curb when he recognized Helen's sweater.

"I'm relying on your sense of civic responsibility, now." He guided us to a vent and leaned out his window. "Island tour? Fort St. George has the best views."

Dave shaded his eyes, smiled, and stepped up to the cab. "What'll it set us back?"

Professor Cleave considered the quiet street. "Pay according to your conscience."

"You won't make anything that way."

Professor Cleave tensed, and we scurried beneath the hood. On the way to Fort St. George, he incessantly picked at his thumb, pausing only to wave at groups of women standing on the curb, comparing the contents of plastic grocery bags, and old men gathered on street corners, passing around loose newspaper pages.

"You know so many people," Helen said.

Professor Cleave startled at her voice. She'd been quiet since climbing into his cab, seemingly consumed with her misshapen sleeves.

"If you follow the road we just passed, you'll find a village called Stokes Hill. That's where I live. Where those people are from." At the outskirts of Portsmouth, he nodded at a woman sweeping dust from a stoop.

"She's right, though. You know everybody," Dave said.

"I drive a taxi and belong to two unions, so I know people, for better or worse. Someone once wrote, 'Hell is other people.' He was only partly right. I argue with them about politics, but in the end, we all live together. I go to their children's baptisms and I help bury their parents."

"Sartre wrote that," Helen said. "It's from *No Exit.*"

"You know the book?"

"I was an only child. I spent a lot of time alone, reading."

Professor Cleave opened his mouth to speak but then glanced at his rearview mirror and lapsed into silence. Soon, the road curved around sheer cliffs battered by surf. Halfway up the coast, Professor Cleave turned onto a gravel path darkened by drooping vines and the broad leaves of rubber trees. The sky vanished and ditches disappeared beneath bracken. A troop of monkeys loped through underbrush and into the gloom. At the top of a hill, the sky reappeared, and Professor Cleave parked in a clearing before a desolate stone fort crowned with crenulated ramparts and dead cannons.

"This fort has had many lives since 1720," he began. "At first, it housed British soldiers. In 1840 it became a workhouse for freed slaves, those arrested for vagrancy between harvests." He squinted at a nimbus of sunlight edging a bell tower. "It became an overflow prison in 1985. Now, it's a museum."

"Doesn't seem to be anyone here," Dave said.

"People come in the afternoon. From the ships." Professor Cleave said. "You'll find maps inside and most rooms open to the public."

He'd just delivered the pithiest of lectures, we thought, as Helen and Dave climbed from the cab. We emerged from the vents, grateful to be spared the superficial nonsense that belied the deeper history of a place we'd known all too well, before every sack of millet had been removed from its cellars and every manacle buried in its courtyard. As we settled throughout the car, Professor Cleave turned his attention to *Capitalism and Slavery*, only to curse its fine print.

"The sun has twisted things." He rubbed his eyes and considered us. "In 1969, this man Williams said, 'It is our earnest hope for mankind that while we gain the moon, we shall not lose the world.'"

Wise sentiments, we might have said, more exquisitely expressed in Gil Scott-Heron's "Whitey on the Moon." The point seemed moot, though. As we'd begun to sense, no one would be going anywhere anytime soon.

Professor Cleave peered through the windshield. Helen was wandering along the edge of a parapet, balanced unsteadily with her arms outstretched in sharp relief against the sky. She appeared ignorant of gravity and poised for a doomed flight. And yet, Professor Cleave thought, no harm could come to one so unburdened by history, like so many of the tourists who reveled in the ruins of his past.

"Not long ago, this was no place for tourists. Your relations who once scaled these walls would tell you the same." He looked up at a rampart with a haunted expression. In place of dead cannons and mounted placards, he saw ghostly rings of razor wire, for in his mind, the walls before him would always be those of a prison.

※

The day of Professor Cleave's arrest began like any other. He awoke before his wife and daughter, and after a quick breakfast of tea and bread, he sprayed his cab and turned on its radio to drown out the sounds we made crawling for cover.

"Someday, the meek shall inherit the Earth," he said, snapping a plastic cap onto an aerosol can. "But today is not that day."

That day was the last he'd later count among the happiest days of his life. To say he'd been happy in the years leading up to his arrest would be to overstate the case. He'd never shed his ruminative ways or overcome his social ineptitude. Still, he had a wife who tolerated him more readily than she resented him. He had a father who confined his nocturnal socializing to his own stoop. He had the love of his beautifully bookish daughter.

On the night that ended these, his most hopeful days, he'd been driving along the harbor, where Portsmouth's shops gave way to the collapsing houses of Tindertown. The woman had stumbled into the street, and he might have hit her, if not for her arresting pallor. As he later recounted to a jury, she slurred no more than most late-night passengers when she gave him an address. In the back of his cab, she rested her head against the window. He spoke once or twice to stir her, drawing from a worn repertoire designed to hold the waning attentions of nodding drunks. When the odor of urine filled his cab, he pulled onto the shoulder, turned on his dome light, and took in the bluish cast of her skin. All he remembered of the drive to the hospital were the streaking headlights of passing cars. In the lobby, he screamed for help, knowing she was already dead.

The police came to his house at dawn. The woman had been an American heiress enamored with cocaine, and amicable international relations demanded the appearance of justice. Professor Cleave was the perfect patsy. He was sitting at the table, drinking rum straight from a bottle when the police arrived. While Cora and Irma cowered in nightclothes, the police overturned every piece of furniture in the house, rifled drawers, and produced tiny bags of white powder. They shoved Irma against a wall when she screamed. In the police van, Professor Cleave felt his fist swelling below a steel cuff and grasped the hopelessness of his situation.

At a farcical trial held after the bruises on Professor Cleave's face faded, a prosecutor depicted him as a sociopath. Through tracts such as *Kapital, Cabs and the Coming Crisis*, he asserted, the defendant had promoted extremist ideologies of the most corrosive nature. Reading from a notecard, he provided the jury with an abbreviated catalogue of titles in Professor Cleave's collection of books. Lamentable works such as *Crime and Punishment, As I Lay Dying, Slaughterhouse Five*, and *The Naked and the Dead*, he argued, provided clear evidence of a criminal mind and morbid predisposition, while *Civilization and its Discontents* disparaged the foundations of society.

"He waged a single-handed attack on our nation's values. He is a social abomination."

"Abomination," Professor Cleave blurted, drawing a small burst of applause from the crowded gallery.

"Did you hear that, you stupid, fat goat?" Topsy shouted in an ill-advised show of support. "My son is a social abomination."

Professor Cleave's fate was sealed, not by his pedantic outburst, taken as evidence of his blithe disregard for the judicial process, or by Topsy's impromptu testimonial, but rather the delicate sobs of the heiress's well-preserved mother, who insisted her daughter had never ingested any drug before making the defendant's acquaintance. The hastily assembled jury spent less than one hour in deliberation.

"Crime and communism are no strangers," the judge said before sentencing Professor Cleave to ten years in prison. "And they have no place on this island."

Cora crossed herself. Irma shrieked. Topsy lowered his face into his hands. Idiots rule, we thought from the rafters. We'd seen it all before.

Professor Cleave spent his first hours in prison sitting on the cot bolted to the wall of his cell. In alternating states of shock and agitation, he picked at the seams of his orange jumpsuit and read graffiti containing misspelled claims to notoriety and references to sexual positions that defied his comprehension—violent and vulgar statements that underscored the extent of his alienation from prison society. Panicked, he lapsed into territorial behavior, measuring the dimensions of his cell and taking inventory of its scant contents. He examined his urine-stained mattress and pressed his face against a grated window, fingered a roll of coarse paper beside a steel toilet bowl and weighed a bar of soap in his palm. We scaled pocked concrete walls and circled the drain in a tiny sink, wondering at the boldness of his intrusion.

He shuddered at the sounds of us clawing through cracks and clogged pipes, stripped a shoe from his foot, and threw it at the sink. We scuttled down the drain, and by the time we reappeared, he'd spread a thin blanket over his mattress and stretched out on his back. Until the naked bulb above his head flickered and died, he kept his eyes squeezed shut, too overwhelmed to battle those of us brushing against his neck to take in his scent. Frankly, we considered him hopelessly unqualified for prison society.

The following day, though, he joined a roll call of pickpockets and male prostitutes, artless forgers, small-time drug dealers, and wet-brained brawlers, and to our amazement familiarized himself with routines that would guide his passage through a version of hell with intellectual isolation at its core. Beside men too muddled to masticate, he ate boiled cassava and bits of vermin with a plastic spoon. On a kitchen detail, he mopped lumps of gruel from flagstone floors. In a rudimentary workshop, he glued wooden legs to coconut piggy banks destined for duty-free shops. He suffered the company of convicts given to abusing fixatives—people even we'd learned to avoid. The spasms of your average huffer can be unpredictable, and for fear of thrashing limbs, we kept to the workshop's far corners. From a safe distance, then, we heard Professor Cleave delivering his first prison lecture.

"Let me tell you, that's no good for the brain," he said to a baby-faced burglar flaring his raw nostrils over a tube of glue.

"Helped me kick drink," interjected a toothless man struggling to open a can of epoxy.

Professor Cleave lifted a finger and started in about "enslavement to infernal adhesives." We should have read the writing on the wall and skittered like hell!

During calisthenics, he upheld pretenses of exercise, marching back and forth across the courtyard under the watch of impassive guards, led and followed by huffers too dazed to remember their crimes. Amidst twitching souls lost in phantasmagorical scenes, he rubbed his fingers to strip away flecks of dried glue and tried to suppress memories of a ghostly woman caught in headlights. Only packages sent by his daughter sustained his spirit. Every evening, he lost himself in books Irma had pulled from rotting boxes behind Portsmouth's shuttered library. His world, during these respites from reality, expanded to fit the dimensions of his roving imagination. Transported, he read aloud.

"'The frontier trail snaked past copses of tall cottonwoods along the arroyo and into the scorched desert,'" he read from *The Treasures of Apache Canyon*. "'Suddenly, he saw the dark war-painted stranger sitting on a dappled palomino. He clutched his reins and prepared to defend his saddlebags of gold with his short life.'"

Those of us lazing on the sink turned in Professor Cleave's direction and twitched. He clutched his book and leaned toward us, unnerved by our electrified antennae. After a moment, he settled back on his cot and contemplated the possibility of insanity's onset. If only we'd calmed ourselves then. Anyone who has read *The Treasures of Apache Canyon* can certainly understand our enthusiasm. The following night, he started reading where he'd left off, and we gathered on the sink. He watched our antennae strain toward the book and dragged his palm down the side of his face.

"'He surveyed the bloody horizon obliterated by saguaro and lowered his rifle, ready to do violence to the feathered stranger until he realized the stranger was his old guide and friend,'" he read, tacking back and forth between narrative and exposition. "It's a desert, you see, and the sun has gone to his head, although you can interpret this as you wish."

The Treasures of Apache Canyon wasn't a complex novel, for fuck's sake, but we could hardly complain, for no one else had ever bothered to read to us. In any case, he was in the throes of adjustment to prison society, so we went easy on him.

Professor Cleave's fear that loneliness had corrupted his senses waxed and waned. At times, he dreaded the advent of madness. At others, he placed his faith in the soundness of his mind, duly recording our physical responses to different literary genres. Bound by the limits of speculation, he eventually conceded an inability to explain our behavior, contented himself with our ostensible gestures of interest, and nurtured hopes of someday delivering recitations to more sophisticated listeners.

"The lowest aspects of things always seduce the unschooled masses," he declared when we disappeared down the drain during Sartre's *No Exit*. "American cowboys and gunshots, I see, are your opiates."

As if we needed a depressing play about three miserably contentious humans facing an eternity of imprisonment together in a tiny room! About humans' inability to escape each other's judgments! If humans want to spout "Solidarity Never," to crave and then detest the company of others, who can blame us if we throw up our antennae and lament the strange ways of the world?

However frustrated by our inconstancy, Professor Cleave read aloud every night until the light went out. In darkness, he weighed the relative merits of literary interpretations, addressing his conclusions to those of us perched on the folds of his blanket. Then he whispered thanks to his daughter and thought of his wife more fondly than he ever would again.

Prison only added to Professor Cleave's intellectual pedigree. The steady arrival of Irma's packages established his reputation as an eccentric bibliophile.

"Why you always carrying those?" asked a terminal insomniac with speckled teeth. He pointed to the book in Professor Cleave's hand. "Just words, words, words. Can't lay down with words. Can't eat words. Don't your girl send things a man can use?"

"*Black Jacobins* is about the Haitian Revolution. A slave uprising that gave birth to a republic."

"Nothing to do with us. Except it's dead. Dead paper. Dead words."

Professor Cleave extended the book. "You should read and digest it."

Two days later, he found several pages of the book, slick with excrement, lying in the courtyard. After that, he concealed his intellectual endeavors from all but us, fearing that in his retreat from glue addicts, he was stepping ever closer to his own form of madness.

Twenty-nine months into his sentence, he stopped receiving packages from his daughter and violently creased letters from his wife. Professor Cleave—all of us—missed the former more than the latter. Cora had always confined her brief remarks to village scandals, recounted in the pithiest of terms, and to the weather, as if she and Professor Cleave no longer beheld the same sky. In her final missive, she stated without explanation that Irma had moved to New York.

From the moment the letter slipped from his fingertips, Professor Cleave underwent a metamorphosis. He picked at the pads of his fingers, as if he might slough off the sickness surrounding him. He paced with renewed intensity, as if he might keep the walls of his cell at bay. He reread well-worn books, fixating on their authors' most trenchant observations and darkest insights into the human soul. He entertained desperate thoughts and held wandering conversations with himself. He might have fallen apart, if not for a storm of Biblical proportions that brought salvation, if only to Fort St. George's inmates. Thirty-seven months into his prison tenure, news of an incoming hurricane began to circulate among the guards, and then the alternately glazed and animated convicts in the workshop.

"The storm will sweep everyone into the sea," one hopeful sociopath said, struggling to affix a pirate flag to a plastic Spanish galleon. "Drown everyone."

Professor Cleave stared at the sticky ejaculate drying at the tip of a metal tube in his hand, and that evening stood at his window and watched the sky darken.

"Maybe it's good she went away." He placed his fingers on the sill. We rose on our hind legs and peered through the grating. "She'll have a life we never will."

Thirty-six hours before landfall, he awoke to the sound of whistles. He dressed in darkness, and moments later fell into a line of inmates stumbling into the glare of spotlights. Surrounded by apprehensive, freshly deputized guards, he watched a cement truck dump sand in the center of the prison yard. He was leaning forward, hoping to glimpse a familiar face, when a guard pressed a shovel into his hand.

"By day's end, there shouldn't be a single bit of sand left in that pile."

"Left of that pile," Professor Cleave muttered as the guard moved down the line. "If there were no sand remaining, there would be no pile to call by the name."

"No sandbags in Portsmouth," the man beside him said. "They don't have nothing ready."

"They don't have anything ready," Professor Cleave stated. "The double negative suggests they have something ready."

The befuddled huffer scratched his cheek, a whistle sounded, and the benighted citizens selected to save Portsmouth began shoveling sand into burlap sacks. At daybreak, the huffer held a crumpled tube beneath his nose and nodded at a new member of the bagging detail, a man in a stained jumpsuit and ankle chains.

"They let John Bowden out of the hole. Nobody but the body come from the hole once it goes in the third time. But they need hands now."

Professor Cleave lowered his shovel and stared at the man in the stained jumpsuit. When John Bowden met his gaze, Professor Cleave turned back to the pile of sand before him. All afternoon, he listened to swells breaking against the cliffs below the prison and thought of Cora and his father.

As the wind gathered force, the smell of seaweed filled the air. The prison's most cognitively addled addicts shoveled erratically and whistled through rotted teeth. Fearing the insidious creep of madness, Professor Cleave watched them in terror. That night, he suffered violent twitches that jerked him from the edge of sleep every few minutes. Anticipating flood surges in every drainpipe on the island, we hardly fared better.

He awoke the next morning with a dim sense of his surroundings. A sheet of cloud had obliterated the horizon. In the harbor, whitecaps formed beneath heavy drizzle and dying grey light. Professor Cleave was straining to see through the window grating when a siren sounded in the distance and the world outside vanished behind a wash of rain.

We emerged from the shadows beneath the sink, and he regarded us in the gloom. "Together, we are left to our own devices."

As he spoke, torrential rain pounded the window. To the sound of screeching wind, he wrestled his mattress across the cell and propped it against the grate. When the glass beyond the grate shattered and the mattress toppled, he huddled beneath the sink, shivering to the sound of uninterrupted squalls while sideways rain pooled around his shriveled feet. Darkness became tangible and time lost all meaning until the next morning, when the wind abated and faint light appeared on the horizon.

Over the next few days, pools of water in the yard became reeking repositories of garbage and drowned rats. During rare musters, inmates with badly pruned feet exchanged news gleaned from the overheard conversations of guards.

"Prime Minister stole the emergency fund," announced a thief riddled with tics. "Doing bad math for years. Left on the plane to Mexico when the first wind blew."

In bits and pieces, Professor Cleave and his fellow convicts learned of food shortages and outbreaks of waterborne illnesses. As discredited cabinet members found asylum in Miami and San Paulo, guards resigned in rapid succession, fearing the rage of inmates confined to moldy cells. Those who remained did little more than deliver foil pouches of rations donated by humanitarian organizations. Professor Cleave spent his days in fever and delirium. We survived on streaks of multivitamin paste.

One month after the storm, Professor Cleave heard a key in his door. His head lolled sideways and he found himself facing Lyndon Buttskell in summer tweed, a silk cravat and impeccable leather shoes unsullied by the filth covering the floor. What an ass, we thought, flicking our antennae in Butts's direction. That said, his suit was stunning. He was, when all the votes were counted, one good-looking man.

"My good friend, I'm happy to see you again, even in such unpleasant surroundings."

Professor Cleave lifted himself on an elbow and lowered his feet onto a mass of rotting pulp. "What are you doing here?"

"News travels slowly, I see. Last month's mudslide set us up for last week's landslide. Now, I've made it my mission to remedy the abuses of previous administrations."

"The SDA? In office?"

"As prime minister, I intend to redress a gross miscarriage of justice."

Professor Cleave rubbed his head. "Prime minister?"

"I've granted your pardon."

"I'd rather appeal the verdict than accept a pardon." Professor Cleave's cheeks were hollow and his eyes sunken. We thought he'd finally gone mad.

"Different paths to the same destination," Butts said with a wave of his hand. "This is no time for old fights about past injuries. This is a new day."

On poached feet, Professor Cleave followed Little Butts into the yard and squinted into blinding sunlight, at a banner strung from coils of razor wire. "'Reconciliation and Regeneration,'" he read. "'The Social Democratic Alliance, an Alliance of All for the Future of Everyone.'"

"That, your cousin James wrote. We'll have our photograph beneath it."

As Butts's arm slipped over his shoulder, Professor Cleave turned to face a dozen reporters clutching cameras, and in his filthy jumpsuit, became the dazed subject of a politically priceless photo.

That afternoon, he returned home in a manner befitting an expendable hero, in a taxi van shared with fourteen newly pardoned and politically apathetic addicts. He found Topsy sitting on the stoop, holding a newspaper.

"They said it might be today." Topsy cast the newspaper aside. "They're now saying you were put away for political expediency. Took this filthy rag three years to come to it."

"Thirty-eight months," Professor Cleave said.

Topsy struggled to his feet and gripped his son's shoulder. "You look terrible. Worse than before."

"I feel worse than before." Professor Cleave's breath caught. Fearing he might cry, he pulled away from Topsy and considered a pile of cigarette butts on the ground. "It looks like you've done a fair job minding my stoop."

"I've been fixing things. Even houses up here felt the storm." Topsy gestured to a heap of branches and warped boards in a corner of the yard.

Professor Cleave regarded an empty bottle lying in the grass. "Have you been keeping your health? You'll be in the hospital with your carrying on."

"Forget about me and look out for yourself. I hope you've had enough of your communism."

"Those communists, as you call them, just gave me seven years of my life."

"They gave you years that already belonged to you. Why wouldn't they? They see a fool prepared to carry their signs." Topsy patted his shirt pocket in search of cigarettes. "At least Butts had the sense to tone down his rhetoric, even if he sometimes still wears that Castro cap. Just like the other clown he followed around as an ass-sniffing pup."

"He secured my release—"

"What did they do for you when it mattered?"

"You were in the courtroom—"

"And now I'm going down the road. The neighbors will want to know you're back. I'll give you time to settle into things."

"Where is Cora?"

"The chapel. Her prayer book's been glued to her hands. She does everything but sleep in church."

"She was never one for church outside of Sunday."

Topsy glanced at the house. "I'm glad to have you home."

Little in the house had changed during his absence, Professor Cleave thought, at first. He stood beside a shelf and caressed the spines of his remaining books, marveled at rows of canned fruit in the pantry and the polished forks in the buffet. As he reacquainted himself with the house, though, he realized everything had changed. In his room, he found his clothes shrouded in plastic beneath the bed. A wedding portrait once on the nightstand was nowhere to be found. He turned to a mirror mounted above the dresser, and for an awful instant wondered if another man's reflection had grown familiar to it.

He entered his daughter's room and found comfort in the disheveled sheets hanging down one side of the bed. In a hopeful moment, he imagined Cora at night, finding refuge from loneliness in the memory and lingering scent of their absent daughter. Then he smelled the traces of rum rising from the sheets. Everything came into relief—the shapeless underwear strung over the back of a chair, his father's Sunday suit dangling from a hook on the door, the stacks of newspapers against the wall, the dirty glass and tarnished UGG pin on the floor.

When Cora came home, he was sitting at the table, staring at his callused hands. He took in her appearance in one sweep. She'd lost too much weight and cut her hair, he observed, noting the tiny twist at the base of her neck. Her face had settled into an expression of permanent accusation that didn't change when he rose from his chair and grazed the corner of her mouth with his lips.

"Why has he put his clothes in her room?" he asked.

Cora stiffened. "He's been helping with things."

"If he's been trying to fix things, he's only broken the place."

"He helped out after she left. We had nothing, and there was no work. So she left. He knew I couldn't ask her for money."

"There's no sense in this. How does he have any money with the way he drinks?"

"He sold his house. He lives here now."

Professor Cleave fell back into his chair and placed his head in his hands. "And when she comes back, where will she live?"

Cora took a deep breath, and he lifted his eyes.

"She met someone. A Jamaican. They are living with his family. In New Jersey."

"You let this happen in three years?" He pounded his fist on the table. "Where was your sense?"

Cora lifted her fingertips to the corner of her mouth, where his lips had brushed hers. "You don't know what it was like. We lived the best way we knew."

"This was your best?" He picked a cigarette butt off the floor and threw it on the table. "There's nothing in your heads. Nothing but excuses echoing back and forth in emptiness."

In that moment, a nearly unremitting silence settled between Professor Cleave and Cora. It remained so laden with mutual resentment that, in years to come, Professor Cleave even found occasional relief in Topsy's commentary when he was at home, which wasn't often. He spent every day driving his cab and every night mixing drinks. He suffered bouts of anxiety related not only to the impersonal aspects of his personal life, but to the disorienting effects of St. Anne's rapid transformation. In the year following his release, billboards advertising new restaurants and spas at restored plantations appeared along the roads. Massive houses vacant for all but two months of the year sprawled over the southern half of the island. Little Butts, confidently poised and perfectly coiffed, led a ribbon-cutting ceremony at St. Anne's first cruise ship terminal.

On the morning of the ceremony, Professor Cleave found his father sitting at the table, tugging a split sock over his heel. "You're a strange sight up at this hour."

"I'm going to the port. They say you wouldn't believe the size of those ships. I suppose you'll find fault in all of it, even though your man Butts can take credit. If this is his socialism, fair play to him, fool that he is."

"This is anything but socialism." Professor Cleave yanked a shirt over his shoulders.

"Your mother and Morris should have lived to see this. Generations of cane cutters and banana boxers should have seen it. Butts will ruin us, but not with houses and hotels."

"What about the tax exemptions given to every foreigner?" In his distraction, Professor Cleave struggled to button his shirt. "They'll want new roads. Electricity. Clean water. The burden will fall on those with the least."

"You won't complain making money driving them around."

"No one's complaining, but we need to take the long view of things."

"Let me tell you, I knew a man who said good things come to those who wait. He died alone in bed the next day, with a full bottle of rum in his cupboard. That's your long view. You must think I'm deaf as a stone and dumb as a goat."

"It's one-step chess playing," Professor Cleave said. "Only a fool would do it."

"You're both fools," Cora said from the kitchen doorway. "In that way, there's not a bit of difference between you."

Professor Cleave snatched his watch from the kitchen table and stormed from the house. In the cab, he listened to our patter as we spilled from the vents.

"You can talk sense to no one in that house. They're like little children." Halfway to Portsmouth, he parked on a gravel shoulder overlooking the harbor. "So, this is the future. This is what reconciliation and regeneration look like."

We pressed against the windshield to observe an enormous white ship entering the harbor. We marveled at its massive hull and grew frenzied speculating on the output of its industrial kitchens.

"The minister of tourism says that, from now on, every citizen must do their patriotic duty and refrain from behavior that could tarnish St. Anne's reputation." Our antennae stiffened as Professor Cleave continued. "It hardly seems our six-legged citizens are up to the task of pleasing our new visitors. In lieu of erudition and proper manners, perhaps invisibility would be sufficient."

Bristling, we turned our backs on him. He'd become distracted, anyway, by the ship dwarfing Portsmouth and spiting the soft landscape with its uniform decks.

"My father will find it a bit Stalinist. But he'll never admit that."

He looked down at a line of tiny boats along the shore and imagined their solitary captains, sinewy fishermen casting nets with callused hands, throwbacks to the past—and, like him, near strangers to the present.

❈

Over two decades later, most of the small fishing boats had disappeared. Ships larger than any Professor Cleave could have imagined on the day of the ribbon-cutting ceremony docked at the terminal. Larger tourists crowded the duty-free mall. Taller gates surrounded bigger houses on the southern peninsula. Professor Cleave had owned three cabs, each shorter of Desmond's exacting standards than the last. His idealism had become a rebuttal to every insult and injury. His intellect had become a refuge from difficult emotions and disturbing memories. Helen Mudge, in that sense, had trespassed. When he emerged from his troubled reflection, she was still on the rampart, gazing out at the sea with her arms held aloft, walking with the careless step of one who could just as easily float away as fall.

He closed his eyes and massaged his temples. "Hell is other people."

When he looked up again, she was gone. He shook his head and considered us.

"Someday, the meek will inherit the Earth, if the next storm does not sweep us all into the sea." Our antennae probed the air for hints of disturbance. "Perhaps then everyone will pay according to conscience, whatever has not been dulled by repeated blows."

The irony! An hour later, when Helen and Dave appeared, he hustled us beneath the hood without a hint of ceremony and flipped the vents closed. Hell, we thought, is *people*, with their irrational fears and crude manners.

"Anyone ever escape?" Dave asked, when the prison disappeared behind a line of trees.

"No one ever escaped, and very few tried. There would have been nowhere to go. Here, everyone knows everybody else. Nothing goes unnoticed." Professor Cleave paused. "One can't be acting the ass on the street, my father says. If you do, make sure the man next to you is acting the bigger ass."

"Just got to choose your company carefully. Still don't think I could last long. In a place like this. With nowhere to go if you mess up."

"People mess up all the time." Professor Cleave slowed to let a troop of monkeys cross the road. "They just stay among the same people they've always known."

Dave remained quiet until the forest gave way to scrub. "I always like to think there's somewhere new. To start over."

The idea of starting over seemed a bit pie-in-the-sky to us. We've spent millennia crawling from one disaster to the next, cursing the world's indifference. Still, clinging to the cab's oily struts, with sunlight glinting off the ocean and the road opening up before us, we could understand his feelings.

Past the stone tower of an abandoned sugar mill, Professor Cleave pulled onto the shoulder before a derelict estate house. We crawled onto the cab's bumper and splayed our wings. Graffiti and scorch marks covered the house's stone foundation, and empty bottles littered its sagging porch. Trees rose from a gaping hole in the roof. Triangles of lead glass clung to the frames of windows overlooking untended fields. It was a glorious sight, a cornucopia of refuse and rot.

"That was once the largest plantation on this island," Professor Cleave said. "In the 1930s, sugar prices dropped, and the owners lost their fortune. No one on the island could afford to buy the house, so they abandoned it. You can find the furniture all over St. Anne. I know a man with a piano in his chicken coop. He can't read a note of music."

"Reminds me of home," Dave said. "Gutted houses. People who'd had their electricity cut off would be taking chandeliers from places like this. Burning them down."

"My father and his friends would come here to drink. He claims they started the first fire. An accident, he says. A storm prevented the whole place from burning. He finds humor in it."

"We'd probably get along," Dave said.

"You'd be fortunate to avoid making his acquaintance. You can walk around the property, if you'd like."

Dave glanced at Helen's sleeves. "We should get back. See about flights." He said little else until Professor Cleave parked before the terminal. "Streets always this empty?"

"Everyone must be inside. In the shade." The furrow in Professor Cleave's brow deepened. "I'll wait here and take you back to the hotel when you're finished."

A few minutes later, Helen and Dave emerged from the terminal. On the way to the cab, they passed a man stumbling along the curb. The man tipped a can of beer in Helen's direction.

"Pretty lady." He drained the can and threw it to the ground. "Maybe not a healthy lady."

Helen slid into the cab after Dave and twisted around to look through the rear window.

"The office is still closed," Dave said. "Wasn't anyone around."

"The clerk at the Ambassador should be able to help you," Professor Cleave said.

As Professor Cleave pulled away from the terminal, Helen was still staring out the rear window, and the man on the curb was still watching her. The still ship hadn't moved. Our antennae quivered, and we felt a familiar sense of desperation—one we'd felt on the brink of so many upheavals.

SICKNESS

WE OFTEN WONDERED IF we'd erred in encouraging Professor Cleave with our enthusiastic response to *The Treasures of Apache Canyon*, a classic of its genre, but hardly recompense for some of the history lectures we later endured. The things we've done for a taste of pulp! Quite frankly, we got suckered. We'd already witnessed, firsthand, most of the events Professor Cleave recounted. We'd occupied barricades on the streets of Paris in 1789 and raced behind suffragettes shattering windows with sledgehammers in 1912. We'd napped with Leon Trotsky while Frida Kahlo painted monkeys in the next room. We'd seen it all, in a manner of speaking, including some things too dreadful to mention.

To be fair, Professor Cleave's lectures allowed us to experience, however vicariously, the few places we've yet to venture. We viewed mountains of ice through Ernest Shackleton's eyes and trailed giant squids through Jacques Cousteau's undersea world. We floated weightless in outer space. The cost of our tuition, though, sometimes became too much to bear. Professor Cleave only rarely, and in the most begrudging fashion, tuned into Kingston's 103.5 Jams. Then there were his recitations of *The Flora and Fauna of the Lesser Antilles*. At times, some of us dropped from the gaskets and made our way onto a cruise ship, if only to get a break from him.

In our worst moments, we had no interest in learning about ports of call or the ocean surrounding us ("Screw the undersea world!" we drunkenly declared, dunking our antennae in gin fizz). We craved the distractions of glittering window displays, glass elevators, and mindless musicals. We bathed in residue at the bottom of fondue fountains. Entirely against our natural inclinations, since scarcity was hardly a concern, we spent an inordinate time foraging. We ate to forget. We lost our good sense in endless buffets, consuming empty calories in our ongoing search for something new and better coagulating in the next chafing dish.

We were always disappointed. In each kitchen drain and dish tub, we found the same soggy tacos, iceberg lettuce, and bits of cake smothered in lard. This was the least of our problems. The ships' cleaning crews, more murderous than Cora Cleave, routed us from every public space with insecticidal sprays. Truth be told, we spent the bulk of our "holidays" brooding in moldy air ducts beneath the waterline.

On fumigation days, when neurotoxins floated through the vents of every cabin and kitchen, some of us sought refuge in the engine room. Our wings slick with oil, we slid into drain pipes and septic bilges, only to be expelled and drowned in the ship's filthy wake. The most fortunate among us sheltered in massive trash compactors, cozily pressed between mountains of garbage, gorging on waste and regurgitating in ways that recalled the vomitoria of ancient Rome's most noble classes.

In the end, boredom and existential distress drove us from every ship. The same conversations and tasteless entrées wore on our spirit, and with no object of attention but the ship itself, we felt helplessly adrift, plagued by an odd sense of moving without going anywhere. We'd find ourselves ruminating on Sartre's most despairing passages, drinking to excess and exposing ourselves to as much secondhand smoke as possible—doing anything to loosen our grip on the mortal coil. Then a small breeze or a bit of music would rouse us from despondency and remind us of hospitable shores and neglected possibilities. Some among us would disembark at the first opportunity—in Basseterre, Nassau, Kingston, or Portsmouth. In Portsmouth, at least, we could always find one unfumigated car, our classroom, waiting at the terminal. One cannot put a price on air conditioning, really, unless that price is education.

CHAPTER SIX

A FTER LEAVING HELEN AND Dave at the Ambassador, Professor Cleave parked at the end of the street and dialed Desmond's number twice. We paced the dashboard, wishing he hadn't, in one of his moralizing fits, removed the ashtray to discourage Desmond's habit. Some of us might have ingested a few shreds of tobacco to quell our anxieties. By then, our antennae were receiving dreadful visions of sanitizing stations brimming with isopropyl, canisters of deadly chemicals, and rows of insect traps (veritable coffins for unsuspecting cockroaches). As so-called vectors of disease, we were already suffering.

"He's too busy smoking to answer." Professor Cleave searched the radio for news and muttered at a public service announcement promoting sexual abstinence. At the end of the dial, he paused. We drew our antennae inward.

"There's not a bit of taste among you. Mighty Sparrow is one of the greats, but I confess there's no time for him now. It's the news we want, and we'll be driving to town to get it." He surveyed the dashboard. "You are shells of yourselves in this heat." He took a deep breath and tuned the radio to 103.5. "I wouldn't indulge your liking for this rubbish, but you've been model citizens today."

In our anxiety, we scaled the windows and batted our wings against the glass. Naturally, he misread our mood.

"I'll never understand the appeal of this music, but with expediency in mind, I am conceding to the philistines among you. If you have any honor, you will return the courtesy and behave around Desmond. He'll know things with no small bearing on us all."

Desmond, unfortunately, proved a perfect exemplar of the scapegoating behavior we've come to expect from humans. Professor Cleave found him smoking beside the terminal gates. We backed against the windshield when Desmond slipped into the cab.

"This car is a scandal, with these filthy things crawling about," he said. "You should get them to move on."

"You think I have them trained? Like circus fleas?"

"They're a pestilent lot, and I'm of no mind to relax. All day, everyone's been looking for news. I ignored them, but I'll tell you things you'll hear soon enough."

Professor Cleave glared at those of us squaring off with Desmond, and we calmed ourselves. We were, if nothing else, attuned to the gravity of the situation.

"There's an outbreak of some kind on that ship," Desmond said. "There were twelve passengers dead this morning. Now eighteen. Bloody noses. Trouble breathing. Fevers."

"They don't know what it is?"

"There's talk of terrorism. Anthrax and that kind of thing. Maiden Cruises requested clearance so sick passengers could go to the hospital, but Butts isn't letting the ship into port."

"They won't infect the real cash cows of the Caribbean, but they'll bring it here."

"That ship wouldn't be given clearance anywhere."

"But they expected it here. Because St. Anne is already infected."

"You're getting ahead of the situation. They don't know how it's spreading."

"That's my meaning, Des. They don't know. Yet they'd come here. And no one here has any voice in it."

Across the street, shopkeepers stood in shaded doorways, contemplating the wasted afternoon. "None of them know," Desmond said. "But they will. Port Authority is getting calls from networks.

Passengers are already sending pictures. Giving interviews on their phones. Butts is making an announcement this afternoon."

We lifted our antennae, hoping to pick up an odd transmission.

"When we're in the news, it's always bad news," Professor Cleave said. Two police vans pulled to the curb, and he shook his head. "It won't look good turning them away, but they must have a better hospital on the boat."

"The infirmary's full, and they're low on supplies."

"It could be all over St. Anne soon enough. We'll need beds for our own people."

"It starts like a cold, they say, and then you're on fire."

"So many of us have touched them in one way or another." Professor Cleave pressed his fingertip to the cut on his thumb.

"A thousand came through duty-free yesterday," Desmond said.

"Those two I picked up. The woman was pale."

"You're all right, Professor. We can't assume anything."

Professor Cleave rubbed his temple. "Butts should be getting the hospital ready to quarantine people. Drafting public health measures."

"You should have been prime minister. Butts isn't fit to handle a thing like this."

"I was never so good-looking as Butts, and the years haven't been kind."

"To any of us." Desmond patted his bulging stomach. The radio hanging from his belt crackled. "It's time."

Professor Cleave gripped Desmond's hand. When he released it, he felt the chill of perspiration evaporating from his skin. We quivered, sensing the fear and mistrust spreading through the ship and making its way to shore, bouncing off satellites and moving through television screens and sweaty phones. Desmond's cigarette smoke had left us cold, too, calling to mind the fumigations starting aboard the *Celeste*. It started with a cold, Desmond had said. For us, it would start with a stinging fog and end in paralysis and suffocation.

❈ ·

When Professor Cleave returned to the Ambassador, he found several Americans sitting in the lounge, staring at the television.

"The ship out there. It's the one from yesterday," the daytime bartender said. "There's some kind of sickness on board. A regular plague."

"I just heard it on the radio." Professor Cleave contemplated televised images of overflowing trash receptacles and yellow quarantine tape and listened to three people at the end of the bar.

"Can't believe the CDC's flying down," a woman remarked.

"It's routine," her companion said. "The CDC flies people all over. Anywhere you get an outbreak like this."

"All that diarrhea. It must be something they ate."

"But nosebleeds?" a second man said. "They don't know what the hell it is. Closing kitchens and pools. They're covering every base."

"And rationing water. Strange asking people not to flush if they're worried about germs."

"I'd flush ten times in a row just to tell them where to stick it."

"They said everyone's making a run on stores for packaged food," the woman said. "Shoplifting because lines are so long."

"I'd steal water," her companion said. "That'll be the hot commodity before this is over."

Professor Cleave peeled a sticker from a pineapple and watched an outline of Florida curl in upon itself at the tip of his thumb.

Little Butts appeared on screen, and the woman leaned forward. "He'd get my vote."

"I'd cut my nuts off first," her companion said. "Not letting passengers go to a hospital? Hell, they might have gotten it here. Something people here have all the time." He examined a water stain on his glass. "Like malaria. They're just used to it."

The daytime bartender loosened his apron and glanced at Professor Cleave. "He'll be another Patsy Williams if he keeps the port closed."

"Butts just pulled out his best English accent." Professor Cleave paused. "But he's stirring the pot, and he'll bring it to boil soon enough."

He felt a tingle in the back of his throat, and without thinking, lifted a finger to his neck to palpate his glands. At a call for a Cane Cutter, he lowered his hand, and for the rest of the afternoon he battled urges to feel his forehead for signs of fever. When the sun set, he turned up the lights to block out the *Celeste* with the room's reflection on the patio doors.

We were grateful. He'd softened our awareness of the world outside, even if the television continued to project images of deserted decks and perishable food rotting in orange plastic bags, and our antennae were still overwhelmed by visions of legs stiffening above upended shells. We eventually left the lounge to wander empty hallways. By then, the Ambassador's guests had retreated to their rooms and closed their windows against nonexistent breezes, as if they could seal themselves away from illness, from each other, and from us. Who better than cockroaches to explain that the Ambassador's cracked walls and warped windows were practically illusions, porous barriers against diseases that had little, if anything, to do with us?

The only guests who'd abandoned precautionary measures were Helen and Dave. Any precautions would have been post hoc in their case, or so their logic went. They spent the evening in their room, processing missives from panicked passengers and macabre footage captured in a crowded infirmary. At nightfall, they ventured onto the balcony. Dave rested a plastic cup on the railing and leaned into the glow coming off the pool.

"Lawsuits already. Nineteen dead, and everyone's just working out how to spin it."

Helen fingered a button dangling from her sweater. "Should we tell anyone we were on board?"

"Why would we? It's here or it isn't." Dave contemplated the dim lights along the *Celeste*'s upper decks. "Looks like they're trying to conserve power."

"I was in the infirmary. You were everywhere."

"If we were sick, we'd know. And who would we tell?" He tightened his grip on the railing. "I've spent enough of my life with people assuming I'm sick. The gay disease."

"There's an incubation period. We might have gotten it right before we left the ship."

"We feel fine. I do, at least." He turned away, shaken by intimations of illness in her sunken eyes and her skin's bluish cast in the television's watery light.

"We might be spreading it," she said. "We should get checked."

"For what? They don't even know what it is. And if I'm sick, I'm sure as hell not going to a hospital here."

"I just feel guilty. Being here."

"Want to swim back out there? They did us a favor when they kicked us off."

"It's what happened." She hesitated. "What I did. I'm alive, and they're dying."

"Your situation's got nothing to do them."

"Did you know people who were sick?"

He looked at the lights just above the *Celeste*'s waterline and remembered his cabin mate curled up in a nest of musty sheets, staring at a steel bed frame through glassy eyes. "I do know people. People who are sick."

"I didn't mean—"

"One of my friends was sick when I left. Slept three feet above him. Good way to get to know someone. Now he's by himself, burning up. Wish I could help him, but I'm here. Don't wish I was there."

She fingered the hem of her sweater. "They're obligated to treat him."

"The *Celeste*'s registered in Somalia. They don't need to do a damn thing for him." He sat down and braced his feet against the railing. "Why did you do it on the ship?"

She turned away from him. "I didn't want anyone to find me."

A helicopter cut through the haze above the *Celeste*. Dave lit a cigarette. "Maybe no one who knew you, but someone found you. Probably one of my friends. Someone like me."

He didn't say anything when she pulled her sweater across her chest and withdrew into the room. He listened to the rustle of sheets and felt an impulse to flee, but he'd gotten too drunk to pack his things or form a plan, so he refilled his cup again and again until the wavering spears of reflected light beneath the *Celeste* blurred together. At midnight, he went inside and drew the curtains. He stretched across his bed and listened to her shallow breaths, the faint inhalations of someone taking life in tentative measures. Her breath caught, and he soothed himself with memories of Miami and the bronzed skin of beautiful men, and then he drifted into uneasy dreams.

While they slept, we gathered on the folds of her sheet to examine her savaged arms and the threads of her sweater. She was, for us, a source of fascination, her twitching as unsettling as it was familiar. She'd been trampled underfoot, in a manner of speaking. At one point, she opened her eyes, considered us, and drifted back into sleep. We left her, then, to dream the dreams of cockroaches.

❖

Professor Cleave closed the bar early. He'd spent the evening mopping the counter with a towel soaked in bleach and thinking about Helen's blotched skin and the deep shadows beneath her eyes. He wiped down every bottle, scrubbed his hands, and examined his conscience, as well as his face, for blemishes. There was, he decided, no way around confession.

"Awake from the sweet repose of ignorance," he said, settling into the cab. "The situation has worsened since we saw Desmond."

We bristled, and he snapped his fingers.

"This is no time for malicious chatter. There are now twenty-one dead on that ship, and I don't need to tell you what it means that we were driving two of its passengers this morning."

As he shared the muddled analyses of perplexed epidemiologists and related stories of overworked septic systems, we scrambled to the windshield to view the harbor.

"We need to consider the insidious nature of this pestilence and act according to our conscience." We turned to face him with curled antennae. "Given our exposure to certain elements, it is incumbent upon all of you to confine your nocturnal wanderings to the car, suffocating as it is."

To his credit, Professor Cleave considered himself, as well as us, a potential vector of disease. "For my part, I will sleep on the couch. Cora will not find that exceedingly strange."

His unexpected disclosure put us in a strange humor. We tapped each other's antennae and fluttered our wings.

"Madness has taken hold, and your gallows humor has taken an inappropriate turn." He fulminated against the improprieties of dashboard degenerates until he arrived home, where he found Cora and Topsy sitting at the table, listening to the radio.

"Butts has his headlines now," Topsy said. "He says he's prepared for the worst, but your man isn't fit to fart."

"He's not my man," Professor Cleave said.

Topsy brushed cigarette ash from his pants. "It's no matter now. He'll be on the first helicopter out if things get bad. Someone should tell him there's no point making pointless speeches on his way to the airport, but then there's no sense talking to the senseless."

"It could be everywhere," Cora said. "The Reverend said there's nothing we can do but pray."

She folded her hands together and fixed Professor Cleave in a clinical gaze. She examined his eyes for signs of jaundice, scrutinized his neck for suggestive lumps, and studied his nostrils for telltale traces of blood. He blamed her for neither her fear nor her inability to comfort; he forgave her for everything except sitting with her hands so tightly clasped in her narrow lap, her small-mindedness, and her empty talk of faith.

"I'll sleep on the couch. There are things we can all do beyond praying." He said nothing when she rose from her chair and withdrew into her bedroom, her quiet sanctuary, and Topsy retreated into Irma's bedroom, his squalid preserve.

In the bathroom, Professor Cleave pulled a chain dangling beside the bulb and silenced the mating calls of a solitary cricket. He looked into the mirror, pressed his fingers to his neck, and repeated Cora's exacting search for signs of illness. He extruded the last toothpaste from an exhausted tube and brushed his teeth with violent intensity until his gums bled. He slid his tongue across the soft tissue lining his palate, peeled off his clothes, and felt his armpits for swelling. He stepped into the shower stall and rubbed his skin raw.

After making his bed on the couch, he turned off the last light in the house. Each time he neared the edge of sleep, violent twitching jerked him awake. He pressed his fingers to his temples to mute the sound of rushing blood, twisted in his sheet and broke into a sweat, heard Tremor talking about old shoes and saw the shadows beneath Helen's eyes. He sat up and felt the side of his neck. Finally, he drifted into sleep, stirred occasionally by the light pressure of Topsy's hand on his forehead and the brush of our wings against his cheek.

In the morning, he tripped over Topsy's overflowing ashtray and left for the taxi stand, where we nestled beneath old newspapers and shuddered in the presence of drivers cursing the latest breaking news. He sat down beside James Brooks, still known as Brooks Brother with much less irony than in years past, and strained to hear a radio.

"Some Americans jumped from the ship at dawn." James adjusted the band of a straw fedora resting in his lap. "They were trying to swim to shore and disappeared."

"I heard nothing coming here," Professor Cleave said.

"It's just out. Butts had boats patrolling the harbor. Playing the big man. The police fired in the air to keep more of them from jumping. The Americans are calling it an act of aggression."

Professor Cleave rubbed his forehead. "This can only end in tears."

"Butts said it was a deterrent."

"That won't be the news of the world."

"You'd think Butts himself had shot them, by what the Americans are saying."

"They need someone to blame." Professor Cleave trailed off to listen to the report of three desperate passengers resigning themselves to unknown currents to escape the relentless spread of sickness. "They'll be pulling bodies from the water soon enough."

"He'll be up to his neck in this one."

"And there's not much above Butts's neck." During a commercial for detergent, Professor Cleave studied the smooth planes of his cousin's face. "You almost look younger than back in Patrice Williams's day."

"The beard gave me years when I needed them to meet a woman. Now I'm trying to give those years back to keep that same woman."

"Who would have seen the way things would change?"

"But things did change." James rubbed his chin. "We got better tips once we shaved."

"And now they will change again," Professor Cleave said. "The fat is in the fire now. It will be hissing away until we can hear nothing else."

By the time he left the taxi stand, news of the morning's most spectacular deaths had spread across the island. It moved through the open windows of parked cars, over backyard fences, and between somber friends and erstwhile enemies reconciled in the spirit of sordid speculation. It consumed shopkeepers on street corners, maids at bus stops, and young men in corner bars. The ghastliest strains of information spread with the greatest virulence, feeding on macabre curiosities and rising resentment. Professor Cleave tapped his thumb on the steering wheel until it throbbed. Whatever it was, he thought, it was already inside him, moving through his bloodstream and settling into his lungs. We huddled behind the vents, knowing it was only a matter of time before bipedal mobs turned their fury upon us, flushing us out of every dark corner and pouring rivers of pesticide over everything we touched.

❈

In Room 504 at the Ambassador, no one had slept much. We'd been plagued by nightmares about poison gas and the treads of tennis shoes. Dave had slept sporadically, unnerved by Helen's presence and the sounds of our scuttling. Helen had awoken several times to strange visions and the sounds of helicopter blades. Hours after daybreak, she stirred to the sight of Dave sitting on the edge of his bed, staring at the muted television.

"What's going on?" She gathered her sheet around her.

"St. Anne's been quarantined. Every airline's canceled flights." He lifted a remote control, and a newscaster's clipped voice filled the room. "The CDC called for the quarantine. The State Department's backing it. We're stuck here."

She studied pixilated images of garbage bags leaking onto a basketball court and shaky footage of flooded bathrooms and feverish faces.

"They don't know where to put garbage," he continued. "Thirty-four people are dead. A few jumped overboard. Said no one was doing anything for them. Guess the police shot at them."

She looked out across the harbor. "What are those helicopters and boats doing?"

"Looking for survivors. Probably broke their legs and couldn't beat the current. Search party's wasting time."

She drew her sheet around her chest and stepped onto the balcony. She studied the bands of dark blue beyond the harbor and imagined indifferent forms turning in cold currents, past dead reefs and the unblinking eyes of curious fish. She looked over the railing and imagined a fall, the release of one last breath, a weightless drift and gentle dissolution. She saw Tremor, then, standing beside the pool, holding a net and staring up at her. When he didn't turn away, she backed into the room.

"The bellboy. He was staring at me. Like he was disgusted. Maybe he heard—"

"Just ignore him," Dave said.

"He probably knows we came off the ship."

"How would he? And what's he going to do if he does?"

Helen drew her sheet over her exposed shoulders. "We need some groceries. To stock up on supplies."

Dave rubbed his eyes and shut off the television.

They walked slowly and spoke little. When they reached the top of the street leading into Portsmouth, a Cessna passed overhead, banked sharply and headed out over the sea.

"I didn't think any flights were leaving," Helen said. "Maybe the airport opened."

"Ain't open to us. No one's getting on a plane unless they own one."

At the bottom of the hill, they followed the harbor road past cinderblock houses. Barefoot children throwing empty bottles into a sinkhole fell silent as they passed. Old men playing dominoes on porches watched their progress. Two women coming from the direction of town lifted their collars to their mouths. A man in torn pants regarded Helen through eyes clouded by cataracts, raised an unlabeled bottle, and pointed at a man kneeling over a gutter, retching.

"He has the American disease." He staggered to the curb and spat on the ground.

"He thinks we're sick," Helen whispered.

"He's not thinking a fucking thing. Just keep moving."

A Learjet ripped through the sky. The children feeding the sinkhole watched its vapor trail dissipate. To the sound of glass shattering,

Helen started again toward town, carrying the memory of faces hardened by fear. Dave trailed behind her, trying to lose himself in dreams of primordial trees and mountain streams, of some place far removed from worsening headlines and uncertain moods.

❈

Dave had lost himself in a postcard world as flat and fantastical as the world imagined by the ignorant scurvy-ridden captains who'd cursed the doldrums centuries before. We couldn't entirely blame him. We were dreaming, too, of times long past, when we'd spread functional wings and enjoyed the luxury of unimpeded flight. Dave was more deluded than most, though. That afternoon, he wandered from the Ambassador's air-conditioned lobby without a single thought to the heat, hoping only to escape Helen. Halfway down the street, he leaned against a wall and looked up at the scorched hills receding further, it seemed, with each step he took. As the first thoughts of water crossed his mind, he smelled something pungent drifting over the wall. He stepped up to a wooden gate and peered between two planks. In a small enclosure filled with flattened cardboard boxes, Tremor stood beside a crate of bananas at the end of a service ramp.

Dave pushed open the gate and stood at its threshold. "Got a minute?"

From a short distance, Tremor studied Dave's skin and eyes.

"The other night, I got the impression you could help me out," Dave said.

Tremor took a small step forward. "Depends."

"I'm looking for some weed. Not much."

Tremor pulled a plastic bag from his pocket. "Fifty dollars, American."

Dave whistled through his teeth. "That's a hell of an opener."

Tremor shrugged. "That's the price."

"That's twenty, at most."

"Fifty's the price of doing business. With people I don't know."

"Didn't seem like a problem the other night."

"That was the other night."

"This is bullshit."

Dave backed onto the sidewalk. A young man with short dreadlocks was walking in his direction, taking the small steps of one accustomed to extreme heat. As he neared, the man peeled his shirt from his back and lissome arms.

"Beautiful day. American?" The man stepped onto the sidewalk. "Maybe you need company. Someone to show you around on holiday. Beaches. Whatever you want."

Tremor slipped through the gate and spat on the ground. The man stepped off the sidewalk and continued down the street, kicking up dust with the tips of his leather sandals.

"He's confused. Crazy like a woman or castrated goat." Tremor dragged his thumbnail across his lips to strip away a fleck of spittle. "People say he's got a disease. It's a risk to be seen with him. I won't do business with him. You know?"

"I get it." Dave dragged his hand around the back of his neck. "Look, I don't have cash on me. I'm in 504."

Tremor's face twitched. "Everybody has money when they ask for things."

"Didn't expect to catch you down here. Didn't expect the price, either."

Tremor gestured toward the crate. "I'll be finished in ten minutes."

"Throw in some rolling papers."

"Five dollars."

"I'll get some in town."

"Long walk on a hot day."

Dave looked up at the sun and nodded.

He was standing on the balcony, with a shirt draped over his bare shoulder, when Tremor knocked twice on the open door. He turned to face the room and rested his elbows on the railing. "That a decent beach over that bluff? Or is something better nearby?"

"I don't know the beaches. I don't swim."

"You live on an island and you don't swim?"

"The water can be dangerous."

"Still." Dave arched his back and looked down at the patio. "Poor Helen. She's another one. Sunning in her sweater."

Tremor conducted a quick inventory of the room, noting a small purse and a leather wallet on the nightstand. "Is that lady your wife?"

"My wife?" Dave drew away from the railing. "No wife in my life, brother."

"A girlfriend?"

"Not my type. Not even close."

Dave entered the room and glanced at Tremor's nametag. "Trevor. I'm Dave."

Tremor averted his eyes from the soft hair covering Dave's chest. "Trevor's nothing. Tremor's my name."

"Tremor?" Dave sat down on his bed and reached for his wallet. "What's the story? Name like Tremor, there's got to be a story."

Tremor tossed the bag onto the bed. "There's no story."

"Just asking. It's not a big deal," Dave said, extending a fold of bills. He tensed at the sight of Tremor's arms and the money slipped from his fingers. "Sorry about that," he began, but Tremor had already swept the money from the floor and turned to leave.

For most of the afternoon, Dave strolled along the beach beneath the hotel, stepping around patches of soft mud and bits of garbage, too high to think about Helen's mutilated arms or their dark counterparts. High above, Tremor cursed castrated goats and sunburned devils in green sweaters, and rubbed his fingers where they'd brushed Dave's.

Those of us on the roof shuddered. Some of us disappeared into drains and air ducts, for there was no saying which way Tremor's mood would turn. The patio, as it turned out, was no great shakes, either.

By then, dozens of hotel guests had congregated around the pool to escape the claustrophobia of their rooms, and to comment on the missing passengers and the posthumous fates of those who'd succumbed to illness. For fear of the contagion's spread, the dead had been consigned to the *Celeste*'s meat lockers. Under the onslaught of dreadful news, the Ambassador's guests traded their fragile sympathies for the secret jubilation of survivors. Unwilling witnesses to misery, they engaged in strange psychological feints to justify their good fortune. Helen was the sole exception. She leafed through a magazine filled with photos of celebrity rehab graduates and let her attentions drift between indistinguishable starlets, the sutures poking through her sweater, and the conversation of two men sprawled on nearby deck chairs.

"Things must be quite desperate if they're jumping," observed a finely wrinkled Englishman. Beside him, an American balanced a sweating beer can on the rise of his stomach.

"Or they're really stupid. I heard those assholes jumped with their shoes on. Doesn't matter. You'd be busted up hitting the water from that height. Wouldn't have a chance to drown."

"All around, it's terrible luck."

"Nothing to do with luck. Dumber than dog shit."

"One wonders if they'll wash up at some point," the Englishman mused.

"Better if they don't. Who knows how long this thing lives in its host?"

"It's the end of our snorkeling plans, though we'd certainly negotiate a good price now."

The American scanned the harbor with a pair of binoculars. "That garbage piled on the decks must smell like shit. Don't know how they can keep people locked in their rooms. No need to impose martial law just because a few jackasses cashed their chips."

"The only person worse than the captain is this Buttskell character," the Englishman said. "A bit of a fascist, from the sounds of it."

"Ought to be strung up from a tree."

"Loathe as I am to admit it, I'm relieved they're not transporting passengers to the hospital here. It would be absolutely mad."

"But shooting at people, stupid fucks or not, wasn't right."

"I entirely agree. It's a police state."

"Might as well bunker down and drink." The American opened another can of beer and cursed. Flecking foam from his chest, he followed the Englishman's gaze to a young woman staring at the sun through mirrored glasses. "Keep it in your trunks, pal. She can't be more than sixteen. They lock you up for that shit."

"If there's grass on the field, play ball. Isn't that an American expression?" Even our jaded antennae twisted, and we pitied those humans fated, like us, to suffer fools. The Englishman inclined his head toward Helen. "I hope we haven't disturbed you with unpleasant talk."

"You should lose the sweater," the American said. "It's hotter than hell, in case no one told you."

"It is hell." Helen tossed the magazine to the ground and rose from her chair.

She entered the lobby with no particular destination in mind. She thought of leaving the hotel and walking until she grew too exhausted to think, but then there would be the severity of strangers' stares, clinging dust, and the suck of liquefying asphalt beneath her blistered feet. She slumped against the wall beside the elevator, stared at a crack in the plaster and dreamed of slipping into some dark space. All she could do, she thought, was retreat to her room and wait, or turn herself over to some authority. She drifted in indecision and tried to focus her thoughts.

She was staring at a baseboard when Professor Cleave found her looking as withered as the potted palm beside her. His mood had deteriorated over long hours trolling the streets, and her unseasonable sweater seemed, more than ever, suggestive of some hidden illness. He looked around the empty lobby and approached her.

"You understand the gravity of the current situation, so you should understand why I need to ask about your health."

She drew away from the wall. "My health?"

"People here are very anxious. With your talk of the ship two nights ago, I have every reason to be concerned. You spoke of an infirmary. And you look ill."

"You have no right to talk about my appearance."

He pointed at her face. "Everyone talks about rights when they want to justify some selfish concern. It's not your right to endanger so many others."

Helen summoned the elevator. "Then you have no business."

"It is exactly my business. I went home to my wife and father last night, and I could offer them no assurances. You saw things on that ship. You were irresponsible to come here."

"Hundreds of people left the terminal. We weren't the only ones."

"But you walked everywhere, knowing what you did. You rode in my cab." He took in Helen's ragged hems and the button dangling from a frayed thread. "They say the infection causes chills. If you're sick, you should have kept to yourself. You and the man you're with."

The elevator opened, and Helen backed across its threshold. "I have no reason to think I'm sick."

He blocked the door with his foot. "You've been selfish. Playing with the lives of so many people."

Helen looked down at his foot, baffled. "Suicide's not contagious," she said.

He thought he'd misheard her until she pulled up one of her sleeves, extended her upturned arm, and repeated her words. She withdrew to a corner of the elevator and pressed her arm against her chest. He staggered backward, and when the elevator doors closed, he collapsed on a couch. He tried to hold onto the image of her arm, now a strange source of hope, and retain what he could of an exchange too strange to fix in his mind. She'd seemed surprised by her own actions, more ashamed than hostile, and more exhausted than indifferent. Still, he felt no less angry for knowing what she'd done to herself.

He bent over a newspaper on the table before him. Beneath a full-page photo of the *Celeste*, a tiny inset referenced a murder in Tindertown. He looked into the lounge, at a group of tourists watching television. Then he tucked the paper beneath his arm and walked to the elevator, realizing how much he needed to be alone, and realizing, too, that the last time he'd gone to the roof to read, he'd raced up eight flights of stairs without once losing his breath.

He found Tremor staring down at the water. He expected to feel renewed anger but felt himself deflating instead. If a little closer to the edge, the boy was sitting where he'd sat years ago, when he'd let his thoughts wander beyond the horizon, to places he'd mapped a thousand times in his mind. The boy, though, had come up in a different world, one filled with new strains of sickness, strange storms, and unpredictable droughts. When Professor Cleave stepped up to the roof's edge, Tremor considered him through narrowed eyes and then turned away.

Professor Cleave unfolded the newspaper. "Jumping when they have so much. At the first sign of problems."

Tremor looked up again, stirred by the depth and direction of Professor Cleave's anger. Together they watched a solitary figure walking along the shore.

Professor Cleave struggled to find words. "With this quarantine, there will be lean days ahead."

"Whole island's Rocky Point, now. Nothing different for most people I know."

"This sickness could change everything."

Tremor picked at the edge of a plastic card in his hands. "How does it spread? By touching?"

"I don't know."

"Does it move through the air? In the breath of sick people?"

"That's of no matter to us," Professor Cleave said. "We have no choice but to breathe."

"Will the water make people sick?"

"No one is certain."

"How long are they sick before they show it?"

"They don't know. About the incubation period."

Tremor twisted sideways to look at Professor Cleave. "Doesn't the paper say?"

"If you want to know what they know, go on and read it." Professor Cleave folded the newspaper and tossed it to the ground beside Tremor.

Tremor drew his knees to his chest and wrapped his arms around his shins. His face had become a register of fear and confusion. "If no one knows anything, they should let them drown. Shoot any that don't."

Professor Cleave thought of Helen's sunken eyes and tried to stir his own conscience. "Then they'll be guilty, too."

"People say we'll all get it in a few days. They brought it here."

"They might not have known."

"They were in your taxi. You touched their glasses. I carried her bags." Tremor placed the card on top of the newspaper. "I brought him a towel."

Professor Cleave looked at Dave's employee badge and rested his fingertip on his upper lip to steady his expression. "Did you tell anyone?"

"No woman will touch me if I'm sick."

"You're getting beyond the situation. We don't know anything."

"Is that why you aren't telling anyone?"

"I didn't know anything." Professor Cleave faltered. "When I picked them up."

Tremor trailed his fingers along his arm. "I should kill them myself."

Professor Cleave looked out at the *Celeste* and realized that Helen's features and those of another woman had become indistinguishable in his mind. "We need to refuse violence, or we become morally deformed."

Tremor lowered his head between his arms, and Professor Cleave knew he'd stretched his meaning over too many syllables. He struggled, in vain, to clarify his thoughts, and then left Tremor sitting on the edge of the roof. Standing behind the bar, he imagined Tremor recoiling from words swimming on newsprint and looking out, in fear, at an unforgiving world. He felt that same fear nesting in his chest and making it difficult to breathe.

At the end of the night, he carried a sack of garbage to the loading dock, where feral cats were fighting over scraps of food. He stamped his foot, and the cats scattered beyond the light falling past the open kitchen door. As he turned to the dumpster, he saw a white uniform shirt floating in darkness. He slowly discerned the shape of Tremor standing near the entrance to the service stairwell.

"What are you doing in the dark? Passing the time, I suppose."

"Killing it. That's what Americans say. Nothing to do."

"You can help me get rid of this garbage."

Tremor sauntered to the dumpster and propped open its lid while Professor Cleave tossed the bag onto a bed of decomposing lettuce.

"Shut that thing now or we'll both suffocate," Professor Cleave said. "Their mountains of garbage never stop piling up."

"Things they don't eat," Tremor said. "Things they won't eat."

"We'll hope it passes soon. The heat. The sickness. The whole miserable lot of them." Professor Cleave wiped his hand on his pants.

"You're afraid you got the American disease." Tremor pulled a lighter from his pocket. Tendons rippled beneath his skin each time he batted its flame with his fingertips. "I'm burning it away." Tremor spat on his fingertips and held them to the flame again. Professor Cleave recoiled from the sizzle of saliva.

"That won't do a thing. It's foolish."

"You said they don't know anything. So, you don't know anything. You just pretend to know things."

Professor Cleave studied Tremor's expression in the flickering light. "You're clouded, again. Wasting time in stairwells. Do you think you don't need a job?"

"The job pays enough for the bus to get to the job."

"You make money for more than the bus by doing everything but your job. Sneaking around rooms. And then you take a paycheck for the job you don't do. You steal in different ways, and they're all the same in the end."

"I'm not working in this place until I'm an old man."

Professor Cleave pressed his fingernails into his palm. "What you think about this place is no excuse for thieving and lying. And the manager is no matter. At the end of each day, you answer to your conscience. It's all you have."

"That's all you have if you're the manager's nigger." Tremor brushed past Professor Cleave and slipped through the gate.

Professor Cleave spent several minutes in the company of feral cats, rubbing his hands where they'd become sticky and trying to compose himself. He felt gutted and frail, and for the first time, afraid of Tremor. He stepped out onto the sidewalk, looked over his shoulder once, and berated himself for doing so. At the corner, a man holding a bloody shirt staggered across the street.

"No work tomorrow," the man slurred, weaving through a streetlight's orange glow. "A carnival without the cruise."

Professor Cleave watched him disappear and started walking to the sound of a woman cursing in the distance. He didn't slow his pace until he reached his cab. He didn't lower his windows until he reached the edge of Portsmouth.

Stirred by warm currents, we emerged from beneath the seats and gathered on the dashboard to view the harbor. We recoiled momentarily from the lurid lights of helicopters and then fluttered our wings, intoxicated against all reason by hints of garbage.

"A fetid feast for the less fastidious." Professor Cleave reached for the radio and then drew his hand back to the steering wheel. "Nothing will have changed, except for the worse."

As the harbor receded, he wondered if exhaustion had finally rendered his senses unreliable. He shuddered at the sight of crooked headstones in neglected cemeteries, chipped grey teeth rising from

rot, stray dogs with gleaming fangs and goats with mirror eyes glinting in headlights, riotous roadside weeds and brooding volcanic
mountains—features of a familiar landscape made nightmarish by
the news of the day.

※

Professor Cleave wasn't alone in seeing the nightmarish aspect of
things. Those of us crawling through the gutters of Portsmouth had
grown disoriented, overpowered by tantalizing scents of decay in-
separable from the suffering of our peers. We felt addled, too, by
static—the erratic thoughts of Tremor in the throes of self-hatred,
more confused than ever as he tried to find his way beneath once-
familiar constellations muted by the glare coming off the harbor.

Tremor had set off in the direction of Portsmouth, too sickened
to think of anything but flight. He didn't even stop to trade his stiff
uniform for the clothes he'd stored in a basement locker, or to re-
spond to the garbled comments of a drunk stumbling up the hill,
slurring about the American disease and pointing at his starched
shirt. He might have bloodied the man's face, but the man's smell,
the infectious reek of a parasite rooting in dumpsters, repulsed him.
He felt the sticky residue of something he'd touched and stumbled
down the sidewalk with gravity tugging at his chest until he felt he
was falling.

At the bottom of the hill, he pressed his palm to his forehead, dizzied by the pounding of helicopter blades, the spotlights sweeping the
harbor for broken bodies, and the smell of rot. He'd heard rumors of
garbage piled on upper decks, falling into the sea in small avalanches.
All of it would wash up somewhere, much of it in Rocky Point.

He leaned against a wall to steady himself, sick at the memory
of six letters he'd spit at a man wearing the same uniform clinging to
his own back. He'd used the word to resist the deadly undertow of
hours slipping away, hours that could become a lifetime spent skim-

ming litter from swimming pools. If he'd left Professor Cleave looking like a slack-jawed old man broken by a single blow, he reasoned,
he'd saved himself by renouncing servitude in the most unqualified
terms he could conjure. Now he wanted to disappear in a crowded,
smoke-filled room and forget the rotted core of each losing argument
with himself. He started in the direction of EZ's apartment, alert
to the sounds of bottles clattering somewhere. The streetlight's hum
merged in his imagination with the buzz of graveyard flies, and he
scratched his face to dispel his sense of tiny insects tracing patterns
across his cheeks.

He slowly gained an awareness of warmth spreading across his
shoulder blades, the retaining wall at his back and the sidewalk beneath his fingertips. He reached around his ribcage and felt torn fabric
and fresh blood, examined his teeth, and felt his head for lumps.
Then he pulled himself to his feet and paced in short turns to restore
feeling to his legs, sensing that something inside of him had broken.
He reached for his phone, thinking to call someone, and realized
he had no name for himself. He tried to will himself into being by
speaking, to remember the sound of others speaking his name, and
heard nothing.

Panicked, he started down the street. In the center of town, he
boarded a crowded taxi van to escape the malevolence he'd unleashed.
He turned to the window and stared at his dim reflection, peering
into the pools of darkness around his eyes until his name returned,
six sequenced letters to exorcise the six he'd spat in a man's face earlier that night. Tremor, he whispered over and over, oblivious to the
exhausted maid sitting beside him.

He wanted, more than anything, to reach home. He paused on
the last word, circled it warily, and dwelled upon its bewildering associations. He wanted to lose himself in predictable routines among
people too addled to judge. Among broken people, he told himself,
he could live with himself. He leaned back in his seat, indifferent
to worsening radio reports of contagion and impending economic

downturn. If the world could recede from his mind without warning, none of it mattered, he thought.

When the bus left him beside the road, he went to his garden. He stripped his shirt from his back and dropped to his knees. He touched the crusted blood at the base of his spine and then buried his fingers in earth to cleanse them. He inhaled deeply and let his eyes slip out of focus. The moon waxed and melted. Tremor, he whispered.

Before daybreak, he made his way into Rocky Point, tripping over exposed roots and alive to every sensation—the touch of overhanging branches scratching his bare shoulders, the sound of a turning tide and the taste of salty air. He looked at the trailers and shacks lining a narrow road, the brooding shapes of tethered boats, and the scales of reflected moonlight upon the sea. He quickened his pace when he passed Mary's reliquary, determined to return home, to the smell of cane liquor and the stirring of his father in the throes of alcoholic dreams.

Those of us in Mary's house watched him pass. Overcome by his volatility, we scurried along shelves and skittered around wooden crates. Mary calmed us by stroking our antennae and blowing gently on our wings. She left potato peels on her floor and watched us eat. She held us in her hands and rocked back and forth on her heels. At midnight, she stepped out into the moonlight and hummed. We clung to the folds of her skirt and let our antennae rest in the trough of a deep vibration Tremor couldn't hear.

MADNESS

Mary's house was our favorite place on St. Anne, a refuge from Professor Cleave's recitations when we had no tolerance for cruise ships and they none for us. We much preferred the fruits of Mary's garden to fondue and fondant, and her dirt floor to polished decks reeking of disinfectant. Mary never once menaced us with cigarettes, badminton racquets, or aerosol cans. She spoke kindly and cooed to us. She let us be ourselves. In her home, we wandered openly, uncensored and according to our wont. But it was the siren call of her voice that always drew us to Rocky Point.

If Mary was out gathering stones or bits of shells when we arrived, we'd wait for her. We never felt as though we were trespassing, for she always left her door wide open in expectation of her husband's return. Mad with longing, we'd nestle in her burlap sacks and examine her Mason jars and dusty crates. We'd trail our antennae along the contents of her baskets and makeshift shelves—broken necklaces and candle stubs, bits of frayed ribbon and a compass with a cracked glass face. We'd touch the things she'd touched and take in her scent. She was, in life, our beloved saint, long before others claimed her for their own purposes; she remained so in death, after she faded from almost everyone else's memories.

When Mary returned, we'd gather within the pale of her lantern's glow and gaze upon her. She'd rub dirt from potatoes unearthed behind her house and mesmerize us with the movements of her rough fingers over their golden skin. She'd cook dinner in a skillet, place some portion in her garden, and leave something for us on the floor. After dinner, she'd sit in her wooden chair and examine everything she'd gathered from the beach. She'd rub stones between her palms and bundle together twigs and feathers. She'd wet shards of clouded sea glass with her spittle and hold them to the light to study different colors fading behind salty patinas. She'd string shell fragments on old fishing lines and hang them beside her door. We followed her every gesture. She could have done anything and kept us watching and waiting, desperately pining.

Toward the end of the night, she'd rise from her chair and rock back and forth on her heels and clutch the loose folds of her skirt. Then she'd smile, and we'd sense the first vibrations, the low hum that filled our minds with madness. She'd let strange syllables spill forth, and then without warning, hold back and draw us, straining, to the very edge of her shelves and our sanity, our antennae tingling and aching in intolerable anticipation. Finally, mercifully, she'd take us in her hands and bear us outside, hold us up to the moon and then close to her face. She'd stroke our quivering wings with her rough fingers and blow on the tips of our antennae until we lay exhausted, spent in the palms of her hands, in a state of unrivaled bliss.

She had us trained like circus fleas. We were the willing channels of her love. Most people ascribed her behavior to insanity, though that's hardly of interest to us now. It didn't keep us from her then. To live, as she did, in the presence of death and to continue loving is certainly a form of madness. Perhaps that's why Professor Cleave never spoke of love. To love is to surrender oneself to madness. Mary chose madness. She hoped, against all reason, for the return of love.

CHAPTER SEVEN

MARY HOPED AGAINST ALL odds—and what lousy odds they were in Rocky Point, where ongoing scarcity had engendered a certain meanness of spirit. At times even we fell prey to insecurity and strayed from Mary's house to root around in washed-up garbage, mindlessly consuming more than we needed simply because we could. Transfixed by the trash on Rocky Point's beach, we wandered with downcast antennae, oblivious to radio transmissions and matters loftier than our search for new and improved varieties of filth.

Tremor could hardly be accused of ignorance when it came to long odds, yet he awoke the next morning feeling convinced he'd finally found home. He squinted into the sunlight piercing a broken shutter and considered a glass standing on a plank shelf and two rusted pans hanging from hooks, finding comfort in the solidity of familiar things. Then he saw the single plate and chipped cup on the table, a spare setting for a man without a wife, and without a son. In tentative steps, he crossed the room to a mattress bearing the impress of his father's body. A creased photograph of his mother hung from a piece of tape curling from the wall. He knelt down and trailed his fingertips over his mother's face, absorbed the quiet of the house, and for the first time grasped the enormity of his father's solitude. He rose to his feet, quickly gathered a soccer jersey from the floor, and stepped outside. He shielded his eyes and counted a dozen men dragging nets from small boats onto the pier. Then he started toward the water, drawn by his father's voice.

Halfway across the beach, he paused before a patch of soft brown mud. All around, gulls were shrieking and pulling trash through the split seams of orange garbage bags. Amidst unrivaled excess, they pecked and batted us each time we approached. While they snatched bits of withered lettuce from one another (Black Friday, indeed!), we watched and waited, hoping to sample what remained after their violent frenzy. We'd feel worse saying that if we hadn't been so unnerved by news of the *Celeste*, and so grasping on account of our fear. Still, that hardly changes the fact that we abandoned Mary that morning to forage for dregs, thwarted less by conscience than sharp bills and the menace of massive wings.

Like all of us, Tremor found himself distracted by the gulls and a rising din at the end of the beach. He rubbed his temple and squinted into the sun's glare. Surrounded by a flock of gulls, Mary was standing beside a piece of driftwood, howling and carving lines in the sand with a crooked stick. A short distance from her, a small group of children had formed a loose circle around her. The children limped and staggered in a ragged line and beat the sand with palm fronds in crude imitations of Mary's movements. Sickened, Tremor turned away. Only the men pulling nets onto Rocky Point's crumbling pier seemed indifferent to the unholy noise at the far end of the beach. Their banter ceased, though, when Tremor stepped onto the pier and made his way to a single-engine boat with a badly splintered gunnel. His father stood above the boat, looping a rope around his upper arm and hooked thumb.

"Early for you." He glanced at Tremor.

Tremor studied his father's face, lined by wind and salt spray, and the muscles along his father's wiry arms.

His father nodded at a pile of nets. "If you remember how I taught you."

Tremor lifted a net and pulled its edge taut. Without a word, his father set down the rope and drew a second net from the heap. Slowly,

Tremor mirrored the movements of his father's practiced hands, disentangling knotted cords and stopping every few seconds to pick scales and bits of seaweed from frayed lattice. As the steady rhythms of work resumed, conversation settled on worn topics, stale gossip and the morning's dispiriting business.

"Everyone's afraid fish have the American disease."

"Messing with that woman, you look like you got the American disease."

Tremor listened to grim speculations and salving jokes and avoided his father's gaze by looking down at the water lapping against the pier. Dizzied by shimmering oil slicks and the rocking of his father's boat, he turned to the horizon to steady himself, only to become disoriented by the enormity of the sky. He backed away from the edge of the pier, into a puddle tinged by the innards of gutted fish.

"You'll ruin those town shoes," one of his father's friends said.

Trevor pressed his forearm against his lips.

"You want a job on a boat, you can have mine," the man continued, carried by a ripple of laughter. "Make lots of money. Wear clothes like the big man, Little Butts. Get greased with more than fish oil."

"Let him be," Tremor's father said.

Tremor tried to adjust the net in his hands, and his fingers grew tangled in its loose weave. He struggled to find symmetry in its grimy folds, overwhelmed by incongruous angles and the smell of discarded bait, and distracted by the sound of John Bowden sharpening a knife at the end of the pier with the same dead expression he'd worn years before, carrying the weight of ankle chains and shoveling sand into the wind.

The sound of metal scraping stone filled our antennae with dread, even though John Bowden had never threatened us. He'd never bothered anyone in Rocky Point, for that matter. He'd said little to anyone since he returned from prison, walking unsteadily but walking nonetheless, confirming Mary's belief in resurrection. Over the years, his clothes disintegrated, growing seamless as sleeves fell away and hems turned to filthy fringe. He spent his days alone in his boat, chasing away waking nightmares with cane liquor and reminding everyone in Rocky Point of the future awaiting any expendable member of society—any patsy or scapegoat (any cockroach!) who strays too close to respectable establishments.

Too young to remember John Bowden's return from prison, Tremor simply envied the awe John Bowden inspired. He listened to the sound of scraping metal and imagined himself rising from repeated beatings, an outlaw hero able to silence children with a glance. When he sensed John Bowden's eyes upon him, he looked involuntarily at Crazy Mary crossing herself and spitting on sand, praying and cursing with equal fervor. He turned away from Crazy Mary to find his father looking at the tangled net dangling from his fingers.

"Give me that, boy." His father stripped the net from his hands. "Be quicker without you."

Overcome by the stench and the sun and John Bowden's unbending stare, Tremor stumbled from the pier, tormented by the sound of children howling in a collective echo of Crazy Mary. He dragged his hand across his mouth and looked to the end of the beach, helplessly drawn to the spectacle of Mary kicking sand at the gulls encroaching upon the driftwood. In loose and shifting formations, the children mirrored the birds' movements, advancing upon Mary, scattering each time she faced them, and then regrouping. Tremor pressed his fingers to his temples and started to turn away when several children broke through the flock, only to fall back screaming about a dead body.

One by one, adults made their way to the beach and saw in place of driftwood a man's twisted form. They raced along the shore, toward their children, toward Crazy Mary. Tremor followed.

At the edge of a small crowd, Tremor watched parents gather children into the folds of their clothing and cover tiny noses to ward off the effusions of a bloated body laced with seaweed and covered in flies. He glanced at a pale hand half-buried in sand and pressed his lips together. As he wiped a trickle of sweat from his face, a small girl strayed toward the body. Her mother lunged forward and grabbed the girl's arm, yanking with such force that everyone heard or imagined the snap of a growing bone. The mother pressed the girl to her chest, as if to will away her child's pain, and Tremor shuddered.

He saw Mary, then, clutching her stick and drawing away from the body. He averted his eyes and gazed at a tangle of muddy blond hair and a swollen leg covered in bruises. Sickness welled in his stomach. He was taking a step backward when John Bowden brushed past him, edged through the crowd, and kicked a gull pecking the eyes of a dead fish beside the body. As the gull limped away, John Bowden glanced at the girl shivering in her mother's embrace. The girl might have been in shock, for the pale imprint of her mother's fingers hadn't faded from her disjointed arm. When two more gulls wobbled toward the dead fish, John Bowden started walking back toward the pier.

Moments later, he reappeared with a rusted gas can hanging from his fingers. He made his way to the center of the crowd and drew a small cardboard box from his pocket. Screeching gulls scattered in every direction as he doused the body and tossed a lit match. In a blinding instant, a sheet of flame rose in the air, folded inward and enveloped the body in a skein of blue light.

Mary screamed. Tremor staggered backward, wiping tears from his eyes as strips of glowing fabric spiraled upward, carried by the heat of their own burning, blackened and then drifted down as ash. Without a word, John Bowden collected the gas can, walked back to the pier, and lowered himself into his boat. He spent the rest of the afternoon staring at the horizon, smoking cigarettes and drinking from an unlabeled bottle.

Almost everyone who watched John Bowden burn the body felt, in turns, unspeakable gratitude and rising dread. From a safe distance, Tremor fell madly in love with the idea of John Bowden. We drew our antennae beneath our wings and trembled.

�֎

No one called the police. All but three people in Rocky Point hid themselves behind closed doors and broken shutters, bemoaned the misery visited upon their village and prayed the next tide would carry it from their shores. Mary, alone, remained near the body. Tremor and his latest girlfriend sat in the weeds above the beach, watching her trace signs in the sand at the water's edge.

"Crazy Mary's crazy as ever today." Tremor's girlfriend drew her knees to her chest. "Gonna get herself sick."

"Can't catch nothing. John Bowden burned it away."

"John Bowden's crazy as Crazy Mary."

"Better to get rid of it. Burn every last one that makes it to shore." Tremor snapped a twig between his fingers. "If I had a can, you'd have seen me do it."

Mary crouched beside the water. With tiny waves lapping at her ankles, she collected broken shells and examined each one before casting it back into the sea or dropping it into her lap. Using a fold of her skirt as a strained sack, she finally made her way back to Rocky Point.

"Take a photo," Tremor said.

"Take it yourself."

"Don't want just the body." Tremor wrapped his hand around his girlfriend's wrist, pulled her from the weeds and pressed his phone into her hand. "I want to be standing next to it."

He edged toward the body until he was looking down at patches of blistered tissue around two empty eye sockets. A wave of nausea passed through him, and he turned to the pier, where John Bowden sat in his boat. Then he turned his back on Rocky Point. His girlfriend squinted at his phone and struggled to steady her hands.

"Get it all." Tremor cocked his head and lifted two unsteady fingers in the air.

His girlfriend took a picture and staggered back into the weeds, holding a hand over her mouth. When he caught up with her, Tremor grabbed the phone and ran his fingers over his own image. He sent the image to EZ, pulled his girlfriend to the ground, and placed his hand on her trembling thigh.

Within an hour, the image had traveled across St. Anne, passed through sweaty hands in barbershops, bars, and bakeries, and beneath disbelieving eyes in small mountain villages and towns along the ring road. It finally reached St. Anne's police chief, who squinted at the charred body and the jagged outcropping of rock behind it. By that time, the image had returned to Rocky Point and ignited fearful conversations among those who knew better than to celebrate their own notoriety, and among all of us, who hid in the scrub or sought refuge in Mary's house. Unlike Tremor, we'd seen it all before.

When Tremor went home, he found the windows shuttered and his father sitting at the table, running his fingers along the edge of a worn leather belt. Without speaking, his father rose to his feet and brought the belt's buckle down on Tremor's shoulder. Tremor fell to the floor and pressed his hands to his face. On elbows and knees, he crawled to a corner and shrank from the blows falling on his back and shoulders. When he began to shake, his father spat on the floor.

"Go away." His father dropped the belt. "You've caused too much trouble here."

Tremor remained on his knees, holding one unsteady hand in the other and seeking words to explain himself until his father's silence drove him from the house. At the edge of Rocky Point, he sat down on the edge of a dry streambed. He traced his welts with his fingertips and struck the side of his head with his palm. His thoughts raced, and in his panic, he heard movements in the branches above him. He looked up at a tree riddled with holes and felt termites boring through his skin, slapped his arms and realized that his brain had again betrayed him, and that he could no longer rely on anyone, including himself.

He'd been sitting in the dirt for an hour when he heard the sound of strained engines. He flattened himself in the streambed and watched two police SUVs moving down the path from the bypass, snapping overhanging branches and crushing saplings. After they passed, he crawled through underbrush to a pile of overgrown concrete blocks on a hill above Rocky Point. When the SUVs parked before his father's house, he collapsed on a bed of nettles. Twenty minutes later, four policemen emerged from the house and made their way to the beach. Tremor waited in vain for a sign of movement inside his father's house, for the parting of shutters or the closing of the door. Then he clawed at the dirt and wept.

A moment later, he lifted his face from the ground. The scales of a familiar song were moving through the trees. Mary had returned to the beach. She was beating shredded garbage bags with a stick and cursing six policemen heading toward the pier. She dropped her stick as they passed and followed them at a distance, falling back each time they turned around to face her, and quickening as she neared John Bowden, still smoking beside the empty gas can. While they pulled John Bowden from his boat and cuffed his wrists, she waited at the base of the pier, violently scratching her arms. Then she followed them through Rocky Point, wailing and cursing and stumbling over loose asphalt as she drew her sandals from her feet. She slapped the soles of her shoes together, shattering the air with each crack. One by one, women appeared on stoops to watch John Bowden walking unsteadily, but walking nonetheless, between two policemen. When the policemen pushed John Bowden into an SUV, Mary lunged at the strangers who'd trespassed on the ground near the body, the site of her most recent heartbreak, and stolen John Bowden, her proof of resurrection.

One push changed everything. With one push, the police sent Mary to the ground. Stunned, Mary sat in the middle of the road with her legs splayed across warm pavement. Slowly, she began to hum and rock from side to side, and then pulled her skirt up over her thighs to expose the indignity of scraped knees.

There was much debate, later, about who threw the first rock. It didn't matter in the end. Dozens of rocks followed the first, raining down on a young policeman foolish enough to stoop for a dropped baton. Women spilled into the road, cut into his face with jagged nails and punched his shoulders, tore at his clothes and smothered him with filthy dresses and decades of unadulterated hatred. At the sound of gunshots, the women fell back, tripping over one another and crawling from the road. By the time they stopped screaming, the police had fled. Mary was lying in a pool of blood.

Tremor tore himself from the dirt and retreated into the cover of trees, scraping himself on branches and gasping for air. Near the bypass, he abandoned caution and followed the fresh imprints of tire treads leading from Rocky Point. He stopped only once, to retch in some weeds with the violent contractions that attend birth. We understood his shame and misery. During Mary's last moments, we'd been mired in garbage. All we'd ever wanted was gone, leaving in its place a terrible silence and sorrow.

At any other time, Mary's death would have attracted little notice beyond Rocky Point. It would have inspired, at most, momentary head-shaking and muted comments about the latest tragedy, or worse, offhand remarks about barbarity. That afternoon, though, with nerves frayed by talk of contagion, the people of St. Anne closed ranks as Tremor's image made its way to New York, London, and Atlanta and reports of tropical savagery began to dominate international news. In the burning of the body, they saw the grim dictates of survival. They saw something they would have done to protect their own children. When they encountered police in the streets, they saw the traitors who'd killed Mary. Unknown to most and a cipher to all, Mary was the perfect martyr for uncertain times.

Within hours of her death, Crazy Mary regained her nearly forgotten name, Mary Clay, a rallying cry for the motley members of a discontented chorus. Stolid ministers of every stripe, ignorant of

Mary's divinations and nocturnal raptures, praised Rocky Point's dearly departed soul and called upon their congregants to contribute to the cost of a simple coffin. Politicians railed against Little Butts' delinquency and demanded accountability for Mary's death. Shopkeepers and the leaders of splintered unions called for a public funeral procession to honor Mary and a one-day general strike to protest the ineptitude of Little Butts.

We might have taken some comfort in the remembrance of Mary, but so many people singing her praises had distorted her voice. Professor Cleave presented an odd specimen. He seemed genuinely disturbed by Mary's death, and more consumed than most with John Bowden's fate. That afternoon, he nearly swerved from the road several times while driving to the taxi stand. There, in the absence of their ostensible leader, members of the General Transport Workers Union had assembled to vote on a motion of support for the self-indicting strike.

Professor Cleave met James Brooks Brother on the curb. They stood in silence at first, leaning against Professor Cleave's taxi and listening to the radio. As an English newscaster reported on the mutilation and possible murder of an American on an isolated beach, Professor Cleave recalled Tremor batting a flame with his fingers and talking about disease. He pulled out his phone and considered the image of Tremor standing over a charred body, struck by the disconnect between Tremor's triumphant pose and fragile expression.

"Maiden Cruises needed a distraction. Thanks to the boy, they found one." He slipped his phone into his pocket. "I suspect he had nothing to do with the burning. But his stupidity got a woman killed and a man thrown in jail."

"If Bowden's the man I think, he's the roughest of the lot in Rocky Point," James said. "The perfect man to charge with murder."

Professor Cleave rubbed the hem of his shirt between his fingertips. "No one's saying much about him. It's easier to pray for the dead than redress injuries to the living."

"He likely doesn't have a lawyer."

"He likely doesn't have any teeth after this morning." Professor Cleave scraped a callus with his thumbnail. "That boy has caused so much damage."

"The police would have gone into Rocky Point anyway. News of the body would have gotten out."

"But that picture. It turned conversation away from things that matter. That woman's death. John Bowden." As an ambulance and a convoy of jeeps passed, Professor Cleave turned his back on the street. "They're fools to go into Rocky Point now. They'll be stirring a very hot pot. And they'll stir it again tomorrow."

"They'll know not to provoke a crowd during a funeral procession."

The convoy rounded a corner, and Professor Cleave faced the street again. "At this point, we're the only union that hasn't come out behind the strike."

"We'll be striking against one of our own."

"Butts is hardly our man now, if he ever was. If we lay down with him, we'll get up with fleas."

"The police belong to Butts. Because of that, they don't bother us," James said.

"But they'll bother us in time. Butts will be out of office someday, and they'll be in the pay of someone else. And there's a time to criticize one's own. They have a woman's blood on their hands."

"But this is no time to fill the streets. Tempers are high."

"Then we should give the anger a focus," Professor Cleave said.

"We'll be putting our necks in the noose for this stupid boy."

"The boy doesn't represent Rocky Point. He doesn't represent anything."

James tapped his phone and held it up. Professor Cleave squinted at an image of a wall spray-painted with Tremor's name.

"You must have come by the ring road," James said. "Drive **through town and you'll see his name everywhere. The little man** from Rocky Point is the man of the hour among the worst sorts. Because of him, they'll be out on the streets. Thinking he's a hero. The issues that matter to us don't matter to most people."

Professor Cleave placed his hand on the hood to steady himself. "Any one of us could end up on the wrong side of a gun. Any one of us could have been that woman." He paused to listen to the radio. The Minister of Defense was providing assurances of the government's unwavering commitment to law and order. Professor Cleave dragged his thumbnail across his palm. "And this is about John Bowden, who will get a monkey trial if he gets a trial at all."

"And after tomorrow? Some won't be taken back to their jobs."

Professor Cleave looked up and down the street, at lowered awnings and darkened storefronts. "Between the ship and that photo, we won't have jobs to lose."

James stroked his chin and nodded slowly. "If I follow your lead, the motion will pass. If we support the strike, it would be best to avoid political slogans. Big ideas have no place in this. Only grief and anger are holding people together right now."

"Grief and anger are an unstable foundation for things to come," Professor Cleave said.

"Without them, the streets would be empty. I'll vote with you so the anger doesn't come to our doorstep. That's the best we can expect."

"So, we'll vote together. For different reasons." Professor Cleave studied the clean lines of James's face. "You were an idealist the day you introduced me to Patrice Williams."

"I had a beard. But I wasn't an idealist. I couldn't afford it. It can drive a person mad."

Professor Cleave leaned through the cab's window and turned off the radio. Scapegoats, though never scabs, we dropped from the gaskets and followed him into the taxi stand, where he called for justice as if he wanted to storm every plastic castle crowding his tiny fishbowl. Had we been less consumed by sadness, those of us who witnessed his extended oration would have been proud to call him our professor.

The afternoon was waning by the time he left the cabstand, feeling relieved by an outcome won with far too much difficulty. His conversation with James and the sight of Tremor's spray-painted name had unsettled him, but the vehemence of his own arguments had given him the clarity he needed to face Desmond, smoking in the shadows behind the terminal's padlocked gates.

Professor Cleave nodded at two soldiers standing on a street corner. "I see they expect the worst. If they act like they expect it, they'll get it."

"They're preparing for the worst, whatever they get," Desmond said.

"Those soldiers were policemen just hours ago. They've put on different uniforms, but they don't have a bit more sense."

"They're nervous. Their fingers have been twitching on triggers all day."

"You look nervous, too," Professor Cleave said.

Desmond lowered his voice. "We've been told not to speak of the incident in Rocky Point."

"The incident. Is that what they're calling it? What else are they asking?"

"To keep out of this. To stay off the streets."

"What will you do tomorrow?"

"I'm thinking only about tonight. My family. Whether they're safe," Desmond said. "It's not just the sickness. It's this uniform. I mixed with visitors more than most, and now I'm protecting foreigners' shops. There's bad feeling all around."

"You can't believe everyone telling stories. They're just talking loud."

"This morning, a man spit on my feet as I was crossing the street."

"People are always spitting on the street."

"On my shoes. That's what I'm saying."

Professor Cleave rubbed his forehead. "There's always been too much rum and foolishness among certain elements."

"Melvin Jones turned his back on me when I entered his shop. Didn't have a single word when he took my money. He let me drop it on the counter. That's not his character."

"Will anyone from Port Authority be on strike tomorrow? On the streets?"

"I wouldn't be able to say," Desmond said.

"Because you won't, or because you don't know?"

Desmond ground his cigarette into the sidewalk. "The police. They won't forget tomorrow."

"And Rocky Point won't forget today. There needs to be a public reckoning."

"There won't be the kind of reckoning you hope for. Too many people just want a headline. You've seen that picture."

"We can't think about him." Professor Cleave gripped the gate to steady his hand. "He's a distraction."

"We have to think about him, because everyone else is thinking about him."

"We need to think about the woman who was shot."

"She must have been crazy to be called Crazy Mary in Rocky Point."

"She's fast becoming Saint Mary."

"Nobody will care about her by next week," Desmond said. "Or about Rocky Point. Those people live in their own world."

Professor Cleave thought of Tremor sitting on the rooftop, staring out to sea. "This morning, they didn't. The world washed up on their shore."

Desmond pulled a small bottle from his jacket. "Did you come here to see if I was safe, or to find out what everyone at the Port Authority will do tomorrow?"

Professor Cleave took a deep breath. "Both."

Desmond uncapped the bottle and considered its label. "I took this from duty-free. It's overtime pay you won't see on my stub. I hope you'll spare me the lecture." He took a drink and passed the bottle between two bars. "So, you support this foolishness."

Professor Cleave took a long swig of rum, much to our surprise. "Whatever that boy did, this is bigger than him."

He handed the bottle back to Desmond and felt himself growing angry. So few people, he realized, could imagine facing a loaded gun. If there'd been some way to communicate with him, we could have told him that the imagination required for empathy was in drastically short supply. Alas, Professor Cleave, however odd a human specimen, had no antennae.

Humans say we're insensate, too primitive to feel grief. They'd hardly understand how we felt huddled in Mary's reliquary at sunset, when soldiers and medics in hazmat suits entered Rocky Point to collect the burned body. At the sound of the convoy, women stepped from Mary's house to cast silent maledictions at the strangers making their way down to the beach. When the jeeps and ambulance passed again, and their taillights disappeared in the trees, the women withdrew into the house that had, in a matter of hours, become Rocky Point's only church. They tended to Mary's body, fulfilling sacred tasks hurried by the heat. They drew Mary's eyes shut, dressed wounds that would never heal and bathed Mary's body with the tenderness of devoted lovers. They wiped dirt from Mary's face and picked bits of gravel from her hair, mended her dress and softened her cracked lips with red gloss offered up by one of Tremor's girlfriends. They anointed her feet with oil.

Before a hearse arrived, the people of Rocky Point gathered at Mary's house to pay their respects, delivering cane liquor toasts and half-remembered prayers to their beloved saint. Emboldened by alcohol, they spirited away rags, amulets on broken chains, and yellowed pages torn from a Bible and covered in scrawl. They took cracked dishes, tarnished spoons, shell fragments, and bits of glass. No one spoke of stealing from the dead. Love alone guided grasping hands over lopsided shelves and the stony ground of Mary's ransacked reliquary. Love provided dispensation to almost everyone brought into fragile communion by shock and grief. Tremor was the sole excommunicated exception.

Huddled in a field above the bypass, he'd watched the ambulance leave Rocky Point, knowing he would never again set foot in his father's house. He retreated into the hills when night fell, tripping over the uneven ruts between stalks of feral cane and slipping deeper and deeper into his mind. In his garden, he collapsed on the only ground he'd ever called his own and sobbed, tormented by the sensation of insects crawling up his arms and the weight of a dead phone resting on his chest. He heard a siren in the distance and imagined unspeakable cruelties in basement jail cells. When the moon rose, he grew unnerved by the play of light and shadow and clawed his way through a labyrinth of stalks. A sudden breeze rustled brittle leaves, a cold breath brushed his neck, and then the air grew still again. For the first time, he imagined Crazy Mary liberated from her body to haunt him. He started running as if he were trying to outrun death, as if he were trying to outrun himself.

By the time he reached EZ's house, the world was listing. He caught his breath and stepped into EZ's yard, surrendering his fate to the acquaintances and strangers drinking on the porch.

"EZ," he called.

EZ twisted around on a railing. "Man, you're the talk of the town." He stepped down from the porch and slapped Tremor on the back. "Get yourself inside."

Tremor looked over his shoulder and then followed EZ into a crowded room smudged with fragrant smoke.

"Looks like Bowden started early on the bottle," EZ said, opening a beer for Tremor. "Crazy fucker to do what he did."

A woman sitting on the floor recognized Tremor and struggled to her feet. "Got rid of the American disease. Nothing crazy about that."

"They'll be beating him all night." EZ sat down on the arm of a ripped couch and passed a joint to Tremor. "And you were right there when the shit happened."

"On the beach," Tremor stated, realizing he had no way of knowing how he fit into stories that had been evolving all day. Fidgeting, he parsed out details, modifying his voice and choosing words in response to shifting expressions. "Stood right next to the body."

"What did it look like when it burned?" the woman asked, fingering her braids.

"Nothing like in movies."

"Fool had it coming, coming here," EZ said.

"Had to do something," Tremor continued, letting names and pronouns slip from his speech. "Stood right beside Bowden. Knew what had to be done."

By the time Tremor finished telling the story for the third time, anyone could reasonably have assumed he'd discovered the body, and through his own resolve convinced John Bowden to burn it.

"One whole can for one man," EZ said. "That's bad."

"Stood right there. Made sure it burned."

Visions of spiraling ash and John Bowden pressing a cigarette between blistered lips flooded Tremor's mind. He thought that, if there were such things as souls, his was dying with every incremental revision of the day's events. Then something like feathers brushed his arm. He met the woman's soft brown eyes and felt himself melting into her.

"I gave him my lighter," he said, lying outright for the first time.

Flushed, he rehearsed the burning again, dwelling on sulfurous sparks and flames rising from a diabolical pyre. As he grew more intoxicated and new questions prompted new fabrications, he changed up phrases and details, subtly and then wildly embellishing his imagined role in the burning.

"You never gonna get into hospitality management school now." EZ jabbed Tremor's shoulder. "You and Bowden can open your own school on the beach."

"Burn every last one," Tremor said, accepting another beer from another stranger. Hours later, he passed out on a stained mattress in the back room of EZ's house. EZ woke him before dawn.

"Time to take you to town."

"Why you talking about town?"

"They'll be looking for you, asking questions. Been enough trouble here."

Tremor propped himself on an elbow and rubbed his eyes. The woman behind him shifted beneath the sheet, and he tried to remember her name, hoping she wouldn't speak. As he dressed and left the room, he felt her eyes upon his back.

He looked up at the bleeding edges of stars when he stepped outside and realized he was still drunk. Exhausted by imagined acts of heroism and fitful dreams, he slipped into a rusted car and slid down in the passenger seat. In Portsmouth, he lifted his eyes above the dashboard and saw, in a shop window, a flyer featuring a grainy photograph of Mary Clay as a smiling young woman. Sickened, he slid down in his seat again until EZ parked before a stairwell leading to a second-story apartment.

Alone in the apartment, Tremor parted a set of shutters and watched headlights sweeping through intersections all over town. Distant voices carried hints of urgency, and he tried in vain to discern phrases with some bearing on his situation. He watched a man across the street tape a poster of Mary Clay to a wall, felt a chill along his spine, and heard Crazy Mary whispering incomprehensible words. He pounded his forehead, collapsed on the floor, and cradled himself in his arms, overcome by longing for his father, who'd wounded him less with beatings than a final, unbending judgment. Then he cursed a filthy tide for ensuring his fall from what little grace he'd known. Hell, in that moment, was solitude for Tremor, unaware that we were sitting beside him in the darkness, bemoaning the foul-tasting garbage delivered to our shores.

❈

Professor Cleave, too, was suffering in solitude. He'd spent all night at the cabstand, drafting innocuous slogans about unspecified reforms under James's watchful eye. When he wasn't muttering about banners draped over chairs and poster boards piling up on tables, he engaged in silent debates with himself, posing questions about the basis of solidarity and the nature of justice, and fashioning long answers for imagined audiences. In odd moments, he allowed himself to dream about leading the union, despite the obvious impediments of his erudition and ill-fitting wardrobe. He allowed himself to hope. When he left the cabstand, though, he found dozens of flyers—each bearing the same image of Mary—affixed to shop windows and telephone poles. He considered the varied messages on flyers produced by different organizations and associations, including St. Anne's Anti-Communist League, a "pest control" company, and a church known for its virulent opposition to gambling and gays. Then he saw Tremor's name spray-painted on asphalt. By the time he climbed into the cab, he'd fallen into a mood as foul and desperate as our own.

"Their slogans say nothing, and the photo from her youth even less." He dropped his keys and cursed. "No one will see her poverty or the violence done to her. Desmond is not alone in ignoring it. And he's afraid. As anxious as all of you, by the looks of things."

We had, in fact, been jittery all evening, stirred to near frenzy by sightings of jeeps and an ambulance, and later a hearse backlit by the setting sun. We only calmed ourselves in hopes of gaining some insight into the afternoon's apparitions. Unfortunately, the demoralizing nature of crafting empty rhetoric had left Professor Cleave somewhat incoherent.

"'The tragic incident,' they're calling it," he said. "Tragedy had nothing to do with this. It began with that stupid boy and his phone. James talks about keeping big ideas out of things, and maybe he has his point, but if not now, when?" He fished his keys from between his legs. "I understand this is no time for incendiary rhetoric. But shouldn't there be some middle ground between big ideas and no ideas at all?"

We curled the tips of our antennae and paced the dashboard, pondering his reasonable, if rhetorical question, at first stymied, and then distracted by his agitated movements.

He reached for the radio. "They normally wouldn't broadcast anything but your Jamaican program at this hour, but these are exceptional times."

As he drove past storefronts plastered with flyers, pundits discussed the political implications of the shooting and the viral photo inspiring international censure.

"Everyone is exploiting misery. The boy no less than these foolish people. He's young and stupid, but nothing explains irresponsibility on the order of what he did." Professor Cleave shook his head. "But the boy isn't the worst. So many are using today's events to elevate themselves. Or to turn the news away from this sickness. The criminals are not just in Rocky Point."

We huddled on the dashboard and watched Portsmouth disappear.

"If Desmond is right, this will end in tears. But then, tears have already been shed." He felt the gravel shoulder beneath his tires and eased the cab back onto the road. "And Desmond fears for his safety while he smokes himself to death."

He turned off the radio and opened his window. We folded our legs and watched moonlit fields streak past, trailed our antennae in warm currents of air, and tried to follow his racing thoughts. He spoke, once, about the seeds of revolutionary change falling on disturbed ground. We remained quiet, too mired in grief to imagine anything new arising from the ruins of stormed plastic castles.

At home, he found Topsy sitting in the front room, rubbing his union pin between his thumb and forefinger.

"They're saying this thing is at ten o'clock," Topsy said.

"So you're going?"

"Why wouldn't I?" Topsy coughed into his fist. "I wouldn't miss the chance to tell your man how to fuck himself. So he'll know how after he's shagged off to some other island."

"That's the extent of your reasoning?"

"I'd say that's good enough reason." Topsy rose from his chair and dropped his pin on the table. "Goodnight, or so there was such a thing at one time. There will be others, when the misfits stop their dirty business."

Professor Cleave was studying the worn surface of his father's pin when Cora emerged from her bedroom. He watched her twist her hair into a knot and wondered if the shadows beneath her eyes had grown deeper since he'd last seen her. She pulled two bowls from a shelf, and he struggled to divine her meaning.

"You didn't eat?"

"I let him eat and waited," she said.

"So you wouldn't suffer his conversation, or so you could eat with me?"

"Neither." She paused. "Both."

She stepped into the kitchen and returned with a pot of stew. She set the pot on the table and sat down beside Professor Cleave. When he reached for a spoon, she took his wrist and slipped her upturned hand beneath his palm. He tensed and tried to draw his hand from hers.

"What if you don't have it?"

"Then we'll have it together," she said, lacing her fingers between his.

That night, they stood beside one another at the bathroom sink, brushing their teeth and staring at their paired reflections in the mirror. Then they lay down together, and for the first time in years, fell asleep facing one another, drawing from a pool of mingled breath. Too exhausted to crawl behind the baseboards, we collapsed beneath their bed and drifted into dreams about the world when it was young, and then into nightmares about some terrible fall, an accelerating descent without end.

SOLIDARITY

Professor Cleave often propounded on the subject of solidarity, encouraged, we suspect, by our peaceful cohabitation within the confines of his cab. One dreary afternoon, during a rainstorm, he read the entire *Communist Manifesto* through to its concluding phrase, "Working Men of All Countries, Unite!"—this delivered emphatically, above the din of water splattering on the windshield. If we grew restless, it was because we'd heard it all before, straight from the source.

Many of us had squatted in Karl Marx's apartment during the six frenetic weeks in 1848 when the great political economist penned his famous manifesto on a nearly impossible deadline. Writing for the masses, ironically, wasn't Marx's strongest suit, and he struggled terribly to produce an easily grasped call to action for an awakening proletariat. He cursed the impossible task of establishing a united international workers' front and forging solidarity among "beer-drinking philistines" hopped up on ale and the ferment of nationalism. "*Was kann ein Kerl tun? (What can a guy do?)*" the beleaguered author lamented, tearing at his beard and cursing the deficiencies of each simple, declarative sentence. "*Mein Gott! Diese schrecklichen Sätze! (My God! These frightful sentences!)*" cried the atheist in his agonies. So, we'd heard it all before.

We had other reasons for being restless during Professor Cleave's recitation. Even in 1848 we'd been perplexed by the odd and, we would think, unnecessary enjoinder at the end of Marx's tract. One can hardly imagine Marx having written, "Roaches of All Countries, Unite!" Such a call might have consigned Marx to the dustbins of history and his manifesto to the chronicles of literary flops; it would have been grossly redundant, if not ridiculous. Cohabitation comes naturally, or at least by necessity, for those of us crowded together in sewers and air ducts. Nationalism and its hollow pretensions have never been our opiates. We could waste a lifetime—or more to the point, many lifetimes spent together—scraping by and scrapping with one another, but why bother? The entire world is our shared oyster. Conversely, garbage is much the same everywhere.

Marx, arguably, should have written a manifesto specifically for chimps, beating their chests and thrashing one another with sticks (Chimps of All Nations, Unite!), or snarling dogs marking territory at every turn, or bees and their corpulent queens stealing honey from others' hives. At least Marx wrote his manifesto for humans, a nearly cannibalistic lot, judged by the way they tear into each other, and certainly the most savage and superstitious, with their strange religions and complicated rationales for hating and hoarding, as if there weren't enough garbage to go around. In times of scarcity or fear, they tend to seek scapegoats. Cockroaches conveniently serve their purpose. Once news of the *Celeste* broke, hotel managers, shopkeepers, and taxi drivers on St. Anne did everything to exterminate us, driven by unfounded associations between cockroaches and contagion.

To give credit where it's due, Professor Cleave stood out for his sobriety and restraint, even after news networks seized upon stories of bloated bodies and necrotic vapors and ignorant gossips began to circulate rumors about cockroaches' role in spreading pestilence. Who could blame us for capitalizing on his aversion to traps and sprays? Still, we found ourselves a bit affronted by his lectures on solidarity. He always extolled the collective, placed his faith in it, but he had so little faith in us. He harbored, too, a quiet disregard for most people, as well as an inhibiting sense of human failure, his own above all others. We often considered hiding in Mary's house for good, but as we're ashamed to admit, we opted for his cab because no one in Rocky Point had air conditioning.

CHAPTER EIGHT

D URING THE FUNERAL PROCESSION, some of us sequestered ourselves in Room 504, and not only because of its air conditioning. We couldn't bear the thought of attending a dog and pony show for jockeying politicians. We scoured the floor for crumbs and tried to ignore the television, always the television, stunting everyone's imagination and threatening to undermine the very foundations of empathy and compassion. Unable to mourn properly, we assured ourselves that we'd inherited Mary's moral example, even if strangers had claimed her body and name. We also had the small matter of survival to think about. The safe spaces for cockroaches were shrinking and Helen, at least, seemed indifferent to our comings and goings (we'd become careless in our grief!). Mercifully, Dave was too preoccupied to notice us.

All morning, he'd been ingesting American news about soiled linens heaped in stairwells, overflowing toilets, and a planned airlift of provisions. Over and over, he saw the image of Tremor standing beside a charred body. He listened to pundits denouncing acts of savagery and calling for a murder investigation, St. Anne's police chief assuring reporters that Trevor Prentice would be apprehended, and American politicians lauding the *Celeste*'s heroic captain and courageous passengers, who would never be surrendered to foreign aggression.

How terrible it must have sounded to Helen, who'd been so rudely abandoned in such a sorry state. She spent the morning pacing, feeling hemmed in and exposed all at once, and for the first time in years, angry.

"We should stock up on food. Before we piss away another day."

Dave turned from the television. "What, you want me to go?"

"I don't exactly want to deal with anyone's shit by myself."

He considered his reflection in the mirror. "Meet you downstairs in a few minutes."

Helen found the lobby disquieting in its hints of sudden dereliction. Beyond a set of French doors, upended chairs rested on tabletops. A broom stood against a wall and a dirty rag lay on the floor, as if abandoned in the middle of unfinished tasks. She looked at the unstaffed reservations desk and felt much like we did, scouring the Ambassador's kitchen for the odd scrap. A bug-out, indeed! If we hadn't known better, we might have said she had antennae.

She sat down on the couch and leaned over the coffee table to consider a pamphlet bearing a photograph of parasails. As the phone on the reservations desk began ringing, the elevator opened. A heavy-set man wrestled two large suitcases over its threshold with a series of blunt kicks.

"Christ it's hot. They already shut off the AC," he said, sinking into the couch. "At least they'll have a luggage porter at the Plantations."

"You're moving to the Plantations?"

"Who wouldn't? Hasn't been a damn soul working here all morning." He rubbed the white sunglass shadows beneath his eyes. "You'd think they'd at least have someone answering the phone."

"It is strange."

"Whole place is strange. Hired that kid, after all. Never saw him around, but I'd sure as hell notice him now." The man wiped the side of his neck with a handkerchief. "If I were you, I'd grab your things and get on the first shuttle."

"I'm not sure it's worth moving," Helen said, as the phone went silent.

"The Plantations is a hell of a step up, even if it's owned by the same company that owns this place. Far as I'm concerned, we should get reimbursed for every dime we've spent."

"You complained?"

"To anyone who'd listen. They just told me to catch one of the shuttles. Just as well. In three hours, I'll be playing nine holes." He stretched his arm along the back of the couch and drummed his fingers behind her shoulder. "Seriously, I'll hold a seat. By noon, we could be knocking back Cane Cutters and getting massages."

The phone began ringing again. "I'll think about it."

"Nothing to think about. Massages. A few drinks."

"I'm not looking, actually." She edged away from his hand. "For anything."

When Dave emerged from the elevator, the man struggled from the couch. "Don't waste too much time thinking." He walked to the reservations desk and unplugged the phone. "In places like this, you got to take charge. Initiative's everything."

Outside, Helen tugged at her sweater. "That creep asked me to go to the Plantations with him. For a massage."

"Way he looked, give him credit for trying."

"It was getting to me. Maybe it's the vibe here. Thinking about the bellboy."

"That guy on the beach probably washed up dead. The kid just took a picture."

"But who would take a picture like that?"

"A bored young guy. The same little fuck who ripped me off."

"Can you imagine yourself doing something like that?"

"Not really," Dave said. "Doesn't matter. He won't be showing his face around here."

They walked in silence, consumed by thoughts of the day's misery. In town, they wandered past gated storefronts and parked cars covered in flyers. Elderly women in wide-brimmed hats, old men in worn suits, and young children in starched shirts milled at the edges of intersections.

"What the fuck's going on?" Dave said. "Everything's closed."

Helen picked a flyer off the sidewalk and backed into the doorway of a shuttered bakery. "Says some woman got shot by the police. Her funeral procession's this morning. There's a strike—"

"Who was she?"

"Somebody's beloved wife. That's all it says."

He shook his head. "They aren't wasting any time getting her in the ground."

"They can't draw it out in places like this. In the heat."

"Probably for the better. Just get it over with and move on."

Helen met the stare of an old man crossing himself. "People are afraid of us."

"Worse things than having people afraid of us."

As he spoke, a slow dirge became audible, and a small boy standing on a corner shouted. A vanguard of men in black suits turned onto the street, followed by a hearse blanketed in white lilies. Cloaked in car exhaust, the people of Rocky Point followed in stained shirts and hastily mended dresses, surveying alien surroundings and staring at the sunburned strangers standing in a doorway. Helen imagined a sleek black coffin behind the tinted windows and drew her sweater close. Dave stepped up to the curb, strained to see the end of the procession, and cursed the unending heat.

"Solidarity Never," we might have muttered, had we not been so preoccupied with our own problems. We spotted Cora Cleave in the ranks of taxi drivers straggling at the rear of the procession, beneath drooping banners and crooked signs. Aggrieved by her powder-blue pumps and the blisters forming on her heels, she'd fallen into a foul mood worsened by the sight of two Americans.

"What are those white people doing here?" she whispered, tugging on Professor Cleave's sleeve. "They are dressed for the beach."

Professor Cleave glanced at Dave and Helen and lifted his fingers to his neck. "They don't know better."

"They don't care. That is worse than being ignorant or illiterate."

"They have different ways." Professor Cleave placed his hand on Cora's back.

"It is basic respect. If one has the means, one should dress properly," she said. "The people living in shacks are one thing. Those white people have no excuse. They have money but no class."

"Speaking of people with no class," Topsy began. "Did you see your man Graham Douglas grandstanding in his expensive suit? Already making his political bid."

"He's not my man."

"Don't you belong to that hotel union?"

"In name," Professor Cleave said. "Are you already starting in on this?"

"He's ugly as mortal sin but not half as interesting. Eulogizing strangers to get a place in the papers. Someone should push him into the hole and cover him up," Topsy said. "He'll be prime minister or a hide-licked dog by the end of the week, depending on what Butts does."

"This is no time for loud commentary," Professor Cleave said.

"His father was a scabby bastard. He didn't have a care for the labor movement, back when it was something to be proud of."

"I see your leftist leanings have returned."

"I used to box that fellow." Topsy nodded to a man hunched within the folds of a baggy suit. "A champion banana weight, even if he doesn't look it now. A real fighter in his day. An artist. Not one of these brawlers you see in the ring now. He showed me a few things back when we used to spar, and I shined the side of his face once or twice."

"This is no time for your stories," Professor Cleave said.

"His wife passed recently. I should join him for a drink after this is over."

"This is no time for drinking in the street. The police don't know who they're working for."

Professor Cleave trailed off. He looked at the backs of sagging banners and the road winding toward a cemetery that had once been a potter's field, where the bones of debtors and slaves, prostitutes and paupers, and now Mary, would share a tiny patch of common ground. He wondered how much time would pass before weeds overran Mary's grave, and how long Tremor's name would remain on walls all over town. We gathered wherever litter provided cover, knowing that the longing for closure had already produced certain forms of forgetting. At the cemetery, politicians in linen suits would distill the most unlikely elements of Mary's life into a cheap liquor to numb raw nerves. From a place of ignorance, they'd speak of love for a woman they would have shunned on the street. We shuddered, truly, at humans' insatiable desire for soothing stories, and failing these, for scapegoats.

After the procession passed, Helen and Dave wandered back to the harbor and sat on the retaining wall. Dave looked out across the water, as if meditating on the *Celeste*.

"I did some math." He pulled a joint from his shirt pocket. "We've been off the ship as long as we were on it. We'd be showing symptoms by now. We won't be dying in this shithole."

"People are still getting sick," she said.

"But they say it's slowing." He took a drag off the joint and extended it to Helen.

"Some people started showing symptoms yesterday," she said.

"I'm not going to worry anymore."

She held the joint loosely between her fingers. "There's something strange about smoking his weed."

"Where it's from doesn't change what it does. And it's paid for."

She inhaled deeply and passed the joint back to Dave. Then she looked up at the cemetery, closed her eyes, and lost herself in the sound of breaking waves.

"I'm going back," he said. "It's hotter than hell."

He dropped to the ground. By the time she opened her eyes and lowered herself from the wall, he was well down the sidewalk.

In the Ambassador's lobby, they found a manager pacing behind the reservations desk. He glanced in their direction and started taping the flaps of a cardboard box. "Perhaps you didn't take time to read the notice. In light of the disruption to services here, we're accommodating all of our guests at the Plantations at St. Anne."

"The strike—" Helen began.

"This hotel is closing. That was explained in the notice delivered to your room."

"This thing's slowing business," Dave said. "Makes sense. Lump us together and turn off the lights here. Saves money."

The manager fixed Dave in a hard stare. "I'll arrange a shuttle for seven o'clock tomorrow morning. Please be in the lobby on time, this time." Without another word, he started pulling file folders from a desk.

Dave found the notice and a brochure on the floor behind their door. "Saw these yesterday. Thought they were junk ads and kicked them aside."

Helen sat down on her bed. "I don't understand. The strike's just one day."

"Tourist season ain't happening now, and the folks at the Plantations sure as hell aren't moving here." Dave began reading. "'The Plantations at St. Anne, where colonial elegance meets modern living. The restored estate house showcases period-piece furniture—'"

"That guy in the lobby wasn't a creep. He was just making small talk."

Dave dropped the brochure on Helen's lap and turned on the television. "Don't be sad. You'll have your pick of creeps at the Plantations. Rich creeps."

She tossed the brochure aside and stepped onto the balcony. The cemetery was empty and groups of people were filtering into the streets of Portsmouth. A second ship, a speck of battleship grey, was growing on the horizon and heading toward the harbor.

She turned to Dave, now propped against his headboard, drinking beer and watching television. "I can see the airlift. Aren't there people actually starving somewhere?"

She waited for him to say something, knowing he just wanted to get away from the claustrophobic room, and from her. She gripped the railing and looked down at the pool, finding familiarity in the shadows lengthening beneath its surface.

Those drinking on Portsmouth's streets saw the second ship through unfocused eyes, as an ill omen waxing on the horizon. Small crowds gathered along the harbor to better apprehend it—a dreaded apparition slowly assuming the appearance of a military transport. With its ill-timed arrival, the ship compounded the grief of Rocky Point. Bringing salvation to the sources of so much misery, it mocked the sanctity of Mary's day and renewed thoughts of injustice at a moment of possible healing. As the sun set behind the *Celeste*, the groups of people standing at the water's edge wandered into the center of town, observed by dwindling numbers of police.

Tremor watched them pass beneath the window of his spare refuge. Hours earlier, he'd parted the loose slats of a shutter and beheld a hearse covered in sprays of wilted lilies. He'd imagined Crazy Mary's eyes, sealed shut but seeing everything. He'd seen his father in sagging pants, walking unsteadily with his bruised face lowered and his shoulders bowed. He'd curled his fingers over his own shoulders, touched his welts and cried, and then he'd slumped against the wall and raged in silence until his mind went blank.

Throughout, we'd kept our distance, shaken by his volatility and his unwitting role in Mary's death. When he began seizing, though, we remembered all the times we'd huddled among weeds, stunned by unfathomable loss, and we edged toward him. Then something in the atmosphere shifted. We lifted our antennae and realized that Tremor, too, had sensed a violent movement in a symphony of voices. He lifted himself from the floor and parted the shutters. People were massing in intersections and standing on the hoods of parked cars. He discerned the guttural slang of Tindertown and the shouted names of friends. When he heard EZ's voice, he abandoned all caution, leaned over the sill, and drew a breath of disturbed air. On the far side of the street, EZ was approaching a man wearing leather sandals, the same man Tremor had seen outside the Ambassador.

"Confused like a castrated goat," Tremor whispered.

"Got the American disease," EZ shouted, stepping into the man's path. "No one wants your kind of business here." EZ turned to two policemen standing at a distance and spat on the ground. The police fingered their batons and then lowered their hands. Emboldened, EZ pushed the man into the gutter. "Beach boy washed up in the wrong place. Messing with white people and infecting everyone."

The man began to rise from a bed of litter, and EZ kicked him in the ribs. Within seconds, glass bottles started raining down upon the intersection, and people began shattering windows in the wake of the retreating policemen.

In our terror, we crawled into wall cracks and the spaces between floorboards. Some of us scrambled onto rooftops, madly seeking higher ground, as if it all hadn't begun to break apart. Tremor tore himself from the window and fled the apartment, leaping over stairs in his rapid descent. At the bottom of the stairwell, he stood in the doorway, captivated by the feverish faces of strangers racing past. With a pounding heart, he slipped into an undertow of sweaty bodies and latched, almost by chance, onto EZ's shirt. EZ spun around, and in one fluid motion pulled Tremor onto the sidewalk. He picked up a loosened cobblestone, pressed it into Tremor's hand, and nodded at a store window.

"You know the man who owns this," EZ shouted. "Talking to the police about things he sees and giving them names."

The streets receded from Tremor's vision until all that remained of the world was the stone resting in his palm and EZ's expectant expression. His hand trembled, and before his mind could revolt, he squeezed his eyes shut and forgot about dirty towels and dumpsters and the shame festering in the welts upon his shoulders. When he opened his eyes, triangles of glass were dropping from the window's wooden frame. EZ slipped through the frame and reappeared in the shop's doorway, shouting about cash registers and cans of kerosene.

When Tremor and EZ left the store, they found the street aglow in orange light. All around, fires were spreading, taking on a life and logic of their own. They leapt from one roof to another, lapped at weathered shutters and wooden shingles. They blackened walls and gutted cars and devoured bags of garbage in glutted alleyways. They scaled telephone poles and left power lines writhing on the ground in showers of yellow sparks. They cast shadows across the face of a woman picking scattered bars of soap off the street. Tremor watched the woman and recalled so many maids bending over bathtubs, picking sticky residue from drains, and with the same sickening efficiency, kneeling before him and wrapping their callused hands around his hips. He turned away from the woman, looked into EZ's glistening eyes, and then ran toward the harbor. He didn't stop until he came upon six friends burning a couch.

"We're burning something bigger," he shouted above a deafening roar.

He started running again, thinking of Professor Cleave's brittle books and thousands of dirty glasses rimmed with saliva. Halfway up the hill, he turned to watch columns of smoke bending in the disturbed atmosphere, drifting over the harbor and obliterating the *Celeste*. He lifted his phone to take a picture, saw that it had no signal, and realized almost everything beyond Portsmouth lay in darkness.

"It's dead," he said.

"Electricity's out," EZ said. "The only lights are in the south."

Tremor turned around and gazed at the reflected light of Portsmouth flickering upon the Ambassador's face. Unsteadied by a familiar sense of vertigo, he continued up the hill and down a sidewalk, past a gated enclosure reeking of garbage, and to the Ambassador's front doors. He tried a locked door and pounded on the glass. Behind him, his friends unearthed rocks from a flowerbed.

He left EZ in the lobby and made his way to the lounge. Alone, he marveled at luminous mirrored walls alive with the light of Portsmouth's burning. He stepped behind the bar and stared at his reflection above a row of bottles, admired the cast of his features and the play of shadows beneath his eyes. He dug his heels into a rubber mat and imagined Professor Cleave brooding over third-hand books.

"When you steal, you lose yourself," he said. "You're deformed."

He drew a bottle from the shelf and held it up to the light coming through the patio doors, enchanted by the glow of amber liquid. The bottle seemed a magical lantern illuminating the only path open to him, now that circumstances had closed every other. He was dousing the bar when EZ found him.

"What you doing? This place is going up. We're leaving."

Tremor narrowed his eyes, unable to grasp the urgency of EZ's words.

"What the fuck's wrong with you?" EZ said.

Tremor pulled out his lighter and conjured a river of blue flame that snaked along the counter, sweeping over stacks of matchbooks, napkins, and cardboard coasters. He stepped away from the bar and held the lighter to the drapes framing the patio doors. A sheet of fire rose to the ceiling, and bits of blackened fabric drifted through the air. EZ shouted when the first ceiling tile crashed to the floor. Tremor registered his name, and for once at one with himself, he followed

EZ through the lobby, over broken furniture and shattered glass and pieces of cracked ceramic. Outside, he gripped the bottle in his hands and waited for the Ambassador to burn.

Most of us, by then, had fled the Ambassador. Some of us lingered in Room 504, transfixed by the sight of Portsmouth consuming itself, and like the Americans, stunned when the hotel went dark. In too many cases, we retreated too late, scaling down blistered walls, crawling into smoking elevator shafts, and in utter desperation attempting flight from the rooftop.

The Americans, remarkably, escaped the flames. Tremor rose from the curb when they staggered from the Ambassador, coughing and rubbing their eyes. Every thought fled his mind. Before he realized he'd raised his hand, he felt the sickening resistance of splitting flesh. He stumbled backward, away from the man collapsed on the pavement and trying to stanch the flow of blood with splayed fingers. He looked at the ghostly woman, a pale incarnation of Crazy Mary, moving her lips without speaking and clutching the folds of her ragged clothing. Then he dropped the bottle and raced down the street, driven by the sensation of Crazy Mary's hands clawing at his neck. Soon, he was lost to us, leaving terror in his wake.

Dave looked up at Helen and the burning hotel, recognizing neither. He tried to make sense of disjointed perceptions—auras of purple light around bits of garbage, twisting metal shrieking, and warm asphalt seething beneath his knees. He felt his eyes liquefy and slide down his cheeks and grew bewildered by his capacity to see. The only mercy was his inability to retain a thought beyond the instant of its inception. He flinched at Helen's touch and just as quickly forgot his fear, rose on unsteady legs and followed her around the hotel. At the top of the bluff, he looked down at a narrow beach, a desolate isthmus dividing two regions of Hell. Above, palm fronds hissed in a sulfurous firework burn. Below, Portsmouth formed a crescent of fire beneath a charcoal sky. With a dim sense of Helen's hand beneath his arm, he stumbled forward, terrified by the sensation of sand swallowing his feet as they staggered down the bluff. He collapsed beneath a copse of trees at the end of the beach.

Helen pulled off her sweater, pressed it against Dave's head, and prodded him into wakefulness each time he slumped. When she peeled her sweater from his face, he shuddered violently, wracked by chills and an awareness of something evil passing through his broken skin and nesting within his skull. He backed against a tree, only to recoil from the skeletal fingers of its exposed roots. He retched and seized for hours and finally grew quiet when the fires in Portsmouth began to burn out.

Helen looked across the water, at the smoke dissipating above the harbor and the *Celeste* floating upon its inverted reflection. She considered its illuminated decks and the indecorous lights strung between its bow and dead funnels, and further south, an isolated glow at the tip of a peninsula. She walked to the water's edge, crouched down, and urinated on the wet sand. Pinpoints of electric light glimmered and vanished on the waves. In her delirium, she imagined constellations of dying stars extinguished by the sea, lost souls cast by indifferent angels into a watery abyss.

Were religion our compass, we might have imagined as much. Some of us had fallen that night, and in a last glimpse of the world seen little more than a steel air duct beneath a water line, paint vaporizing on the Ambassador's face, or the collapsing timbers of a tinderbox slum. Those of us who'd escaped the Ambassador huddled beneath singed wings and cursed the *Celeste*. The bravest among us finally drew our antennae from the sand, extended them toward Portsmouth, and wondered what life there remained.

Professor Cleave, too, had spent the night in torment, obsessed with the orange glow in the sky. He sat at his kitchen table and stared at his hands, stunned by how quickly a peaceful march had devolved into violence. He returned again and again to the fact that he'd felt uneasy leaving Portsmouth with Cora beside him, fussing over a blister, and Topsy in the backseat, searching for cigarettes. He'd thought to stop by the terminal, but he'd been too disappointed in Desmond. He'd been too angry. Now he was trying to remain calm while Cora recounted half-spent batteries and searched the radio for news.

"Our stations are dead," she said. "If we walked up the hill, we could see something."

"My father's been up there. He said there's nothing to see through the smoke."

"We might see something from the church."

"Perhaps there's nothing left to see."

Professor Cleave met Cora's eyes and regretted his words. She straightened the wick of a guttering candle and fell silent. By the slight movement of her lips, Professor Cleave knew she was either praying or conducting mental inventories of canned goods. At midnight, he rose from his chair.

"Desmond is by himself," he said.

Cora rose from her chair. "You're a fool to go out there now."

"They'll leave me alone. We marched this morning."

"So did everyone else lighting fires."

"They've spent themselves by now."

She slammed her palm on the table, and a stream of tallow spilled from the candle. "You've been putting your neck out for years."

"He would do the same for me."

"What if you're seen? By the police. By others. You don't know what they'll do."

Professor Cleave drew his keys from his pocket. "This is Desmond."

"This is us." She blew out the candle and disappeared into her bedroom.

Outside, Topsy was staring at the glow above the trees. He slid to the edge of the stoop to let Professor Cleave pass.

"I've already been up the hill. There's nothing to see except that minister sitting in his chapel, talking to himself about the evils of drink. The only thing genuine about the man is his ignorance. I've had more to drink than that whole lot down there, and you won't find me tossing matches."

"I'm not going up the hill." Professor Cleave started toward his cab. "Desmond's at the terminal."

"It's too late to go down there," Topsy said, struggling from the stoop.

A moment later, Professor Cleave looked into his rearview mirror and saw his father in crimson taillight, beating his thighs with his fists. He didn't roll down his window until he'd passed beyond the reach of his father's voice. With stinging antennae, we assembled on the dashboard, sickened by our sense of acceleration without flight.

Near Portsmouth, odd particulates accumulated inside the car. Some of us turned from the windows, tripping over one another in our haste to escape the stench of burning rubber. At a bend in the road, the trees parted to reveal the smoldering center of Portsmouth, scattered fires at the edge of town, and closer still, the wreckage of the Ambassador. Professor Cleave took in the Ambassador's scorched face and the smoke trailing from its incinerated rooms. He rubbed his eyes, and in his momentary blindness grasped the enormity of the destruction ahead.

He had no sense of his hands on the steering wheel as he skirted overturned cars and the springs of burnt couches. He reached the first impasse at an intersection blocked by a burning mattress and twisted bicycle. He climbed from his cab, gripped a set of warm handlebars, and tossed the bicycle from the road. As three men emerged from an alley, a bottle shattered at his feet. With chunks of concrete raining down on his windows, he fell back into his cab and sped through the intersection. When he looked at his rearview mirror, he saw a fractured world coated in ash.

At the terminal, he tripped over a broken padlock and raced past ransacked stores, stopping to catch his breath only once, before a cracked window covered in streaks of pale cream. He looked at a bottle of tanning lotion on the ground, became aware of a profound silence filling the spaces between distant shouts, and started running again.

He found Desmond lying on the pier. He fell to his knees, tugged at Desmond's jacket, and felt the sickening strain of dead weight. His fingers grew sticky when he slid them beneath Desmond's head. He felt for Desmond's pulse and then pounded his fists on concrete until his hands lost all feeling. Finally, he lowered his cheek to Desmond's chest and beheld the world on its side, strewn with perfume bottles and shot glasses and plastic key chains.

"There is no reason," he whispered.

For the rest of the night, he sat beside Desmond, remembering their secret pacts and countless disagreements. He gripped Desmond's hand and felt the calluses crowning its palm and the jagged edge of a bitten nail. He remembered Desmond's fingers moving nervously around a cigarette during their last conversation. Every abstraction had failed him.

With the ground still warm and the sky clouded over in the most infernal way, we were incapable of consoling him, or of comforting each other. Each of us existed, at that moment, in near isolation. We almost felt human.

ANTHROPOCENE

WE REMEMBER WAITING IN Professor Cleave's cab in the hours before dawn. Smoke had obliterated every star from the sky, but in the light of dying fires, we saw shattered glass strewn across the deserted street and violent slogans painted on the walls of gutted shops. It was difficult to believe that kindness had ever existed, or that anything but hatred and mistrust could arise from the wreckage. Viewed through the cracked windshield, the world might have been extinguished of all human life. We sensed, not for the first time, that we were witnessing the end of the Anthropocene.

One commonly hears that cockroaches will survive any disaster that befalls the planet, that we'll inherit and even thrive in what remains. In his influential 1897 study, *New World Arthropods*, Antonio Pelegri postulated that "cockroaches possess an incomparable resilience that will ensure their survival during periods of dietary deficiency and destruction of habitat." Cockroaches, Pelegri added, "prehistoric in origin, will assuredly outlive *Homo sapiens*, thereby demonstrating the relative evolutionary advantage of physical adaptability over cranial development and brain mass, the latter nearly nonexistent in this order of arthropods." Utter rubbish, to be sure.

If Pelegri's present-day acolytes routinely overstate our resilience, Hollywood filmmakers fuel regrettable forms of sensationalism by depicting cockroaches as enormous mutants ravaging radioactive landscapes, picking over the steel bones of dead American cities and trampling crowds in Tokyo. One need only think of *Infestation* and *Roach Rampage!*, which some of us saw as a double feature at Cine Internationale in Guadalajara. Perched beneath the dusty beam of an overworked projector, we consumed stale popcorn and cheered our takeover of the world's subways. It was all just entertainment, though, at odds with our realities, or more to the point, our vulnerabilities. That, we knew at the time. That, we knew the morning after the riots.

Many of us had died during the night. Some of us didn't make it from the Ambassador's roof. Some of us suffocated within the walls of burning houses. Others escaped the flames, only to be trampled underfoot. People never account for times like those when they write of cockroaches' limitless resilience or concoct stories about roach triumphalism in the wake of humans' demise.

Pelegri (remarkably, an Endowed Chair of Natural Sciences at the University of Turin) and his ilk failed to attend to symbiosis, which bears upon our species no less than any other. Even if we survive some oddly selective apocalypse, what sort of life will we have? We imagine we'll live on the contents of cupboards until the cupboards are bare, and then off the rot of dying plants. We'll eat through wallpaper and books and ingest dollar bills found in the streets, scraping by in the meanest of ways. When the last paper disappears, we'll sift through dirt for edible matter, hoping to avoid whatever poison has wrought the end of all others. Then, in the long days of slow starvation, when only dust and ash remain, we'll reign over a kingdom of silence, for there will be no radio—just orphaned transmissions moving between dead satellites.

How quickly it's passing, the Anthropocene.

Humans sense their end coming and seem to accept it as a given. This might explain their predilections for films about catastrophic events. We suspect they're trying to envision the new order that will arise after the wars and floods. As we've been troubled to observe, the new order projected on screen seems much like the old one, between cruel leaders controlling scarce resources, widespread slavery, and marauding motorcycle gangs clinging to outdated ethnic identities. Humans seem unable to imagine the world transformed by a period of chaos. Talk about limited cranial development! What might Pelegri have written had he foreseen the development of modern cinema?

Rhetorical questions aside, we've spent enough time sneaking into movie theaters to know that post-apocalypse films of the "Roachploitation" genre are of the lowest possible grade—little more than training videos for sadists and barbarians committed to vilifying insects. If Hollywood has any predictive value, "hordes" of cockroaches will continue to serve as scapegoats for feeble-minded and emotionally unsound individuals long after the world, as we know it, has passed. If it were within our biological capabilities, and if the implications weren't so disturbing, we'd yawn.

Arguably, humans' inability to conceive of the future as anything but an exaggerated version of the present suggests not only a preponderance of pedestrian intellects, but a troubling resignation. Even if humans (and cockroaches) have passed a tipping point, there's an argument against fiddling and filming while Rome burns. Willful ignorance and despair are unaffordable luxuries, and for us, unattainable, for cockroaches are extremely sentient beings.

CHAPTER NINE

IT WOULD HAVE BEEN easy to fall prey to despair the morning after the riots, as daybreak revealed Portsmouth's ruins and the harbor deadened by a stratum of ash. Helen considered her filthy sweater and the flies swarming above it. Dave touched his cheek and struggled to sequence the events of the night before. Over and over, his fragmented thoughts returned to Tremor.

"The kid. How bad is it?"

"You had a concussion. Have one, maybe."

She pulled her sweater from the sand and carried it to the water's edge, rocked on her heels, and sunk into silt and soft mud. At the sound of a helicopter sweeping the harbor, she looked at the *Celeste* and contemplated the possibility of succumbing to thirst within sight of a shopping mall and a stock of airlifted supplies. She dragged her teeth over her parched lips.

"People do it all the time," she whispered.

She sloughed off her bandages and cast them to the ground, wet the sleeve of her sweater, and walked back across the beach. When she knelt down and dabbed the side of Dave's face, bloody water fanned across her wrist, and she realized she knew nothing about the man, a stranger even to himself, staring at her with unfocused eyes. She lowered her hand to her lap and rubbed her fingers together until a gritty red seal formed between them. Then she considered the damage she'd done to herself, the irony of her fear, and began wiping crusted blood from his cheek. After she wiped down his face and neck, she lifted her face to the sky.

"We need to find clean water," she said.

They trudged across the beach, stopping at short intervals to catch their breath. At the top of the bluff, she looked once at the Ambassador's scorched face and then continued walking, using her back teeth to scrape saliva from her inner cheeks and leading Dave with impossible promises of relief.

In Portsmouth, they found roof beams collapsed into blackened foundations, houses and ransacked shops spared the ravages of unpredictable fires, signs announcing a sundown curfew, and groups of women sifting through bits of broken jewelry and pausing, without fail, to stare at two strangers covered in dirt and the marks of disease. They identified the grocery store by its trampled sign. Helen approached a door hanging from loosened hinges, called out, and hearing nothing, stepped inside. In the spare light passing through a small window, they made their way around toppled shelves and a rifled cash register upended on the floor to a dark cooler with open glass doors.

Helen pressed the back of her hand to her nose. "Something's gone off."

"I can't smell anything," Dave said.

While he struggled to open a bottle of water, she started gathering plastic bags, small boxes, and foil packets from the floor. A moment later, she sensed a movement and jerked upright. A man stood in the doorway, adjusting his grip on a cricket bat.

"Get out of my shop."

"We just needed water," she said.

The man looked at the bags straining her fingers. "Take what you touched and leave." He entered the store and stepped behind a counter. "Just go. Please."

"I can pay you," she said.

"Please. Just go away."

The man placed the bat on the counter and lowered his face into his hands. When his shoulders began to shake, she took Dave's arm and staggered into sunlight.

They sat on the steps of a padlocked church and ate in silence. Dave studied six letters spray-painted on a billboard advertising beachfront condominiums.

"It's his name," he said.

She heard a question in his voice and nodded.

"I'm having trouble reading," he said. "I feel sick."

"The smell is probably making it worse."

He looked around, as if he might recognize some odor by sight. "I can't smell anything."

"It's burnt rubber. It's everywhere. In our clothes."

He lifted his collar to his nose and shook his head. The bruise on his face had assumed a dark purple cast.

"There must be a hospital." She looked at an overturned car blocking an intersection. "How far can you walk?"

"I don't know. Not far."

"We need to keep moving." She touched his shoulder and he flinched.

"He's a hero," he said, staring at the billboard. "These people are savages." He was still staring at the billboard when he started down the steps.

Near the terminal, she crouched beside a tangle of clothing in front of a souvenir shop. She pulled several shirts from a pile, shook glass from their folds, and read the decals emblazoned on each. We shrank beneath our wings in mortification. It's impossible, sometimes, not to feel an affinity for females of the human species, even if few entertain affection for us. Between *Mean Girls Suck and Nice Girls Swallow!* and *Body Police: Flat on the Ground and Spread Them!*, we shuddered, truly, and crossed every set of legs. Helen and Dave, though, desperately needed something to wear.

While Dave stared at a single shoe lying in the street, Helen held a shirt to his shoulders.

"'Surrender the Booty.' It's awful, but it should fit." She gathered another shirt from the sidewalk, fingered Bob Marley's airbrushed image, and then sifted through beach covers patterned with tropical sunsets. A moment later, she looked down at a spliff visible through the parting in a pastel sky and collected two packs of cigarettes from the gutter. She was pulling a small flag from a storefront display when a man passed on a bicycle. Dozens of watches encircled his arms and a lopsided stack of straw hats upon his head swayed from side to side.

"Look at that, two white niggers looting," he called.

When he rounded a corner, Helen wrapped St. Anne's flag around Dave's head and knotted it. "Let's keep walking."

They headed south, along the harbor road, until they encountered an overturned van blocking the street. Three men in sleeveless shirts stood beside the van, watching their approach. As Helen and Dave neared, one of the men hurled a bottle in their direction. Helen stepped away from a spray of shattered glass, took Dave's arm, and turned around.

"Maybe there's another road south," she said. "Further inland."

In the center of Portsmouth, Dave took a sip of water and retched. He cast an empty plastic bottle to the ground and sat down on a curb. Helen blinked salt from her eyes and measured the sun's distance from the treetops.

"Our cab driver. I think I could find the road to where he lives. He said he lives in a place called Stokes Hill. He might give us a ride. We won't make it anywhere else before dark."

Dave rested his forearms on his knees and lowered his head. "I can't get up yet."

She sat down beside him. To the buzz of circling flies, they closed their eyes and drifted in and out of waking nightmares. When a barking dog startled her, she prodded Dave, and they started walking again, announcing themselves to every stranger with a desecrated flag and looted shirts emblazoned with a vulgar demand and pirated lyrics about one love.

We rested on beds of singed newspaper and turned our antennae toward Stokes Hill, wondering how Professor Cleave would react to their arrival. He was in bad form that morning, and in fact, hardly himself, which might not have been the worst thing. No one had the patience for lectures, and he didn't have the energy or conviction to deliver them.

All morning, he'd been sitting on his stoop, staring at the cracked earth between his feet or looking at the sky with closed eyes and letting the sun bleed through his skin. He barely heard the door open behind him. Topsy coughed once and shuffled past, cradling a radio.

"I just picked up that program out of Kingston." Topsy fiddled with the radio to steady his hands. "They say your man Butts is stepping down."

"He's not my man." Professor Cleave lowered his head.

"No, he wouldn't be." Topsy softened. "He was his own man, out for himself and no one else. He was never a communist. He was just like the rest, getting fat at the feedbag."

Professor Cleave lifted his face. "He wasn't a socialist, either."

"No, he wasn't." Topsy started down the walkway. "I'm going to see Morris's daughter to get some batteries for a few cigarettes. She's desperate with addiction."

"Bring your cane."

Topsy brushed aside a fly. "I always stick to solid ground. I've never fallen once."

When Topsy disappeared down the road, Professor Cleave contemplated his surroundings with bloodshot eyes. He formed fists and then stretched his fingers, felt skin cracking at his knuckles and the stiffness of swollen joints.

"Desmond showed me a few things back in the day, when he and I used to spar." He envisioned himself as an old man in a baggy suit, attending never-ending funerals and growing more alone each day. "You won't find the likes of him anymore."

In one night, he'd grown mortally afraid. As difficult as things had always been, he thought, perhaps the truly lean years and loneliness had just begun.

He struggled to his feet and walked around the house, appraising grapefruit trees and bartering their fruit, in his mind, for a host of imaginary goods. He surveyed Cora's garden—tomato plants with yellowed leaves, shriveled pea pods, squash warming on cracked clay, and so many thriving weeds. He peered into a small shed and considered a crate filled with sprouting potatoes and the jars of honey and pickled vegetables crowding a sagging shelf. He took a potato in his hand, inhaled its earthy scent, and placed it back in the crate.

He felt his chin and considered shaving. Then, as he walked back toward the house, he stiffened at the sight of his battered cab. There would be no work for a long time, and no reason for routines beyond a hopeless search for normalcy. As quickly as he'd been calmed by Cora's providence, he felt stricken by the thought of empty months and years stretching before him. He stood beside his cab and studied its dented roof and pocked hood. He drew a line across its cracked windshield and considered the soot clinging to his fingertip, opened the door and collapsed on burning vinyl. Soon, sweat began to pour from his body, and his kidneys throbbed.

We emerged from beneath the hood and crawled across the dashboard, leaving tiny footprints and the trails of dragging antennae in a thin layer of ash. Professor Cleave opened one eye to regard us, anxious students nearly indistinguishable from the dark spots clouding his vision.

"Desmond was the last one who should have suffered," he finally said. "He'll never bother you with his cigarettes again."

We drew our wings inward and buried our antennae in ash. The only feeling more powerful than our shame was our fear that Professor Cleave had become unmoored by grief.

"As it turns out, the meek might not inherit the Earth. If they do, they'll inherit its shell. You, my friends, might inherit this car, but it's in very sorry condition."

At a sharp rap on the window, we scattered into the alleys between seats and doors.

"She's not interested in fumigation today. There's been too much death already."

As he lifted a finger, Cora yanked open the door and dragged him from the cab, cursing for the first time in her life. He staggered into the house with her arm around his waist and took tiny sips of water under her watchful eye. When he regained his bearings, he removed a roll of bills from the biscuit tin on the mantle.

"We have so little," he said.

"We have enough to get through, here and in the bank."

"If there's a bank left." He measured the roll between his fingers and placed the bills back in the tin. "She'll want to send us money."

"We have always said no, and we will say no again," Cora said.

He turned to a faded photograph of his parents hanging on the wall. It had assumed the appearance of an antique, but his father had barely changed, he thought, since posing for the picture, even if he'd grown stooped and a touch cynical. He had the disturbing sense that he'd surpassed his father in years over the course of a single night. Exhausted, he went into Cora's room and slipped into unconsciousness.

He didn't snore. He didn't move at all, and we feared he'd surrendered to despair. We hadn't been prepared for talk of inheriting the cab, and we struggled to sleep beneath the bed, only to suffer visions of picking stuffing from the car's decaying vinyl seats until only a rusted frame and dead radio remained. We were hardly prepared, ourselves, for the Americans' arrival.

❈

They reached Stokes Hill as the sun began to set. Dave surveyed his surroundings with the gaze of an amnesiac, as if trying to remember something he'd left somewhere. Helen stopped at each rise in the road to catch her breath and lowered her eyes each time they passed a shuttered house. She might have thought Stokes Hill uninhabited, if not for the woman crouched beside a car engine in the middle of a patchy yard. As they neared, the woman rose to her full height and narrowed her eyes at Dave's shirt.

"'Surrender the Booty.'" She tossed a wrench to the ground and considered the bags straining Helen's fingers.

"We're looking for someone named Wynston," Helen said. "He told us he's lived in Stokes Hill his whole life."

"He's dead?"

Helen stiffened. "No, he isn't."

"Then he hasn't lived here his whole life. Still has some life to live."

Helen cleared her throat. "He works at the Ambassador Hotel."

"No one works at the Ambassador. That hotel burned."

"Is there a man named Wynston here, who worked at the hotel that burned down?"

"Just up the road. Someone usually out front. The elder Cleave, if you're lucky." The woman turned back to the engine. "Don't know what business he has with dumb white folks now."

Morris's daughter often raised the tips of our antennae with her hard speech. To be fair, the Americans were a miserable sight, trudging up the hill with soot clinging to their legs and exhaustion clouding their vision. If not for Topsy, sitting on the stoop and massaging his knees, they might have missed the house. Helen saw the taxi's cracked windows and thought to turn away, but Topsy had already risen to his feet.

"You must be lost." He squinted at Dave's shirt. "But then, everyone's lost these days."

"We're looking for Wynston. We rode in his cab a few days ago." Helen glanced at the taxi. "Is he all right?"

Topsy ran his fingers through his sparse hair. "Despite everyone's efforts."

She drew her beach cover close. "He doesn't know we're coming."

"That's one thing he doesn't know."

"We came off the ship," she said. "But we're not sick."

Topsy studied Dave's face and opened the gate. "But you're not well." Near the house, he hesitated. "He's not at his best."

As he spoke, the front door opened, and we scattered from the stoop.

"What is this noise? He's sleeping." Cora considered St. Anne's stained flag and a wan face that recalled the worst of all years. "Why are these people here?" she said, clutching the small cross hanging around her neck.

Professor Cleave appeared beside her, rubbing his eyes. When he saw Helen and Dave, he staggered slightly and gripped the edge of the door.

"He was attacked outside the hotel," Helen began. "He had a concussion. We didn't know where else to go."

Professor Cleave shook his head. "They said everyone left the hotel."

"We missed the shuttle. We were in our room."

"That kid. The bellboy started the fire," Dave said. "He came after me on the street."

Professor Cleave let his hand slide from the door. He rubbed his fingertips together and felt something sticky, the insidious thread of an inextricable web. He stood quietly for a long moment, staring at the two strangers intruding upon his grief with their suffering and need.

Topsy placed a hand on his shoulder. "Your mother wouldn't have let them stand there."

Professor Cleave stepped aside. Cora pressed her cross to her lips.

"How did you find me?" Professor Cleave glanced at the open gate and closed the door.

"You showed us the turnoff. When we were in your cab," Helen said. "Your neighbor pointed out your house."

Cora backed toward a corner. "People will be spreading stories. Shunning us."

"People would talk anyway," Topsy said. "We don't get many visitors."

"We don't get white visitors. Dressed this way. Looking this way."

"The roads are blocked. And there's a curfew," Helen began.

"The curfew is not for white people."

"But it's no time be out," Topsy said. "There's no shortage of bad elements at the best of times."

"We don't talk of these things in front of strangers. This is no business of theirs."

"It was their business last night. The lady said he's had a concussion." Topsy pulled batteries from the radio and slid them into a flashlight. He tested a dull beam against his palm and pointed it at Dave's eyes. "Down at the factory, fellows would get caught by bags of sand coming off the belt. It was worse than boxing. In the ring, you had gloves to protect yourself."

"I have a headache, but the pain's mostly in my face," Dave said.

"You won't be posing in magazines, but your eyes are reacting," Topsy said. "You should clean that scratch before we eat."

Professor Cleave closed his eyes and dragged the flat of his hand down the side of his face.

Cora steadied herself against the table. "What do you think they'll eat?"

"Yesterday's rice and chicken." Topsy carried five plates from the buffet to the table. "The icebox is dead, and you can't take rotten chicken to Heaven. Isn't that what your minister says? That you can't take it with you? Morris died with cigarettes still in his pocket. That's all the proof needed."

Dinner was a dismal affair. Professor Cleave hunched over and ate in silence, with his head resting in his hand. Obsessed with signs of ill health in her unwelcome guests, Cora sat at a remove from the table, spilling rice onto the floor and resenting each squandered

grain. His sense of smell deadened, Dave searched out tastes and tex-
tures in a manner off-putting to his most reluctant host. Helen held
the hem of her sleeve to her palm with three fingers and picked at
a chicken neck with the tines of her fork. Topsy alone ate with zeal,
sucking marrow from tiny bones and eyeing Helen's plate.

"Are you already finished?"

Helen looked down at her lap. "I'm not a big eater."

"Everyone is always dieting in the States. A strange problem. A
curse of too much." Cora collected her plate and started toward the
kitchen. "Or maybe our food doesn't suit them. They'll have a better
dinner at the Plantations later."

"That would be tomorrow's dinner." Topsy turned to Helen.
"You and your man can sleep in the side room."

Cora spun around in the kitchen doorway. "That isn't your room
to offer."

Professor Cleave tossed his spoon on the table and pushed aside
his plate. He leaned into the light of a kerosene lamp and gazed at
his hands, following the oscillation of light and shadow between his
fingers.

"We should leave," Helen said. "But I don't think he can walk to
the Plantations."

The plate slipped from Cora's hands. She considered the floor
with a bewildered expression and then looked at Helen. "Did you
think he would drive you? Everyone thinks you're contagious."

"We don't know anyone else."

"You don't know him." Cora bent down to collect bits of ceramic.
"You don't know anything about him. About any of us."

Professor Cleave watched Cora sweep the floor with the edge
of her hand. "A curfew means martial law. The police won't make
exceptions."

"We can pay you—"

Cora tossed a shard into a trash can. "You think his life is worth
a handful of dollars?"

Professor Cleave closed his eyes and saw a pale woman slumped in his backseat and a square of sky framed by stone walls. He saw hellish light filling the cracks in his cab's windows and Desmond lying on stained concrete.

"I can't drive you. Anywhere." He pushed away from the table. "In the morning, go on your way."

Outside, he uncapped a bottle drawn from the grass beside the stoop, and a sweet smell filled his nostrils. If there was ever a person who needed a drink, it was Professor Cleave, still reeking of chemical burn-off and ash, but he wasn't a man who could handle liquor. With a great deal of anxiety, we watched him ingest a shocking quantity of the most gastric-sac-burning rot imaginable. When moonlight began to twist his eyes, he pounded his forehead with his palm and cursed himself. We withdrew into the house, braving Cora to spare his dignity and hear one of Topsy's stories. We desperately wanted to dream, if only for a few moments.

Mercifully, Cora had dimmed the lamp on the table. Sitting at the edge of its miserly light, she bristled at the sound of Dave snoring in her daughter's room and traced the shadows of empty glasses with her fingernail. For an hour, she maintained a principled silence and refused to retreat to her bedroom, if only to stand witness to depravity until exhaustion claimed her. Topsy sat in his chair, counting minutes and cigarettes. Helen counted seconds and despaired at the night ahead. We clung to the curtains and tried to control the twitching of our antennae. Topsy saved us all by drawing Cora's ire.

"To hell with austerity." He drew a bottle from beneath his chair and two dirty glasses from the table. He filled both glasses and handed one to Helen. "I can't say who had that last, but what's in this bottle will sterilize anything. We should have poured some on your man's head."

"The man with you," Cora said, turning to Helen. "That shirt he's wearing. I wouldn't think it's something to wear in decent company. At times like these."

"I'd say it suits the times all too well. But it's an ugly thing. Ugly sentiment," Topsy said.

Helen's face warmed. "We picked it off the street. He needed something to wear."

"I suppose a man can't be too choosy when he's stealing," Cora said. "Pulling things from broken windows—"

"Or choosy with the news." Topsy lifted the radio from the floor and placed it on his lap. "Our stations are out. They say the police station and that resort have power. Not a spark anywhere else. There's a rhyme to it, but no good reason." He skimmed static until he heard a newscaster describing a rash of potholes on Kingston's roads. "Jamaicans don't give a pot of piss about this place."

He turned off the radio and set it back on the floor. For a moment, we'd entertained outrageous hopes of catching DJ Xspec. Demoralized, we watched Cora rise from the table and draw a bar of chocolate from the buffet. She peeled a leaf of foil from its whittled edge and used her fingernail to shave tiny ribbons of chocolate onto her palm. Topsy, all of us, watched her transfer ragged curls, one by one, to her barely parted lips.

"You can allow yourself a bit of chocolate," Topsy said. "You might even allow us a bit."

"Parsimony has its place."

"Chocolate won't make up the margins."

"We're rationing now."

"There's a sort of parsimony with no place."

"There's a sort of drinking unsuited to respectable people." Cora returned the chocolate to the buffet. "And a sort of behavior and dress with no place here."

She considered the bottle in Topsy's hands and the spliff on Helen's shirt, slammed the buffet drawer, and went into her bedroom. Helen, all of us, remained perfectly still until she closed her door. When we heard the creak of bedsprings, we dropped from the curtains.

"She has her reasons. Driving a taxi can be a dangerous business." Topsy lifted the bottle. "Have another sniff, now that the censorship board has gone to bed."

Helen tried to read his expression and hesitantly extended her glass. "Wynston told us about you. He showed us where you worked."

"I was the president of the United Gravel Grinders. The most powerful union in its day." Topsy straightened in his chair. "We led this country's independence struggle."

"When was that?"

"Usually from sunset until midnight, but some of the neighbors would tell you it went on much longer." Topsy drew a cigarette from a nearly empty pack on his armrest. "We were a force to be reckoned with."

Helen took a sip of rum. "Does the union still exist?"

"Times have changed." Topsy lit his cigarette. "But we made this island what it is. We laid the Ambassador's foundations. It was the tallest building anyone had seen. When every one of us is in the ground, no one will be left to remember the day we poured the concrete."

Helen recalled the rattle of a dying air conditioner, rusted railings and smudged walls, and flames devouring everything. "It was a great place," she said quietly.

"At one time, maybe. I wouldn't be able to say. I never went inside." Topsy considered the tip of his cigarette for a long moment. "What's in that feed bag of yours?"

She reached into the bag beside her chair, picked through bits of cellophane, and then emptied its contents. "Most of it's crushed or melted."

"Broken or not, get any biscuits. And you're a good girl to bring cigarettes. I traded too many for batteries. But then, batteries are the stuff of life now." He leaned forward to take a small packet from Helen's hand. "Things must have been desperate on that ship."

She followed his eyes to her slipping sleeve and drew her arm to her side. "I left before most people got sick."

"Then things couldn't have been so bad, but you're the only one who can say." Topsy settled back in his chair. "There's always some monkey's ass saying things could be worse. Things could be better, too."

"I suppose," she whispered.

"I always wondered what things were like on those ships." Topsy examined a biscuit in the candlelight. "So many of the people coming off them just want their pictures with monkeys. Strange business. They're good for stew and not much else, if you ask the old people."

"Most people at home would think they're too close to humans to eat." Helen looked into her glass. "They'd worry about diseases."

"Maybe they're eating monkeys on that ship of yours."

"It's not my ship."

"You sound like my son. He's always looking for the finer meanings." Topsy took a sip of rum. "He spent his whole life writing about revolution and he got a riot. And lost a good friend."

"I didn't know." She looked at the floor. "We shouldn't have come here."

"You can't be out there now."

"I'm sorry. This all started with the ship."

"It wasn't your ship. Ugly things." Topsy drained his glass and rubbed the stubble on his chin. "Still, it would be great to go up in one of those kites. Those parasails. I always imagined looking down at the sea with birds passing beneath my feet."

Over the next hour, Topsy told stories about St. Anne's first labor union and its amateur boxing league, and Helen imagined him floating through the sky, far above a gutted hotel. We settled beneath the table and feasted on chocolate dust until Professor Cleave came into the house, grabbed a glass from the table, and filled it with rum. Topsy sniffed the air as he passed.

"When did this start? That stuff will eat you up inside."

"You're doing fine. Haven't you always said that?"

"It's my constitution." Topsy gestured at Professor Cleave with a biscuit between his fingers. "Morris's end is what most can expect."

Professor Cleave rifled through a buffet drawer until he found an accordion fold of yellowed paper. "I'll mark a route to the Plantations." He glanced at Helen, spread the paper across the table, and smoothed its creases. "You won't need to go through Portsmouth."

Topsy struggled from his chair and stepped up to the table. "I haven't seen that in years. That's a British topographical map. Accurate to the inch." He studied tiny numbers and lines indicating elevations and the island's narrowest roads. "They were rotters to the last, but they made a decent map. We used these when we laid down the ring road."

Professor Cleave slid the map out of Topsy's shadow and penciled something onto its brittle surface. "If you leave at sunrise, you'll arrive at the Plantations well before dark."

"When I was young, the only plantations were working plantations," Topsy said. "We walked to work before dawn and we came back after the sun went—"

"I wrote in landmarks." Professor Cleave emptied his glass and handed the map to Helen. "Take water from here or from the pump down the road. It's no difference to me."

"That map wasn't yours to give," Topsy said. "But I suppose my walking days are over."

"Sleep in my daughter's room." Professor Cleave placed his glass on the table and pushed it in Topsy's direction. "In his room. It's what she would have wanted." Without another word, he disappeared into Cora's bedroom.

"It'll be a tight fit with your man," Topsy said.

"He's not my man."

"That's the first good news. You'd have to be desperate to shag a man wearing that sort of shirt." Topsy settled back into his chair.

"Where are you going to sleep?"

"In the room behind the kitchen. Now take the lamp."

He stretched his legs, and she took the lamp, knowing the room behind the kitchen was merely a fiction to dignify charity.

She found Dave sprawled across the narrow bed, breathing unevenly. She surveyed the pared-down belongings of an old man: a framed photograph on a nightstand, a porcelain bowl and shaving brush, wrinkled shirts draped over a chair, and stacks of disintegrating newspapers. Topsy's gestures had loosened something inside her. She fingered her stitches, feeling as though nothing were holding her together, extinguished the lamp and lay down on a woven rug. We gathered in a patch of moonlight before her. She studied the movements of our antennae until the strangeness of her situation became a salve, and then slipped into restless dreams about crooked lines marking a path into the unknown. She twitched like mad all night, as if she were alert to every danger and every possibility, as if she had antennae.

At daybreak, she found Topsy sleeping in his chair with his fingers curled loosely around its armrests. During the night, he'd repacked her bags with bread and jam and Cora's half-eaten chocolate bar. She watched his chest rise and fall, whispered her thanks, and then slipped outside to find Dave waiting for her, tracing the side of his face with his fingertips. Followed by the sideways stares of curious goats, they walked to the bottom of the hill and headed south, with the sun breaking over the trees and warming the ground beneath their feet.

Suddenly, so many people seemed to be on the move, scuttling from one place to the next. Some possessed only the most limited means of flight. That, at least, we had in common with the two Americans, and with Tremor.

FLIGHT

WOE TO US WHO suffer the curse of stubby little wings, ves-tigial appendages suitable for neither flying nor fanning ourselves on a hot day. (One can hopefully appreciate our love of air conditioning in light of this one regrettable aspect of our anatomy.) Fault-finding scholars have spilled rivers of ink caricaturing our limited flight capabilities. In the *Records of the International Entomological Association*, Dr. Jane Weir writes, "Members of the species *Periplaneta americana* are notably awkward in flight, capable only of gliding from higher to lower elevations, and of brief and lurching airborne movements." Other authors of the same bent need not be quoted. Why reward insensitivity? Those possessing means of flight, natural or artificial, would hardly understand the terror or indignity we experienced centuries ago, when we scattered one step ("lurch") ahead of Europeans' machetes and shovels.

Perched on the Ambassador's roof, we experienced the long-lost sensation of flight without lifting a wing. We might never have missed our primordial wings, had it not been for Paul Müller, the chemist who concocted DDT, the progenitor of modern pesticides. In his toxic wake came parathion, pyrethroid, tetramethrin, and difluben-zuron—horrible compounds that sent us lurching once again. We remember our first whiff of the sterilant gas imported by American hotel managers. It inflamed our antennae and turned our gastric sacs. It nearly drove us mad.

Some of us fled St. Anne, only to discover that the same threats plagued us everywhere. Even in New York City, the so-called roach capital of the world, we grew sick from poisons sprayed in subways, four-star restaurants, and corner delicatessens. The sewers became unsafe, for traces of unspeakable things poisoned the water. Certainly, there have always been "safe houses": abandoned tenements and dive cafés and hourly motels. The Ambassador served as one for a while, in the days of Tremor Prentice, when the maids were too distracted to maintain their insecticidal regimens.

For years, cars provided some escape. On St. Anne, we boarded a car for the first time during an unexpected fumigation of the Governor's Mansion. Panicked, we scuttled down the porch steps and slipped into the undercarriage of an idling Bentley. A clutch popped, an engine roared, and a love affair was born. While the governor dispensed *bon mots* to a white-gloved chauffeur, we clung to struts and gleaming chrome fenders and watched the road streak beneath us, giddy with the sensation of flight. For decades, no one thought of spraying toxins beneath seats and dashboards. We lived in James Brooks's Avenger, in Patsy Williams's state car—a Fiat outfitted with massive ashtrays—and air-conditioned tourist vans. We learned to fly with wheels instead of wings. Few of us dwelled on the fact that we'd grown dependent upon those eager to destroy us. We grew comfortable with air-conditioned compromises.

Our glorious flight came to an end in the 1980s, thanks to Fountainhead Chemical Solutions, manufacturer of *Roach Out!*, a neurotoxin approved for use in cars and other closed spaces ("Kills roaches, not kids," commercials claimed). By 1990, the drivers of almost every taxi and luxury car had begun using *Roach Out!* If we'd been thinking clearly, we would have taken to the undersides of bicycle seats. Enthralled by its speed and sheen, though, some of us continued to ride in the prime minister's SUV. We lived in denial, explaining away strange illnesses as hangovers from cocaine dust and spilled champagne. When the shaking became intolerable, we'd leave the car, swearing never to return. Those of us who did return were always worse for the experience. Nietzsche was wrong when he wrote, "That which does not kill us makes us stronger." Some things just leave you gutted and sick, crippled in mind and riddled with tics.

CHAPTER TEN

WHATEVER GLORIOUS TECHNOLOGIES THEY have at their disposal, humans are lurching more and more these days, woefully unable to navigate strange currents or sustain their exhausting flights. Tremor spent the day after the riots on the floor of EZ's house, recounting coups against the police and slowly coming down, dragged by adrenaline's ebb and the gravity of his actions. He sat with his back to a wall, trying to stake his place in dying conversations, distracted by memories of birds scattering from a body, Crazy Mary lying in the road, his father's hand wrapped around a belt and his own wrapped around a bottle.

He touched a trace of blood on his pants and imagined Crazy Mary and a stranger haunting him from both sides of the pale divide between life and death. By evening, he would have given anything to erase the image in everyone's phones and scour his name from every spray-painted wall in town.

He turned to EZ. "They'll be looking for me."

"None of the police are showing their faces tonight." EZ jabbed Tremor's shoulder.

The woman Tremor had slept with shrugged. "Nowhere to hide. Nowhere to go. Not if you can't swim."

Tremor scraped his palm with a bottle cap. "It's just time before everybody's looking to make money off me. Turn me in," he whispered.

EZ looked sideways at Tremor. "Tomorrow, I'll talk to a man who can get you to Jamaica on his boat. Help you disappear. Cost you, but you know how to pay him."

Tremor relaxed his shoulders and felt the sweat on EZ's arm mingling with his own as his latest, nameless girlfriend curled up at his side. By nightfall, he'd smoked enough to slip into a dreamless sleep in EZ's bed, on sheets smelling of kerosene and cum.

He awoke to the sound of screaming and the sweep of flashlight beams. Before he saw their faces, he felt their batons pressing into his ribs and their hands twisting his head, forcing his gaze to the woman cowering in a corner, shielding her breasts. They dragged him from the bed and ordered him to dress, and he struggled to control his hands long enough to zip his pants. As handcuffs closed around his wrists, he looked down at the coins scattered across the floor and a base metallic taste filled his mouth. They led him from the house and pushed him into a police car, and then dragged the woman, naked and screaming, into the yard. She knelt in the glare of headlights, her elbows planted on gravel and her fingers buried in her hair. In the curvature of her spine, he saw his own terror and shame.

He arrived in Portsmouth as dawn broke upon walls spray-painted with graffiti about diseased Americans and pigs and prostitutes. In the shaky, unmistakable letters of his name, he saw the incontestable warrant for his arrest.

We generally avoided the police station, a nest of dread and misery. Some of us had scaled its walls to escape the riots, only to find worse things on the inside. The morning Tremor arrived, we were lost within its confines, lurching deeper and deeper into dark warrens with a misguided sense of direction and dim hopes of escape, only to find ourselves, through repeated missteps, in suffocating stairwells and indistinguishable cells. We had nowhere to run but forward, into a future not of our choosing, spared the bottoms of boots and the force of folded newspapers by sheer dint of our negligible size and inconsiderable crimes. Tremor had gained far too much notoriety to escape anyone's disgust. He walked down a concrete corridor, unbalanced by fluorescent lights and flanked by three policemen. At the end, the man behind him uncuffed his wrists and turned him toward a steel door.

"Now you can work out what happened on the beach. Your friend claims he didn't kill the white man."

He unlocked the door and pushed Tremor into a cell. In the watery light passing through a barred window near the ceiling, he discerned the form of John Bowden lying on a bare cot with his hands upon his chest. Tremor might have thought him dead, if not for the sounds of labored breathing and the slight movement of a head turning his direction. He registered swollen eyelids, a darkly bruised jaw, and the angles of broken fingers—the features of a man so badly marked by beatings that he could only become a suicide statistic hanging from a sheet.

When the door closed behind him, Tremor sat down on a second cot. He spoke only once.

"What will they do to me?"

John Bowden turned to face the ceiling again. Tremor wrapped his arms around his ribcage and dug his fingers into his back, held himself in a solitary embrace and sobbed.

An hour later, two guards came for him. In a spare basement room, they cuffed him to a metal chair. He looked at a faded bloodstain on the concrete floor and tried to remember what had happened on the beach, too unmoored to recover the truths he'd abandoned for lies. We clung to the underside of a steel table, overcome by the smell of bleach and our rising terror in the dreaded maze beneath Portsmouth's prison.

After a sleepless night, Professor Cleave had spent an hour sitting on the edge of his bed, staring at a streak of crusted blood still on his pants. He heard voices outside the house and tried to fathom the simple acts of standing up and taking his first steps, of speaking or eating after the two nights he'd just passed. He considered the objects in his room, so ordinary and unreal. The soft yellow curtains concealing a world strewn with wreckage. The willful clock keeping track of empty time with its insistent springs and gears. The brittle Palm Sunday cross offering hollow benedictions from the wall above Cora's pillow. His redundant car keys lying on the floor.

When he finally wandered into the living room, he found Topsy shouldering his way in through the front door and fastening his belt.

"What were you doing out there?"

"Doing my bit by conserving water in the toilet tank. Starting the day." Topsy parted the shutters and searched for loose cigarettes. "You look like you haven't ended last night."

Professor Cleave turned from the sunlight pouring through the front door when Cora entered the house, carrying an aluminum pot of tea she'd been steeping. She drew a jar of marmalade from the buffet and placed a loaf of stale bread on the table. Without a word, Professor Cleave broke a heel from the loaf and slumped into a chair. Topsy tore into a piece of bread with his back teeth and fixed his eyes on his son.

"You should change that shirt. The smell's an affront to common decency."

"There's no such thing as common decency."

Topsy picked a half-smoked cigarette off the floor. "Then it's an affront to my nose. It's gone a strange way, and your mind will be going straight after it."

"I'll change it when there's cause," Professor Cleave said. "I have nowhere to go."

Cora fanned herself with a church program and watched him nurse his tea. He met her eyes and opened his mouth, and, finding no words, feared that grief had returned to plague their marriage. Only the sound of a punctured muffler dispelled the silence. Topsy shuffled to the window and saw James Brooks climb from a parked car.

"It's that foolish cousin of yours. I hardly recognize him. He used to look like a goat."

Cora smoothed her dress. "Look at us. The dishes and the filthy floor. What would any decent person think?"

"No need to be house proud for that communist. Look at that car he's driving. Some kind of Nissan. A step down from his glory days. But his pants and shoes are smart. Smarter than the man himself."

Professor Cleave brushed past Topsy. Outside, James Brooks was adjusting the cuffs of a crisp shirt. Those of us huddled in the weeds marveled at the strangeness of human conceits. Admittedly, we also marveled at James Brooks's car (an '09 Nissan with a sunroof and spoiler) and momentarily lost ourselves in dreams of radios tuned to tolerable stations.

"I'm sorry about Desmond." James rested his hand on Professor Cleave's shoulder.

Professor Cleave pressed his knuckles to his forehead and looked at the ground. "You were both right. They were on the streets for him. That boy Tremor. And now Desmond's dead." Professor Cleave faltered.

"You can't carry the weight of it."

Professor Cleave pulled away from James and looked up at the sky. "I can see you're not here to talk about him," he finally said. "And I can't talk about him."

"Even the time for proper grieving is gone." James glanced at the house. "Is your father here?"

"Where else would he be?" Professor Cleave turned to the house, and James took a deep breath and followed him inside.

When James entered, Topsy stroked his own jaw. "Without water for a shave, I'm wearing whiskers. They'll be confusing me with your friends, hairy things talking loud and living with loose women."

James stiffened. "There was only one woman, and she wasn't loose."

"Don't mistake me. I don't judge her. She didn't know what she was getting. She couldn't see through the hair." Topsy settled into his chair. "But you discovered shaving suds."

"This is nothing to talk about now." Cora led James to the table and placed a glass of water before him. "We're being rude to our guest."

James took a sip of water and turned to Professor Cleave. "Things are happening quickly. The police are hardly to be seen, except at a few checkpoints. And Buttskell has been at the Plantations for two days."

"Life is sweet in the prime minister's suite," Topsy mused. "But he'll be returning the key soon, getting on the next plane and getting laid on some layover."

"He has learned such shameful talk from American radio," Cora said.

"Parliament plans to deliver a vote of no confidence," James continued. "Butts will be abdicating his official responsibilities in the next day or two."

"He did that years ago," Topsy said.

"And Graham Douglas will lead the provisional government," James continued.

"The strike was against the police," Professor Cleave said. "Not a call for a new government."

"People want a return to normalcy. Butts can't—"

"There was never anything normal here," Topsy said. "All of them have been clowns, from the British to Butts. They've been winding you up for decades with promises and parades."

"Let me get to the point." James raised his voice. "Douglas's deputy came to see me. Douglas needs a driver. He thinks you'd be suitable."

Professor Cleave narrowed his eyes. "He can get a driver on any street corner."

"He needs to broaden his base. As a member of the two largest unions, you'd bridge two parties."

"I'm a member of the Hospitality Service Workers' Union in name. Douglas has pushed for nothing but tax breaks for foreigners. He's never said a word about wages or schools."

"He thinks you'd lend credibility to the new government. You have a reputation for standing against police corruption."

"For being a victim of corruption. And anyone who remembers my case remembers who secured my release. It was as much a sham as my trial."

"No one cares about details. If we work with Douglas, we could have a voice in what happens."

"And a responsibility for it."

"Douglas is willing to talk about renegotiating relations with external stakeholders."

"Of course he is," Topsy said. "The air coming out of him doesn't cost a thing."

"When would I start doing my bit in politics?" Professor Cleave asked. "As a driver."

"You sound uncharacteristically cynical," James said.

"The town is uncharacteristically burned."

James Brooks fingered his watch. "Douglas's deputy wants to see you this afternoon."

"How can he be safe on the streets?" Cora asked.

James handed Professor Cleave a slip of paper. "Show this at checkpoints."

Cora stepped up to the table and read over Professor Cleave's shoulder. "That is Graham Douglas's signature. Who are the police answering to?"

"Certain continuities will ease the transition—"

"The same police in the same uniforms, with Bowden still in jail." Professor Cleave tossed the slip on the table and let his hands dangle between his knees.

"This is your pride," James said. "No one would blame you for taking this."

"Irma has seen the news," Cora said. "She'll want to send some-thing."

Professor Cleave looked at the biscuit tin and dragged his hand across his mouth.

"Be at the Hospitality Service headquarters at three," James said. "And shave. You have a reputation as a man who keeps his head. You can't afford to lose that."

When the sound of the Nissan's punctured muffler faded, Topsy took a long drag off a relit cigarette. Cora rifled through the buffet in search of her chocolate bar. Professor Cleave lowered his face into his hands and blindly promised himself that he'd never take money from his daughter.

How far reputations diverge from reality, sometimes. We wouldn't have said that Professor Cleave had "lost his head," but he was com-ing apart at the seams. We could have told James Brooks (could he have listened) about Professor Cleave's obsession with the flecks of blood clinging to his clothes and skin, the traces of Desmond haunt-ing him, and all of us. It wouldn't have mattered. The only aspect of Professor Cleave's head Graham Douglas cared about was his baby-smooth chin fresh from a shave. Graham Douglas might as well have hired Little Butts to chauffeur him around, but then Butts didn't know how to drive.

Shameful as it is to say, we'd begun to miss Little Butts. Graham Douglas, a regular clean freak, was a misguided bore on his best of days. With his superficial intellect and stunted imagination, he could never have hatched an escape from the torturous maze everyone had entered, much less have defined the zeitgeist. The best he could do was reflect his times. Elevated by chance and the worst of circumstances, his first instinct was to pander. He was a one-step chess player, and in that respect much like Tremor, though he had so many more options than Tremor, and far fewer excuses for playing chess so badly.

For two hours, Tremor had been revisiting his lies and reliving the instant he'd tossed a match onto a body that, from a distance, could have been a piece of driftwood. The body was still when he first saw it, he told himself, and then he jerked in his chair, twisted by memories of twitching fingers and the rise and fall of a chest beneath a web of seaweed. He rehearsed different narratives and in lucid moments recognized his lies. He envisioned eyes swollen shut and bloated fingers half-buried in sand and assured himself that he'd burned all sorts of things, but not a man. He hadn't killed anyone, he told himself over and over, before falling sway again to his own lies and imagining death at the end of a twisted sheet. At points, he feared the onset of insanity and wondered if madness would be his salvation or his final torment. His skin crawled, and he imagined the satiety of soft maggots moving through rotting flesh. He drew his feet from the bloodstain and waited.

The man who finally entered the room was the sort of man given to anonymity, a man with unremarkable features and an infinitely adaptable expression. He leafed through loose papers in a manila folder before addressing Tremor.

"The generator is so much trouble today." He glanced at the bulb flickering above his head. "It would be a shame to lose the air conditioning. To need to open the windows upstairs, with so much garbage on the streets."

He drew Tremor's phone from his pocket and placed it on the table.

"A very expensive phone. You seem ambitious. But, you see, an ambitious boy would be working to advance himself in ways that matter. If you were on the police force, for example, you would be standing here rather than sitting there."

The man moistened his finger and peeled a sheet of paper from the folder.

"You're not someone I want standing at all. But some people think everyone deserves a second chance. Every little piece of garbage." He studied the paper for a moment. "Some people might even think you'd be suited to the police force."

He placed the paper on the table and considered Tremor's down-turned face.

"In your position, you must think everyone deserves a second chance. Or maybe you would think the police force is beneath you."

Tremor shook his head.

"You don't think everyone deserves a second chance?"

Tremor sucked air through his nose and blinked.

"You seem uncertain. Choice would be a luxury. Not everyone can join the police force. We give every applicant a test. Since we have time, you can take it right now. Just to see how you do." The man rested his fingertip on the paper. "Just a few simple questions. Yes or no. We'll pass over the easy ones. You're a smart boy. We'll start with question thirty-four."

Tremor grew faint, and the edges of the room blurred.

"Do you have a propensity to violence? Maybe a Rocky Point boy can't understand that word. Propensity. Do you like violence? This is no time to lie. Witnesses saw you breaking windows. I asked if you like violence."

The muscles in Tremor's legs began to spasm.

"On the police force, you'll face people from Rocky Point. They'll be throwing rocks, bottles, all sorts of things. You'll need to be prepared. I'll ask again. Do you like violence?"

"I don't understand."

"The question is simple. Do you like violence?"

Tremor pressed his feet to the floor to steady his legs. "Yes."

"Then you'll like this." The man hit the side of Tremor's head with the base of his palm. "Why are you crying? You answered correctly." He lifted Tremor's chin with two fingers. "We'll move on. Question thirty-five. Again, a simple yes or no. Is the answer to question thirty-five yes or no?"

"I don't know the question."

"Is the answer to question thirty-five yes or no? That is question thirty-five."

"I don't understand."

"A shame. You were doing so well." The man struck Tremor again. "Your friend John Bowden said you took out a lighter when the white man crawled onto shore, begging for his life. Did you burn the white man? Before you took the photograph."

"He was already burned."

"By your friend John Bowden?"

"Yes," Tremor whispered.

"No one likes a man who spreads stories about his friends. Snitches have no place on the police force." The man drew a lighter from his pocket and held it sideways to heat its metal case in a blue flame. "You should find the lighter familiar." He stretched Tremor's collar and exposed a line of welts. "It seems I'm not the only one disgusted with you. Let me ask again. Did John Bowden burn the American?"

"He didn't do anything."

"You shouldn't lie." The man held the lighter to Tremor's skin.

Tremor screamed and twisted until the flame died. "He didn't kill the man."

"That wasn't the question."

At the sound of scraping flint, warmth spread between Tremor's thighs.

"Not housebroken? Aren't there toilets in Rocky Point? You should wear a diaper, like a little monkey. Tourists will burn you alive and take your picture. Tell their friends they killed the murderer from Rocky Point." The man held the lighter to Tremor's shoulder again.

Tremor slumped forward over a pool of urine and smelled his own terror and traces of bleach. "I didn't kill him."

"I never asked if you killed anyone." The man slipped the lighter into his pocket and unlocked Tremor's handcuffs. "My last question was about toilets in Rocky Point. Stand up."

Tremor struggled to his feet, gripped the table's edge, and looked down at a blank sheet of paper. Senseless, he limped into the corridor and followed the man to a steel door that promised ongoing questions and escalating abuse.

"It's unlocked," the man said.

Tremor pushed into a room lined with dented lockers. A leather belt lay coiled on a bench beside a black beret and brown jacket. A towel hung from a hook next to a concrete shower stall.

"In other times, no one would have time for rioters from Rocky Point. But you have admirers, those who want to see something of their wretched selves in power. For reasons that disgust those who took a real test, you will be a probationary member of the prime minister's security detail." The man pulled two polished shoes from a locker and dropped them on the floor. "You'll stand in the background. Nothing more. First, you'll wash. The animal smell always comes through, but you can disguise it for now."

Tremor waited until the man's footsteps faded from the hallway. In the shower, he spread his hands on the wall, took in their symmetry and recalled John Bowden's twisted fingers. As traces of urine, blood, and ash slid toward the drain, he opened his mouth and tried to wash away a metallic taste, memories of an exposed spine and screams that might have been his own. Then he wrapped himself, shivering, in the towel. He was examining his shoulder when the man returned, carrying a gun and leather holster. Slipping once, Tremor backed into the stall.

The man considered the drain between Tremor's feet. "It would be so easy for me to wash away the blood." The man placed the gun and holster on the bench. "As I said, though, some people think you can be useful."

Tremor clutched the towel.

"Too bad for you, it's not loaded." The man glanced at the soiled clothes heaped on the floor. "Perhaps that will change when you're housebroken. Or not."

When the man left, Tremor dressed hastily, heedless of the scratch of coarse fabric against his welts and burns. His trouser hems brushed the back of his heels; only the thick soles of his shoes kept them from touching the floor. His shirtsleeves covered the tops of his hands, and he moved too easily within the folds of his jacket. His beret slid over his eyebrows. He pulled it one way and another until it rested at a severe angle across his forehead. He winced when he lowered his holster onto his shoulder and tightened its strap across his chest. Dressed, he stood before a mirror and saw a stranger, someone sick with fear, too thin and transparently self-conscious.

He considered the possibility of John Bowden returning to Rocky Point to spread stories about his tears and terror. He imagined his father spitting on the ground at every mention of his name, and to his own shame, he wished for John Bowden's death at the end of a twisted sheet. As he began to sweat into his jacket, he told himself that none of it mattered. He could never return to Rocky Point after wearing a police uniform. He thought of the policemen he'd mocked so many times and realized his survival would depend on their hatred for him fading over time, as he adapted his cruelty and severed parts of himself until almost nothing remained.

He turned from his reflection and beheld the gun. He approached it in small steps and lifted it from the bench. When he wrapped his hands around its grip and felt the impress of cross-hatching against his palm, his breath caught. He massaged its trigger until he knew the extent of its resistance and the pressure needed to force its yield. He turned back to the mirror, touched its muzzle to the double of his parted lips, and shut his eyes. He squeezed the trigger and his heart raced. For the first time in years, he felt immune to Crazy Mary's curses. For the first time in hours, he felt as if he could escape the repercussions of his lies.

We clung to the ceiling, too sickened to witness the brutal amputations taking place, or to watch water laced with blood, sweat, and urine seeping into the clogged drain. Everything that disappears into a drain flows somewhere, usually into some sewer, and becomes ours to bear, the stigma and filth attached to cockroaches. When the deputy collected Tremor, we frantically sought wall cracks and air ducts, desperate to find our way back into the outside world, however ruined. In a misguided moment, we'd sought refuge in a deadly subterranean maze, and despite our nocturnal inclinations, we longed for unfiltered sunlight, something to raze and burn every trace of the sprawling jail from our collective memory.

❈

Professor Cleave, too, felt stirrings of panic, a sense that there was nowhere to run but forward, into unfamiliar and ever-narrowing passages. He leaned against his bathroom sink and considered his face in the mottled mirror. Some of us emerged from the drain to avoid a torrent of soap and assembled around the faucet.

"And so I will shave." Professor Cleave glanced at us and lathered his face. "I have a reputation, you see, as a man who keeps his head. Do you think I can keep my head?"

Some of us scaled the wall to more closely consider his expression.

He reached for a razor and recalled his vague statements about solidarity, and then his hesitation leaving the house during the riots. He'd been naïve, he thought, and then slow to act when the need was clearest. Now, almost nothing of himself remained but the shadow of a man lifting a razor to his own throat. Though we couldn't quite believe he'd harm himself, our antennae stiffened.

He touched the deep creases beneath his eyes. "These, my students, are the wages of sin. Or the wages of working for sinners."

As he scraped away the last traces of soap, blood beaded beneath his lip. He pressed a washcloth to his chin and stared at his reflection, as though trying to commit a stranger's features to memory. Then he held the cloth beneath a stream of water, wrung its worn fabric, and tore out bloodstained fibers, one by one. Finally, he threw the cloth into the shower and slammed his fist against the wall, feeling as though he might go mad listening to his own breathing and the slow drip of wasted water sliding down the drain.

In his cab, he turned his keys over in his hand, dreading the moment of backing onto the road, into a future he'd never imagined. We fanned from the vents, settled in confused formations across the dashboard, and fluttered our wings, wondering if circumstance would force us to abandon the cab.

"The lumpenproletariat has emerged from its slumber." He squeezed his key to feel the sobering pressure of metal teeth against his skin. "Some of you must have seen me drinking. Maybe you can smell it even now, coming from my pores." He paused. "Everyone has their breaking point."

He'd finally pulled the cob from his ass only to deflate, we thought.

"There are degrees of debauchery, and my one misstep shouldn't be taken as license for countless improprieties. Nor should it distract the errant among you from what I am about to say."

He slid his key into the ignition. "I have made the difficult decision to accept a position with a man hardly better and perhaps much worse than Little Butts," he said, backing onto the road. "To keep body, if not soul, together, I will be driving his car. Henceforth, I will serve as your professor in only the most limited capacity."

Henceforth? We turned in frenzied circles and batted our wings. In the bathroom, we'd hoped, perhaps naïvely, that we might retain something of our former life, however stunted by boredom and bad music. For the first time, we faced the prospect of an empty cab and a silent radio, of intellectual dereliction and the death of poetry. Henceforth, Professor Cleave would be driving a car that had wrought the downfall of countless cockroaches and moving in social circles enamored with insecticides.

"Perhaps you'll be happy to revert to your delinquent ways," he said, noting our agitation. "Or perhaps you'll find a way to edify yourselves in my absence."

We lowered our antennae and huddled at the base of the windshield. Like Professor Cleave, we couldn't grasp our losses. We remained pressed against the glass all the way to Portsmouth.

In town, Professor Cleave glanced at two policemen standing on a corner. "Next to those men, you are model citizens. But would you behave any differently with badges and batons? With two legs and tailored suits?"

We briefly wondered what we might have been in other, less toxic circumstances, and then turned our attention from speculative musings to the reality of the streets. Professor Cleave had come upon an overturned car blocking the road.

He pulled alongside the curb and turned off the engine. "You can wait here or take your leave. In the absence of reason or restraint, the world and all its wreckage is your oyster."

He climbed from the cab and faced the end of the street, where three policemen stood before the barricaded entrance to the Hospitality Service Workers' headquarters. He drew the slip of paper from his pocket and studied the signature of the man who'd granted him passage through a town he'd once called his own. Those of us crawling through the rubble knew just how much he'd lost.

Preoccupied as he was, he might have passed the makeshift barricade without recognizing Tremor if he hadn't noticed the familiar slouch accentuated by the sag of an oversized jacket. Tremor ran his thumb beneath his holster strap, and Professor Cleave stopped in his tracks. He considered Tremor's uniform and gripped an unsteady board spanning two sawhorses.

"Everyone's suffering because of you," he said. "And here you've found yourself a job. There will be no end to the need for police now."

"And you'll always be cleaning up after tourists." Tremor struggled to control his voice. "Diseased Americans."

The pass slipped from Professor Cleave's fingers and fluttered to the sidewalk. Tremor gripped the strap across his chest, and the two policemen standing behind him smirked.

"The man you cut with a bottle?" Professor Cleave said. "Was he too dirty for your business? So diseased you couldn't take his money?"

"I don't know the man you're talking about."

"If no one takes a picture, it didn't happen? Is that what you think? Did you take pictures at the terminal? Where your friends left a man dead?"

Tremor's expression shifted in alternating currents of hatred and fear. "I wasn't at the terminal."

The edges of Professor Cleave's vision went black. Only when his knees met the sidewalk did Professor Cleave realize he'd pushed aside the barricade and fallen to the ground with his fingers pressed into Tremor's neck. He felt damp skin and corded muscle, a wild pulse against his thumb and the edge of a baton beneath his ribs. He felt weightless, and then breathless and bruised, as two policemen dragged him to his feet, pressed the paper slip into his hand, and pushed him down the sidewalk. He stumbled forward, disoriented by the sun's glare, leaving Tremor on the ground, gasping for air.

Inside, he slumped on a couch, rubbing his hands to control their shaking and trying to obliterate the lingering sensation of Tremor's pulse. We watched him from the air ducts, for it would have been sheer madness to show ourselves in the headquarters of the Hospitality Service Workers' Union. We'd ventured into the very bastion of sanitation crews, the command center of countless insecticidal regimens and "hygiene" campaigns. Overwhelmed by the static filling Professor Cleave's mind, we welcomed the gradual return of his attentions to the room, finding unlikely relief in the renewed workings of his intellect.

"'The Future is Here.'" He squinted at a poster featuring a wall of high-rise hotels along a Jamaican beach. "'Prosperity and Pride through Progress.'"

He leaned over a polished glass table and considered a pamphlet bearing a glossy photo of Graham Douglas. Studying a composite of unremarkable features, he realized that weary voters would welcome a sexless antidote to the philandering Little Butts and a prosaic counter to the mythical extremes of Patsy Williams. Then he felt a cold breath on the back of his neck.

"Air conditioning," he whispered.

He twisted around and looked at a vent above his head. For the first time, he heard the hum of a water cooler and a phone ringing behind a closed door. He was struggling from the couch when Douglas's deputy emerged from a back room.

The deputy extended his hand. "Wynston Cleave."

"You have phones. Electricity. Air conditioning," Professor Cleave said. "This can't all be from a generator."

The deputy lowered his empty hand. "Lyndon Buttskell disabled cell towers to keep the disturbances from the news. One of his better decisions. As for electricity, certain lines have been repaired and not others. You understand these things take time."

"I understand all too well."

"There needs to be a center of government during a state of emergency."

"People with something to gain have prolonged this state of emergency," Professor Cleave said.

"You, too, have gained from our efforts to establish order."

"And that boy outside? It's inconceivable."

"If he went to jail, people would say Graham Douglas condemned a hero. Many people believe that boy defended this island against an epidemic."

"He's done nothing of the sort."

"Then let people believe in nothing. This isn't the time for ideological battles."

Professor Cleave placed his hand on a wall to steady himself. "He was throwing bricks only two nights ago."

"Like so many others."

"One man at the terminal was doing anything but throwing bricks."

"I was sorry to hear about that. About your loss," the deputy said. "But there's no evidence that anyone on our security detail was involved."

"He's not fit to carry a gun."

The deputy narrowed his eyes. "Do you think his gun is loaded? It's as empty as the gesture of putting him on the force. A gesture that will ease tensions and cost nothing."

"In the short term. In the long term, it will cost everyone. And it's a hollow gesture, with Bowden still in jail."

"The Americans see Bowden as a murderer."

Professor Cleave scrutinized the deputy's expression. "Is that what you see?"

"I see a man who's been favored with a job in lean times and still criticizes political gestures. Who talks about the long term when he needs to eat now."

A moment later, Professor Cleave stood beside a Land Rover parked on a fenced gravel lot. "This is Lyndon Buttskell's car."

"This is the prime minister's car. Lyndon Buttskell is no longer prime minister." The deputy picked a dead leaf from its hood. "You'll wipe down the interior between every trip. You'll clean the exterior at the end of every day. Once a week, you'll spray the car to prevent infestations."

"They find their way in," Professor Cleave said. "Always."

"They'll find their way out, now. Tomorrow, you'll drive Prime Minister Douglas to the Plantations to meet the U.S. cultural attaché. You'll need to purchase new shoes."

"When the shops open."

"In the meantime, someone in your acquaintance must own shoe polish." The deputy turned away and left Professor Cleave beside the car.

Alone, Professor Cleave wet the car's dashboard with a disinfectant wipe, massaged scented oil into its leather seats, and cleaned the gearshift with a felt rag. Kneeling to vacuum sand from its floor mats, he experienced a sickening sense that he was indulging the perverse obsessions of an impotent and dangerously incompetent man.

When he returned to the street, Tremor was nowhere to be seen. With a pressed uniform draped over his arm, ammonia stinging his hands, and keys to a battered car in his pocket, he felt like the last of a dying species driven from its shrinking refuge. Those of us gathered in the gutters drew away from trampled images of Mary and lurched behind him, through litter and rubble, back to our classroom, desperately longing for the radio and sensing, no less than Professor Cleave, the imminence of extinction.

❀

The places of refuge open to Tremor were shrinking, too. Everywhere, shock was fading and anger taking its place, spreading like a foul weed. If Professor Cleave had taken a different route home, he might have passed Tremor sidling along defaced walls and pausing to look over his shoulder at every corner. Dismissed early, Tremor had been sent into the empty streets at evening's onset with nothing but the uniform on his back. He gave no thought to direction, taking random turns in his desperation.

Near the center of town, he paused in a doorway. He saw six letters painted on a twisted fence and imagined the shopkeepers who now hated his name—people with so little to lose that his uniform would mean nothing to them, just as retreating police had meant nothing to him. There were those in Tindertown, too, who hated the police more than they hated anyone else. His uniform, salvation hours before, had already become a curse. With a downturned face, he slipped from the doorway, carrying the dead weight of a gun with no bullets.

On the street where he'd lit his first fire, he was stunned to find EZ's apartment still intact above a ransacked shop. He paused at the base of its stairwell, considered the door above him and decided he'd break its lock, if he had to, just to sleep on a familiar floor. He ascended the stairs, encouraged by predictable creaks and the sight of a rolling paper beside a baseboard. Near the top, he placed his hand on his holster and called EZ's name. The door opened, and EZ peered into the stairwell, as if trying to discern the elusive shape of a ghost in the dusty light.

"We thought you'd be dead. What the fuck you doing in that uniform?"

"I got to get off the street. People are looking for me."

"Looks like you're the one looking for someone. You alone?"

Tremor nodded, and EZ backed against the doorframe. Inside, Tremor found people he'd once called friends sitting on the floor, staring at his uniform with confusion and contempt. He felt relieved, if only for the absence of the woman he'd last seen curled in on herself in the sweep of headlights.

EZ closed the door and circled Tremor. "I asked what the fuck you doing."

Tremor shifted his weight from one foot to the other. "I got a job."

"You're messed in the mind," EZ said.

Sweat ran down Tremor's neck, and he felt himself dissolving within the confines of his jacket. He looked around at foreheads coated with perspiration and discarded clothes lying in corners. Taking a deep breath, he unbuckled his holster and slipped out of his jacket and shirt. He sat down on a crate and pointed to the welts and blisters covering his shoulders.

"Crazy shit's happened." Averting his eyes from EZ, he recounted his day, distorting and omitting scenes ill suited to his needs. He stumbled only once or twice over quickly conjured details.

"Burning the white man. That's all they asked about."

"They ask about us?"

"Just once. Didn't want to hear about how they ran and hid themselves."

EZ leaned against a wall. "So after you put your name all over town, they gave you a uniform and a gun?"

"They're afraid." Tremor dug his fingernails into the crate. "They think people will leave them alone if I'm with them."

"That what you think?" EZ studied Tremor's face.

"You got someone with them now. Watching what they do. Making sure nobody bothers us."

"They. Us. You. Them. You sound confused."

"I'm saying things just got easier. For us."

EZ cocked his head. "So they had you with Bowden? Haven't hung him with a sheet?"

Tremor looked at the floor. "Beat him so bad he lost himself. Was lying there staring at the ceiling, talking crazy. Seeing things. He don't even know what happened to him. Don't think he'll be right again."

Gripping the sides of the crate, he closed his eyes and saw a shrinking passage, a concrete cell, and a twisted sheet strained by the weight of a dead man. As John Bowden opened his swollen eyes, he opened his own to find EZ staring at the burn marks on his shoulder.

"What they did to Bowden, they can do to anyone." EZ pushed himself from the wall and drew Tremor's gun from its holster. He ejected its empty magazine and placed it beside Tremor. "When they say they're behind you, that's when you need to watch your back. An empty gun's asking for a bad end."

EZ reached beneath his shirt and pulled a gun from his belt. He scrutinized Tremor's face and spilled six rounds into his own palm.

"You're not ready," he said when Tremor held out his hand.

For the next half hour, EZ showed Tremor how to chamber rounds and hold himself when he pulled a trigger. "First time, no one expects the weight. They shoot dirt. And check the safety," EZ said, fingering a small lever. "This is the EZ lesson. Aim high, not low. A red dot means blood's ready to flow. Lucky you found me."

"Didn't think I'd find anyone here."

"Serious, thought this was a bust when we heard you."

"Maybe it is." Tremor raised the loaded gun and swiped a pipe from the top of a speaker. "Confiscating shit. Get used to it."

Everyone but EZ lifted their hands to their faces.

"You think I'm serious?" Tremor said. "You should see yourselves."

Staring into Tremor's eyes, EZ wrapped his hand around the gun and pointed it toward the floor.

"I'm asking again. Why'd you come here? Acting this way."

"Nowhere else to go."

"Keep that in mind when you start waving shit around."

Tremor let the gun slip into EZ's hand. He sat down on the crate and looked at his wrinkled uniform jacket, a shed snakeskin lying limp on the floor. Haunted by visions of twisted sheets, he sat half-naked before strangers, consumed by fear and shame and wondering how much time would pass before everyone turned against him. When he got high, he felt as though he were running along the edge of a sheer cliff giving way beneath his feet, breaking apart in increments and forcing him into endless and exhausting flight.

PARADISE

THE PLANTATIONS OF ST. Anne was a dreadful place, but you'd never have guessed from the rubbish published in magazines like *Resort Life* and *Luxury Traveler*. Only months before various fires ravaged St. Anne, Jacqueline Whitford of *Sophisticate* described the Plantations' estate house as a "testament, par excellence, to *haute culture* at its most eclectic and experimental, a celebration of Britain's imperial aesthetic in a bold pastiche of hallmark colonial styles and modern design elements." The most omnivorous among us should hardly be expected to digest such thoroughgoing nonsense. "History aficionados and golf enthusiasts alike," Whitford wrote, "will delight in tea trolleys laid with eggshell china and teak chests that provide unique glimpses into the island's charmed past."

There is pulp (much of it admirably written), and then there is rot. This was rot of the lowest order, barely fit for compost. The trolley so beloved by Whitford had been diverted from a discount outlet in Biloxi. The brass pots hanging in the Sugar Mill, "the Plantations' premier restaurant," had acquired their patinas in a chemical bath north of Bantangas. Honduran sweatshop workers in Miami had distressed the teak chests with industrial sanders. Whitford understood her audience, if nothing else. Whatever their need for modern conveniences, many of the Plantations' guests (especially those who paid a handsome sum to rent the master's chamber, a high-ceilinged suite overlooking the golf course) wanted something of an "authentic plantation experience." This we found more than a bit odd, but then, so much depends on perspective.

We witnessed the Plantations' violent birth. We witnessed slaves arriving in wagons, chained at the ankles and bleeding from fresh brands. At harvest time, we watched them toiling in the sugar mill, day and night, extracting juice from stalks of cut cane. We saw grinders and rollers crushing hands and stripping muscle from mangled arms. We saw slaves scalded by spilled molasses in the boiling house. We witnessed more suffering than we can recount.

Of the original Plantations, little remained by 1990, when a developer from Cincinnati bought the derelict property and sent us "lurching" again, this time from the path of bulldozers. Contractors demolished the boiling house, mulched disintegrating beams at the site of a long-abandoned slave village, sodded over cemeteries, and buried rusted manacles beneath the sand traps of a new golf course. They razed banana trees and rows of feral cane to build gingerbread cottages and condominiums, duty-free shops and a tanning spa. They built pools with swim-up bars where guests could sip cocktails called Clipper Ships. They built the Molasses Shack and Pizza Paradise, where guests could order pork sandwiches called Hogsheads and pepperoni slices imported from Idaho. Where they didn't lay cement, they planted alien species of flowers and ersatz forests. They erected walls ringed with concertina wire. They imported vast quantities of insecticides. These they used liberally, with wild abandon we might say, if they'd been anything but obsessive in their efforts to exterminate us.

We found our way to the Plantations by accident, at first, and then lured against our better judgment. The first among us to explore its grounds slipped from the gaskets of Little Butts's car, dazed by *Roach Out!* and delirious from champagne. We thought we'd discovered Paradise. Ah, to recall the perfume of strange flowers glistening in the silver mist of sprinklers and oozing sweet nectars— honey-colored meads and dusky opiates that served, for some time, as panaceas for all our woes, drew the veil from our antennae and revealed earthly delights never before imagined. Awakened, we floated on silken wings over shimmering pools, mirrors of infinity beneath the endless sky. We nestled in emerald grass and napped on the leaves of resplendent trees. We discovered baskets of exotic fruits, trays of liquefied fat, stacks of pancakes, and mountains of whipped cream. We bathed in streams of cool air spilling from magnificent vents and nearly drowned in pleasure.

Had we only known of the venom tainting each bloom! The corruption at the core of each fruit! Over days and weeks, we languished, consumed by a sickness never before known to us. Strange spots appeared on our legs and fever overcame us. Perfume once heavenly stung our eyes and perverted our senses. We lost ourselves in a labyrinth of air ducts, trailing mucous and suffering unimaginable torments of the soul. We wandered through gardens, afflicted by monstrous scenes and the unnatural colors of sickly, overfed blooms. We tread in horror over the bones of ancestors, Professor Cleave's and our own, pursued by nightmarish visions of verdant graves. Heaven became Hell, and we languished within its walls, confined by razor wire and stung by phosphates. Most of us eventually escaped, seizing and shaking beneath the seats of departing airport shuttles and Butts' car. A few of us returned, helplessly drawn by the siren call of incomparable air conditioning. *Sophisticate*'s columnists described the Plantations' gardens as tranquil. That isn't the word we would have chosen, but again, so much depends on perspective.

CHAPTER ELEVEN

THOSE OF US AT the Plantations when Helen and Dave arrived had spent the week muddling through mazes of golf courses and condominiums and restaurants nearly indistinguishable from other golf courses and condominiums and restaurants at other all-inclusive resorts lodged in our collective memory. (You'd think humans had all joined in a perfect harmony of opinions, only to bring forth a utopia for the fatuous and feeble-minded.) We had just enough clarity to recognize how degraded everything and everyone had become. Sure, we were messed up six ways from Sunday. Still, observations made under the influence aren't, by definition, fucked up or wrong. Logic 101 (*ad hominem* fallacies)!

When Helen and Dave appeared, dragging their feet on their way to (Pizza) Paradise, we hadn't yet succumbed to the tremors and narcoleptic fits that attend excess of the worst kind. We were mourning the murdered monkeys dumped beside the road to the Plantations, even regretting the times we'd called them "chest-beating, knuckle-dragging bipeds." It was the right thing to do. And appearances aside, monkeys and cockroaches were in the same miserable stew.

Helen and Dave found the first monkey in a thicket of weeds a kilometer from the Plantations. All day, they'd been following deserted roads past stretches of feral cane and the stone towers of abandoned sugar mills, sheltering in shade whenever possible and dreaming of sleep. In the afternoon, the hills leveled into a stretch of scrub dissected by fresh asphalt roads, stacks of sewer pipes, and fluorescent flags. They might have missed the monkey rotting in a newly excavated ditch if not for the flies swarming above its bloody fur. Its fingers had curled inward and stiffened. A milky film covering its eyes recalled the memory of clouds. They drew away from the ditch and continued down the road, only to find a heap of dead monkeys at the edge of a razed lot.

"Looks like they attacked each other," Dave said.

Helen considered a tangle of shattered limbs and pressed her sleeve to her nose. "It looks like they've been shot. Just keep walking."

In silence, they followed dusty tread marks multiplying in the impressionable asphalt. The marks led all the way to the Plantations.

They shuffled forward, indifferent at first to the rings of concertina wire crowning a massive wall, and the soldiers in blue surgical masks monitoring their approach. As they neared, a soldier cradling an automatic rifle stepped into the road. His sleeve bore a corporate logo, an abstraction of wings and rifles.

"No one had permission to leave the premises."

Helen tried to place the man's accent and read the expression suggested by the deep creases framing his eyes. "We were never on the premises." She faltered, distracted by two soldiers dragging a dead monkey onto a tarp in the distance. "We missed the shuttle from the Ambassador. We walked."

The man nodded at Dave. "What happened to your face?"

Dave touched his cheek. "Hit with a bottle. Two nights ago."

The man pulled his mask from his mouth and spit on the ground. "You'll find savages running riot all over. We should finish the job they started. Put things right." He looked up into the hills. "They're not fit to solve their problems. Same everywhere I've been."

"Why are there so many dead monkeys?" Helen asked.

"We're exterminating the ones that try to cross the perimeter. No more than rats with thumbs. You don't want to nick them, or they shriek." He nodded at the tarp. "Like that one. Nasty business cleaning them up."

"But they're everywhere. Almost a mile out."

"If we see them out there, we get them before they come here. If they come here, we send them back where they belong. I'd do the same with every one of them rioting." He pulled a plastic bottle from his pocket. "Report to the main house."

He drew a line of sanitizing gel across his palm, rubbed his hands together, and turned his back on Helen, a distraction from his endless mission to pacify the planet, one privatized war at a time. We'd seen similar mercenaries in so many places, using so many variants of *Roach Out!* Had we been Helen and Dave, we might have sought alternative accommodations, but who can resist the siren call of comfort, or relief?

Beyond the gates, fountains and electric waterfalls feathered mist over birds of paradise, English tea roses, and the Kentucky grass carpeting an empty croquet pitch. Golf carts overran a sprawling course beyond a line of Italian cypress trees. What unholy shades of putting green and daiquiri pink! Oblivious to everything but the pain in their feet, Helen and Dave shed their plastic bags and limped toward a sprawling two-story house with broad shutters and shaded porches.

In the days of slavery, the estate house had been a termite-riddled mess illuminated by crystal chandeliers and littered with empty wine bottles, the castoffs of the aristocratic wastrels who gathered in its drawing room to laud each other's excellent taste. It had since become a sanitized museum laid with polished marble and hung with sepia photographs of white men in jodhpurs and barefoot women carrying baskets on their heads. At the base of its winding staircase, Helen rested her arms on the desk of a concierge with heavily painted hazel eyes.

"We missed the shuttle from the Ambassador."

The concierge regarded Dave's face and turned to Helen. "Do you have a voucher? You should have been given one on the shuttle."

"I just said we missed the shuttle. We walked."

"I'll summon the executive manager." The concierge made two notations on a spreadsheet and spoke quietly into a phone.

When the executive manager arrived, we squeezed beneath a line of baseboards and cowered. In crisp beige linen and understated accessories, the executive manager rebuked eccentricity of any kind. In lieu of beauty, she possessed unshakeable poise. Her skin glowed without color. Her chameleon hair shifted from silver to blond, depending on the tilt of her sculpted chin. She was a terrifying specimen, responsible for every insecticidal campaign waged at the Plantations. She commanded an army of groundskeepers and had, at her polished fingertips, substances even deadlier than *Roach Out!*

"Ms. Mudge. Mr. Fowles. I have been in close communication with the CEO of Maiden Cruises, and he's been very concerned for your well-being." She turned to Dave and appraised St. Anne's stained flag. "I understand you sustained injuries, and I've arranged for an examination by our resident physician. Our reservations associate can take you to him now."

The concierge stepped from behind the desk and gestured to a hallway. Helen pushed a strand of hair from her face and watched Dave follow the woman from the lobby.

She turned back to the executive manager. "Concerned with our well-being?"

"He made it clear that you should receive any medical assistance you require."

"Maiden Cruises didn't seem too concerned when they kicked us off the ship."

"From what I understand, there were questions about passenger safety, Maiden Cruises' main consideration."

"About liability. And what about liability now? What if we're sick? I suppose it would be bad press to send us back into a riot."

The executive manager folded her hands together at her waist. "The Plantations would take appropriate precautions if there were reason to believe you might compromise the health of other guests. We're just relieved that you arrived safely."

"We didn't arrive safely." Helen dug her nails into the concierge desk. "I don't understand. You're not worried about infections, but you're shooting monkeys."

The executive manager considered the desk's marred surface. "We're taking every precaution. Bringing in a professional security team is part of that."

"Shooting monkeys is part of that?"

"We're accounting for the very small possibility that certain species carry communicable human diseases. We understand vendors near the terminal released their monkeys rather than destroy them. It would be easy to exaggerate the threat of invasive wildlife, but some guests have expressed concerns."

"Those men at the gate are supposed to prevent an outbreak?"

The executive manager's face assumed the appearance of a plaster mask. "We've chosen to err on the side of caution. I trust you'll report any symptoms, should they develop."

Helen felt the chill of sweat evaporating from her skin. "Air conditioning." She looked up at a ceiling fan churning cold air.

"Is there something wrong?"

"I saw the lights during the riot. You never lost power here."

"Fortunately, our guests have been able to enjoy all of our amenities. Tonight, we're hosting a football tailgate-themed party on the main patio. There will be a free buffet for guests. Including those from the Ambassador."

Helen slipped her hand beneath her sleeve and rubbed her arm. "How do I get to my room?"

The executive manager considered the airbrushed spliff between the folds of Helen's beach cover and drew an envelope from the desk. "Your keys. Our staff is reduced at the moment, but we'll try to make your stay as comfortable as possible." She started toward the staircase and then turned around. "I understand you received thorough medical treatment aboard the *Celeste*, but our physician is available, should you want follow-up care. Of any kind."

We barely relaxed when the executive manager disappeared. We never felt at ease in the estate house. As for the rest of the Plantations, it was hardly a comforting place, between its artificial streams, decorative footbridges to nowhere (how often we fell for them!), and impenetrable beige tiles so tightly sealed with grout that we felt trapped within its massive bathrooms. If not for the Plantations' lavish kitchens (and the cocaine in Butts' car), we might have opted for the worst dumpster in Portsmouth.

Room 612-C, like all of the Plantations' guest rooms, was the sort that neither offends nor charms most humans. It had been swept of every crumb and immunized against complaints by cold cleanliness. An abundance of boring! We could understand Helen's relief, though, as she settled into a massive tub to drain the weeping blisters on her heels. Mercifully for her, she had only two feet.

When Dave entered the room, she tensed, sensing, as we did, the agitation in his movements. By the time she stepped from the bathroom, he'd fallen asleep. His sheet was twisted around his legs and he was twitching violently. She studied the bandages taped to his face and recalled his expression on their first morning at the Ambassador. He'd been disgusted by her injuries; she'd been humiliated, and much angrier than she'd allowed herself to admit. She thought to leave him, but he'd become a liability, a mutilated man about to wake from nightmares in a room full of mirrors.

She stepped onto the balcony and watched two mercenaries crossing the grounds, leaving the imprints of heavy boots in wet grass. One of them lowered his surgical mask and lit a cigarette. They stood beneath a tree and passed the cigarette back and forth, talking quietly and pausing occasionally to look up at her. She listened to a coarse joke and fragments of clipped speech until they tossed the cigarette into a flowerbed, and then she backed into the room.

She found Dave sitting on the edge of his bed, turning a small plastic bottle over in his hands. He was wearing a green polo shirt with yellow golf clubs stitched across its pocket. A matching baseball cap rested in his lap.

"Was having nightmares," he said.

"Where did you get those clothes?"

"The manager gave them to me. Decent of her."

"She's worried we're bringing down property values."

"Still, it's a good thing." He shook two pills onto his palm and nodded at a paper bag on the dresser. "The nurse gave me painkillers. Antibiotic ointment and bandages. Said they were for both of us."

"What did she know?"

"Not much. Don't think it matters."

"Maybe. Maybe not." He stiffened at the edge in her voice, and she turned away. "We should get something to eat," she said. "There's some free buffet."

She looked outside. The sun had almost set. Sidewalk lamps had given form to a world of silhouetted trees and white glare.

"Don't tell anyone we were on the ship."

"You think I was going to announce it?"

"People don't need to know."

"I get it." He pulled on his cap and swallowed another pill. "I got it already."

We shuddered. On more than one occasion, we'd raided the Plantations' dispensary after Butts' cocaine had worn off, desperate for anything to numb our antennae. Mad with craving, we'd scoured the floor for spilled serum and the contents of broken capsules. We'd sampled every sort of existential analgesic, psychic expectorant, and nerve-numbing agent available. Dave, we knew, was about to cop the lowest sort of high.

For the Plantations' guests, and for all the refugees honored with an invitation, the tailgate party provided a familiar forum for numbing every extremity with bizarre cocktails and sugary punch. We went in for the crumbs of hot dog buns, hoping to line our gastric sacs and get a grip after our latest misadventures. Helen and Dave ducked beneath crêpe-paper streamers and edged through the crowd to a table cluttered with crusted plates and plastic cups. Above the table, a bunch of blue and yellow balloons strained its tether. One of its deflated members had settled on the frosting of a half-eaten cupcake.

"Michigan," Dave said, adjusting his cap. "Ain't exactly home, but there's room."

They sat down beside a man and woman with the appearance of inveterate tailgaters. The woman took a sip of punch and smoothed a plume of silver hair rising above her duckbill visor. A ruddy testament to digestive derring-do, her husband had just cashed in his last potato chips for a pork sandwich.

"You should have worn a football shirt," he shouted. "They're giving free drinks to anyone wearing a team logo. Shirts. Hats. Hell, they'd probably accept football-themed underwear. There's one in every crowd."

Dave noted the heavy class ring cutting into the man's finger. "Hopefully there's more than one."

"That's the spirit. Take it you're a Michigan man."

"Born and bred. Hancock. Name's Dave. This is Helen."

"Bud Anderson. Michigan. Class of '69. This is my wife, Gerry. Class of '72. Retired from GM management after thirty years."

"Still live in Michigan?" Dave asked.

"Michigan plates is about it. We spend winters in Phoenix and travel every fall. Can't take Michigan weather. Hell, I can barely stand the weather here. This vacation's run its course."

"He's being a sourpuss." Gerry slapped Bud's knee. "At least they gave us lots of coupons. I guess they feel bad everyone's vacation's ruined. It's funny, but you wouldn't even know all these terrible things were happening if it wasn't for CNN."

"Don't say that too loud, or we'll all be paying for our drinks," Bud said.

A middle-aged man with gleaming teeth pushed up to the table. "Hey, Bud, let us shove in with you."

Behind him, a woman in a University of Illinois shirt surveyed the crowd. A second woman, straining the seams of a strapless dress, gathered her hair in an alligator clip.

"These are some good friends we met last night," Gerry said. "Jim's a contractor, and his fiancée Sarah's a pediatrician. And that's Marianne from Lansing. She works for the fashion industry. She's been helping build factories all over Asia."

"Site scouting," Marianne hooked her thumbs under the elastic tubing of her sundress and adjusted her breasts. "Not that anyone here needs to give a shit. I left work behind."

Over the next few minutes, Dave eased into the familiar rhythms of drunken banter beneath a constellation of string lights. Helen settled back in her chair and watched two women at a nearby table comparing pedicures. She startled at a familiar name.

"This place is overrun by those people from the Ambassador." Sarah wet her fingertip to taste her punch. "We paid four times what they did."

"She's been calling them welfare cases," Jim said.

"I'm just saying, I didn't come to an all-inclusive resort so everyone could be included."

"The only one getting any service is that Buttskell," Bud said.

Jim grabbed two cups of punch from a waiter's tray. "Getting serviced, more like it. I hear he's been here for days, getting blown by Australians."

Gerry shuddered. "Throw a rock and you'll hit someone, I heard."

"Someone should throw a rock," Bud said. "Part of me has to hand it to him. He probably doesn't spend too many nights out in the cold."

Marianne picked a cherry stem from her hair. "What's up with his entourage? I've never seen so many black people on a golf course."

"One of them couldn't even clear the fairway this afternoon," Bud said. "I teed off before he moved on just to send a message. Someone said he was the defense minister, but he couldn't have turned tail faster. At least the private security is on the ball."

"Bud was talking to some of them," Gerry said. "They flew in from South Carolina."

"Tough as hell. Some of them were in Afghanistan. Making a hell of a lot more in private security than regular Army grunts humping it."

"The one we talked to didn't sound American," Helen said.

"They're from all over. Post-Soviet Stans. Africa. All trained by Americans."

"We met one from South Africa," Gerry said. "Really nice guy."

"Deals mainly with third-world clusterfucks like this one."

"The shooting's a bit much, but I suppose they know what they're doing." Gerry rested her hand on Bud's knee. "Someone told me monkeys carry human disease, or maybe it's the other way around. Anyway, I can't imagine shooting one. If I did, I'd be drinking like those boys."

"Work hard, play hard. Nothing wrong with that."

"Speaking of playing hard, you need a rum punch." Jim pointed at Bud's empty cup.

"I'll give you a rum punch. What's that you had last night? A Smoking Cherry Bomb? Goddamn girlie drink."

"I'd squeeze into a skirt right now, but the bartender's only got punch on tap."

"That bar's fully loaded," Bud said. "He just doesn't want to sink to your low."

"Just need vodka, grenadine," Dave said. "151. One or two other things. Used to bartend."

"All last night, Jim was daring us to join his asshole antics." Bud struggled from his chair. "It's time to pay the bartender to stand down so Dave can show us how it shouldn't be done. Anything to shut you up."

"Don't be stupid," Sarah said. "They only have plastic cups."

"Most people blow them out," Dave said. "Or use a straw."

"Only way is to shoot it back and swallow," Jim said. "Don't think. Just sink the pink."

Helen watched Dave adjust his cap. "Don't you need to sleep?"

"I need to do something normal for a change."

When Dave disappeared with the rest of the group, Gerry rested her hand on Helen's arm. "You're shivering, dear. Are you all right?"

Helen looked at the diamond ring nestled in her sleeve, inches from her sutures, and smelled something cloying, talcum powder or lilac sachet. "We've had a rough few days."

"I was going to ask about your husband's bandages, but I didn't want to be nosy."

"We missed the shuttle. From the Ambassador." Helen looked into Gerry's eyes and lowered her face. "Some people set fire to the hotel and attacked him. We walked here."

Gerry traced a broad circle on Helen's back with her palm. "I can't imagine."

Helen wiped her cheek with her sleeve. "We'll be all right."

"But you're not all right now. Let's go to my condo. I'll get you something nice to wear. I'd rather do this than wait for Bud. I can tell you, he won't be crawling into bed anytime soon."

"I can't take your clothes."

"You need clothes. Nice clothes. Who knows when we're going home?"

At the mention of home, we felt as Helen did, stirred by yearning for a place long gone. Swept along by soothing chatter, we lurched behind her, forgetting momentarily that Paradise has been destroyed. The condo jarred us from our reverie. It was engulfed by the sort of electric haze that generally fucks up circadian rhythms and makes it impossible for us to keep civilized, nocturnal hours. It was an abattoir for ants and anyone else incautious enough to nick a spot of jam in the fluorescent light of late evening, when humans are most inclined to snack.

"I told Bud not to leave the jam out." Gerry used a paper towel to shift a jar from the granite countertop to the garbage can. "The ants are going crazy. If there's even a crumb, they swarm. The maids are useless."

"I hadn't noticed."

"With everything you've been through, I shouldn't complain." Gerry swept the sink with a sponge and watched an ant slide down the drain in an eddy of scalding water. "It's just not as nice as some of the places we've stayed."

"I suppose there's good and bad in every place."

"I guess we always try to stay in the good places. By the way, I apologize for what they were saying about welfare cases. People say things and don't mean them."

"I couldn't really hear them."

"People can be so cruel." Gerry wiped down the toaster. "Bud laughs at me for cleaning up on vacation. It's a losing battle. Just keeping things in order." She drew a bottle from a wine rack and set two glasses on the counter. "When we're done trying clothes, we'll have a drink."

Upstairs, Helen stood beside a poster bed while Gerry pulled blouses and skirts from a walk-in closet.

"It's like playing dress-up," Gerry said. "I used to do it all the time with my daughter. She never did learn how to shop. I had to lend her a suit for her first job interview." She held a wraparound skirt to Helen's hips and set it beside a sleeveless linen blouse on the bed. "That would be a really cute outfit."

"Really, a sweater or jacket's all I need."

"The blouse is way too small on me." Gerry leaned over the bed and smoothed the linen. "Funny, but it never fit, even the day I bought it. I don't know why I always pack it."

"It's too nice to borrow."

"Nothing's too nice." Gerry slid a beige sweater from a hanger and guided Helen to the bathroom. "My daughter could get away with anything. I don't know where she got her genes. So thin, just like you. You're going to look darling."

Alone in the bathroom, Helen examined scented soaps wrapped in lace ribbons, bottles of lavender bath salt, and delicate silver chains spilling from a small box. She held a set of pearl teardrops to her ears, opened a tube of red lipstick, and resisted a mad impulse to paint herself as someone else. Finally, she slipped into the blouse and sweater, wrapped her hips in silken folds, and studied the reflection of a woman who could pass for pretty in the pages of a mail-order catalogue. This is self-preservation, she thought. Red wine and well-lit solitude. Shedding the weight of filthy clothes and forgetting.

"You look adorable," Gerry said, when Helen stepped from the bathroom.

"I feel strange taking these."

Gerry squeezed Helen's shoulders. "You can't survive with just that T-shirt. It doesn't flatter you. Take off the sweater so I can see what the blouse looks like."

Helen drew away from Gerry. "It fits perfectly. It's nice of you to lend it to me."

"Don't be shy." Gerry brushed past Helen, leaving a trace of talcum in her wake. "I have a necklace, too. Just some cheap thing I bought at the airport, but it would be cute with the blouse. You'll look like a runway model."

"I can't." Helen sat down on the bed and slumped forward.

Gerry turned around. "What's wrong? You're shaking again." She placed her hand on Helen's shoulder. "You can tell me."

Helen looked up and studied the soft lines of Gerry's face, smelled something familiar, something from a recurring dream, and felt her own limbs grow limp. She turned a palm to the ceiling and pulled back her sleeve, heard a sharp intake of air and felt Gerry's fingers slide down her back. When she looked up, Gerry was standing at the top of the stairs. Helen drew her sleeve down, rose from the bed, and began gathering hangers.

Gerry folded her arms across her chest. "Just leave everything."

"I can help." Helen looked at a hanger in her hand.

"You should keep them covered. People might. They might get infected."

In the kitchen, Gerry returned one wine glass to the cupboard. "The sun goes down so early here. It always feels later than it is."

"I'll return your things."

"Just keep them." Gerry turned to a trail of ants beside the sink. Her face was drawn from exhaustion. "I've never worn the blouse. I didn't even try it on in the dressing room. I must have been thinking of her. She was just like you. So cruel. Such a waste." She pulled a paper cocktail napkin from a drawer and began crushing ants. "I assume you know your way back."

Helen fingered the hem of a linen shirt bought for a dead daughter and left Gerry staring into the drain. She retraced her steps past interlocking pools, sickly aortic shapes aglow in red light. At the sound of breaking waves, she stumbled from the sidewalk and down a dark path, berating herself for fashioning a fantasy of love from a stranger's pity, for making herself an object of charity and then revulsion. When she reached the beach, she collapsed at the water's edge and stripped the sweater from her back to expose her arms to salty air. Until midnight, she sat on the beach, following the erratic movements of bats flitting along the shore, trailing her fingers over her arms, and ruminating on departed mothers and dead monkeys.

Those of us gathered around her were grateful to have escaped the tailgate party. The stench on the patio had been enough to conjure the worst sorts of collective memories. We'd witnessed Rome burning when it was less the subject of moral platitudes than a place of real pain, a ruined city filled with the music of a madman's fiddle, the sort of music that, back in Nero's day, had made us long for someone like Calypso Rose to rise from the ashes.

Post-traumatic stress, indeed! It's as common as disturbed dirt among those who have beheld the rise and fall of empires or lurched down streets running with blood. Those of us on the patio were scurrying like mad from rivers of spilled maraschino cherry juice and hideous concoctions bubbling around bits of char.

At first, Dave thought nothing of his inability to detect it—the stench, everyone said, of blackened plastic. He felt unsteady on his feet, dizzied by the heat and too many drinks, but relieved to be back in a familiar element. When he'd first stepped behind the bar, he'd grown anxious, struggling to read a label. His eyes were strained by exhaustion, he told himself, and then poured five shots, dispensing generous measures and garnering attention with his flair. With something close to relief, he fought a tremor in his hand to light a match, lifted his cup, and extinguished a blue flame in his mouth with all the theatricality he'd acquired in countless clubs.

"In for a penny, in for a pound," Bud declared. "Down the hatch."

Seconds later, Bud yanked his hand from his cup's sagging rim, stomped on a puddle of flame, and kicked off his sandal. As his sandal drifted toward the center of the pool, he stood on one foot, massaging his toes with an ice cube fished from a stranger's punch.

"No point walking around in one shoe." He tossed his second sandal into the water, sat down at the pool's edge, and submerged his feet. "Chlorine will sterilize everything."

"I told you to use a straw," Sarah said, when he hobbled back to the bar.

Bud placed a damp bill in front of Dave. "No more Molotov cocktails. It's whiskey from now on."

Dave smiled against the pull of surgical tape and settled into the role of bartender. He felt as though he were looking at the world through a pane of liquefying glass, pleasantly detached from his surroundings and oblivious to the smell described by everyone laughing and backing away from snaking flames and melted cups. As the night wore on, though, his senses became uncertain conduits of disjointed perceptions. His fingers tingled at the touch of strangers pressing money into his hands. Stars and strings of electric lights occupied the same flat plane, a dull expanse obliterated by smoke and haze. Women in bikini bottoms and football jerseys staggered past, shrieking, and static filled his ears. He recalled flickering orange light catching a jagged edge of glass and tried to retain an instant already slipping from his mind. He pushed back his cap and dragged his palm across his damp hairline.

"Don't mean to get into your business, but what the hell happened to your head?"

Dave considered Bud's face, florid and sickly beneath a string of green and red lights. "Walked into something a few nights ago."

"Ain't that what they always say? Hope that little lady isn't roughing you up. Shit, you hear about that sometimes."

Marianne pressed against the bar, and Dave pulled his cap down over his forehead.

"Gimme a cherry. A flaming shot an' a cherry."

Dave fished a cherry from a jar and placed it on a paper napkin. She peeled it from the napkin and pushed it through her lips, indifferent to a shred of tissue clinging to its underside. Without thinking, he reached into the jar again and placed a cherry in his mouth. He broke its candied skin, tasted something metallic, and wondered if the stench had soured his saliva. He was sniffing the air when Bud spoke.

"I smell like a goddamn gas station. A Manhattan to end the misery."

"Sorry. Thought you were talking to the bartender."

Bud brushed a streak of ash from his shirt. "I thought you were the bartender."

Dave turned a bottle over in his hands, trying to arrange the words breaking apart on its label. He thought of walking away, but leaving because he couldn't make a drink, because he'd grown tired before a man twice his age, would set an unacceptable precedent. He just needed a prompt.

"Can't remember the last time someone ordered one of these."

"About a minute ago. That would have been me."

"This last call?" Jim said. "Hit me with a drop shot, girlfriend."

Dave heard an erratic buzz, the sound of a fly suffocating inside a sealed jar.

"The hell with it," Bud said. "If I can't get a real drink, make it a shot of fruit juice. Tomorrow, we're sticking to whiskey or beer. No more girly drinks."

"If it's a girly drink, get me some high heels, brother," Jim said.

"Bet I'd find some in your closet. See your little lady left without you."

"Flaming shot is right." Jim wrapped his arm around Bud.

"Keep your pants on, Jim," Marianne said.

"Don't worry, sister," Jim said. "I'm a lot of things, but I ain't queer."

Dave pressed his fingers to his temple and closed his eyes. Bud coughed, and Dave recalled the feverish face of someone nesting in damp sheets. When he opened his eyes, a shattered bottle was lying at his feet, and he was holding his cap in his hand. His bandage dangled from two strips of surgical tape.

"What the fuck happened to your face?" Jim asked.

Marianne looked at the jar of cherries and staggered toward a hedge. Dave touched his cheek and studied his darkened fingertips. He felt his bandage dragging down the side of his face and pressed it back into place, pulled on his cap, and stumbled from the bar.

He walked without direction, catching on branches and trampling flowers until his legs gave out. Damp earth swallowed his knees. A legion of mosquitoes massed around him. He clawed his skin and forced himself to walk again, shying away from bright lights and doubling over whenever pain shot through his head. He stopped before a row of identical buildings. Disoriented by the glare of a sidewalk lamp, he feared their resemblance to so many other buildings in so many other places had conditioned a false sense of familiarity. He pulled a small envelope from his pocket and struggled to read the number on its flap. When he found a door bearing the number, he stood paralyzed until his fear of drawing attention overcame his dread.

He found Helen lying beneath a sheet, her upturned arm exposed to the light filtering through a drawn curtain. Even after he saw her stitches, he panicked, wondering if he'd entered the room of a stranger who might wake and scream. He shut himself in the bathroom, placed a towel at the base of the door, and turned on the light. When he turned to the mirror, he recoiled. Slowly, he leaned over the sink and considered the man standing before him, searching for something familiar, something of himself, in the man's disfigured features. He removed his cap, peeled away a square of gauze and ran his fingers along sutures pinching discolored skin. Imagining the scars that would forever define the man's face, he spat at the mirror and watched a streak of saliva slide down the glass. He registered the stunned expression of the man before him. He loathed the man and saw his loathing reflected back.

He dragged his fingers across the glass, knowing he'd always situate his memories on either side of a jagged line. He'd measure every future disappointment and heartbreak against the happiness of a life extinguished in the time it had taken a stranger to break a bottle against his head. He remembered Tremor's cheeks streaked with soot and saw in the mirror a face deformed by thoughts of murder. He slid down the wall, collapsed on the floor and curled his hands into fists to control their shaking.

In that moment, we truly empathized with him. Time and again, we'd stumbled into the Plantations, drawn by false hopes of regaining Paradise, only to fall prey to despair. We knew only too well what happens to those who stray into places where difference inspires disgust.

SOLITUDE

WHEN HUMANS ENCOUNTER US in kitchens or showers, they sometimes hesitate, if only briefly, to use violence. They study the movements of our antennae, shudder, and remark that we "almost seem to be thinking." More circumspect ("squeamish," they say) humans wonder aloud if we're sentient, as if causing pain weren't enough to deter them from squashing us with tennis shoes. Often, the last thing we see in this life is a pancake of stale gum caught in a rubber tread. There is no dignity in death.

Humans go to remarkable lengths to rationalize acts of barbarism, usually by claiming that other species lack certain forms of intelligence—the advanced reasoning and self-consciousness that supposedly distinguish human beings from the "lower orders." They do this through intelligence tests grossly marred by bias and the spurious logic of insecticidal maniacs. In the *Journal of Cognition*, neurobiologist James Nolan (a consultant for Fountainhead Chemical Solutions!) concluded that "cockroaches demonstrate remarkably limited recall and very little to suggest problem-solving capabilities, or even intelligence beyond that associated with automatons' unthinking responses to physical stimuli."

Complete rot, from stem to stern! Nolan based his opinion on an absurd test that involved placing individual cockroaches in an extensive maze and observing their failed attempts to locate a sugar cube. Nolan's unfortunate subjects completed these tests in the afternoon, despite the fact that cockroaches, unless routinely disturbed or driven by scarcity, sleep during the day. Mired in anthropocentrism, Nolan failed to account for our circadian rhythms, and more importantly, the compound intelligence enabled by collective behavior. Had we been tested in Nolan's insidious maze as we naturally act, *en masse*, we would have scored higher than comparably sleep-deprived humans who hobble themselves by hoarding information and working alone.

Nolan and his ilk would undoubtedly dismiss the results of more carefully designed intelligence tests. There's too much money to be made in *Roach Out!* Stooges of the insecticide industry routinely insist that animals lack sentience—the individual self-awareness that generates existential meaning. They have on their side the studies of crackpot scientists who shove dogs in front of mirrors to see if they recognize their own reflections, and then cite any perceived indifference as evidence that animals lack the *self*-consciousness and *individual* subjectivity necessary for metaphysical reflection. The mirror test reflects little more than human vanity. Where is the genius in staring at one's own gob and ruminating over wrinkles? Why should dogs stand in judgment because they're content with their appearance? Because they'd rather gaze upon others than ogle themselves? Because they lack the self-absorption humans identify as a hallmark of higher intelligence?

Even Descartes, however brilliant a philosopher, was encumbered by a preoccupation with isolated individuals. Faced with the possibility that the physical world is illusory, the product of dreams or hallucinations, he concluded that only his own thoughts could confirm his existence. He might as well have lifted a glass to Narcissus's reflection when he wrote, "I think, therefore I am." Humans, so smitten with "I," seem perfectly willing to exist as brains in vats, steeping away in solitary thoughts. What a bitter brew! What is the basis for empathy if everything outside of one's mind is subject to doubt and suspicion? How different humans might be if they had antennae, if they could say, "We think, therefore we are." They'd know and feel so much more. They wouldn't be so lonely.

CHAPTER TWELVE

H ELEN AND DAVE HAD tasted the most bitter of brews. They started the next morning popping pills behind drawn curtains, less to mute any physical sensation than to dull their awareness of mirrors, the sources and reflections of their shared misery. They left their room in search of food, less to satisfy hunger than to escape the closeness of each other's company. The pills had only produced a superficial indifference to misery, a dreadful sense of inconsequence and terminal slowing, and distorted the sounds of distant gunshots. The sun appeared filmy and fixed in the unchanging sky, the heat intolerable for having no end.

"This where we were last night?" Dave stepped onto a pool patio.

"It looks different." Helen tired at the effort of speaking. "Without shit everywhere."

Her attentions drifted to a masseuse working oil into the bronzed arms of a woman lying face down on a table. At the sound of a gunshot, the woman lifted her head, regarded her surroundings with heavily lidded eyes, and stretched out again beneath a layer of fresh lubricant. Helen touched the sleeve of her borrowed sweater and her mind emptied itself of everything but the memory, now a fantasy, of sunlight upon her bare skin. Dave leaned over to study his reflection on the pool's surface, transfixed by his own image. Helen considered him for a moment and started walking toward the estate house, relieved, if wearied, when he followed her.

They ate in the Sugar Mill, beside an open window. Dave flared his nostrils over the tip of a sausage. Helen looked out across the terrace at languid guests sipping iced tea and perusing menus to the sound of gunfire.

"I grew up around hunters, and this is getting to me," Dave said, dropping his fork. "Don't these people have fucking silencers?" He noticed a young woman staring at his bandages and threw his napkin onto his plate. "I'm too hungover for this. I got to find a bathroom."

"I'll wait outside," Helen said.

At the edge of the terrace, she settled into a chair and contemplated the slow bleed of hours and days. Her limbs grew heavy, and she might have been sleeping, she realized, when she heard ice cubes hitting glass. A waiter was leaning over her table, filling a goblet with water.

She waved away a menu. "I'm just waiting for someone."

Dave appeared behind the waiter. "Bloody Mary for me."

"I don't know if you should. Your head."

Dave scratched his bandages. "Bloody Mary," he repeated.

He drew a plastic bottle from his pocket and sat down. As he shook a pill onto his palm, our antennae twisted in doubt. The throbbing in his face would momentarily fade, but nothing would allay his agitation, or his sense that life had suddenly become unfair.

The unfairness of life, we could hardly dispute. Those of us huddled beneath the hood of the prime minister's SUV were feeling queasy from the smell of disinfectants and unsettled by Professor Cleave's behavior. Professor Cleave had become a touch unhinged. In his mind, he was still holding class. At one point, he addressed us—or more accurately, the vents, for only fools would tempt fate by appearing on the dashboard of an insecticidal (but otherwise petty) despot like Graham Douglas. Fortunately, he came to his senses, in the way of people who wake themselves from troubling dreams with their own outbursts. He glanced at the rifle propped between the knees of the bodyguard in the passenger seat and looked into the rearview mirror. The deputy narrowed his eyes. Professor Cleave knew, then, that he'd spoken, and feared his senses had betrayed him. The car had been fumigated, or so he'd been told, and yet he'd just seen an antenna poking from a vent. If reason had defected, he assured himself, it had done so momentarily, in the face of incomprehensible folly.

When he'd first glimpsed Tremor's face in the mirror, he'd found it no less despicable for being contorted by anxiety. Against his better judgment, he'd battled disbelief by looking into the mirror again and again. Finally, he'd withdrawn into his mind, only to lapse into ingrained habits. He'd addressed us, madly enough, as "his students," driving us away from the vents in fear that he'd blown our cover and jeopardized his job.

We might have been relieved about the latter. However low-fidelity the speakers in Professor Cleave's cab, there was no music at all in the prime minister's car. No Calypso Rose. No Skatalites. Not a single beat of DJ Xspec's *Heavy Vibes Hour*. Since Butts's warmth had faded from the car's leather seats, the speakers had become silent showpieces. Any unmeasured speech was bound to stand out.

Professor Cleave gripped the steering wheel and forced his attention to his surroundings. Young women sweating into stolen dresses stared sullenly at the car as it passed. Young men carrying bottles of cane liquor spat on the sidewalk. Professor Cleave realized that he recognized none of them, and that any one of them might have murdered Desmond.

"They're animals," the deputy said. "Every single one of them."

Professor Cleave tensed, knowing he'd just heard an echo of his own thoughts.

"They belong in cages," Graham Douglas said. "We should have used tear gas."

We quivered and crawled closer to the vents to learn what we could of the future unfolding before us. In the back of the car, Tremor fingered his holster's strap. After an uneasy sleep on EZ's floor, he felt grateful for the windows' dark tint. He leaned against the glass to watch an old man pushing a shopping cart full of radios up a dirt road. He was staring at the man's cinched pants when the deputy spoke again.

"A disgrace to this nation. When children see these things, they become animals, too."

"In the future, you won't see these kinds of people on the streets," Douglas said. "The police won't allow it. The economy won't encourage it."

Tremor recalled his father spitting on the floor and decided he'd never cede the strap across his shoulder or let the impress of a gun fade from his hands. For the rest of the ride, he listened to the deputy and Douglas.

"The U.S. attaché is a spotted lizard." The deputy trailed his fingers over the top of his own hand.

"Years ago, when we threatened a strike, he invited me to the Plantations. He offered women and liquor and spoke of being reasonable."

"You refused, I presume."

"The days of corruption are over," Douglas said. "That is my answer."

"After today, the attaché will make appointments to see you at the Governor's Mansion. This will be a very different place."

"In so many ways. The attaché spoke of American interest in expanding the terminal. He needs to understand that our workers should gain from any proposed schemes."

The deputy gazed at a line of concrete sewer pipes. "What was Buttskell's phrase? 'The Future is Now.' A slogan unfulfilled. But these are different times." He fell silent as the first dead monkeys appeared beside the road.

Douglas leaned against his window. "They're covered in sores."

"They've been shot," Professor Cleave said. "They're riddled with bullets."

Professor Cleave looked into the rearview mirror and met the hard stare of a man contradicted by a subordinate. He turned his attention back to the road.

When the Plantations came into view, Douglas pointed to the mercenaries standing at its entrance. "Those men will need to clear the animals from the roadside. The Plantations owns the land, but the roads are public."

"I suspect those are the men who shot them," Professor Cleave stated, bringing the car to a halt before the gate.

Douglas smoothed his tie. "Then I will insist upon it."

A mercenary pulled a surgical mask over his mouth and approached the car. When Professor Cleave lowered his window, the man rested his arm on the door and surveyed the car's occupants.

"What's your business here?"

Professor Cleave noted the crude insignias inked across the man's sun-scarred arms. "Prime Minister Douglas has an appointment with the U.S. cultural attaché."

The mercenary stepped back and waved the car through the gate. When Professor Cleave parked, Douglas remained in his seat. Professor Cleave hesitated and then stepped from the SUV and opened its back door.

"When we come to the Plantations, you will always remain beside the car," Douglas said. "Only today, you will follow me inside."

Douglas started toward the estate house, and Professor Cleave followed, as unsteady on his feet as Tremor walking in his stiff, oversized shoes. In the lobby, Professor Cleave stood with his back to a wall and studied the veins running through the marble floor tiles.

"I am here to meet the U.S. attaché," Douglas said to the concierge.

The concierge lifted a phone and rested a pen on her lower lip. "Mr. Douglas is here to see the executive manager."

Douglas placed his hand on the desk. "I am the prime minister. Here to see the U.S. attaché."

The concierge placed the phone on its cradle and turned to a spreadsheet. "The executive manager's secretary has been informed that you're here."

"This is a disgrace." Douglas dabbed his forehead with his handkerchief and paced, pausing to mutter at the deputy, "To be addressed as Mr. Douglas. To be treated with such disrespect."

Professor Cleave averted his eyes from Douglas and studied an arrangement of photographs on the wall—images of stone towers, wagons loaded with cane, and a flatbed truck parked beneath a banana tree. He squinted at the last photograph, genuinely dumbfounded by his surroundings and Douglas's behavior. When he turned back to the room, he found Tremor peering into a framed wall mirror, oblivious to the executive manager's approach. By the time Tremor turned from his reflection, the executive manager was standing before Graham Douglas.

"It's a pleasure, Mr. Douglas." She folded her hands together.

"Prime Minister Douglas. I understand the former prime minister is staying in the Presidential Suite."

"You're referring to Lyndon Buttskell, the current prime minister."

"I am referring to a man who abdicated his position. I need to know what financial arrangements he's made to retain the suite. It's my job as prime minister to prevent the misappropriation of public funds."

"It will be your job when you are prime minister."

Douglas's face flushed. "Any uncertainties regarding my position should be resolved as quickly as possible. The attaché has privately acknowledged the vote of no confidence in Lyndon Buttskell, but a public statement would do much to restore order."

"We'll address your status during a conference call with our primary stakeholders."

"This is a diplomatic meeting."

"One that will affect investors. Right now, they need assurances of political stability. An attractive economic climate. The attaché needs to know that you can provide these."

"This is extortion," Douglas said.

"This is negotiation at a critical time for your country." The executive manager looked at Tremor. "I was told the police arrested him. Then one of our security associates informed me that he'd appeared on the grounds. As part of your detail. You need to understand what stakeholders are willing to accept."

"There's a man in custody being questioned about the events in Rocky Point."

"John Bowden is not my concern. This is the man everyone has seen. Our guests know him as the person who murdered an American."

"There is an ongoing investigation—"

"St. Anne's image has suffered. The Plantations' census projections are down. If our meeting is going to be productive, you need to remove him from your service immediately. Beyond that, dispense with the problem as you see fit."

Douglas turned to the deputy.

The deputy turned to Tremor. "Wait near the car."

Tremor looked at Professor Cleave, a man in badly polished shoes observing him with disdain and pity, and the executive manager, considering him with the quiet contempt he'd seen on so many strangers' faces. He imagined her, all of them, backing away at the sight of the gun, doubting him at first and then falling to their knees at the first shot. He pressed his fingers to his temple, lost in a profusion of red and black spots bleeding into one another. He struggled to bring everything into focus—the concierge's painted hazel eyes, the two bodyguards, and Graham Douglas. Failing, he looked again at Professor Cleave and then reeled across the lobby, past faceless forms and into blinding sunlight.

He shrank beneath the sky, feeling like a shadow erased by the midday sun. The prime minister's polished black car now resembled a hearse waiting to convey him to a dark cell strung with a twisted sheet. He looked at the flowers surrounding the house, smelled a sickening perfume masking accelerated rot, and then something of Crazy Mary—exhumed soil embedded in disintegrating fabric and the ferment of moldering fruit. He studied the loops of concertina wire crowning the Plantations' walls and counted five mercenaries standing beside the front gate. He was close enough to the mercenaries to hear their voices, guttural and cutting, and discern the features of a man in a surgical mask observing his movements.

He turned from the gate, surveyed an exposed fairway and a line of trees in the distance, lowered his face and walked around the side of the house. Beneath an elevated terrace, he seized at the sight of waiters in white jackets lowering silver pitchers to stare at him, and the American man, recognizable even in bandages, overturning a chair as he struggled to his feet. Tremor touched his gun and stumbled backward, gripping the strap across his chest as if it could give him balance. Then he started running.

He fled without thought, deafened by the blood rushing in his head. He followed winding sidewalks into a dense grove of trees, to a shaded flagstone path spotted with fractured sunlight. The strap across his shoulder pressed against his blisters and his beret slipped over his eyes. He tripped once and waited for the pounding in his chest to subside. A bird shrieked. He looked over his shoulder, at the path leading back to a polished black hearse, picked himself off the ground and started running again, toward a sliver of blue visible through the trees, drawn by the sea and the promise of drowning.

By then, the beach had been cleared of sunbathers by accretions of soft mud and shredded orange plastic. Tremor stood at the water's edge, watching the erratic movements of gulls skimming the ocean's surface. A wave broke over a distant sandbar. He saw his fate beyond its glittering crest, in unfathomable depths beyond shame and regret.

"Nowhere to hide and nowhere to go," he whispered. He tried to remember the woman who'd spoken those words. "Not if you can't swim."

He imagined the moment of letting go, when he slipped beneath the waves, lifted his toes from sand, and allowed an undertow to carry him from shore. The sun would waver and recede beyond a watery ceiling. There would be terror, but there would be forgetting, too, as his thoughts narrowed on his last breath. He crouched down, wrote his names in wet sand with his finger, and watched each of them disappear. He carved Trevor first, and then Prentice, and then Tremor, feeling more disembodied each time an incarnation of himself dissolved.

He remembered Crazy Mary walking along the shore, dragging a stick along the ground and carving strange symbols in the sand, and children trailing behind her, taunting her. He remembered her shaking beneath a mantle of rags and issuing demands to an empty sky, hoping and grieving in ceaseless cycles. He tried to grasp the kind of love measured by indifference to the world, to all the objects she'd surrendered to the elements in her endless bartering. Despairing, he sat down in the sand and fingered the laces of his shoes, wondering if she'd follow him into darkness when the weight of the gun drew him beneath the waves.

In a moment of doubt, he tried to lift himself from the ground, only to collapse. Tiny waves crested the sandbar, rolled into shore, and broke against a fragile ridge of sand and shell fragments at his feet. He followed the movement of silt trailing away in tiny riptides and realized he'd exhausted himself. There was nowhere left to run.

Professor Cleave was still running, or at least pacing, looping back and forth across the lobby and ignoring the concierge's sideways glances. Before going upstairs with Graham Douglas, the deputy had asked him to wait beside the car. The request had been cruel and foolish, less because of the heat or the deputy's pretenses than the boy's volatility and his own disgust. Fearing his own temper, Professor

Cleave had remained in the lobby to ruminate on a boy who'd stolen so much and gained nothing, and those who'd been foolish enough to enlist him in their ill-advised political campaign. At the far end of the lobby, he paused before a set of French doors and peered into a sunlit room. For a moment, he forgot Tremor's face and the slouched shoulders of the provisional prime minister. He forgot himself.

A Persian rug covered all but the edges of a hardwood floor. A chandelier hung from the molded-plaster ceiling. Upon a teak desk inlaid with ivory, a quill yanked from the ass of some poor goose rose from an empty inkwell. An umbrella stand fashioned from an elephant's hollowed foot stood in a corner. What a room! What a world! None of that mattered to Professor Cleave. He saw only hundreds of books arranged on mahogany shelves, rows of leather spines and the calligraphic curves of embossed titles. As he entered the room, those of us watching him lamented the transient nature of transcendent joy. He drew a book from a shelf and turned it over in his hands, mesmerized and then perplexed by its tight stitching. When he split the gilt sealing its pages and cracked its resistant spine, the scents of glue and bleach filled his nostrils. He replaced the book and examined the stiff spines of other volumes dressed in factory-distressed leather.

"I have found the only library on St. Anne, and it is a decorative library staged for indolent intellectuals smitten with the trappings of art."

Realizing he'd again addressed us, he gripped the edge of a shelf. What could we do but reassure him that he had not completely lost his head? Reluctantly, we emerged from the dusty spaces behind books, where we'd been napping for weeks, undisturbed by the Plantations' incurious guests. Professor Cleave dragged his hand across his forehead and leaned forward to study our antennae. As if he couldn't help himself, he lifted a finger in the air.

"There is such a thing as cultural capital acquired through intellectual labor. This collection, however, is a thin veneer that disguises more than edifies."

We'd already arrived at that conclusion. The guest library at the Plantations at St. Anne had never provided us with anything but a place to sleep. As for edification, its nearly inedible contents—thousands and thousands of alkaline-soaked pages embalmed in glue and strips of synthetic leather—hardly constituted proper food.

"The only thing worse than the false pretenses on display is the loss to those who would gain an education, were these books in a public library. There was once such a place."

A set of frayed volumes between two ivory bookends caught his attention. He drew several books from the shelf and fingered the unraveling stitches of *Queen Victoria's Glorious Empire*, the crooked cover of *Missionaries Among the Pygmies of New Guinea*, and the tattered *Cultures of the British Raj*. He considered the faded library stamps inside of each.

"One wonders why they keep these, if not to celebrate strange ideas." Imagining we might have found, in his remark, some sanction for ignorance, he composed himself. "But perhaps there is something of worth to salvage from the rubbish."

Or an organic snack, we might have added, but we'd always taken care to preserve the worn volumes between the bookends. Their earthly scent always recalled fond memories of napping peacefully in the stacks of Portsmouth's library.

Professor Cleave drew a slender cloth-bound book from the shelf and squinted at its cover. We lifted our antennae as he leafed through *The Wonder That Was Ours: Colonial Days on St. Anne, from the Perspective of a Loyal Crown Servant*, by Winthrop Markeley, O.B.E.

"His was a rarified world, a rarely seen wonder. The days of Markeley were lean for most."

He turned brittle pages riddled with brown spots, skimming passages about high-society pastimes and inspecting photographs of molasses vats and plantation managers in linen suits. He paused to consider an estate house vanishing from the grains of disintegrating paper.

"He'd find humor in this one. The UGG's first meeting place in all its glory, or as he'd say, before they brought it to its greatest glory by drinking more than the British on their worst days."

We crept to the edge of the shelf and strained our antennae toward the photograph of the old Markeley place, wearied by memories of sleepless nights and then stirred by thoughts of "boxing," as Topsy had called it.

"He'd say they lit up the sky when they burned it, and then he'd find some way to connect it to the independence movement."

He trailed off, envisioning the world his father had known. Then, recalling his own injunctions about stealing, he slipped the book into his jacket. "That we need to steal a book to save it from obscurity is the real abomination. It once belonged to all of us."

We fluttered our wings as he walked through the lobby, past photographs of plantation managers mounted on horses, feeling as though he'd just reclaimed a small measure of stolen dignity.

When he stepped onto the porch, Tremor was nowhere to be seen. Professor Cleave looked at the polished car, and at a group of mercenaries near the front entrance, smoking and talking over lowered surgical masks. As he touched the railing at the top of the steps, he heard his name and turned around. Helen was rising from a rattan chair beside a tea trolley. Between her insistent pallor and the way she adjusted the folds of her skirt, she looked as though she'd stepped from the pages of the disintegrating memoir tucked in his jacket. Behind her, Dave was leaning against the armrest of a second chair, drawing from a cigarette and surveying the grounds with disgust. Like her, he had the look of a ghost, part of a bitter history forever unfolding into the present.

"Your father said it would only take until afternoon to get here," Helen said. "He was right."

Professor Cleave released his grip on the railing. "Of course he would have been right. When he was coming up, only the Governor had a car. You walked because that's what you did."

Dave stood up and scratched his bandage as if it were a second, hated skin. "We saw that fucking kid. Half hour ago, behind the house. Came out of nowhere in some kind of uniform and pulled a gun on me."

"He didn't pull it," Helen said. "He put his hand on it."

"To pull it." Dave ground his cigarette beneath his shoe. "He was looking right at me, with his hand on it."

Professor Cleave scanned the grounds. "Where did he go?"

"Who the fuck knows? And what the fuck is he doing in a uniform?"

Professor Cleave massaged his forehead. "Certain people erred in judgment. They know this now. He'd just been dismissed when you saw him."

"Who the fuck hasn't been fired before? He's got a gun."

"The woman at the front desk called security," Helen said. "The manager's coming down to talk to us."

"She's taking her goddamn time. I told those guys at the front gate. Told them what happened at the Ambassador, too. They got it. They said he should be strung up with razor wire."

Professor Cleave looked at the mercenaries. "His gun isn't loaded. They should be told that."

"It doesn't matter. He's waving it around. He's dangerous."

"It matters a great deal," Professor Cleave said.

Helen started toward Professor Cleave. "The woman at the front desk seemed to know it wasn't loaded—"

"He burned down the hotel and tried to kill me," Dave said. "He probably murdered that guy on the beach. Who knows what else he did two nights ago?"

"We might never know," Professor Cleave said quietly.

"Are you defending him? Think about everything he's done."

"I've thought about nothing else for days."

"Someone should bust his skull open. String up what's left and let everyone take pictures." Dave collapsed into a chair and buried his face in his hands. When he sat up, his jaw was hanging slack, and his fingertips were moving along a strip of surgical tape.

Sickened, Professor Cleave started down the steps. On the bottom stair, he gripped the railing to steady himself. Helen stood above him, cradling her arms.

"Is there something we can do to pay you back? For letting us stay."

He flinched, imagining something pecuniary and crass, something deeply American, in her question. "Send my father a letter. From the United States. He liked to get them. A very long time ago."

He walked to the car, pulled the book from his jacket, and began to read. The sun was blazing, and yet he was suffering the heat, she knew, rather than bear their presence. To the sound of distant gunshots, she touched her cracked lips.

Dave looked at her and shook his head. "He was defending him. What the fuck is that about?"

Helen said nothing. From the top of the steps, she stared at Professor Cleave, standing in front of a polished black car, cradling a book in his palm and occasionally lifting his eyes to look into the distance, as if he were delivering a sermon.

❈

Professor Cleave squinted at faded letters and struggled to distract himself from thoughts of a man picking at his bandages and talking about lynching. He leafed through brittle pages, pausing on the photograph of a house that had lit up the sky and then slipped into dereliction. When he looked up, the two Americans were sitting quietly on the porch, surrounded by the trappings of an empire moldering away in memoirs.

The sound of a gunshot drew him back to his surroundings. He remembered Tremor staggering from the lobby, blinded by a slipping beret. The boy, he thought, had lost his last protection. Certainly people in Portsmouth had seen him in his police uniform, and stories had begun to circulate. Rocky Point would exile him. His friends would shun him. Someone in Tindertown might kill him. The car was now as good as a hearse, and the boy would soon be sitting in its backseat, ignorant, if he were lucky, of the fate awaiting him. He imagined delivering the boy back to the streets, or to jail. He recalled Tremor on the Ambassador's roof, brutalized and deeply afraid. The boy would never survive prison, if he even made it to trial. Most likely, he'd end up hanging in a solitary cell. Professor Cleave twitched at the memory of a wild pulse beneath his fingers and feared he might be sick.

He looked at the mercenaries standing near the gate, recalled their dead expressions and the crude tattoos covering their arms. He considered the tall windows fronting the house, overlooking the short drive to the entrance. He imagined Tremor's terror, felt it in his own chest, and turned back to the gate. He counted three mercenaries. The others were nowhere to be seen.

"Beyond that, dispense with the problem as you see fit," he whispered.

Professor Cleave surveyed a series of exposed fairways and patios, a small cluster of cottages, and a dense grove of trees obscuring the shore. He pressed his knuckles to his forehead and tried to imagine what had passed through Tremor's mind when he staggered from the house. In his panic, the boy had likely run himself into a dead end on the beach. Professor Cleave cursed and started walking, trailing loose pages in his wake, dropped the book, and then broke into a run.

He found Tremor staring at the waves breaking along the shore. He called out once and walked to the water's edge. At the sight of Professor Cleave, Tremor fell back on his palms and heels and crawled sideways across the sand like a retreating crab. Then he struggled to his feet and placed his hand on the gun. Sand clung to his pants, and his face was slick with sweat.

"I know it's not loaded." Professor Cleave took a step forward. "They're looking for you. The police. Soldiers."

"I didn't kill the man on the beach," Tremor said. "He was already dead."

"I can drive you through the gate and take you down the road. Anywhere."

"I wasn't at the terminal." Tremor lifted his hand to his own throat. "I didn't kill anyone."

"If you have anywhere to go, you should leave now."

Tremor looked up the coast, at the jagged outcropping of land beyond Rocky Point, the furthest reach of the only world he'd ever known, and out to sea, at oil tankers and barges distant enough to appear sedentary. They seemed otherworldly, shimmering pieces of an interrupted dream about to resume. He imagined, among them, splintered boats with hidden compartments.

"Do you understand what I'm saying?" Professor Cleave said. "You need to leave."

Tremor stood motionless, in suspended flight, imagining a sinewy man in a wooden boat bearing him across the waves. Professor Cleave took another step forward. Tremor slid his fingertips beneath his collar and felt the edge of a welt on his shoulder. Then he remembered the last words his father had spoken to him, stepped away from the shore, and followed Professor Cleave, the man who'd tried to strangle him, into the trees.

When they reached the car, Tremor looked at the three mercenaries standing beside the front gate. His chest grew tight, and he forced himself to breathe, only to grow faint from the smell of rot and the sight of two Americans, the witnesses to his worst crimes, rising on the porch.

"Don't stop," Professor Cleave said, unlocking the car. "Just get in."

Tremor climbed into the passenger seat and twisted around to look through the rear window. The man with the bandaged face was stumbling down the porch steps, and the woman was following him.

"I didn't kill anyone," Tremor said again, turning to Professor Cleave.

Professor Cleave looked into Tremor's eyes, unfocused by fear, and down at Tremor's hands, faintly scarred and dusted with sand. For a fleeting instant, all that existed was the space inside the car, the boy sitting stiffly beside him, the sounds of uneven breathing. He thought of his daughter, of Cora and his father, and imagined wasting away in a jail cell for what he was about to do, for what he'd already done. He fumbled with the gearshift and the car lurched forward.

Halfway down the drive, a mercenary stepped into the car's path. Professor Cleave braked and lowered his window. The mercenary placed his hand on the side mirror.

"This is a government car." Professor Cleave gripped the steering wheel to control the shaking of his hands. "We need to leave the premises."

The mercenary leaned forward. The smell of putrefaction moved through his mask. "Seems one of these rioters is running loose. Threatened a guest." He looked at Tremor. "But you must know that already. Being on the police force. Maybe you can help us out. Mate."

"We have business in Portsmouth," Professor Cleave said.

"No business in Portsmouth now. Nothing left of it." The mercenary addressed Tremor. "I need you to get out of the car. To answer some questions."

Professor Cleave's breath grew shallow. "We have government business. It's urgent."

"You could say this is urgent." The mercenary took a step backward and angled his rifle toward the ground. "It'll take just a minute. Turn off the engine."

Professor Cleave struggled to speak as Tremor opened the passenger door and lowered himself to the ground. He was fumbling with his seatbelt when two soldiers came around the side of the house. He dug his nails into the steering wheel and listened to the mercenary leading Tremor toward the gate.

"What we can't understand is how a rioter got over a wall," the mercenary said. "With all the razor wire."

Tremor faltered and then stopped in his tracks. He watched a flock of birds merging into a dark mass against the empty blue sky.

The mercenary turned to face Tremor. "Say, you're the one who burned the body. Seen you on the news. Every bloody channel."

Tremor looked into the man's face, and his mouth parted around a broken word. He trailed his fingers across his cracked lips.

"Good on you. Taking preventative measures. No different than what we're doing." The mercenary pulled his mask from his face and spat on the ground. "Had monkeys in South Africa. Have them there still. They're everywhere, moving from one place to the next. Diseased, the whole lot of them."

Tremor grew dizzy at the sight of a dead bird caught in concertina wire.

"We're no different, really. Except you're a celebrity."

Tremor's fingertips slid from his lips.

"I didn't hear you, mate," the mercenary said.

"I just saw the man burned."

"You need to speak up."

Tremor took a step backward. "I didn't burn him."

"You don't have to lie to me. But you're right to worry. You don't have many friends here. But you have friends somewhere. Gave you a uniform. Even gave you a gun. What is it?"

Tremor pressed his fingertips to his cheek and tried to speak.

"Your weapon. What is it?"

Tremor started to turn around.

"I'm still talking to you, boy."

"I have orders." Tremor's voice broke. "To leave."

"You still haven't told me what kind of weapon you're carrying."

"It's not my gun."

"If it doesn't belong to you, you'll need to turn it over. You need authorization to carry a weapon here. Remove it from your holster and place it on the ground. Then you can leave."

Tremor imagined making his way through Portsmouth, past shops and houses marked with his name. He thought of EZ and all the hard bargains he'd have to make, of how little left he had to trade. A wave of nausea passed through him, and he feared he'd lose control of his bowels. The gun's dead weight seemed his only ballast. When it was gone, he'd have nothing, but the man was standing before him, forcing a decision.

The gun seemed more unwieldy than he remembered. Its weight twisted his fingers into odd angles. He angled its muzzle toward the ground, envisioned himself curled within a fishing boat's splintered hull, and then he crouched down. As he placed the gun on the grass, he lifted his face and looked into the mercenary's eyes. He feared the mercenary would see that he'd released the safety and kick him in the head. The man took a step backward and leveled his rifle.

In that instant, time lost all meaning. The past slipped away, and with it, all regret. The future vanished, and with it, all responsibility. The world became a puzzle of shifting shapes. He heard a jumble of voices and whispered Mary's name, and silence settled upon everything. In her silence, his last fear dissolved. He told himself he'd only imagined the power of Crazy Mary's prayers and curses. Without the fear that had always defined him, he became nothing. He'd already stopped being a man when the bullet tore through his jacket.

LEGACY

IN THE END, EVERYONE leaves St. Anne. Most do it by dying. They leave their brittle wings and hollow bones behind, in neglected cemeteries or the stony ground beneath a golf course. Some—usually humans advantaged by canvas sails and gleaming wings—learn to master polluted currents and create new lives elsewhere. Humans comprise an opportunistic species adept at exploiting disequilibrium to colonize new niches, much like weeds sprouting amidst the stumps of a clear-cut forest. The Spanish built an empire on the graves of smallpox victims and the ruins of our homes. The British indulged sweet cravings until their teeth and souls rotted, and when they went bankrupt, Americans supplanted their Union Jack with a pink hotel. When the Americans leave, others will come.

Cockroaches also bear the hallmarks of opportunistic species: the ability to subsist on disparate food sources and exploit moments of disruption. Professional exterminators typically discuss cockroaches' opportunism in pejorative terms. They write of "dietary indiscretion" rather than "adaptability" when noting our ability to subsist on anything from crème brulée to stamp glue. If only humans could register their own failings—the traits that distinguish their own opportunism from that of the so-called lower orders.

The alphas of the Anthropocene, however adept at capitalizing on accidental advantages, rarely adjust well to new environments. They transform each new niche to satisfy their ever-expanding appetites. They drain rivers to water golf courses in Phoenix and burn mountains of coal to maintain indoor ski slopes in Dubai. They exile the night with neon and repel the heat of day with air conditioning (a remarkable invention that regrettably introduced us to the depravities of addiction). They destroy the conditions of their own survival and then move on, leaving behind boarded-up shopping malls and dead radios. In flight, they're remarkably adept, graced with wheels and functional wings—objects of envy for "lurching" cockroaches, the inheritors of more inedible waste than one can imagine.

Not all humans possess the same abilities and inclinations, of course. Some can barely lurch. For every deposed prime minister sailing off in a private jet, billions of humans huddle in the crowded steerage of listing ships. Those with nothing to barter for wings live in the shadows of dead factories, nest in condemned houses, and rummage in dumpsters. They dream of leaving. Who can blame them?

More and more, the wealthier and winged members of the human race have been migrating upward rather than outward, building towers of steel and glass to remove themselves from the smell of sewers and the sounds of traffic. They sense what the poor have long known: the world is getting crowded. Professor Cleave still insists that rampant irresponsibility will come home to roost, that "those elevated by greed or accident of birth won't be able to ignore" (or fumigate, we'd add) "the dispossessed forever." At the risk of sounding cynical, we'd argue that those with functional wings have inured themselves quite well to others' misery. Their willingness to scuttle what they've damaged knows no bounds. Now they talk of colonizing outer space, as if they've already given up on Earth and packed their bags to leave a dying planet.

We've been inclined, as of late, to give Professor Cleave credit where it's due. He's one of the few of his species who could have bartered his wheels for wings but chose to stay. He was afraid of flying, certainly, but he was determined, too. He would never have abandoned his imaginary garden to see it choked by real weeds. If we stay in his cab, it's not simply because of its air conditioning, which has been more erratic than ever, or because we know that most of the world has been poisoned. Though Professor Cleave is a curmudgeon, a bipedal pedant of the highest order, there is much about him to love. And in any case, our odds of sneaking onto a space shuttle are slim indeed.

CHAPTER THIRTEEN

WE WOULD NEVER HAVE abandoned Professor Cleave that afternoon. He could barely stand upright as two maids draped a sheet over Tremor's body. He whispered to himself, trying to order his thoughts, watched a perverse red bloom spread across the sheet and struggled to guard his memories against clouded accounts of what they were calling an incident. For twenty minutes, he'd been listening to the new prime minister, the deputy, and the executive manager construct a narrative already distorted by conflicting testimonies. The longer they argued, the more desperately he struggled to fix certain details in his mind.

"He drew a loaded weapon on two guests," the executive manager said. "Our security associate responded appropriately to an established threat."

Graham Douglas traced a line across his forehead with his fingertip, as if drawing the outline of a simple argument. "It's not possible his gun was loaded. My deputy saw to that."

"There must have been an oversight on the part of your personnel."

"It's impossible, and entirely remarkable that—"

"What's remarkable is that you thought it wise to bring him here. Given what is known about him. Our security associates had every reason to consider him a threat. He refused to surrender his weapon."

"My driver said he was placing it on the ground." Douglas turned to Professor Cleave. "He had a direct view."

Professor Cleave lifted his hand to his own throat. At the sound of a gunshot, hundreds of birds had scattered from the trees. The woman had screamed. He'd fallen from the car and started running, thinking little beyond each instant he recalled in isolation, as disparate frames in a film slipping from its reels. He'd stopped short of Tremor, arrested by slate-grey eyes above a surgical mask and the tension in an arm bearing the weight of a rifle. He'd fallen to his knees. He felt himself falling still.

"The attaché isn't alone in being concerned about your indiscretion," the executive manager said to Douglas. "This incident will impact our image."

"There are implications for all of us," the deputy said. "Feelings are high, and now another person from Rocky Point is dead. Who will answer?"

"Our security associates responded to an individual with a history of violent behavior."

Douglas looked at a group of people standing at the edge of the golf course, pointing at the sheet and holding up phones. "Tonight, people will burn what remains of Portsmouth."

"You have no need to corroborate rumors," the executive manager said. "By tonight, people will be thinking about other things. This afternoon, you'll restore electricity. You'll announce that the quarantine has been lifted. That the outbreak on the ship never posed a threat to public health here."

Douglas dabbed his forehead with the end of his tie. "Where there was fear of sickness, there will be fear of scarcity."

"You'll announce plans to rebuild the terminal. To build a casino. You'll talk about St. Anne's growing position in the regional economy. About employment."

"People will still want to know what happened today," the deputy said.

"People want to move forward and forget. There's an expression. Raise the flag and declare victory."

Douglas looked at the stained sheet. "People in Rocky Point don't think that way. They don't care about simple declarations."

"Today, the U.S. Secretary of State will acknowledge your government. You'll soon have drafts of his statement and your response. Right now, your detail needs to remove the body. Our staff will deliver a stretcher to expedite matters."

The prime minister turned to the deputy.

"That's the prime minister's car." The deputy's voice grew hoarse. "We can't."

"We need to finalize things inside," the executive manager said.

The deputy looked at Professor Cleave and gestured toward the car with the expression of a man making an inexpressibly sordid request. "Make a place for it in the back."

We turned our antennae to Professor Cleave. His tie was askew, his shoes were scuffed, and he had grass stains on his pants. He rubbed his fingertips together, rocked on his heels for the assurance of solid ground beneath his feet, and started toward the house, pausing every few feet to collect yellowed pages from the grass. When he reached the car, he folded the pages into his jacket. He pressed his hand against the rear window to steady himself, insensate to the burn of hot glass. Two maids were wheeling a stretcher across the grounds. The deputy and Douglas had disappeared into the house, but the executive manager was standing on the porch, speaking with Helen and Dave. Professor Cleave strained to hear their voices.

"This morning has been extremely upsetting for everyone." The executive manager placed a hand on Helen's shoulder. "You're dealing with an enormous shock. I'd like you to meet with our resident physician."

"I don't need a doctor." Helen slipped from beneath her hand.

"Some people experience shock after traumatic events. There's no shame in discussing difficult feelings."

Helen walked to the top of the steps and looked at a group of mercenaries smoking near the front entrance. "I was standing on the driveway. I was close enough to see it."

"You were under extraordinary stress on the ship. And you've experienced a great deal over the past few days." The executive manager took a step toward Helen. "It might be best to discuss your feelings now. Things probably seem very confusing."

"He was putting the gun on the ground when they shot him."

"You said he threatened you this morning. That he was a violent individual."

"He didn't pull a gun on us," Helen said. "He never pulled a gun."

Dave spat into a hedge below the railing.

The executive manager studied his expression. "My concierge said you'd encountered him before today."

"He came after me two nights ago. Tried to kill me. Pulled a gun on me this morning. Whether he put it on the ground's just details. He had it out." Dave shook his head. "He was a murderer."

"At some point, we'll have a better understanding of how he was involved in the incident at Rocky Point. There's every indication he was mentally disturbed." The executive manager regarded the beige cotton sleeves bunched at Helen's wrists. "I'm certain that will come out in the record. It always does."

"What do you mean by that?"

The executive manager met Helen's gaze. "The quarantine is being lifted. The *Celeste*'s most infirm passengers will be ferried to St. Anne's airport and flown to Miami on a military transport. I'll be happy to secure places for you on the first commercial flight."

Dave tried to recall a feverish form on a lower bunk, but his head was throbbing, and the itch beneath his bandages had grown intolerable. "The sooner the better. I just want to get the fuck out of here."

"The quarantine," Helen said. "I don't understand."

"The CDC discovered contamination in one of the *Celeste*'s water storage tanks. The spread of illness here is no longer a concern. Of course, every precautionary measure made sense. They made sense this morning."

"He was putting the gun on the ground," Helen said.

"I'll deliver your flight information to your room." The executive manager turned her back on Helen and disappeared into the house.

Helen shook her head. "He was putting it on the ground. You know that, don't you?"

"He cut up my fucking face."

"I know that," she said.

"But you don't get it. I didn't cut myself up. I was attacked. It's different." He stumbled down the porch steps, keeping his head down to avoid the attention of people taking pictures of a bloody sheet.

He found the beach nearly deserted. The incoming tide had asserted itself and shell fragments, driftwood, and bits of garbage had massed on shore. Speckled gulls pecked at beached fish and bits of seaweed and left thick white streaks across the sand. He followed a set of footprints to the water's edge and pulled his sandals from his feet. In the distance, the *Celeste* was heading toward Portsmouth beneath a cloud of black smoke. Further north, a jagged outcropping marked the location of Rocky Point, a place he'd spend the rest of his life hating. If he'd resented the weight of Helen's sadness, he hated her now. By planting uncertainty, she'd dispelled the illusion of justice he desperately needed. It was a small matter, the gun, but something in her expression wouldn't leave him. With everything they'd seen together, she still seemed certain that some new wrong, worse than any other, had been committed.

"He tried to kill me," he whispered.

A wave broke over the shore and slid back into the sea.

It didn't matter, he told himself, whether or not the kid had pulled the gun. The kid had been a murderer, or would have become one soon enough. Still, she'd been so angry, and so obsessed about one detail. He closed his eyes and tried to imagine what she'd seen, and saw only his own face, brutalized and monstrous. Consumed by his own suffering, he realized, he'd been lost in ruminations about his face when he heard the gunshot and she started screaming. He was thinking of his face now, and he'd think about it for the rest of his life. Whatever she said, the kid had murdered in his own way, stolen something he struggled to understand.

The word innocence came to mind, but it wasn't exactly innocence; he'd lost a certain sense of invulnerability. He'd never again laugh about forgetting a name or losing his way home after having too much to drink. He'd never assume the best of anyone or find it in himself. He'd lost something other than innocence, but he'd lost his innocence, too. He'd sacrificed honesty for revenge. He scratched the tape clinging to his skin. He would never forgive, he knew. At best, there would be forgetting.

He lifted his face to the sky and let the sun raze everything from his mind, trailed his fingers over his cheek and remembered his face as it had been. He imagined what it might be again, when it healed, and he held the image as long as he could.

A small riptide eroded the sand beneath his toes. He felt a sickening sense of vertigo. Tiny waves washed over his feet and deposited shell fragments and soft brown mud onto the shore. He imagined currents bearing the contents of emptied septic bilges and backed away from the water, sinking into muck that rose between his toes and then disappeared in the suck of an undertow. The earth suddenly seemed to be shrinking, dissolving beneath his feet and forcing him into endless and exhausting flight. For the first time in his life, he felt there was nowhere left to run.

From a distance, we listened to him whispering, knowing he could hear no sound but that of his own voice. We wondered if his expression would slowly twist into something hateful, and if the fearful reactions of those around him would only confirm his self-loathing. But even with antennae, none of us can see the future. Unable to rouse him from his waking nightmare, we turned our attention to the detritus on the beach and dodged the gulls' endless strafing in our desperate search for food. The lean times would soon be upon us. Of that, we were certain.

❀

Thankfully, most of us made it off the beach that afternoon. Some of us even managed to escape the Plantations altogether, "lurching" through an ersatz jungle to reach the prime minister's car. As we crawled into its wheel wells, Helen stood beside the car, watching Professor Cleave fold a leather seat forward. They didn't speak at first, silenced by the sight of mercenaries smoking in the distance and the prime minister's bodyguards lifting Tremor's body onto a stretcher.

As the bodyguards pushed the stretcher across the lawn, Professor Cleave and Helen backed toward the house. On the golf course, small groups of people were holding up cell phones.

"They have no respect. No decency. There are so many bloody hands." Professor Cleave pulled loose pages from his pocket and sequenced them with trembling fingers. "They'll say he was mentally unbalanced. They'll vilify him, and then they'll forget him." He drew a book from his jacket and pressed the pages between its covers.

She drew her sweater close. "Was he mentally unbalanced?"

"He's dead. That's all that matters."

"He didn't pull the gun. I saw everything."

"Everyone will see something different." Professor Cleave paused. "He was troubled. Dangerous. The shred of truth will support their lies. But no one should die as he did. Violently. Alone."

She fought the impulse to touch him, sensing he might flinch. He spared her by crouching down and collecting a loose page from the ground.

"The old ones are coming apart." He brushed the cover of the book in his hand. "So many of them burned with the hotel."

He turned away from the car as the bodyguards loaded Tremor's body into the space behind the backseat. She trailed her fingertips along her wrist and then drew her sleeve over her hand.

"What's going to happen now?" she asked. "When people find out."

"I don't know. There's no way I could know," he said, bewildered by her question. He slipped the book into his jacket and fingered the cut on his thumb. "Maybe everyone is exhausted. Tired of the violence. Maybe they're already forgetting."

"What will you do?"

"I'll drive him to the morgue. Then I'm going home."

For a few minutes, they stood in silence in the shadow of the house, holding vigil for a man slipping into obscurity behind plastic and black tinted glass. When the deputy appeared, Professor Cleave left Helen standing in front of the house. She watched him close a door behind Tremor's body and open another for the prime minister, and then she watched the car until it disappeared down a road littered with massacred monkeys.

When the crowd on the golf course dispersed, she returned to the porch. Soldiers at the front gate were loading dismantled barricades onto the back of a jeep. She studied a set of stretcher tracks running across the lawn. She closed her eyes and sequenced events, distilling impressions and committing each to memory. A mercenary had spoken of savages running riot, of putting things right. She'd been too exhausted to say anything. She'd been afraid, too, when he'd slicked his hands with sanitizing gel and dispensed with her. Beyond the biting scent of alcohol, she'd smelled decay. And yet, she'd found everything—the disinfectants and decay, her fear, his violence and dismissal of her—all too familiar. To too many people, including herself, she'd been a dead woman walking, going nowhere. To too many people, she'd been expendable.

She opened her eyes and looked at the tracks fading in the grass. The mercenaries had disappeared. She cradled her arms and started pacing. At the end of the porch, she collected a pack of cigarettes and a book of matches from the tea trolley. Struggling to steady her hands, she tapped a cigarette between her fingers. She withdrew to a corner of the porch and lifted a match to the cigarette, sickened by the tug of stitches along her arm. A slow burn filled her lungs, and she let the cigarette slip from her fingers. It rolled between two planks and into the dark space beneath the porch. She considered the ash clinging to the edges of two knotted boards and lit another cigarette. She inhaled deeply, dropped the cigarette onto the porch, and pushed it between the planks. She imagined the slow hiss of dried leaves and debris burning beneath her feet, a wall of flame crawling up the front of the house. Then she lit another cigarette.

With burning tobacco raining down on us, those of us beneath the porch decided to scuttle the house once and for all, little knowing what our future held (but having a good guess, for where there's smoke, however thin and insubstantial, there's often fire). We just wanted out. When Helen finished the last cigarette, we followed her from the porch to a patch of shade beneath a banana tree. We examined the ground as we gathered around her, helplessly drawn to the flesh of fallen fruit. Still, we like to think that noble sentiments, above all others, guided us, and that she felt less alone as she contemplated her future for the very first time.

"It will all come out in the end," she whispered. We turned our antennae toward her.

She crouched down on her elbows, blew on our wings, and observed our movements. Perhaps she was testing some strange theory about cockroaches. Or perhaps she hadn't ingested the sort of rot published in most entomological journals and could actually see something of herself in us. Maybe, after years of suffering, she'd finally surrendered to madness. Maybe she just wanted to impart to us the momentary sensation of flight.

With strange particulates starting to move through the air, we'd be taking flight again soon enough. But when she leaned back against the tree, we snacked on bits of soft pulp and waited. Her expression softened, and her legs twitched. She was dreaming, we knew, of herself as a gloriously failed suicide floating far above a gutted world. We left her to float on borrowed silken wings, looking down at the sea with nothing but birds beneath her feet. It had been years since she'd slept peacefully, so we nestled in the dirt and settled down for a nap. It seemed right, after so much horror, to doze, if only for a moment, in preparation for everything ahead. And we didn't want to disturb her dreams. Insofar as her future was ours, our dreams were the same.

If Helen had actually been graced with flight, she might have seen some of us below, earthbound exiles in the prime minister's car, fleeing with wheels instead of wings. Behind the vents, we batted our wings for all they were worth, trying to capture wafts of fresh air and dispel traces of something too terrible to countenance. Graham Douglas, the deputy, and the two remaining members of the security detail had been spared the smell of blood by the miracles of modern science. The plastic tarp had allowed them to close the windows, to mute the sun with tinted glass and flood the car with cool air. It had allowed them to ignore the dead man lying behind the backseat.

Professor Cleave, though, had at his fingertips the insistent memory of a beating pulse. He kept his eyes from the mirror, fearing he might see Tremor's face upon the glass.

"We'll need to inform certain people this afternoon," Douglas said. "Did he have a family?"

"Being from Rocky Point, I assume not much of one. None of them do," the deputy said. "You must know something of his circumstances. You worked with him."

Professor Cleave didn't realize he'd been addressed until he felt a hand on his shoulder.

"I said you must know something about him. Whether he had a family."

Professor Cleave considered how little he knew of Tremor, the person who had, more than anyone else, cast his own convictions into sharp relief. Tremor, he realized, had been little more than a mirror for his own moral vanity. "I don't know anything about his circumstances."

The deputy settled back in his seat and watched the withered landscape slip past. "He's one more card in their hand. Bowden can be ours."

"It would be madness to release Bowden now," Douglas said.

"It could ease tensions. Those who arrested him worked for Buttskell."

"Those men now work for me."

Professor Cleave glanced at the rearview mirror. Douglas was struggling to loosen his tie with one hand.

"Rocky Point will always be Rocky Point, and Bowden will disappear into it," the deputy said. "We don't need to give them another martyr."

"They said Buttskell was a terrible golfer," Douglas said suddenly. "They laughed and said I would improve my game in time."

Professor Cleave felt the deputy's hand on his shoulder again and looked up to see Douglas pressing his fingertips to his lips. He pulled the car alongside a stack of concrete sewer pipes and then averted his eyes to spare the only dignity left to a gutted man getting sick in the weeds beside a ditch.

We dropped from the gaskets the moment Professor Cleave pulled the empty car into the lot behind the Hospitality Service Workers' headquarters. For a long moment, he stood with a hose in his hand, watching oily water soak into the gravel beside the car. He thought of the hospital morgue, still without electricity, and the dark stain left in the back of the car, where Tremor's body had been. He turned off the hose, then, and locked the prime minister's car for the last time.

He was relieved to find his cab where he'd left it. When he took his place behind the wheel, we gathered on the dashboard. Our only regret about the cab was that it didn't have a cylinder to spare. We fluttered our wings, knowing Professor Cleave would exercise his usual caution pulling away from the curb. We wanted to speed through every intersection, to accelerate until it seemed that gravity held no sway. He turned a worn key over in his hand and peered through the windshield at trampled flyers lying in the gutter.

"They'll be washed away when it finally rains. Rain will bring relief, but it will bring forgetting, too." He slid the key into the ignition. "I know you dream of digital displays and satellite radio. Of tinted windows to shield your scandalous behavior."

We must have confirmed his impression by skittering across the radio dial.

"Let me tell you, few can survive in such a car. There is no future in it, my students. It reeks of corruption. That car is a damnable hearse."

He drew *The Wonder That Was Ours* from his jacket and placed it on the seat. Several of us rounded its edges, brushed its loose pages and fluttered our wings, as if we might fan the flames of so many years ago.

"You have no need to fear a lecture today." Professor Cleave rubbed his eyes. "Perhaps you want to know where I found a book in circumstances such as these. I admit taking liberties in the Plantations' library. Their disregard for learning is more shameful than anything you have devised in your rudest moments. They have a wealth of knowledge at their disposal, and they are happy to dispose of it."

We dipped our antennae into weak currents of recycled air, content with the sound of Professor Cleave's voice.

"If it eases our conscience, we saved this book from obscurity. It was once in our library." Professor Cleave faltered. "I sound like he used to, and you are right to think so."

He hung his head between his arms and listened to a rattle beneath the hood. When he lifted his face, he considered a burned couch upended on a sidewalk and pulled away from the curb.

Out of respect for his feelings, we remained quiet until we reached the harbor. At the sight of the *Celeste* churning jetsam and belching smoke, we crowded against the windshield to watch policemen overseeing the disembarkation of sallow forms slumped in wheelchairs.

"For them, it's over. I almost expected to see Des standing there, smoking his cigarettes."

We flattened ourselves on the dashboard. Professor Cleave left us to our ruminations and regrets, and we left him to his.

At the edge of Portsmouth, he grew animated at the sight of a man limping along the road, holding up his pants with one hand. "Already they've released him." He leaned forward to better see through the dusty windshield. "That he's still standing is the wonder. We can't pass him without offering a lift."

He snapped his fingers and gestured toward the vents. We scurried out of his reach to behold one of our few human connections to Mary. John Bowden had always brought salted fish to Mary's house in the middle of the night, and while he'd never paid us much heed, he'd never menaced us with anything beyond his stare.

"Damn you to the last," Professor Cleave said. "I would not be using such foul language but for such foul behavior. The man has suffered, and this is no time for your provocations."

We barely registered his words as he pulled to the side of the road and pushed open the passenger door. As if his bones had been fused, John Bowden turned toward the car in tiny increments. He considered Professor Cleave through the slits between swollen eyelids.

"I can take you to Rocky Point," Professor Cleave said.

John Bowden took a halting step forward and lowered himself into the cab. With his working hand, he reached over his lap and pulled his door closed. "I remember you. From years ago." He rested his broken fingers on the threads spanning a tear in his pants. "In the prison yard. Before the storm."

He regarded those of us gathered on the dashboard. We drew our wings close and remained perfectly still.

"I saw the light when it burned," he said, once Portsmouth had disappeared. "It filled the cell. But seeing it in the day. His name everywhere."

"He's dead," Professor Cleave said.

"I know. He was with me. They took him. They'll say he did it to himself."

"They let him out of jail," Professor Cleave said. "He was shot this morning." Over the next few minutes, he related what he knew of Tremor's last hours, fearing his composure might dissolve. "He made a bad bargain."

"They made him look death in the eye," John Bowden said. "And he had nothing to bargain."

For the rest of the way to Rocky Point, Professor Cleave and John Bowden remained silent. We studied John Bowden's crooked fingers and remembered so many traps, so many corners we'd backed into, and all the sewers we'd called home. At the Rocky Point bypass, Professor Cleave turned onto a dirt road. He stopped at a dip where the road had washed out years before. John Bowden gathered his pants at the waist and pushed against the passenger door with his shoulder.

"They always take your belt," Professor Cleave said.

"I didn't have a belt. I had one, once. A long time ago."

Without another word, John Bowden struggled from the car and started toward Rocky Point. As he disappeared into the trees, Professor Cleave tried to imagine the village at the end of the overgrown path—the polluted beach, the rusted trailers and splintered boats, the children in shapeless clothes.

"I never knew a thing about him," he whispered. "About any of them."

Professor Cleave was talking to himself. We'd been driven to distraction, but not for the reasons he suspected: hints of rotting fish and washed-up garbage. We'd glimpsed Mary's house through the trees. It had been emptied by then, sanctified and then stripped. Still, as Professor Cleave backed onto the ring road, we scaled the windows and crowded one end of the dashboard, straining our antennae in the direction of Mary's door, desperately hoping to recapture the sensation of her rough fingers brushing our wings.

"Gravity has no sway in this car, I see. Your holiday has hardly restored your intellectual energies, and you've lapsed into your usual mischief." He eyed the dashboard. "Much to your distress, my students, classes will soon resume."

The announcement, however couched in needless offense, drew us from the edge of despair. Those of us given to sober reflection mingled the tips of our antennae in quiet dialogues. Some of us paced, contemplating the intellectual exercises that would invariably impinge upon our noontime slumbers. All of us, admittedly for reasons not entirely laudable—boredom beneath the hood and a strange sort of nostalgia—felt roused, if not entirely rallied. Professor Cleave sensed our mood and rose to the occasion.

"We are all facing lean times now," he said. "We'll be turning stony ground full of weeds, but let me tell you, we will treat it with care, as if there is no other."

He spent the rest of the drive home reimagining Geoffrey Morrow's splendorous garden. For our part, we dreamed of clear puddles and soft pulp and the most incredible weed ever known spreading across every hillside, the smoking ruins of plantations and the end of all pesticides; of Mary whispering to the tips of our antennae. We dreamed of paradise.

At home, Professor Cleave found Topsy sitting before the house, trying to light the tobacco shreds clinging to a cigarette butt. As he stepped from the cab, Topsy moved his cane and shifted to the side of the stoop.

"I can get past you well enough," Professor Cleave said.

"I wasn't moving for that reason. Sit down after a day driving that miserable bastard around. You look terrible. Worse than ever."

Professor Cleave drew the tattered book from his jacket and placed it on the stoop.

"Where did you get this thing?" Topsy took the book in his hands.

Professor Cleave planted his elbow on his knee and rested his forehead on his upturned palm. "The Plantations. They have a library there."

"I don't understand. It didn't belong to them."

"I know. There's a stamp. It was in the Portsmouth library."

"I was talking about the title," Topsy said. "It doesn't make a bit of sense. *The Wonder That Was Ours.* My father always said this man Markeley was a real monkey's ass. Nothing of this place ever belonged to him. But Markeley, all of them, acted like it was theirs to raise or ruin."

Topsy leafed through the book, picking out loose pages and discarding all but those with photographs. "This is a good one," he said, holding up a page. "It shows you how they lived. What sort they were."

Professor Cleave looked at the photograph of a sprawling estate house.

"We were mostly drinking, but you could say it was the first headquarters of the United Gravel Grinders. We started the labor movement there. We didn't have your man Marx, but we had a manifesto. We had class in every sense of that word."

"I never saw a manifesto. Nothing of the sort existed."

Topsy picked a shred of tobacco from his pants. "Your ma started the first fire. I was up there with her. We drank some beer and she kicked over a lantern. We weren't married, but it was love. That was the night you came into it."

Professor Cleave drew his tie from his neck and tossed it onto a pile of cigarette butts.

"She was extravagant when it came to hats and shoes," Topsy continued. "Otherwise, we scraped the bottom of the bowl. But we got by. That was the wonder. Let me tell you, the union led this country to independence, and the wonder became ours."

"To raise or ruin," Professor Cleave said.

Topsy braced his hand on his knee and stood up. "I'm going to get a few cigarettes off Morris's daughter. She always spares a few. She's not a bad sort, underneath it all."

Professor Cleave lifted the cane from the grass and handed it to his father. Topsy wrapped his stiff fingers around its handle.

"Morris didn't raise a fool," he said. "And I didn't either, even if he thought he knew something about everything. Now you know something about yourself."

Professor Cleave listened to a fading soliloquy about professors and pulpits until his father disappeared down the road. Alone, he leaned forward and lowered his head. His father's story had loosened something inside him. For the first time in years, he wept. He felt himself losing definition, giving way to grief and exhaustion. He lifted his face and examined the cut on his thumb and the cracked skin around his knuckles. He longed to wash himself clean, to lie down in a shallow stream on a cool evening. He tried to imagine the stream and realized his memory of rain had nearly evaporated.

He considered the book lying in disarray beside him. He picked up the grainy image of the plantation house and envisioned the first members of his father's union drinking in an abandoned drawing room and conceiving manifestos inspired by a clouded sense of possibility. He imagined his mother kicking over a lantern, stunned by the sight of flames eating away the polish on hardwood floors, and then laughing with his father, once the smoke dissipated, at the destruction that would stand as a testament to their first love. He imagined all of their wonder as the same he'd felt flying down a road on a rusted bike overloaded with books, carried aloft by fantastic ideas. He rested his face in his palms, and in the quiet space folded within his hands, tried to capture something of the wonder that still remained. We sat with him, our useless wings resting on our backs and our antennae raised, listening to Mary and waiting for rain.

LOVE

WE ENTERTAIN FANTASIES OF flight, still. Who can blame us? How could we forget perching at the very edge of the Ambassador's rooftop, at the edge of the known world, it sometimes seemed, with wind stirring our wings and the sensation of flight stirring our imagination? That sensation carried Professor Cleave through the long hours and days he bartered for books. It allowed Trevor Prentice to imagine a weightless body liberated from hunger and hard stares. It recalled, for all of us, something of innocence, as we imagined it, right before a terrible fall.

Now that the Ambassador is gone, we sometimes perch on the ramparts of the deserted Fort, lift our antennae to the breeze and recapture something of that sensation. We catch the scents of distant shores, knowing there's no escape from the damage that's been done, that paradise has been lost, and that it might always have been an illusion. We sit above the courtyard, which has been silent for some time, and dream about what might have been and what could someday be. We look up at the clouds and remember what it was like to fly so long ago, in bygone eras forgotten by most. Eventually, we always crawl back to Professor Cleave's cab, our classroom and air-conditioned sanctuary.

One day we'll inherit the Earth, they say. They've been wrong before. However resilient we become, insecticides will kill many of us, and so much else. For now, we'll continue to live where we can, in houses built upon our homes, sewers and drainpipes, deep cupboards and fast cars, and landfills and luxury resorts. Some of us might just survive to inherit the shell of the Earth, with all its jetsam and ruin, and if we do, we'll fill it with whatever love remains.

ACKNOWLEDGMENTS

I AM IMMENSELY GRATEFUL to everyone at Dzanc Books, including Steve Gillis and Dan Wickett, for giving this book a great home, and especially to Michelle Dotter, editor extraordinaire, whose insights and suggestions made this a much better novel than it was when she found it, and its author a much better writer. Dzanc's judges, readers, and interns provided invaluable input and suggestions, and I owe more than a few people beers.

I am deeply indebted to numerous friends who amaze and inspire me with their creativity and kindness and far too often talk me down from the cliff. For friendship and support, many thanks to Sandie Maxa, Sue Maxa-Hofmann, Meghan McCarthy, Kate Mudge, Ged Gillmore, Anne Fisher, Karen Coleman, Chris Scott, Michele Strong, Lia Paradis, Deborah Wallace, Daniela Triadan, Linda Greene, Gunther Ding, Maureen and Ray Noeth, Dick Derick, Jean Emrick, Amanda Quinby, Bryn McFarland, Andrea Piomelli, Robin Israel, Summerson Carr, Sarah Womack, and Helen Faller. Emma Blake did overtime by reading an early draft and reminding me that cockroaches dig Prince. Dev Ashish, Blake Ashley, and Michele Rivette gave me the tools I needed to mine sources of gratitude. Two wonderful teachers, Meg Files and Juliet Niehaus, reminded me that the process of learning and growing never ends.

RAW provided an intellectual home and source of salvation more times than I can count. Stephen L. Russell and Bill Adams helped form the core of a fanatical reading group and rallied behind the cockroaches from the very start. I hope we get seats near one another on the Mother Ship when it finally arrives. Philip Ivory, Rebecca McSwain, Marilyn Spencer, Linda Brewer, Barbara Kapange, Becky Pallack, Tom Prinster, Dave Dickerson, and Victor Hightower provided invaluable feedback, a safe space to be weird, and endless inspiration through their unwavering focus on craft.

Many other friends shared the wisdom and resources I sorely lacked stumbling into the final stretch. Reneé Bibby, Adrienne Celt, Lilian Vercauteren, Dana Diehl, and Morgan Miller converged on cafés every Write Wednesday, and thanks to all of you, and to everyone else who showed up to get down to biz, I feel much less adrift in a sea of Arizona sand. I owe a special thanks to Michelle Ross for reading closely and helping me keep my priorities in order when I started losing my way. Eric Besté, an amazing correspondent, never let me forget why I was doing this.

This book is dedicated, in part, to Melissa Noeth, my first human contact in Tucson. I still miss the warmth and laughter you brought to the world. Thank you to Brenda Pentland for serving as an intellectual beacon and spiritual guide in the psychic wilderness, and for listening to my rants and rambling drafts. Riley Hardesty pulled me out of countless ruts and, just as I was about to toss in the towel, reminded me of a certain cockroach-infested car and encouraged me to have faith in the strange. Emily Ignacio, a sister of another mother, alleviated some of the fear of moving forward, even when things seemed dire in the interstate Zey-Hive. Many thanks to my mother for reading to me and sparking my imagination with repeated trips to the library when I was young, and much gratitude to Bob and Florence, who believed when few others did.

Finally, I dedicate this novel to Lars, for his boundless intelligence and insight, and much more importantly, for all of the love, understanding, and patience that made this novel possible. I love you.